# BROKEN JUSTICE
## Justice Brothers, Book One

# SUZANNE HALLIDAY

# Prologue

THWACK. CLINK. THUD. "Aw, suck my balls, Cam!" Draegyn yelled, clutching his crotch with a wicked laugh as his last two horseshoes made contact with the metal stake in the ground about forty feet away in the sand pit that was Afghanistan.

"Fuck you, Drae!" Cameron yelled back heartily. "You totally pussied out last week when the Frisbees were flying with that weak-ass excuse that your neck ached. I think you set me up with all your wah-wah crybaby shit, so don't go thinking this means anything!"

The two men grinned and flipped each other the finger during some downtime at their base deep in the mountains of Afghanistan. All around them, sand bags were stacked high as a shield against every imaginable type of attack, while overhead, an American flag hung limply from its standard in the stagnant air of a blisteringly hot day.

Their special forces compound was a ragtag setup of tents, combat housing units, tin siding, barriers, sand dusted tables, lopsided chairs, and car back seats that had been thrown around an area where the men gathered to forget about where they were and what they were doing.

Dressed in backward baseball caps with sweaty bandanas around their necks and standard issue green military t-shirts that the sleeves had been ripped from, Drae and Cam were fending off the long stretches of isolated boredom that descended upon their team between missions.

Cam was wearing a pair of camo pants, lopped off at the knee, and an old pair of combat boots that were half-laced and covered in the desert sand that clung to everyone and everything. Dark, polarized sunglasses shielded his eyes from the relentless sun, and a serious beard covered the bottom half of his face.

In tip-top physical shape, after eight long years in the military, Cam's tan and muscled arms had a tattoo-wrapped bicep that matched Drae's. Together as brothers-in-arms, they were men of the Justice Squad. A gruff, no-nonsense special ops team who had been sucking in the arid sands of this God-forsaken place for far too long.

Shuffling across the hard-packed sandy ground, they stooped to retrieve their horseshoes and continued to rib each other relentlessly about all manner of things that brought their manhood into question. It was a lighthearted moment in an otherwise deadly serious existence.

The low *woof-woof* of an approaching K-9 grabbed their attention as one of their squad newbies, a soldier they nicknamed 'The Kid', approached with a serious-looking German shepherd on the end of his tether.

Everyone liked The Kid, although at twenty-five and after several long tours in various hot spots around the region, he was hardly considered a greenhorn. A communications expert who spoke several native dialects and handled his K-9 with adroit skill, he'd impressed even the most battle hardened of their squad. He wasn't standard military. Not exactly. Most likely he was CIA or one of the elite, super-secretive counterterrorism operatives deployed throughout the region. One of the norms in this corner of the world was that these men didn't ask questions of each other and rarely, if ever, used their real names. It was as if the time out of place nature of what they were ordered to do required a completely different mindset than the one they'd rely on in the real world.

"Hey Kid, what's up with McLain? He seems a bit tense this morning," Drae asked while he studied the dog on high alert, pacing this way and that, at the end of the tether.

True to a soldiers' habit for creating nicknames and catchy terms for nearly everything, this particular shepherd had been named after the Bruce Willis character in *Die Hard* because he had a small bald spot on top of his head. Their special tactical squad was even called Justice after the Justice League superheroes operating out of a hidden cave with a top-secret mandate to take on all villains who threatened the American way. Seemed oddly fitting in some perverse way.

Tugging on the tether to bring the dog under heel, The Kid shrugged, directing his reply to both men. "I don't know, Sirs. He got all antsy earlier at the south checkpoint, but none of the other canines reacted, so maybe he's just having a bad day." When the animal finally settled at his feet, tongue lolling out of his mouth as he panted and ever watchful in his capacity as a bomb-sniffing guard dog, all three men studied the brown and black shepherd with keen interest.

Never taking anything for granted or at face value, each mulled private thoughts as eyes, alert and ever vigilant, surveyed the scene, looking for anomalies that might explain the dog's tension. Improvised explosive devices and suicide bombers were the enemy's preferred *fuck you* method for striking the coalition forces. Attacks had been more frequent and in unexpected places, coming closer and closer to their secured areas.

Turning his attention away from the dog he had at his side, The Kid held his M-16 rifle protectively across his chest. "Hey, did you hear about Team Matrix? They were doing an overnight near the border when one of those motherfuckers blew a device on the convoy. Killed six, including an imbed from the BBC."

Hearing that bit of news, Cam and Drae looked at each other behind the dark lenses of their sunglasses. *Fuck.* Talking about body counts was usually immediately followed by a swift change of subject that Draegyn was quick to provide.

"Have you been over to HQ yet, Kid? The Major has been holed up there for way too long with a bunch of heavy-vested pussies. Oh, my bad. I mean *politicians* who were making his life hell, last we heard." The disdain Drae felt for those so-called public servants dripped from every word with special emphasis on the *pussy*.

Alex, the third wheel and senior member of their long association, was a brilliant tactician with the body and brawn of a battle-hardened warrior. He spent way too much time these days holding the sweaty hands of the never-ending stream of nervous politicians and state department yahoos who flew in under the cover of darkness. After a dog and pony show visit, they would hightail it back to the safety found on US soil so they could whip up their constituents and department heads with dramatic tales about the sights and sounds of life in a forward-operating base in the middle of what had become a never-ending war. All that PR shit wasn't exactly what Alex thought he'd be taking on when he was unexpectedly promoted last year.

"I saw Badirya headed that way earlier with Asef in tow. He asked where you were, Lieutenant," The Kid said in Cam's direction.

Thinking about Asef and his mother, Badirya, lightened Cameron's thoughts. Asef was nine or ten years old and accompanied his mother nearly every day when she came into their compound to work as a translator and secretary in the HQ. The youngster was bright-eyed and extremely personable. He loved all things American with a special enjoyment for anything and everything connected to Batman.

Cam liked the boy a lot, and he reminded Cam of him at an age before innocence got lost and life became serious. In his case, it was the year or two before his mother stuck one too many heroin needles in her drug-wasted body. She took her last breath on their wobbly stained living room couch, leaving him to an uncertain and complicated future.

Drae cast him one of those knowing looks that bordered on a leer before chiming in. "You've been spending quite a bit of time with the lovely widow and her son, Cam. You find a way underneath that hijab yet, dude?"

"Shut the fuck up, Drae," Cameron snapped. "You're way more likely to go for a pair of brown doe-eyes beneath a veil than either of us would," he added while gesturing with the tilt of his head to where The Kid stood. "Asef is a good kid, and it doesn't hurt to show the boy not all Americans are bloodthirsty dickheads worthy of jihad."

"Hey, leave me out of that argument, Sirs," The Kid added with tongue-in-cheek humor. "My fiancée would seriously kick my ass if she thought for one minute that any of the female locals were fraternizing with the enemy." Mention of his fiancée gave pause to Cameron and Draegyn. They'd seen pictures of the couple during happier times and had listened to many heartsick stories from the lonely warrior during his time assigned to their squad.

From Cam's deep-seated mistrust of women and ability to compartmentalize sexual encounters to Drae's man-whore behavior and Alex's cold-hearted view of romance, the three of them made quite a trio. Truth be told, each of them envied The Kid in his own way. The battlefield hadn't robbed him of the ability to feel or diminished the desire to forge a future beyond the shitstorm they lived in now.

Suddenly, McLain jumped up from his at-ease position and lifted his snout in the air. All three men, ever vigilant to even the slightest signal of danger, stopped in mid-thought and actively scanned their immediate surroundings. Something was up; they could sense it. By reflex and from sheer habit, Cam and Drae immediately hoisted their ever-present rifles and began moving toward the other side of the well-protected compound.

Shit got real when the K-9 took off running at a fast clip around a mortar pit with The Kid right behind him. A commotion was building just beyond their view. They could hear angry shouts and commands to stand down being barked out in Arabic.

All hell broke loose in the next ten seconds as gunfire erupted followed by a small explosion and then a massive *BOOM* that knocked Cam and Drae off their feet. Smoke, dust, shrapnel, and debris clogged the air.

Choking from the blast, Cam was on the ground, unable to move as debris covered most of his body. Frantically clawing away from the mess, he called out for Drae in the ensuing chaos.

"Draegyn! Drae! Are you all right? Where the hell are you?" he hollered as fear and adrenaline coursed wildly through his body. Spitting the putrid sand and dust from the blast out of his mouth, he crouched low, on alert, gun pointed in case of attack while the smoke cleared enough for him to finally see something more than the inside of a dark cloud.

Catching sight of Draegyn's unmoving form laying thirty feet away under a pile of tin and wood, Cam immediately sprinted to assist his fallen comrade. As he approached the spot where Drae fell, a sudden movement from the corner of his eye caused him to swing his weapon into a defensive posture, ready to annihilate any further attack that came their way. When four shit-kicking Marines raced by, he stood down, returning his focus to Drae.

With a burst of superhuman strength and determination, Cam lifted a tremendous piece of tin attached to a wooden post from his prone friend and wildly tossed it aside in an effort to reach Draegyn. When his battlefield brother was freed and able to slowly lift to his knees, Cam sighed a relief that equaled none he'd known before.

A heartbeat later, years of training took over. After helping Draegyn to his feet and checking to see that their weapons were ready to go, they started forward again in a fast sprint toward the center of the explosion.

Upon reaching the area of the HQ, the men stopped and assessed the scene before them. Bodies and parts of bodies were everywhere as shouts of, "Medic," and, "Code Red," filled the air. Half the HQ building was gone, and a fire had started in another structure nearby.

"Holy fuck, Cam!" Drae shouted. "Goddamn, motherfuckers," he growled. "We've got to find Alex."

Both men took off in the direction of the building where they hoped their friend would be found unhurt. Along the way, they encountered McLain, who was untethered and clearly in distress, wandering in circles around a clump of brown camo on the ground. Cam's stomach dropped away as he realized that The Kid had taken the worst from the blast while the dog had somehow survived. Fear arced up his spine, propelling him forward in search of Alex.

Drae got there first, shouting, "Alex, Alex! Talk to me, man! Where the fuck are you?" All around them, soldiers were frantically tossing debris aside in search of the dead and injured.

They found Alex, badly hurt, with blood pouring out of every inch of his body and a leg wound that looked like ground meat. He was alive, barely. The instinct to survive, no matter what the situation, had been branded on their souls in such a way that a pulse meant victory in an otherwise horrendous scenario.

Luckily for Alex, it took only seconds for an entire team to descend on the area and take control of the situation. In the end, sixteen military personnel had been killed or injured along with seven civilians. Magically, the visiting politicos had escaped unscathed, having left for the airfield earlier that morning.

After seeing to Alex's care and feeling satisfied he was alive and on the way to the hospital at Ramstein, Drae and Cameron were left to deal with the aftermath of what turned out to be a suicide bomber. In the days and years to come, each battlefield brother would have wounds and emotional scars to contend with. Not only was Alex critically injured and The Kid going home to his fiancée in a body bag, but the bomber also turned out to be the doe-eyed widow, Badirya, who sacrificed her only child Asef in some deranged act meant to re-unite her with her dead Afghan husband.

On that fateful day, the Justice Bothers were born from the smoke, death, and despair of an Afghan battlefield. Things would never be the same for any of them, and each carried demons, ghosts, and nightmares from that time into the future. In the two years that followed, one by one, their team would leave the desert hellhole behind and some would seek a future together, far away from war, in the hot, dusty winds of southern Arizona.

JUSTICE

# Chapter One

I T WAS FUCKING hot. Balls hot. No surprise because it was always hot in this part of the world. Cam had been used to the smell of his own sweat since the years he spent in the arid dust of the Middle East. It made ignoring the perspiration running down his back easier. Using the t-shirt crumpled up in his hands as a towel, he swiped it absently across his chest and face before dropping it to the floor and laying his head on the back of the chair.

Above him, an ancient ceiling fan cranked in useless, lazy circles. From his room on the second floor of the pensión, sounds from the bustling street below choked in the oppressive heat of the midday sun. The only noise inside his dingy, cheap-ass room came from the Hispanic woman leafing noisily through a trashy celebrity tabloid.

Amada, or whatever the hell her name was, sat at a small, rickety table with a folded up matchbook cover shoved under one leg to stop it from wobbling. She studied the American gossip magazine he offered her and inhaled an ice-cold Coke with gusto.

Wrong fucking time to think of his mother, but it couldn't be helped. He was the kid of a street whore whose lifestyle made his earliest years a living hell. Cam recalled a childhood of being shunted aside while his only parent entertained men and got royally fucked up on drugs.

In a weird way, this knowledge gave him a unique perspective when it came to these matters. The working girl sent to his room as bonus for a completed assignment wasn't eager to suck his dick because she wanted to. Her appearance at his door was just one of those things that happened in his line of work; something that was not wise to turn down.

He'd been south of the border for months on a job he knew was just this side of being illegal and seriously dangerous to his health. He would have preferred to wrap things up and silently vanish.

After a troubled youth of neglect and social poverty that lead him nowhere, the military had straightened him out in a hurry. A record of minor scrapes with the law, mostly fight club stuff that wouldn't even get an eye roll these days, his life had quickly careened out of control. He had been headed for a shitstorm of trouble. The military knocked some fucking sense into his thick head and gave a nineteen-year-old in a downward spiral the skills to manage his adult life. Following nearly a decade of a hardened soldier's life and the acquisition of some rather unique skills, he and two battlefield brothers had gone out into the real world and created an exclusive agency specializing in surveillance, protection, and cyber security.

Most of their assignments were straightforward, but at times, their unusual abilities and the promise of a substantial payday brought them to off-the-radar places like where he was today, doing work that required some of those dubious skills learned on the modern battlefield. He'd been in this dingy room for eight weeks, blending in effortlessly. His long, dark hair and beard gave him the appearance of a local and let him disappear into the background. Having completed this particular assignment, he was ready to start the careful transition from undercover work south of the border back to his regular life.

Manuel Santos showing his appreciation and satisfaction with the outcome of their professional arrangement by sending him someone from his stable of working girls presented Cam with a bit of a dilemma.

Turning down the woman's services would more than likely end with her getting an ass kicking, so he looked for a solution and did some quick strategizing in his head.

Fishing into his pocket, he pulled out some crumpled bank notes and pushed them into her hands. "No, no!" she cried in alarm. Her services were gratis per Santos's wishes. Taking money would cause problems.

"Don't worry," he told her in fluent Spanish. "That money is for your family. Use it wisely."

She didn't seem convinced and looked as if she'd start to cry at any second.

He wasn't in the mood for any of this. "It's fine," he bit out. Knowing whatever he said would most likely be reported back to Santos, he chose his words carefully with an eye to paving the road for his departure.

In rapid Spanish, he told her he was gay, thanked her for the offer with a cringe-worthy mock shudder of revulsion and motioned for her to sit down. Pulling the trashy tabloid from his shitty old ruck-sack, he tossed it on the table in front of her and offered the cold soda he'd been about to drink.

"Just between us, okay?" he told her.

She nodded and attacked the soda while he sat in an old chair and kept an eye on the time.

The ability to compartmentalize gave him an edge. The military taught him that, as did years of fending for himself on the mean streets of New York City. He sat there in the oppressive heat, thinking about the rivulet of sweat slowly making its way down his spine as he mapped out his departure from this hellhole. He was more than ready to leave this place and head for the busy urban environment of sprawling Mexico City where he could shed his scruffy local look and re-emerge as a suited businessman for the trip over the border to the US.

Amada flipped another page and studied the pictures in front of her. Sometimes, Cam wished he could be that detached, but in his line of work, it wouldn't do to get lazy or sloppy.

Case in point: it required a Herculean effort on his part to steer clear of Manuel's arm candy wife. She hit all the right notes as a crime lord's piece, including the one where she tried everything in her power to take a ride on his dick. She had made it clear what was being offered, and he could easily have fucked the man's wife and walked away without a backward glance.

The unsettling thought brought him to the ever-widening sinkhole of empty solitude that marked his life.

*Ugh. Where the fuck did that thought come from?*

Shit. Enough was enough. He needed to get the hell out of this God-forsaken place that reminded him so much of the stifling heat and dusty villages in Afghanistan where his military career ended. He wanted a hot shower and a shave. He needed to knock back a bottle of very expensive Scotch whisky, and most of all, Cam needed to get some goddamn air into his lungs. This oppressive heat was messing with his head.

When he figured enough time for a professional blowjob had gone by, he pushed Amada with his formidable presence to the door, and without ever laying a finger on her person, she was through it and forgotten half a second after he swung the creaking wood door shut.

Less than forty minutes later, he had loaded his rucksack into a dilapidated Jeep and was pulling out onto the bumpy backroads that would take him away from this scorching hellhole and back to his real life.

Back to being Cameron Justice.

# Chapter Two

EARLY FALL ON the East Coast during that period when the scenery was bursting with flaming autumn colors was the only time of the year Cam felt like returning to his old stomping ground. The magnificence of an East Coast fall was something that never failed to cleanse his soul. He'd been making this pilgrimage whenever possible for as long as he could remember.

As a New York City kid stuck in the social services system before he was ten, Cam had learned to survive the harsh realities of group foster care and the mean streets of Gotham. The summer he turned thirteen, a chance placement put him on a list of disadvantaged kids chosen to spend time at a summer camp in the Pocono Mountains of Northern Pennsylvania. The experience was life changing. Being able to punch his way out of a street fight didn't translate into being adept at rope climbing or help him build confidence in his ability to paddle a canoe. It was as if an entirely new world had opened up, right before his very eyes.

From that summer on, he made sure to get his name on the camp list. It was a slice of heaven in an otherwise coarse and unforgiving existence. The year before he turned eighteen and got dumped out of the system onto his own, he'd been lucky enough to be chosen as a junior camp counselor. Best goddamn summer of his life in more ways than he could count.

He'd spent the time banging an eccentric craft counselor at the camp, every chance he could. In her tiny cabin in the woods, Bridget Murphy enthusiastically taught him a lifetime of detailed lessons in the art of oral sex . Under her tutelage he learened how to coax the mysterious female orgasm to life during long, sultry summer nights that were the stuff of every teenage boy's fantasies. She'd schooled him on how to get her off and then showed him the many ways he could fuck what he'd pleasured.

Without a doubt, the highlight of this sexual schooling was Bridget's eagerness to blow him. Before that summer, he'd never known what it was like to push his dick to the back of a woman's mouth as he shot his come in endless spurts down her throat.

He looked forward to the nights when he could go down on her and then simply lay back on her creaky metal camp bed. Hands behind his head, he watched her straddle his cock and fuck him senseless. She preferred being on top, and Cam really liked watching her pendulous breasts sway and bounce with each of her frenzied movements. For an endlessly horny teenager, it was heaven.

When summer was over and the campers dispatched home, the counselors hung around a few extra weeks to close up the campground for the harsh weather ahead. The approach of the changing season in the Pennsylvania Mountains was something he was likely to never forget, same as the lessons learned from the naughty Bridget.

Returning to the area over the years, Cam found old towns that had seen better days dotted in the mountains around the ski resorts. On this fine autumn day, he found himself in a backwater village on the far edge of an upstate town with a couple of run-down bars, a laundromat, a bunch of stores, and a few gas stations. The rich folk lived in the fancy vacation homes and outlet shopping zones that reached into the mountains and brought tourists to this out-of-the-way place. However, here in town, he found that the normal hard scrabble, blue-collar life didn't crowd his preference for anonymity.

He'd been staying in a motor court on the town's outskirts for about a week, taking in the crisp air and blazing glory of autumn in full swing. A couple of more days and then he'd have to go home, get back to work, and deal with his day-to-day life. Draegyn was texting nonstop about clients on his queue, a signal from reality that he needed to start reconnecting.

Alex would also get on his case before too long. Cam sighed. With his higher rank than everyone else bullshit, the Major liked to think he knew everything. Immersed as he was in technology and the cyber world, dealing with data and machines sometimes made his former commanding officer an insensitive bully. He and Draegyn had been saying for months that the dude needed some damn human interaction. Not that the two of them should be talking much smack about the need for human connections. Neither he or nor Draegyn St. John, it seemed, were going to win any awards in a 'warm and fuzzy, let's be best friends' kind of way.

Right now, though, he was caught up watching a scene play out that had intrigued him each of the past three days when he'd come to this particular food joint. From his seat in a shadowed booth at the back of the diner, he'd noticed her immediately the first time he'd stopped in for a late breakfast. He had been drawn to her clipped, efficient movements as she sat in a small cramped space at the end of the long lunch counter. Everything about her actions told him she was trying to be as small and unnoticeable as possible. Too many tours of duty and hunting down terrorist bad guys had left a mark on him. Cam couldn't avoid the comparison of her behavior; it reminded him of tradecraft—attempting to avoid detection, something people didn't do without reason.

His gut told him something was up with this one, and he'd been hooked from that second on. When she turned up at the same time on the next day, Cam slipped into watchful mode. Keeping eyes on target was an occupational hazard, he guessed. He wasn't fooled by what he saw on the surface. Years of surveillance work sprang to life as he examined every single detail before him.

The object of his attention was young, maybe mid-twenties, with an air of quiet intensity. Her eyes were downcast but very much on constant guard as they flicked around the room, noticing every movement and every person approaching her personal space. Just like previously, she seemed to be taking great pains to remain small and of no consequence.

She was more than average in height but not too tall. Dressed in nondescript clothing that did nothing for her figure, she had on tattered sneakers, jeans at least a size too big, and a baggy sweater under an unzipped hoodie that screamed thrift store find. She carried a large backpack that had seen better days, and her movements suggested she guarded the pack like a Fabergé egg. Everything about her intrigued him.

He hadn't gotten near enough to see her features up close, but you couldn't miss the blond hair pulled back in a sloppy ponytail, framing an oval face with arched eyebrows, a pert nose, high cheekbones, and a determined chin. It was her hands that kept drawing his attention, though. In her attempt to be invisible, she kept them still and hidden in her lap. This was no preening female with wild, gesturing flourishes meant to attract the attention of every male in sight. Far from it. This girl appeared determined not to be seen at all.

When her hidden hands came into view, Cam saw she had long fingers and delicate looking wrists. Even from across the room, he found her hands beautifully expressive and wondered what made her keep them hidden away. He struggled to ignore the growing compulsion to experience those beautiful hands as they stroked the hard, angled planes of his body.

Beyond intrigued by the female stranger, Cam had arrived early at the diner today so he could observe her when she entered. He hadn't been disappointed when her ponytail appeared behind a town bus as it pulled away from the stop across the street. She walked directly into the diner and found the most out-of-the-way booth available, where she slid in and secured her meager belongings. Heaving a deep sigh, she relaxed against the back of the old vinyl-covered booth but never looked at the menu and barely glanced around the room.

She'd ordered what looked to be tea and a bowl of whatever soup made it on the daily special. Upon closer examination, he realized the older waitress was furtively loading her up with rolls and butter. *Hmm*. Ponytail, as he started calling her, had found a soft heart in the gruff, smoky-voiced waitress. Things were getting interesting.

He suspected that the diner was a stop-off. Somewhere she could go and sit without much bother. Several possible explanations for her behavior were ticking into place. Maybe she was a student cutting school, or perhaps a silly female with a hopeless crush on some dude working nearby.

The notion didn't sit well with him. Luckily, the fact that she didn't speak to or interact with a soul, outside a few murmured words with the waitress, crushed that scenario.

The way she carefully counted out a handful of change told him she was pinching pennies. He felt a surge of annoyance at the thought that the huge breakfast he'd just inhaled would be an indulgence to Ponytail. Maybe watching her wasn't such a good idea if he ended up all maudlin and soft about the circumstances of another person.

He didn't do maudlin, and he most definitely did not do soft. Cam took what he needed when the fancy struck him and never gave much thought to the aftermath. He wasn't what anyone would call a people person. Too many years in a shitstorm toting an M-16 rifle while decked out in head-to-toe Kevlar made him something of an emotional recluse in the everyday world. His dim view of women, created entirely from memories of his neglectful, selfish, and abusive mother, made him a less than charming guy.

At the end of the day, he got laid when he needed to, which had been pretty often until recently, and didn't bother with social niceties unless directly related to the flourishing security agency he and his Justice Brothers had launched. If no man was an island, the three of them were the exception to that rule.

His reverie was broken when Ponytail discreetly slipped into the ladies' room, hauling her stuffed backpack with her. Her bowl of soup and tea remained on the table, indicating she'd be returning to the booth. Craning his neck, he noticed a wall phone in the dark vestibule outside the restrooms and felt the sudden urge to make a call.

A couple of minutes later, he felt like an idiot as he engaged in basic Surveillance 101 by giving the impression he was using the phone as he scoped out what she was up to. *What the hell was he doing? Jesus.* He knew what he was doing. "The damn woman intrigues me," he whispered into the phone piece.

Before that thought could be followed with another, the restroom door swung open to allow a harried looking mother and her rambunctious kids to exit. As the woman stood holding the door wide, he spotted Ponytail standing at the back of the space along a wall of sinks. Snapping up the opportunity, he dropped the phone and gallantly offered assistance to the beleaguered mom by holding the door.

"Here, let me help you, ma'am," he mumbled, angling his body to prop the door farther so she could navigate a stroller and a hyperactive youngster out into the hallway.

From this vantage point, Cam was able to observe what Ponytail was doing and found her energetically rubbing something under a trickling faucet. Trained to look closer at scenes like this, he instantly recognized several important things.

A small bottle, probably liquid soap, was on the sink. So was an empty plastic bag. Her backpack was open on the floor next to her feet. From this angle, he saw something wadded up, like a t-shirt, and a big plastic bag spilling from the pack. Her attention was focused on something in the sink. Something small and blue. When she stopped for a moment to examine what she was holding, his mind stuttered as he realized that A. she was washing her panties, and B. she was clearly fretting. He heard her mutter sharply, "Well, that's just great. Period stains on the only new undies I have left."

*Fuck, had he heard her right?* He'd been instantly hooked as the sound of her voice struck him like a punch to the solar plexus. Slightly husky but decidedly feminine, her words ended with an exasperated sigh. He wanted to have a conversation with her. Listen to that beautiful, sexy voice and feel more of the squeezing in his chest.

The mother and her kid army wandered off, and the door closed in their wake, leaving Cam standing there feeling even more like an idiot. Man, he had to get his shit together immediately because stalking some poor girl was quite beneath his dignity. Sure, he tried to convince himself, it was an occupational hazard to be wrapped up in watching someone, but a line must be drawn at some point.

Hanging up the phone he'd left dangling and returning to his table, he tried to get his thoughts under control. Five minutes later, she returned from the restroom and slid into her booth without ever making eye contact with anyone.

Cam watched with knowing eyes as Ponytail slowly wrapped leftover rolls in several napkins. His own early experiences reminded him that she was likely saving them for later when hunger overtook the evening and make for a restless night. Maybe that was why he couldn't ignore her. She was striking chords of a memory deep inside from his miserable youth when food was a luxury and liquid soap siphoned out of public restroom dispensers was a smart move. He knew how much effort it took to survive.

The last thing he needed right now, though, was to be distracted by a female. That was not who he was and not at all how he lived his life. Best he remembered that and got his head back in the game before he did something dumb.

Dropping money on the table, he pulled an old baseball cap over his shaggy hair and ambled out of the diner without drawing attention to himself. Looking back over his shoulder at the last second, he saw her turn around and crane her neck to catch sight of the old clock above the lunch counter. Sensing she might be on the move soon, he made a snap decision to follow her and see where she was headed.

*So much for not getting involved.*

The intriguing Ponytail didn't disappoint when she left the diner ten minutes later and headed to the corner bus stop. From his vantage point, he had a perfect view of her as she stood with several others waiting for the next bus. Noting where the bus was headed, he figured that  be the end of Ponytail for today, but Cam was startled when, as the bus approached and people stood ready to board, she quietly and effortlessly vanished into the deep shadows of an alleyway behind the bus stop. *Shit.* She was deliberately trying to cover her trail.

The girl was good but not as good as he was. High-profile clients lined up for the expertise of the Justice Brothers for a reason. He followed her easily on foot, deeper and deeper into what was referred to as the other side of the tracks, where abandoned and sometimes crumbling houses scattered along cracked and worn streets.

When she cut across an empty lot and easily squeezed through an ancient chain-link fence, he was right behind her. With ever-watchful eyes, Cam took in his surroundings. A dilapidated apartment building sat watchful on the corner next to a long row of run-down homes. Two empty lots overgrown with weeds and piles of dirt partially hid several abandoned houses.

In the blink of an eye, his elusive Ponytail slid through a fence around one of the abandoned buildings and headed for a mission center tucked at the end of the dirty alley. Nodding as he processed the facts before him, Cam was hit with a wave of anger followed in short order by a sense of crushing familiarity. She was relying on the mission for shelter, trying to survive, and most likely hanging by a thread. All were conditions he knew too well. His gut knotted as he pushed the memories flying into his brain back into a cold, dark corner of his mind.

Distaste for the person he blamed for leaving him in dire straits made his mouth burn. The woman who had given him life was a selfish waste of humanity. He rarely referred to Lorraine as his mother because she was the furthest thing from being a parent. A common prostitute with an off and on drug dependence, the woman saw to her selfish needs by selling her body, leaving him to fend for scraps and cast-offs to survive.

As a child he'd never known a time when hunger and uncertainty weren't a part of his everyday life. Lorraine collapsed and died of a drug overdose right in front of him when he'd been just a boy. After that, he'd found himself deep in the social services system where the hunger and uncertainty never let up. His so-called mother had done nothing to protect or nurture him, and the only charitable thing he could eke out for her was the simple fact she gave him life.

He wondered who had let Ponytail down because ending up in a filthy alley next to a run-down mission at her young age wasn't a situation that happened without help, usually in the form of an authority figure or adult having dropped the ball somewhere along the line. *Fuck*. He was sucked in now.

Suddenly, Cam caught glimpses of two burly individuals lurking in the alleyway. Seconds later, a scuffle broke out. Assessing the commotion, he saw a flash of light hair followed by a small shout of alarm. Next thing he knew, his long legs were pounding down the alley as he shouted at what appeared to be two older teens while they struggled with Ponytail for the mangled bag she carried.

"I suggest you run for the hills, fellas!" he barked in a booming voice that threatened serious retribution for anyone not heeding what he said as he landed in the middle of a street fracas gotten out of hand. Apparently, she wasn't giving the backpack up without a fight.

"Mind your own fucking business, old man," the biggest of the teens hollered a split second before Cam's fist connected with his face. He could easily have killed the little fucker with no effort, but he held back on the punch and tried not to do any more than just scare the kid off. His frightened accomplice forgot all about Ponytail as he dragged his stumbling friend to safety.

Satisfied her assailants were effectively warned off, Cam turned his attention to the woman jumping up from where she'd been pushed, only to find her grabbing that blasted backpack like it was a lifeline and hauling ass away from him as fast as her shaking limbs could move.

Growling impatiently, Cam bit out, "Hold on there, lady! Are you all right?" She never even looked at him as she continued to put distance between them. Moving into action, Cam leaped forward, grabbing her arm to stop the retreat, repeating grimly, "I *asked* if you were all right."

Pretty much the last thing he expected was a cry of pain when his fingers wrapped forcefully around her forearm to stop the attempted escape. Glancing where his hand was gripped, he saw blood seeping through the sweatshirt sleeve.

"Take your hands off me," she screamed in his face as surprise and hesitation loosened his grip. "Let me go."

Ponytail appeared two seconds away from being hysterical, not that he could blame her. She'd been mugged in an alley, gotten bloodied somehow, and even though he was, in fact, rescuing her, from a victim's standpoint, she must be terrified by his less than friendly demeanor and dark, menacing appearance.

Not having much experience when it came to being reassuring or friendly, Cam was out of his league on this one. Years in the military and deliberate solitude did that to a man. He probably should have gentled his behavior, but he was in uncharted territory and feeling a tad out of sorts, so he resorted to tried and true tactics and went with the He-Man approach.

"Settle down, lady," he snarled, pulling her closer to inspect the bloodied arm. Her gasp of pain barely found its way into his conscious mind, but the way all the color leeched from her face did. Unfortunately, when he yanked her, she had been forced into his personal space by the fact that she weighed next to nothing. The terror on her face as she collided with his hard-muscled physique surprised him.

When shit happened, it usually happened quickly. The whispered anguish in her husky voice pleading with him, "Please don't hurt me," echoed in his brain as she collapsed in a dead faint. Luckily, his swift reflexes stopped her from hitting the pavement.

This was the first time he'd gotten a really good look at her up close. She was awfully young with flawless skin and fair coloring. Celebrity women paid surgeons thousands for what she came by naturally—a pair of plump lips that looked bee-stung and about as delectable as a woman's mouth could be. Even out cold, her chin angled in a way that dared the world to mess with her. However, it was the smattering of light brown freckles across the bridge of her perfect nose that melted his brain into his socks. With her hair swept back into that tight ponytail, she looked more kid than woman, a thought that made him uncomfortable.

A frozen spot in his soul suddenly heated up, making Cam all too aware of how unfamiliar he was with anything that resembled actual feelings. A chance encounter with a young ponytail was throwing his carefully detached demeanor into the shredder. Deciding that he was simply moved by her obvious struggles after what he'd experienced in his own life, he tried to bring his thoughts back into focus. This was not the time to let a pair of pouty lips distract him. Those lips and the freckles, though, had the power to stop his thoughts dead in their tracks.

Some of the color was returning to her face, suggesting she'd be coming around soon, so Cam quickly inspected her bloody forearm before she came to her senses. He wasn't sure if the slight gash he found was the work of a blade or an accident but it didn't matter. His first-aid kit and battlefield training could handle the injury, but he wasn't so sure he had anything that would solve the problem presented by having gotten involved in her life.

When her eyes fluttered open, it took a handful of seconds for her head to clear, but even that didn't stop the protective instincts that he appreciated all too well. With the grace of a cat, she leaped from the ground, grabbed the worn straps of her backpack, and made a supersonic dash away from him. Unfortunately for her, he was prepared and, being a great deal faster, effectively blocked her hasty retreat with his physical presence.

Stopping dead in her tracks, Ponytail eyed him warily sneering, "Go away." Cam was partially successful at trying not to enjoy the sound of her voice but lost out on projecting an air of disinterest when she fixed a pair of bright baby blue eyes on him. Having never seen eyes that color before, he was fascinated by the long fringed eyelashes blinking at him. He knew his presence scared her, but all he could wrap his mind around at that moment was how stunning her eyes were.

"I'm not going to hurt you," Cam murmured, removing the ball cap that shadowed his face. He watched her eyes dart, seeking a secondary route of escape. The last thing he wanted at that moment was for her to disappear, a thought as uncomfortable as it was shocking since he never gave two seconds of emotional thought to anyone or anything.

Going for clinical and straightforward, he nodded toward the arm in the bloodstained sweatshirt. "I'm guessing one of those idiots had a knife because there's a slice in the hoodie and you've got quite a gash. I have a well-stocked first-aid kit in my truck a few blocks from here. Let me help you out. *You're safe with me.*" He didn't analyze why he added those last words. Her alarm and panic made him want to set her fearful mind at ease.

"Please," he added, indicating with his outstretched hand that she should follow him as he led her away from the dark alley.

It took an eternity until she nodded her consent, while continuing to eye him cautiously. Cam was impressed by Ponytail's control in such a difficult predicament. *Down but not out*, he mused.

Interesting.

# Chapter Three

IT DIDN'T TAKE long to locate where his truck was parked. Convincing her to go with him to the motor court so he could attend to her injury took a bit longer. She said not a word when he promised to help her with no strings attached although she appeared to wobble a bit. Cam remembered what it was like to be cautious and suspicious about offered acts of kindness.

In his motel room, she sat warily at a table by the window while Cam gathered his first-aid kit. That she never relaxed her grip on that old bag she carried told him, while she might accept his offer of his assistance, she also kept one foot firmly out the door at the same time. Clearly, trust was an issue … something he understood.

Keeping her bag stuffed under one arm, she pushed back the bloody sleeve on the hoodie to inspect the injury. Her heavy sigh told Cam that she was surprised and probably a bit frustrated that she had one more thing to deal with. Turning her baby blues back to him, she kept silent when he moved to the table and began setting the first-aid supplies out.

Cam was struck again by how young she looked and kicked himself for being his usual gruff self. She'd been through an ordeal, and he should at least try to be civil and unthreatening. Unfortunately, a headache bumping around the corners of his brain and a deep achiness overtaking every inch of his body robbed him of the ability to feign friendliness. Being the loner he was, it took effort on his part to go through the motions expected in polite society of civilized people. Right now, he was feeling less than civilized.

Aware that her watchful eyes didn't miss a thing and deeply conscious of her wariness, he cleared his throat and gave polite a try. "By the way, my name is Cameron." *Jesus, was he actually waiting with bated breath for her to answer with that deliciously feminine voice he'd heard earlier?*

Instead of offering her name in return, she calmly said, "You chased those guys away in the alley." The sound of her voice reached into Cam's empty heart and took up residence. Unsettled by his reaction, he nodded but didn't say anything else as he held up a tube of antibiotic ointment to indicate what he was about to do. Putting a folded towel down on the table, he motioned with his head for her to lay her injured arm on it. When she cautiously complied, he grabbed a bottle of water and poured some of the liquid on the bloodied gash. Noting how Ponytail tried to silence a gasp of pain and suddenly fisted her hand, he wanted to reassure her but kept on with the task at hand against a backdrop of silence.

Upon closer inspection, he realized the gash was pretty deep but knew better than to suggest she seek emergency room care. He was intimately familiar with the wall of denial she'd build at the suggestion. People in her circumstances did everything they could to stay away from even the most basic of social services, usually out of an abundance of caution born of previous experience. He'd have to try suturing it himself to stem the bleeding and avoid infection.

He'd stitched himself up plenty over the years. Another battlefield skill learned through expedience. But stitching up this *younger-than-he-was-comfortable-admitting* girl was not something he relished doing. Especially not while a bone weary ache moved in waves through his body. Because there was no other choice, he completely ignored the stirring in his groin, and a growing heat that told him he was sporting a swift hard-on.

He studied her face. An anxious frown formed when she realized the wound was more than just a simple cut. Shoulders tense, she sighed and bit her lip. "Just wrap it up. I'll be fine." Though she tried for a determined air of invincibility, he caught the slight waver in her voice that offered a glimpse of the vulnerability she tried to disguise.

Jesus, but she was stubborn. "Wrapping isn't going to do it. You're bleeding, and a stitch or two will be necessary to close the wound. I've done this before," he added while pulling down the collar of his shirt to show her an old scar. "It's going to hurt like a son of a bitch, but luckily, I have some topical cream to numb the area first."

Raised eyebrows and a hastily spoken, "You up for this?" hung in the air for only a second before she shrugged and nodded for him to continue.

Twenty minutes later, Cam was relieved to be finishing the task at hand as he wrapped a length of bandage over the two stitches needed to close the nasty wound. She hadn't so much as moaned when he pierced her skin with the surgical needle although she'd gone rigid and turned white as a sheet. He'd seen bigger and tougher men in the midst of battle all but faint over similar experiences and felt a surge of admiration for the way she handled herself. The girl might be young, but Ponytail was no piece of fluff.

She sat quietly, rolling the bloodied sleeve over her bandaged arm while Cam put the medical supplies away and washed his hands. He noted her color beginning to return and was glad she hadn't tried to bolt for the door. Not entirely sure why but some reflex had him reaching for one of his old sweatshirts before tossing it her way.

"That hoodie is toast. There's no way to get all the blood out without leaving a huge stain, and besides, the slash left a tear in the sleeve." As he said the words, Cam remembered her standing at the washroom sink in the diner as she tried to rinse her panties of bloody stains that had nothing to do with being injured.

"You can put that on in there," he suggested with the tilt of his head toward the tiny bathroom that he knew was littered with the towels he'd tossed over the shower rod and a pile of discarded jeans and t-shirts left on the floor. She watched him silently with a cautious wariness that tugged at emotions he didn't want to think about. She hesitated and then hesitated some more.

"Look, I can see you don't exactly trust me, and I understand. But you are safe here, for real. It would help a lot if you told me your name, so we can talk to each other in more than nods and grunts."

Her blue eyes instantly shuttered, and she wavered, as if deciding whether to give him her real name. "Umm, well," she finally answered with a great deal of lip biting and fidgeting. "My name is Lacey."

Satisfaction mixed with a high-powered jolt of attraction moved through him at her answer. She wasn't sure if he was a threat or not, but apparently, she was willing to communicate, albeit on a need to know basis.

"Well, Lacey, you've had quite the day, and my hat is off to you for fending off those two thugs in the alley. I'll just slide out for a bit and grab some coffee at the snack bar to give you some privacy. Can I get you anything?" he added while she vehemently shook her head in the negative.

"Use of the bathroom is enough for me, thanks," she mumbled while gathering her bag and his well-worn sweatshirt.

Nodding, he told her, "I'll be back in about twenty minutes. Feel free to use whatever you find in the bathroom."

And with that, he eased himself out of the motel room heading for the snack bar across the driveway that offered an unimpeded view of the room in case she decided to try to scurry away once she thought his attention was diverted. For whatever reason, that thought did not sit well with Cam. As he stomped across the asphalt in search of hot coffee, he tried to come to grips with the unfamiliar, protective impulse the freckle-faced Ponytail had lit up inside him.

She also inspired a warm tightening in his groin that made him feel like a pig when he considered that she'd done nothing more than try to keep space and silence between them. *What the hell was wrong*

*with him that all he could think about once he'd heard her soft, femi-*
*nine voice was how she would sound surrendering to a mind-blowing*
*orgasm?* An orgasm he wanted to wring out of her.

By the time he had downed a mug of black coffee liberally mixed
with an abundance of sugar, Cam was juggling two realities. First, he
was undoubtedly getting sick as a dog. The uptick in his body temperature was letting him know a fever was on its way, and second, that
his curiosity about and uncharacteristic desire to help Ponytail was
messing with his emotions. He accounted for the tightening in his
chest at the mere thought of her pouty lips and bright baby blues to
the onset of a fever. *What the hell else could it possibly be?*

Grabbing a couple of sad looking sandwiches, a container of hot
tea for her, and another steaming coffee for him, Cam pocketed a couple of granola bars at the last second. He nodded at the attendant in
the motel snack bar and headed back to his room.

The minute he stepped inside, his senses were assailed with the
scent of soap and something else decidedly female wafting from the
confines of the bathroom. Noting that the door was still firmly shut
and probably locked, he set the food and beverages on the rickety table and then took a moment to check the text messages on his phone.
Drae was letting him know he'd be off the radar for a few days while
Alex texted twice about a technical glitch he was working on with an
admonishment not to bother him unless it was an emergency.

*Typical Alex*, he thought. Nothing got through the man's defensive shields except the machines and technology that made up his
world. Cam shouldn't judge since the Justice men were each damaged
in their own way. Drae, the martial arts expert and unabashed play-
boy, dealt with his inner demons by womanizing his way across every
continent on the planet. Alex was all but unreachable as he immersed
himself in the cold and impersonal world of cyberspace and artificial
intelligence. Cam rounded out their triad of emotional dysfunction
with a dark, brooding, and silent approach to life that didn't allow for
anything that even remotely approached real emotion.

*Jesus, was it hot in here?* Cam wondered as he checked the old thermostat on the wall. When he saw the temperature was actually on the cool side, he swore aloud, realizing the heat was from the fever overtaking him. He hated being under the weather and couldn't remember the last time he'd been honest-to-god sick. Being the ornery fuck he was, he'd always held to the belief he was too mean and cantankerous for germs to get close enough to stick. *Yeah. Not so much this time.*

Moments later, the bathroom door swung open and out stepped Ponytail; only this time, her hair was more wet than dry and hanging on her shoulders. The sweatshirt he had given her with the faded Marine Corps logo was several sizes too large and hung to mid-thigh. Her jeans had seen better days as had the ratty sneakers on her feet. Dressed as she was, with the hair he was used to seeing pulled tight against her skull now falling about her shoulders, this Lacey looked more girl than woman. As that odd thought thumped in his brain, he also realized his insistent hard-on was heating up at the sight of her. Feeling his dignity slipping away, Cam rationalized that it must be the fever.

Glancing sideways at him as though unwilling to spend more than a scarce second under his regard, she mumbled, "Thanks for the use of the bathroom," while making a beeline for the door. He couldn't believe she tried try to slip away with damp hair and a stomach he could hear growling from across the room.

Completely ignoring her attempt to run, Cam sidestepped the escape attempt by waving the sandwich and tea at her. "Sit down and eat something before you fall. The snack bar had slim pickings, but I grabbed us a couple of sandwiches, and there's hot, sweet tea for you." Noting her surprised hesitation, Cam motioned to a chair and away from the door as he sat down and began unwrapping one of the sandwiches.

"I'm guessing mystery meat," he said as he tried for amiable before taking a large bite. Making a face that said, *not so bad*, he sincerely hoped his nonthreatening manner was enough to persuade her to stay since that deer caught in the headlights look she had was rubbing his nerves. He fully understood where the wariness and reserve came from, but his curiosity and desire to get to know her better was something of a big deal. Cameron Justice didn't want to get to know anybody better. That was until Ponytail had wandered into his line of sight.

Her hunger won out, as he knew it would, and she slid economically into the seat across from him without much fuss. He didn't think he'd ever met a woman who was this quiet and uncommunicative. Apparently, Lacey wasn't much for conversation.

Okay, so it was up to him to make the dialogue happen. Not his strong suit by any means. Fantastic. Searching for words, he settled on an obvious question as a starter. "Is that your real name?" he asked. *You're some sparkling conversationalist,* chuckled the voice in his head.

Her blonde head nodded while popping the top off the steaming tea. Taking a delicate sip, he watched her swallow as she seemed to consider what, if anything, to say.

"Yes. Yes, it is," she answered slowly. "Lacey Anne Morrow."

He watched, silently fascinated, as her tongue swiped the tea from her lips. Her lips were fucking amazing. The fantasy-filled vision of those lips opening for his cock momentarily blinded him.

*Give me credit for a quick recovery,* Cam thought as he smoothly continued. "Well, Lacey Anne Morrow, you're the first damsel in distress I've ever rescued," he told her with a completely straight face. "I take it you are." He paused, searching for the right words. "Between places to live," he finished while continuing to inhale the pathetic sandwich. He studied her every move and noted most of the emotions flickering across her just scrubbed face.

Taking a measured bite of the sandwich, she looked at him full on. "More or less."

*Hmph. Lady of few words.* When she didn't offer anything more, he kept on eating, taking in her slow, deliberate movements. While she drank the hot tea and nibbled away, he remembered what it was like, trying not to give in to the hunger he knew she must have been feeling. Noticing she was favoring her injured arm, Cam nodded in her direction and asked, "Any better?"

"Um … well, it hurts a bit, but I suppose that's to be expected," she answered quietly with a shrug.

Rising from the table, Cam grabbed his overnight bag, fishing around until he extracted a container of analgesics. Tipping out two tablets on the table next to her, he said, "Take those for the pain." Retreating to the bathroom, he returned seconds later with a tear sheet of meds. Handing her the sealed antibiotic pill, he murmured, "Just in case an infection sets in."

When she eyed the pills with clear skepticism, he handed her the blister pack and bottle of pain relievers so she could see for herself that he wasn't fucking around. Some serious shit had to have visited this girl, judging by the way she reacted to every little thing. He wondered if she would have eaten the sandwich if he hadn't dug in first.

The minutes ticked by in silence as they finished eating and then sat back to finish their hot beverages. Cam was going over the options of what he wanted to say and do next as Lacey wrapped her hands around the container of sweetened hot tea. She was very good at not looking in his direction, a fact that was starting to make him uncharacteristically edgy. Glancing at his watch, Cam marked the time and made a quick decision on how to proceed.

"Look, I have to go out for a while so you're welcome to hang out here and grab some sleep if you want." When she finally looked at him, her face was closed, but the way she fidgeted told him she was uneasy. When she glanced at the door, he figured she was considering getting as far away from him as possible. He understood. She had learned the hard way, no doubt, to depend only on herself and not to trust anyone else.

Rising to his feet, Cam made to leave the room before she bolted. "I'm checking out some property an hour north of here," he told her while pointedly looking at his watch. "You'll have the place all to yourself for hours." Catching her guarded expression, he hastily added, "Really, Lacey, I'm no threat. Just trying to help."

The shrug of his shoulders, and the way he kept his distance must have eased her fears because she nodded shakily while biting her lip, a hopeful sign that she would accept his offer. Mentally adding to the win column, he deliberately ignored that she still wasn't completely at ease around him.

Grabbing his keys and cell phone, Cam slid on an old leather jacket and reached for his sunglasses. Remembering the granola bars he had pocketed earlier, he tossed one for her on the table with a nod. "For you," was all he said. Surprisingly, he wished she would talk to him. Not known for being particularly loquacious, Cam spent a good deal of his time in silence and preferred the sound of his private thoughts to the inane chatter of others. Hoping for some chitchat with a total stranger was throwing him off.

"I'll be back around nightfall. The door will lock behind me. Try to relax, Lacey, and if that arm starts to bother you, take more pain medication." She attempted a half smile, but it didn't stick on her face for more than a second. *Poor kid*, he thought. She didn't deserve to be so suspicious of basic human kindness. Cam almost laughed out loud at that. He was known for a lot of things but being a purveyor of humanity wasn't one of them.

As he made for the door, he turned around and looked at her one more time. "Get some sleep. You look beat. We'll talk when I get back." With that, he swept out the door and climbed into his truck without looking back. He really did need to check out the fifty-acre farm he'd arranged to tour. Buying property in the mountains was a new whim he'd been tossing around for months. Unfortunately for him, though, he really was starting to feel like warmed over shit as his temperature climbed.

"What-fucking-ever," he mumbled out loud as the truck backed from the parking space. Mind over matter. No way was some annoying bug going to take him down. And with that, he hit the highway and started driving.

Lacey peeked cautiously through the curtains as her rescuer drove his truck out of the parking lot and headed north toward the main highway that lead out of town. An abundance of caution kept her rooted in that spot scanning the area around the motel for several long minutes before she finally stepped back from the window and heaved a deep sigh.

She didn't know what to make of him. Beyond thankful that he appeared in time to thwart a bag snatching that had gotten out of hand, he had also sort of frightened her with a dark knight quality that stole her breath.

Besides the obvious fact that he was big, solid, and muscular, he had an intimidating presence that drew rather than repelled her interest. Vivid green eyes with abundant dark eyelashes on a handsome face covered in several days' stubble, he was definitely a looker. The man had a double dose of bad boy sex appeal going on as well. The shaggy black hair in need of a trim only added to his attraction.

Looking around the motel room, she noted that except for the pile of clothes on the floor in the bathroom, he was as neat as a pin. The somber, dark-haired man who just left was nothing like any who had passed through her life before. Her neglectful father had been an indifferent slob, and the uncle who had nearly destroyed her life had been nothing short of a slovenly pig.

Thinking about her two worthless relatives was a reminder of how rough the past couple of years had been. Technically speaking, she became a runaway when she fled south Florida at seventeen. In the five years since then, she'd been living hand-to-mouth, performing odd jobs, doing seasonal labor, and surviving by sheer luck and gritty determination. When available, she stayed in short-term motel rooms like this one, but mostly, she'd been surviving in campgrounds, the occasional overnights in church run missions, and urban youth hostels.

Relying on her gut for instinct, something that had served her well all these years, she decided to see where this chance encounter went. Trust was not something Lacey had much success with, but the way his presence seeped into her veins with a surprising warmth and ease fueled her leap of faith. He didn't look like a *Cameron,* but he said that was his name, and she couldn't deny there was something special about him.

Her arm ached and she was feeling drained by the past few tumultuous hours. Stretching her limbs, Lacey tried to pull herself together, forcing some of the day's tension to recede. If her rescuer planned to be gone for hours, she was going to take advantage of the opportunity to crash in safety and comfort. It seemed weird to sleep in a strange man's bed, so she plucked a pillow from under the coverlet and instead settled down on the lumpy sofa.

Despite being exhausted from the earlier turmoil, she didn't immediately drop off to sleep. Instead, she saw in her mind's eye the vision of a tall man with shaggy black hair and unusual green eyes beneath dark brows that made him look fierce and dangerous. His mouth reformed time and time again in her thoughts as she struggled to find sleep. Her savior had a full bottom lip and sensuous heart-shaped top lip that made her think of things she had no business contemplating. Things like how it would feel to be kissed by those lips. Words like *devoured* and *consumed* filled her brain while warmth spread slowly through her nervous system.

At twenty-two years of age, she felt aged beyond mere dates on a calendar. Even so, she'd never been kissed. Never felt the warmth of a lover's embrace. Never wanted to, either; at least, not up until this second, a realization that rocked her world.

*How could she sleep when her thoughts were full of the devastatingly handsome hero who oozed masculinity and raw desire?* He'd been uncommonly kind to her, yet something else lurked just below the surface. Something dark and serious. He had eyes that saw too much, as if he could click into her private thoughts at will. Maybe he had his demons too, just like she did, and maybe just like her, he was emotionally damaged and trying to make sense of what life had put on his plate. *Whatever.* A deep yawn emptied her lungs. He was as much a mystery to her as she was to him, and with that last thought,

Lacey drifted off.

She must have slept like the dead because it was well after nightfall when she roused. Waking up in an unfamiliar setting made her jump straight up and off the sofa before she remembered where she was. Quickly darting to the curtain-covered window, she peeked outside, noting that Cameron's truck wasn't there. True to his word, he had been gone for hours, and a quick glance at the clock on the bedside table told her he'd likely be returning soon.

Spying the granola bar he'd left, Lacey inhaled the delightful treat as she replaced the pillow on his bed. Out of habit, she then checked her old backpack to make sure her meager belongings were okay.

Lacey could only walk in circles for so long, so she turned on the TV, clicking through the channels to find the local weather report. Summer was a fading memory and her August birthday in the rear view mirror. Now that autumn was in full swing it wouldn't be too long before the weather turned cold. Almost time to head south to a warmer climate where she'd be better able to survive through the winter.

She would avoid going anywhere near Florida, of course; a place she'd come to hate with a passion as unwelcome memories of her former life there flashed in her mind. Having saved enough money from doing summer work to afford a bus ticket, she was considering Georgia or Texas. Lacey knew the homeless nonsense was getting old so her goal was to find a job and a cheap room in a new town where she could build a life.

That thought was barely spent when she heard the low rumbling of a big vehicle outside the motel room. Standing, she wiped the granola bar crumbs from her lips and peered through the room's door peephole to see if it was her mysterious rescuer returning.

He said they'd talk when he returned, something that Lacey wasn't good at. She'd always found quiet safer than being a motor mouth. Sliding the security chain free, she cracked the motel room door before moving herself to the other side of the room as she waited for him to appear.

A wayward thought danced in her mind. She'd been yearning for a friend, someone she could try her hand at trusting. *Had that person magically appeared in the form of the mysterious, brooding enigma who had shown her unusual kindness on what was one of the worst days of her life?* As she waited for whatever happened next, the old maxim *Be Careful What You Wish For* washed through her mind. *Hmm.*

# Chapter Four

RELIEVED TO BE back at the motel in one piece, Cameron sat in the cab of his truck for several minutes while he struggled to pull himself together. The property tour had gone reasonably well, but as the day wore on, he had become sicker and sicker. A climbing fever and an uneasy rumbling in his gut made the past hour and a half sheer torture as he navigated the mountain roads. Twice he'd had to pull over when his stomach turned on him. Puking out his guts along the side of the road hadn't exactly been a party and he wasn't so sure his legs would even carry him to the room when he got out of the truck.

Lacey and her ponytail had been front and center in his thoughts all day. He hoped she'd still be there when he got back because Cam was pretty sure if she wasn't, he'd track her down in a heartbeat. Something about the woman-child got to him in a way he didn't want to examine too closely. He'd been entranced by her baby blue eyes and seduced by the sound of her voice almost from the first second. She was an unexpected breath of fresh air in his stagnant, walled-off emotional life. He tried convincing himself that the admission was because of his fever.

Trembling fingers that didn't seem to want to do his bidding fumbled with the keys in the ignition before he pushed open the truck's door with his foot and tried swinging himself free of the cab. A long string of pithy swear words lit up his mind but stayed unspoken since he sincerely doubted he had the strength to do anything more than groan. The terse, "*Fuck*," that did find its way from his weakened vocal cords was all he could manage when he leaned against the side of the truck and waited for the world to stop spinning.

Staggering to the motel room door, Cam was surprised to find it unlocked and slightly ajar. Relief surged through him knowing that Ponytail was on the other side of the door. When his stomach made an unfortunate series of spasms and lurches, he picked up his pace, rushing through the open door and charging toward the bathroom before he embarrassed himself by vomiting all over the motel room floor.

Even sick as a dog, he made note of the blond-haired, freckle-faced girl watching him in silence as he ran to the bathroom. Slamming the door a mere second before it was too late, he surrendered to a violent case of the pukes that left him shaking and weakened under the blinding glare of the way-too-bright bathroom lights. If a gun was available, Cam would happily shoot out each of the bulbs.

Lacey was right there when he came out of the bathroom, helping him stumble to the bed. He collapsed as powerful body-shaking chills swept through him. After that, everything became a blur. Somehow, he managed to yank his t-shirt over his head and shuck off his jeans. The last thing he remembered before passing out was the concerned expression on a freckled face that reminded him, for once, he was not completely alone.

*Holy cow*, Lacey thought. *He's a mess*. She'd been stunned when her dark angel lumbered into the room, just barely making it to the toilet before throwing up. By the time he crashed on the bed, his body was shaking uncontrollably with chills as he fell into the sleep of sickness. *Well, looks like one good turn deserves another,* she mused because clearly, her rescuer was more than just a tad under the weather. Judging by his pallor and the way he was shaking, a serious case of the flu was having its way with him. She marveled at his ability to drive in his condition, much less find his way back to the motel in one piece.

Switching into angel of mercy mode, she put a hand on his forehead to check his temperature. He was burning up. She needed to get him comfortable and under a pile of blankets before that fever got completely out of control.

Trying to be clinical, Lacey took in the sight of his half-naked form. After shedding his clothes, Cameron was left in just a pair of snug cotton boxer briefs that did little to cover his masculine attributes. *And, dear god, did he ever have attributes.*

As he sprawled across the bed, she was captivated by the width of his shoulders and the unusual tattoo circling his bicep. His deeply tanned torso, contoured with the distinctive shape of some seriously hard-muscled abs, was covered with a smattering of hair that fed in a diminishing line into his boxers. Powerful thighs and long legs flickered across her glance before her eyes fixed on the clear outline of his sex in the soft cotton molded to his body.

Not having any experience whatsoever in what a real live, fully grown man looked like in his underwear, Lacey couldn't help but indulge her curiosity as she took in the full measure of the man before her. She'd seen a famous sports celebrity in a magazine ad hawking the type of boxers he had on. Even passed out from sickness, he looked better than the guy had in the magazine. Clearly, he wasn't a tighty whities kind of guy and considering what was staring her in the face, she was unexpectedly glad.

The elastic band of the snug gray briefs slung low beneath his navel, revealing v-shaped lower abs that disappeared behind the soft fabric. He was naturally slim-hipped and the boxers molded the top of his bulging, muscular thighs in a way that made Lacey's mind go blank. But it was the pouch where his private parts were that almost made her stop breathing. The snug cotton clung to his manhood, leaving very little to the imagination … even her inexperienced and slightly naïve imagination.

Feeling like a naughty voyeur, she cleared her throat while staring shamelessly. The rounded spheres of his balls supported the outline of a penis. She unconsciously bit her lip. Her visual survey studied the sexy silhouette noting how it lay against his groin, almost topping out of the waistband. Even passed out, his virility screamed loud and clear as she mapped the impressive length and fat head of his staff. Yeah, there was no denying it—he was devastatingly gorgeous.

Lacey's mind screamed as her conscience tapped on her shoulder with a snappy reminder that she was ogling an unconscious man. *What the hell was she doing?*

Well, she was only human, and if truth were told her dark knight was one mouthwatering sight capable of drenching the panties of a nun.

Yanking on her messy ponytail, she cleared her throat yet again and tried unsuccessfully to pull her wayward thoughts back in to line. Fantasizing about some hot guy was a luxury Lacey couldn't allow in her daily struggle to survive. She'd been fierce in her determination to get past the limitations visited upon her life by those who should have been taking care of a young and growing child. All the normal teenage things like having girlfriends, exploring makeup, boys, dating, clothes, pop culture, and even graduating from high school had been totally absent from her life.

With a self-conscious grimace, she admitted that something as simple and innocent as enjoying the sight of a good-looking guy was an extravagance she'd never indulged in. Keeping herself together and safe was a tall order that dominated every waking hour and seeped into her dreams. While young women her age were daydreaming about careers, weddings, a house in the suburbs with a minivan in the driveway, and a hunky husband mowing the lawn, Lacey's fanciful musings were more basic like having a real bed to sleep in, enough to eat, and a few dollars in her pocket. But Cameron's passed out body shot right past all those basics and struck her emotionally in a place she didn't know existed.

Looking around the room, she spied a shallow plastic container that could be filled with water so she could get a cold compress on his head to help lower his body temperature. The bathroom was a disaster, but he managed not to vomit all over the place; a small blessing that allowed Lacey to focus on other things like the sick man she felt compelled to help.

Several hours passed with no improvement in Cameron's condition. In fact, the fever and shivering only seemed to increase. Lacey's anxiety spiked higher and higher as she struggled to stay ahead of the escalating problems. Biting her lip and frowning in concentration, she tried pressing a cold washcloth to his forehead, but the fever seemed to be raging out of control. When that didn't get the desired results, she went one step further, running the cooling cloth over his impressive torso.

He certainly was something to behold. His body was so hard and uncompromising that saying he had abs of steel seemed like an understatement. As she swiped the cool wet cloth across his torso and down his massive, muscled arms, she studied the dark tribal tattoo that wrapped around one bicep. Even the ink marking him seemed dark and dangerous.

She kept up the slow, languid strokes of the cooling cloth across his fevered skin, telling herself all the while that she was simply doing what anyone in her position would. *Liar*, her conscience screamed as she tried desperately not to enjoy the way his skin felt under her fingers. Laying the palm of her hand against his temple to gauge his temperature, Lacey couldn't help but brush the long hair back from his forehead while enjoying the softness she discovered when her fingers swept through his black mane.

He moaned at her touch, turning his face toward her hand as if seeking comfort. She highly doubted that was something he would do if not for the fever. He very much struck her as a man who didn't look outside himself for anything. *Seems familiar,* she snorted wryly to no one but herself.

Lacey glanced at the clock and then back at a severely weakened Cameron, whose temperature was showing no signs of abating. Sitting by his side on the double bed, she considered her options, trying to decide what she should do next. She spied the first-aid kit he'd brought out earlier.

"Oh, thank god," she muttered upon finding a package of liquid fever reducer in handy single-dose packets. She wondered why he traveled with a complete first-aid kit that was something of a mini-triage setup. Deciding it was none of her business, she set about ripping the top off of one of the packets and carefully dribbling the gooey liquid into his mouth. She followed that with a slow, thin stream of cold water to flush the fever reducer down his throat. Relieved to have accomplished this task so easily, Lacey crossed her fingers and prayed that the medication worked quickly.

The next hour passed with his body still shivering even though he was under several blankets. In his delirium, Cameron mumbled and thrashed about on the bed, obviously running from the demons his fever produced.

"Drae, Drae," he muttered in an anguished groan. "Find Alex. Oh, my god! Oh, my god! They're all dead," he cried out as his body shook and shuddered. "No, nooooo!" he choked out as the fevered nightmare took over. Lacey looked around the room, wondering what to do. He couldn't continue like this without possibly hurting himself, and as big as he was, she seriously doubted her ability to restrain him should he get out of control.

Muttering tersely, "Oh, pooh," she came to a hasty decision. Quickly peeling off her jeans and Cameron's old sweatshirt, she slipped under the covers and pulled his sweat covered, cold, and quaking body close to hers, wrapping him in her arms as she willed her body heat to ease his suffering. He seemed to relax almost immediately while Lacey, in nothing but an old stretchy camisole and plain cotton undies, wrapped herself around him as best she could.

Quietly and calmly, she whispered to him so he would know in his fevered restlessness that she was there and trying to do all she could to help him. Cooing to him as a mother might to a sick child, she spoke in hushed tones to try to ease his pain.

"It's all right, Cameron. I've got you. Relax. Relax." Cuddling his body close while stroking fingers gently across his fevered brow, she noticed that he responded to the sound of her voice, by going still and turning toward her.

Holding the huge, muscular man in her arms wasn't all that unpleasant. They fit together in some odd way. As she soothed him with inane words, he calmed even more. Eventually he trapped her in place by curling into her body with his head on her shoulder and a knee thrown over her leg. The crooked leg wedged between her thighs made her pulse race.

While her heart thumped wildly, Lacey cooed, telling him random details of her life, and at one point, desperate for words, she even read the community messages flashing on the local cable channel. She told him about recycling dates and an arts festival coming to town. Whenever she paused, he moaned and became restless. To keep him still, she read telephone numbers for animal control and recited the names of everyone in the school district's administration. It struck her someplace deep inside that the sound of her voice was bringing him comfort from his fevered demons.

Time passed as his temperature continued to rage, but Lacey never stopped her soft words and gentle touches. At some point, he snuggled deep into her neck. She could feel his hot breath against her skin while he gently cupped her breast in the hand that had flung across her. She had to bite back a groan when his sturdy fingers wrapped around the soft mound, causing her nipple to harden and ache from the contact. To add to her already off-the-charts physical awareness of him, when he shifted his thigh over hers, she could feel the unmistakable presence of the part of him that made him so masculine; the part she had been ogling and curious about earlier.

She adjusted her hips to make the contact more direct and flushed with embarrassment at the realization she was enjoying their tangled limbs. Biting back a string of graphic swear words that she would never dream of uttering out loud, Lacey kept up the running dialogue that was soothing the dark knight.

They stayed like that for long hours with Lacey wide-awake and conscious of his every move. At one point in his delirium, he mumbled what sounded like military talk as he fought off the nightmares. She caught words like *ambush* and *IED* and shuddered knowing he'd been through some sort of soldier's hell. She thought it explained a lot.

Trying to ease his anguish, she stroked the muscled arm crossing her chest and much to her horror, allowed her leg to move along his thigh while his manhood pressed intimately against her female core. He seemed to like that and nestled deeper into her, relaxing and murmuring hushed sounds that she couldn't make out. She thought she heard him mutter, "Ponytail," and went completely still.

When he shimmied slightly, causing his thigh to rub sensuously between her legs, Lacey didn't even try to bite back the moan of awareness and full body shudder that rolled through her. He was killing her with a flash of fire she'd never experienced before. That he was unaware of what he was doing brought pangs of regret to her confused mind.

Seconds later, she distinctly heard, "Mmm, Ponytail. Been waiting for you." Her world shuddered to a screeching halt. *Was he talking about her?* Fevers didn't lie and couldn't play mind games. *Was he dreaming about her? A girl with a shaky past and no future who he'd only met this morning?*

Leaning into him, she whispered, "I'm here, Cameron. You're with me, and everything is gonna be all right." His answering groan and the heavy, relaxing sigh that followed sliced through her composure like a hot knife cutting through soft butter. Lacey was undone. She never, ever allowed anyone to get close, so she didn't understand what was happening. *How could she, who rarely relaxed or felt safe, suddenly feel as though she'd found a place that was hers and hers alone while wrapped in an embrace with a man she didn't really know?*

Left alone with her thoughts, she had nothing to do but wait. Wait and see where this strange encounter led. Dawn was long passed when she felt his fever finally break. Waves of relief flooded through her now that the crisis had passed. Satisfied that she'd done all she could, Lacey slipped from the bed, pulled on his old sweatshirt once again, and collapsed in a thankful heap on the sofa before eventually drifting off into a deep sleep.

The all-too-familiar dream turned nightmare had him in its deadly grip as Cam burned through a fever that shut down his body and ignited his brain. As each flickering scene danced in his mind's eye, building toward the black oblivion that waited, his body tensed just a little bit more until, stiff and unyielding, he was thrust backward in time to that awful day.

As always, the unremarkable parts of what had started off as just another sand and dust choked day played out in rapid-fire fashion; a game of horseshoes with Drae, the way a bottle of water he'd been guzzling had warmed in the relentless heat, the muffled sound over-head when the occasional breeze of hot, dry air rustled the American flag raised each day just yards from where he stood. Nothing remark-able stood out because those were the moments of a soldier's life that played on an endless loop.

Then there were the scenes of horror and fear and reliving mo-ments of physically demanding effort when, weighed down by Kevlar and firearms, his mettle was tested over and over.

Even in the throes of fever, he knew, what was coming next. All these years later, the sensation of apprehension racing through his nervous system and the way his senses switched from neutral to high alert never failed to get his heartbeat racing. He remembered with crystal clarity the way his weapon felt in his grip and the sound of gravel and sand crunching underfoot as he and Drae raced toward the danger with no thought of their own safety. A warrior's salvation was found in forward motion; but this time that deliverance was framed in black smoke and an anger that burned deep in his gut, even to this day.

Eventually, the nightmare exploded just as the day had and Cam was thrown into a deep tangle of horror that was infused with treachery and fear. All of it was punctuated with the sounds and smell of death. Blood and terror swam before his closed eyes until revulsion for what had been lost mixed with a steely determination to escape the burning hellhole lifted him from the past a split second before his eyes opened on the present day.

He lay there, letting the past recede from his thoughts while willing his racing heart to calm and return to normal. Minutes ticked by and the memories that had been loosened by sickness slowly faded until only silence was left. Cam blinked heavily once or twice then struggled to sit up before gingerly swinging his legs over the side of the bed.

At first, he could only sit there, with his elbows resting on knees that seemed just a bit shaky. Holding his head with both hands, he scrubbed his fingers back and forth against his skull through hair that needed a trim. His mouth felt dry and tasted downright nasty, plus the aftermath of a high fever left him smelling like an overripe kennel. *Ugh.*

Eventually raising his head, he swiped a hand down his chest and took a deep steadying breath. Looking around, he noting every detail about his surroundings. Down by his feet in a rumpled pile were his jeans along with a t-shirt, some socks, and his boots. On the nightstand lay his pair of Oakley sunglasses, his key ring, the room key, and the old, leather wallet he carried. A plastic container of water was also there with a washcloth hanging over the side. The bed under his butt was seriously rumpled.

Turning toward the flickering TV, he immediately noticed Ponytail with her back to him lying curled on the ancient sofa under the window whose curtains were blessedly closed tight. The light peeking in around the sides told him it was probably midday, but right this second, a blast of bright sunlight would probably cause his head to explode.

The surge of relief that shot through Cam upon finding her still on the scene almost rivaled the sudden tightening in his shorts. He studied her as she shimmied to find a more comfortable position and in doing so caused his oversized sweatshirt to ride up, revealing a pair of no-nonsense white panties.

The sight of those plain panties shot through him like a cannonball of desire that landed squarely in his head, both of them. The one on his shoulders that should know better, and the one twitching between his legs that apparently did not. Unbidden, but definitely in full-on Technicolor, his thoughts created an erotic tableau that showed him moving across the room to strip the sensible white cotton from the deliciously heart-shaped derrière staring him in the face so he could run his big hands along the plump orbs to see if her skin was as soft and warm as his imagination insisted it would be. That mouthwatering thought was immediately followed by an urgent desire to flip her over and bury his face between her thighs so he could lick and probe her damp folds with his tongue while she writhed and whimpered until he'd made her come with a scream that he knew would be as sexy as her voice.

When his dick started throbbing, Cam knew for sure the sickness of yesterday had passed and the current aching of his sex was much, much more than a simple reaction to a morning hard-on. He'd never experienced a wanting as strong as the one turning him inside out now. *Where the hell was all this coming from?*

Having never had a girlfriend or anything that even remotely resembled an actual romantic relationship, Cam's preference was for uncomplicated sex whenever and however he wanted. A direct result of his lifelong impulse never to let down his guard with or put his full trust in a woman. Any woman. His mother had taught him that lesson from the cradle. He didn't consider himself a man-whore, but in all honesty, he didn't get all that invested in whether his sexual partners enjoyed what passed between them. He preferred adult encounters with women who were savvy enough to take control of their own gratification.

Oh, he was great in the sack and had the necessary knowledge and talent to bring any woman to a quivering, moaning completion. But over the past year or so, he'd been more and more unsatisfied with everything surrounding the emotionally empty, sex-fueled encounters that were his norm. He'd been sleeping with a divorced mother of two who he'd met through work. She was a lawyer coming out of an ugly divorce with no interest in romance or relationships. What they did together was about getting laid. She was a terrific legal resource, wanted nothing from him but his cock, and was a high-energy lover with a taste for mild BDSM. They had hooked up every few weeks for more than a year at a motel out in the desert where 'anonymous' was everyone's first name.

Cam hadn't been fond of the heavy-handed caveman antics she needed in order to get off, but his powerful sex drive overrode the dissatisfaction he felt afterward. Until six months ago, they'd regularly indulged in what became increasingly dreary encounters. After his return from Mexico, he simply never contacted her again. Something had happened to him in those long months south of the border. Maybe he'd had too much tequila or maybe he'd spent too much time thinking about the wasteland that his personal life had become. *Whatever.* There'd been a shift in his thinking, and he didn't need to pick apart his emotional life, or lack thereof, at every turn in the road. It was what it was, plain and simple.

Maybe that was why this ponytailed innocent with her huge pile of shit to deal with had gotten to him. He had to get it together before what he was feeling got out of hand. Men like him shouldn't mess with girls like her. He was damaged. *Broken.* Nothing could ever change that.

Cautiously hauling to his feet, Cam headed to the small bathroom, shutting the door behind him with a distinct snick. Upon catching sight of his reflection in the mirror, he was shocked to see how ravaged he'd been by his bout with the flu.

He snorted aloud, "Some warrior." Looking strung out, his cheeks still bore the flush of a raging fever. Hair that no doubt had been drenched by sweat was either slicked to his head or wildly sticking out. The several days' growth of beard he sported made him appear rather menacing. In short, he looked like death warmed over and left to rot.

It didn't take long to use the toilet and wash up as best he could without actually taking a shower. Although he felt with each passing minute that he was getting his strength back, he also knew that unless he wanted to end up sprawled on the floor in a heap, he needed to take things slowly.

About the last thing he expected when he opened the bathroom door was to find Lacey standing on the other side with a worried frown on her face.

"Are you all right?" she asked in that warm, sexy female voice he rather enjoyed.

And just like that, he was back to fighting off an erection with a mind of its own.

# Chapter Five

LACEY AWAKENED FROM a deep slumber the moment she heard the bathroom door click shut. Accustomed to being alert, she immediately sat up and scanned the room for Cameron's presence. Apparently, he was awake and had made it as far as the bathroom.

Getting up, she tugged his old sweatshirt to the tops of her thighs and hurried across the room to stand outside the bathroom door. Hearing the sound of running water, she felt relieved and let some of the anxiety leave her once she realized he must be feeling somewhat better if he could see to his own needs.

Pacing back and forth, she wrung her hands and waited for the door to swing open. When it did, she immediately stepped forward to help him.

"Are you all right?" *Uh-oh! Was that husky voice coming from her?*

She was in no way used to being so affected by someone of the opposite sex. This particular man was making her experience feelings and sensations that until now had been a complete mystery.

His look of surprise at her obvious worry pierced her brain, making Lacey pretty damn sure that her hero was rarely, *if ever*, on the receiving end of someone else's concern. She moved closer, placing an arm around his waist to steady him while the other hand instinctively came up to rest against his chest. That he let her help him was a testament to his weakened state, or so she thought. Guiding him cautiously back to the bed, she helped him sit down and then snagged a second pillow to place behind his back so he could recline comfortably.

Cam was all but speechless when he found her on the other side of the bathroom door and was thrown by the adorable woman's attempts to be his angel of mercy. When she curved an arm protectively around his waist and laid the other hand against his chest, emotions he didn't know how to describe overcame him. That he could have performed cartwheels across the room didn't stop him from acting the invalid by allowing, and actually reveling in, her concerned ministrations.

Walking toward the bed, Cam slowed their approach so he could enjoy the way her warm hand felt on his skin. He remembered with crystal clarity that as he observed her in the diner it was her delicate hands, which had first snagged his interest. He didn't want her to ever remove that hand and was intrigued by how potently male he felt with her gentle fingers resting against his skin. His growing erection was voting on the issue as well, Cam grimly realized as the warmth spreading through his groin turned firm in more ways than one.

Guiding him gently to the side of the bed, she reached across the mattress to grab another pillow. In doing so, she revealed the long, lithe thighs his oversized sweatshirt barely covered and a quick mouthwatering glimpse of her plain, white panties, causing his brain to blank. Just like that, he was fighting the pounding need racing through him to tumble her down upon the bed, spread her glorious thighs, and bury his throbbing cock in her hot, wet depths. Only through a hard-won sense of grim willpower was he able to gain control over his rampant need to fuck her senseless and claim her for his own. Clearly, she had no idea what was going on in his head or with his body.

"You're finally getting some color back. Can I get you anything?" Lacey asked, laying her palm on his forehead. Though he was no longer hot, she had difficulty pulling her fingers away. She liked touching him; she felt little sparks of delicious awareness shooting through her each time they made contact. Before she knew what was happening, she ran her fingers through the tumble of hair falling toward his eyes and pushed it back so she could see him better. Self-conscious of the tactile liberties she was taking, Lacey tried to yank her hand away. But to her surprise, he reached for her at the same moment and actually threaded his fingers through hers, bringing their joined hands against his chest.

"Thank you, Lacey. Thank you for staying with me. Couldn't have been pleasant," he murmured as his eyes bored into hers.

Something about the way he looked at her and being so close to him scattered her thoughts, making her want to melt against him. She stared in silence, fixated on his mouth, while answering words fled her mind. She wondered what it would feel like to have those lips pressed against her own and whether he tasted as wonderful as he looked.

Cam knew he was flying without a net by acting on impulses he'd long ago decided could have no place in his life. He didn't want to examine the rush of need pushing back against years spent in a carefully constructed emotional wasteland. Suddenly, he wanted more than polite conversation from the freckle-faced girl who was looking at him with big eyes filled with questions. Maybe it was the aftermath of the fever or maybe it was the crossroad where he'd been stalled for some time. *Whatever.* All he knew for sure at that moment was that he wanted, no *hungered* for, a human connection with this woman. His heart skipped a beat when his mind, or maybe it was his heart, screamed that he *needed* her.

Watching her while keeping their fingers entwined, he realized she had fixated on his mouth. Completely caught up in his own inner turmoil, he hadn't immediately picked up on the signals she was sending. As his tongue slid along his lips, trying to bring moisture from an otherwise dry mouth, he felt a surge of satisfaction so deep it wrecked his composure when her cheeks flushed and nostrils flared at his provocative move.

So he wasn't the only one feeling the attraction arcing between them.

"Is there any water around here I could drink? My throat feels kinda raw from the fever."

She flinched. His question dragged Lacey from her thoughts, and sent her jumping into action. When her hand moved from his chest she felt an unexpected rush of regret. Grabbing a bottled water, she tore off the cap, and handed it to him.

"Drink as much of that as you can. You had a prolonged fever and are probably dehydrated."

Cam was suddenly never so happy to have been sick as he was at this moment. He was shaken by the unfamiliar tug of a smile playing at the corners of his mouth. Her concern for his well-being was as charming as her encouragement to drink more fluids. They were strangers, yet this girl-woman cared for him. He felt lightheaded from the upwelling of unfamiliar joy powering through him. Even though his conscience told him he shouldn't, he wanted more than anything for her to keep talking and touching him with those delicate, expressive fingers.

When he accepted the bottle from her outstretched hand, Lacey felt fireworks tingle on her skin where his fingers touched hers. With wide eyes, she stared as he tipped his head back and drank deeply from the container of chilled water. The way he wrapped his lips around the bottle had her thinking about that beautiful mouth on her sensitive skin. When he swallowed, she marked the path of the water as it moved down his throat and almost groaned aloud when he finished with a low grunt of satisfaction.

Needing to do something, *anything*, besides acting like a teenager with a bad case of hormones, Lacey moved to arrange the blankets and was immediately thrown for a loop at the sight of the prominent bulge in his shorts.

He was watching her closely, something he seemed to do a lot. Far from being embarrassed by his obvious state of arousal, Cameron challenged her with a quirked eyebrow.

Pretending nothing was amiss proved more difficult than she thought when he moved to take the blanket from her frozen hands. "Here, let me get that," he muttered, swinging the soft material over his hips.

She blushed from the soles of her feet to the top of her head when he rumbled out a very sexy, "Sorry 'bout that," followed by a less than discreet rearranging of the covering so that his erection wasn't *quite* so evident.

*Yeah,* she thought, *fat chance of that.*

Lacey silently muttered, "*I'm in deep doo-doo,*" at the pathetic way she was reacting. She had zero experience in the ways of men, and here she was, losing her cool with this guy. No, this *man.* An older man, if she was judging things correctly. Men like the dark knight lounging by her side didn't get involved with naïve innocents such as her. All this moony-eyed nonsense made her look like a fool. Men like Cameron Justice exuded an intoxicating maleness that undoubtedly made all women swoon. He probably dated supermodels and wouldn't have any trouble whatsoever finding a beautiful, sexy woman to share his bed. She figured he was mid-thirties and so far out of her league it was laughable.

Cam watched the play of thoughts and emotions on her face and noted them all. He didn't think she'd be thrilled to know that he could read her like a detailed recipe. She'd obviously had little experience dealing with the opposite sex, judging by her complete lack of artifice when it came to hiding her reactions. Something inside him warmed at the notion that she was struggling with the same awareness for him that he was experiencing for her. The thought shouldn't be so deeply satisfying, but it was.

He could also plainly see she was embarrassed and out of her comfort zone. Cam wanted to calm her before she panicked and ran. The last thing he wanted was for Ponytail to vanish before his eyes. She intrigued him and shook up his cautious reserve. Made him see shadows of things he dared not dream of. Truth be told, he was also out of his comfort zone. The growing sexual tension sparked in the silence stretching between them. *Say something, you idiot*, his mind screamed. *Say something before she bolts.*

Quickly standing, she snatched her jeans and deftly slid them on with her back to him. Turning around as she worked her hands through the messy hair falling around her shoulders, she pulled it back and secured it with a band all without making any eye contact.

*Get her talking*, Cam thought. *Get her talking and everything will be all right.* "Come back and sit down, Lacey," he rumbled as he moved his legs aside to make space for her next to him. When she met his gaze, he saw clear surprise at his commanding tone etched on her face.

Holding out his hand, he gestured for her. "Tell me what's happened," he said nonchalantly hoping his laidback questions would circumvent her impulse to shut down and run for the hills. "How long was I out?" he asked matter-of-factly and then waited expectantly for her next move.

Lacey's eyes darted, looking everywhere around the room—from the drawn curtains to the TV by the sofa—except at Cameron. She noticed the container on the nightstand filled with cool water that she'd stroked over his burning skin. She saw her backpack on the floor. She stared at his clothes piled on the floor and took stock of how his half-naked presence was wreaking havoc on her nerves.

She was drawn to him, and though she had no idea what the heck she was doing, or why, Lacey let a thread of control slip from her hands when she responded to his command and moved silently to sit by his side. She had to clear her throat twice before actual words came out rather than a raspy, self-conscious bark.

"You were a mess when you got back last night. Judging by how bad things were when you came through the door, I'm astonished you were able to drive," she told him hesitantly. "Don't you remember anything?"

"I remember feeling like fucking shit," he ground out. She tried not to grimace at his coarse language. "Pretty sure I puked my guts up and then face-planted." Twisting slightly to place the empty beverage bottle on the nightstand, he turned back toward her. "The washcloth and water container tell me you had your hands full."

*Busted,* her mind screamed. *Yeah, she had her hands full all right.* Full of touching him, stroking that wet cloth across his torso and along his neck and shoulders. Using her greedy fingers to push his hair back off his forehead, letting them linger against the stubble on his face. She'd all but given him a complete sponge bath and would have gladly done so with her tongue and hands, a thought that exploded in her head with a shocking bang.

Her pretty blush told Cam she was remembering using the wet cloth against his skin, and try as he might to find some remnant of awareness of her administering to him, the blankness that met his attempts frustrated him greatly. He knew he'd been sick, but apparently, he'd also been completely out of it. Her lovely hands had been on his skin, and he couldn't remember any of it.

*Fuck my life*, he thought.

He studied her face. Hiding her expressive baby blues from him, Ponytail shrugged while carefully inspecting a spot on the floor that only she could see. He waited her out, and her husky response obliterated the pathetic show of nonchalance she was trying to affect.

"Your fever got quite high, so I *had* to use wet compresses to cool you down," she began. The emphasis she placed on having to do what she did invaded his brain. She was clearly self-conscious about admitting to touching him. This was new territory for Cam. Despite displaying a serious, kick-ass attitude toward the life she'd been handed, she was apparently off the reservation when it came to dealing with the fact she had run her hands along his body. The lady was embarrassed.

"Thank god you knew to do that, little Ponytail," he muttered. He didn't want her to feel awkward about what she'd done and frankly was hoping to get her to do it all again so this time he could remember.

Lacey's eyes instantly snapped to his while her heart leaped in her chest when she heard him call her Ponytail. So he *had* been dreaming of her in his fever. Suddenly, the world slipped a tad off center, and for a few seconds, she thought she might have half a swoon coming on.

Shifting his big body, Cameron ran his fingers over her knuckles. "I don't ever remember being that kind of sick. Like, ever," he grumbled. Laying his head back against the pillows, he added, "Thanks again."

Keeping her hands passively in her lap was costing Lacey as the thin hold she had over her composure wavered under his light touches. She was drawn to him, but old, self-protective reflexes scrambled her thoughts and brought her up short. *What was she supposed to do?* In the end, the only thing that made sense was just to be honest and see what happened.

Remembering the fever reducer she'd given him, Lacey hastily blurted out one long sentence. "Nothing was working and you were burning up. I remembered the first-aid kit, so I went through it until I found a liquid fever packet." Glancing at the clock, she assured him, "That was about four hours ago, and luckily, there was no adverse reaction."

When she stopped talking, it took a deep breath to calm her nerves.

Seeing her look at the clock reminded Cam he had no idea of a timeframe for how long he'd been out of it. "What time is it now?" he asked.

"Um, well ..." she mumbled while biting her lip, "it's just past two in the afternoon. You came back around nine thirty last night, so I'd say you had a twenty-four hour virus."

Cam ran the numbers and the whole scenario as best as he could in his mind. The craptacular way he felt yesterday afternoon, and how he'd steadily gotten worse as the late afternoon and early evening came on. How he'd barely made it back to the motor lodge in one piece and how god-awful sick he was on the drive. That was what she'd been presented with when he came stumbling through the door.

She'd been left to deal with a sick stranger who she nursed through what must have been one hell of a night. She'd put cold cloths on his fevered skin, had the presence of mind to search his bags for a fever reducer, and had stood watch over him throughout the course of his fever. He saw glimpses of other things he wasn't sure were real or just the fevered imaginings of a sick mind. Things like Lacey wrapping him in the warmth of her arms, sharing the heat of her embrace, and the hushed sounds of her sexy purr against his ear. His hands remembered the feel of a succulent breast that he shaped in his mind's eye with exquisite detail.

Next thing he knew, Lacey asked how he happened to come upon her predicament in the alleyway. Cam considered his answer carefully before deciding to be direct and then wait for the fallout.

"I saw you at the diner," he told her. "You were trying to blend into the woodwork, and it caught my attention. I notice things like that. It's sort of what I do for a living; I notice things."

He saw her look of confusion and just plowed on.

"Couldn't help but piece together the pattern. When you arrived. How long you stayed. The fact that you put on a good show of pretending to get on a bus." She looked slightly panicked at that particular reveal, but he just kept on explaining, deciding it was best to go for broke.

"What I'm saying may sound a bit unsettling, but really, Lacey, it's what I do for a living. Noticing that kind of shit. You struck me as vulnerable, and I guess my hidden inner hero came along for the ride."

Considering what he'd just blurted out, Lacey fixated on something he'd said. He noticed things, and it was what he did for a living. *What the heck did that mean?*

"What are you saying … *you notice things*? I don't understand. What made you even care about what you *noticed*?" she growled at him. "Why me?"

"Yeah, I know it sounds stalkerish and creepy, but that is, in fact, one of the things I do." Reaching onto the nightstand to grab his wallet, Cameron extracted a business card and shoved it at her.

With a slightly shaking hand, Lacey lifted the card and read, "The Justice Agency, Sedona Arizona. Cameron Justice, Associate." She stared at him, frowning and confused.

"There are three of us. Draegyn, Alexander, and me. We have a private agency that does security and investigative work. My specialty is surveillance and analysis. Call it an occupational hazard. I'm here on a break from work, and I noticed you. Plain and simple. I wasn't trying to fuck with your life, Lacey."

He was an investigator. Of course, he noticed her pattern. In trying to stay on top of things, she'd allowed herself to fall into a rhythm. One that anyone who actually paid any attention would certainly pick up on. She stared at the card in her hand.

"So you didn't just happen to be passing by when those guys jumped me?" she asked quietly.

"Right," was all he replied.

The silence stretched while Lacey thought about what she'd just learned.

Going for broke, Cam jumped on an idea brewing in his mind from practically the moment he'd first spied her.

"Look. You've nothing here, right?" he asked quietly. When she shook her head, he tugged on her hand. "What are you going to do when winter comes?"

"Well, actually," she answered smoothly, "I had planned on going someplace warmer. I've saved some money that will help me get a fresh start, and if I head south, it will be easier not having to battle with the weather."

Jumping on the unbelievable opening her declaration of independence had given him, Cam played all his cards in one fell swoop.

"I'm glad to hear you're headed someplace warm and have a desire to start over. It's settled then," he proclaimed with enormous aplomb. "You're leaving with me when I head back to Sedona. It's warm as hell in Arizona, so you'll like it. And I can get you a job when we get there. I know of a security agency that needs a temporary replacement for their office manager."

Feeling mightily satisfied for coming up with a solution that allowed him to keep her near, Cam relaxed against the stacked pillows and waited for her to fall in line. When she didn't immediately say something, he started feeling the slow drip, drip, drip of anxiety at the thought she might turn him down. He wanted to take her with him, wanted to explore the peculiar attraction he felt toward her, and wanted to do a fuck-load more if his hard-on was any indicator.

He hated feeling off-kilter whether from the lingering effects of illness or the quiet indecision radiating off Ponytail. Scrubbing both hands up and down his stubble-covered face and through his shaggy hair to help clear his head, Cam all but groaned aloud in frustration. *Why was she being so quiet?*

Lacey stared at the man who had in just twenty-four short hours turned her world upside down. He was offering her a way out and a chance to start over; the very thing she'd been dreaming about and working toward for a long time. *Why was she hesitating?*

She knew the reasons but didn't want to give them any oxygen. She was acutely aware of the attraction she felt toward him. A delicious blend of mystery and danger with a hefty dollop of **OH MY GOD** thrown in, Cameron Justice was way out of her inexperienced league. Unfortunately, that didn't stop her wayward thoughts and aroused senses from wanting to follow him like a needy puppy.

The conscience perched on her shoulder was tut-tutting her indecision while pushing her to *jump*. Taking a deep breath, she hoped she wasn't making the biggest mistake of her short life. Striving for businesslike, she doubled down on the details to give her thumping heart a chance to calm down.

"You're offering me a ride to Arizona and a job when we get there?" At his quiet nod of affirmation, she hesitated one more time. "Why are you being so nice? I'm practically a stranger to you. It doesn't make sense."

Without any hesitation, he answered, "Hell, Ponytail, I'm gonna give you that. You need a way out and me ... well, maybe I need a chance to prove that I can be human. That too many hard years in the military and a bunch of empty ones on the outside didn't make me a complete bastard. "

She snorted a low chuckle at his answer and nodded. "It's been my experience that most men are complete you-know-whats, but I don't see you that way at all Cameron."

"Don't be fooled, Lacey. I *am* a complete bastard and in no way a gentleman, but I assure you, if you come with me, I'll behave and do everything in my power to help you get on your feet again." His green eyes bored into hers.

"Let me think about it, Cameron," she whispered while her hands got busy clutching and smoothing the corner of his blanket where it draped over her leg. "Are you hungry?" she asked, quickly changing the subject. "I'll run across the parking lot and grab you something. You'll feel better after you've eaten."

As if on cue, his stomach rumbled loudly, and he was hit by a thirst that plain water wasn't going to quench. Grabbing his wallet, he withdrew a bunch of bills and pressed them into her hand.

"Man, that would be great," he murmured. "I need a carbonated soda, preferably one with a shit ton of caffeine, so don't grab any of the unleaded crap. I'll munch down on whatever they have. Make sure you get something for yourself too, Lacey. Later on, I'll drive us into town and we can get some takeout, okay?"

Glad to have something to do, Lacey jumped to her feet, scrambling for her bag before heading to the door when he spoke.

"Leave the backpack, Ponytail. You don't need to lug it everywhere you go."

She hesitated, pondering Cameron intently. Something about the way he looked at her suggested he could read her innermost thoughts. As someone who didn't trust easily, the way she felt driven to believe in him rattled her cage. *How the hell did he do that*, she wondered.

Overcome with indecision and doubt, she lowered the rough and ready bag to the floor as slowly as humanly possible, while she gnawing on her bottom lip. She'd been protecting that bag and her only possessions for what seemed like a lifetime and had even engaged in a street fight to keep from having it forcibly taken from her. She was in no way used to going anywhere without it. Taking a deep breath and squaring her shoulders, Lacey opted for strength in the face of fear as she pushed the bag with her foot to a corner near the sofa. Turning and leaving took all her strength, but she managed to do just that, locking eyes with her dark knight just before she slipped out the door with a softly muttered, "I won't be long."

When the door clicked shut, Cam practically high-fived himself at the current state of things. He had wrung just a hint of trust out of her as evidenced by the ugly rucksack crammed discreetly in the corner of the room. Plus, he had nearly convinced her that going with him was a great idea even though she wasn't completely sure it was the right thing to do. His first reaction at her belief that men were bastards was to throttle every man who'd ever given her cause to feel that way, and the second was to immediately disabuse her of whatever hero status she had bestowed on him.

Now, though, he felt ... *better*. And not just better because he wasn't sick anymore. This kind of better seemed deeper. He even felt stabs of joy at the idea that once he got her to agree to his plan, they'd have several long days together in his truck as they made their way southwest. Time enough for him to enjoy the sound of her seductive voice.

He squashed the surge of happiness that reared its surprising head and pushed away everything except satisfaction at how things were turning out.

That satisfaction came at a cost, though, as the inner voice of his conscience growled at his rejection of the obvious fact that he shouldn't be doing any of this. Everything about his fair damsel in distress screamed innocence, and he should know better.

*Screw knowing better.*

Hours later, after the snack bar food and a long hot shower, Cameron insisted he was feeling human and in command of himself once more. He suggested they drive to a fancy hamburger joint on the outskirts of town, near ground zero for the hordes of credit card toting tourists who stopped along the way to shop while enjoying the fall scenery tours.

It didn't take much for Lacey to give in to his suggestion because she wasn't a complete idiot and realized he would just keep at her until he got exactly what he wanted. He was one of those types of men, and oddly, though she normally avoided alpha types like the plague, she rather enjoyed taking a back seat to his decision-making. It made her feel special somehow.

His truck, while slightly rough around the edges on the outside, was a modern, state-of-the-art vehicle on the inside. Behind the tinted windows, she found herself seated comfortably on plush leather while watching silently as he punched an address into the on-board GPS. He adjusted the satellite radio to an oldies station.

She tried not to react like a kid on Christmas morning, but she really couldn't help herself, turning this way and that in the comfortable passenger seat. There was a cooler in the cab behind their seats, a stack of books at her feet, and a funny looking bobblehead dog perched on the dashboard. While the cab of the truck was big, he was bigger, and no amount of extra space was going to keep Lacey from being deliciously aware of how he smelled after his shower or how strong and capable his hands looked where the gripped the steering wheel.

She'd retreated into silence as the afternoon and early evening ticked by, feeling slightly lost and uncertain about what to do next. He wasn't exactly being a chatty Cathy, either, seeming to prefer his own thoughts. When he suggested they leave the motel to grab some dinner, she let him sweep her along with the least amount of discussion possible. There were questions, a million of them, but long held habits kept her from asking too much. For now, she was going to see where this unexpected change of events took her, and him.

The gourmet burger restaurant had a line out the door when they arrived, forcing the two unlikely companions to place a take-out order rather than wait an eternity to be seated. Lacey was silently relieved because noticing how most of the women dressed made her acutely self-conscious about her ratty appearance. Wearing Cameron's extra-large sweatshirt, she was sporting worn jeans that were at least a size too large for her and a pair of sneakers that had seen better days. Her rescuer was the sort of man who would be the center of every female's attention in whatever space he occupied, and the last thing she needed was for the bitchy negativity she'd be subjected to by being at his side. Once again, she thought of the supermodels he probably dated and the sophisticated, modern women he was most likely acquainted with. Suddenly, she felt like the cleaning lady.

Cam wasn't surprised by her silence. He could hear her thoughts by her body language. She was insecure about how she looked. He marveled at the way a woman's mind worked and spent several long, pensive minutes considering the obvious fact that she didn't recognize her own beauty. He, of course, saw beyond the thrift store clothes and focused only on the fresh-faced attributes that made her so appealing and unusual. Wondering at the sort of transformation she might go through when her existence became less and less fraught with anxiety, Cam hoped she didn't lose any of the all-American, girl-next-door quality she radiated in spades.

When their meal was ready it took but a few short minutes to pay the bill and get back on the road. With the music from a station playing eighties rock in the background, they drove along without talking until Cam suddenly blurted out what was on his mind.

"We'll spend the night at the motel and then head out midmorning. Is that okay with you, Lacey? Will you need to stop anywhere before we leave, or are you ready to get going?" he asked without taking his attention off the road.

She didn't answer right away, so he kept talking over the silence. "It will take about a week, maybe less, to get to Arizona. With so many miles to cover, I don't drive till I drop each day. I aim for a couple of hours each morning with a break for lunch and some physical activity and then drive for a few more hours before stopping for the night. That way I'm not totally ragged out by the time the trip is over.

Sound okay to you?"

"I haven't said I'd go with you, Cameron," she reminded him softly.

Not normally used to justifying anything to anybody much less this slip of a girl barely out of her teens, Cam spoke his mind in no uncertain terms. "Well, Ponytail, I'm not taking no for an answer. I get that you're being cautious, but if you really think about it, you'll see that I'm offering everything you've ever wished for. A chance for a fresh start, a job, and a life that has a future."

Back at the motor lodge it got quiet again and stayed that way all through their shared meal back. After checking her injured arm and finding it healing nicely, Lacey grabbed her backpack and made a beeline for the laundry room at the rear of the snack bar. This left Cam to putter aimlessly, tossing belongings in his bag and generally straightening the room where he'd been staying for the last ten days.

Try as he might to dismiss Ponytail from his thoughts and just get on with the business at hand, he found himself fantasizing about what it would be like to spend hours each day alone with her in the confines of his truck. When she returned a short time later after having laundered her meager belongings, he was struck again by her fresh-faced appeal and the way she tried so fucking hard to be invisible. He was of the general opinion that most women were high-maintenance, but this one seemed hell-bent on being just the opposite. He was curious to find out what circumstances in her life led her to the predicament she was in and hoped he got the opportunity to find out more about her. Somehow, she'd managed to avoid saying whether she'd go with him or not, a reminder that didn't please Cam one bit.

When the time came for lights out, he tried to talk her into sleeping on the bed while he took the sofa, but she would have none of it. He was too big for the sofa, she primly reminded him. Throwing herself on the sofa with her back to him, Cam could only stand there slack-jawed at how neatly she had settled that sticky situation.

*Damn but she was good*, he thought as his head eventually hit the pillows on the motel room bed. He didn't know what had made him try for chivalry by offering her the bed since such gestures weren't a part of his normal repertoire.

His final thought before sleep overtook him was of what she was wearing underneath the hundred sizes too big t-shirt she slept in and whether she changed from the no-nonsense white panties into something with less fabric and more lace.

# Chapter Six

C AM SLEPT LIKE the dead and awoke later than usual the next morning. He'd been dreaming about Ponytail just before waking. Her indecision the night before had left him feeling grumpy and out of sorts. Not like him at all.

He'd decided in a superficially dreamy way that if she didn't want his help, then fine. Screw her. He didn't need a freckle-faced twenty-something to slow his roll. In the time between dreams and reality, Cam had reasoned she couldn't possibly be as inside his head as he feared. If she wanted to go on her way, he would happily drive her to the bus depot and be done with it. After all, he didn't play the white knight for anyone, especially not a woman. He had more important things to do than babysit a blond ponytail with a ratty backpack.

The second his eyes popped open, though, a different reality set in. It took less than two heartbeats to realize he was alone in the motel room. *What the fuck*. He wondered if she had actually bolted in the night. Regret and a sense of loss made his chest burn. He'd blown it with her. Came on too strong and tried to boss her around.

Jumping to his feet, Cam set off across the room to grab his clothes so he could go find her.

*Wait a minute.* What? Go find her? Where had that thought come from? Hadn't he just decided he was better off without her?

He was a fucking mess and had to admit he didn't know how to find the door at that moment without a valet, a GPS, and a personal Sherpa. A low, feral growl of frustration rumbled up from his chest and split the air at the exact moment his bare foot met her crappy backpack. Standing there frozen like an idiot, Cam tried to wrap his mind around the evidence staring him in the face. If not for his heart thumping wildly in his chest, he might have found two threads of reason to string together in quicker fashion.

"Okay, man, *think!*" he murmured grittily. Her backpack was here, but she wasn't. If her backpack was here, she would be returning, right? Hope started spreading through his brain. Sprinting the rest of the way to the bathroom, he washed up and dressed in short order and was putting his wallet in his pocket and reaching for his keys and sunglasses when the door to the motel room burst open.

Cam recovered from his shock at Lacey's abrupt entrance and moved quickly to help her with lord knows what, as bags went spilling everywhere. He tried to push aside the joy that lit up his soul at her appearance. As he reached out to pick up a rather nice-looking pair of strappy sandals, his one thought was that if he knew how to smile, he'd be doing just that right about now.

"What have you been up to, woman?" he asked as he surveyed the pile of stuff on the motel room couch. Noting that everything had hand-written tags, it didn't take a rocket scientist to make out that she'd been to the local thrift stores for what looked like a new wardrobe. Well, maybe wardrobe was a bit of a stretch, but she'd definitely picked up some new jeans, a couple of pretty tops, and an overnight bag covered in blue flowers.

Lacey had a heck of a time getting through the door with her arms laden with plastic bags. Her limbs felt dead from all the carrying and walking from the bus stop to the motel. She wanted to toss everything down on the floor and just collapse, but right at this second, she was struggling with the key to the door. Stomping her foot in frustration just as she finally managed to get the door open, she practically fell headfirst onto the floor from the forward momentum of her actions. Catching herself at the last second, she nonetheless managed to stumble to a halt directly in front of a startled Cameron who was looking at her like she'd grown a second head.

Shifting her bags before they all went tumbling to the ground, Lacey muttered under her breath, "Um … jeez … a little help here would be greatly appreciated," as she began to unburden her load on the sofa by the door.

After an agonizing, sleepless night that had Lacey tossing and turning for hours, she finally just let herself succumb to the inevitable decision. The only choice she could reasonably make. So much unhappiness had been visited on her young life that having hope seemed like a fool's errand. But somehow, someway, this man named Cameron Justice had burst upon the scene and completely shaken up her carefully orchestrated life of invisibility. And in doing so, he caused a tidal wave of optimism to creep into her soul.

What else could she do except put her big girl knickers on, stop being such a wuss, and tag along to Arizona with him, fingers crossed?

With the hard part of the decision behind her, Lacey was swamped with practicalities like getting some real clothes and preparing herself for a new life. She'd been hoarding every penny she could from odd jobs picked up with an eye to finding employment and a decent place to live. With a figure in mind of what she could frugally spend, she was up and out at first light to troll through the downtown second-hand stores for items she needed. She was, after all, operating on a deficit. She could barely remember a time when she wasn't obsessed with where her next meal came from or whether she had a roof over her head.

On her way back to the motel, she wondered what Cameron

would make of her spontaneous shopping spree. She was relying on him to provide the transportation to her new life, and while she doubted he'd let her chip in for gas, he would have to accept that she wanted to pay for her own food and whatever else she needed along the way. Lacey knew the funds she had would start to dwindle quickly, but starting out by putting her best foot forward was the only way she knew how to proceed. She'd never relied on anyone, knew better than to even try, and wasn't about to start now.

Right this second, though, Cameron was helping her pick up several items that had spilled off the sofa and was, in fact, holding up her single extravagant purchase—an almost brand-new pair of strappy sandals with a chunky heel that was going to look great with the new pants, tops, and skirts she'd found. His look of astonishment made her stop and pause. *Did he think they were too … too?* She hated feeling unsure. When she was around him, it was like every single female insecurity ever recorded bloomed in her mind.

"Hmm." She heard him rumble as he carefully considered the shoes he was dangling in the air. "I like these," he informed her solemnly with the briefest suggestion of amusement coming from his eyes. He was joking with her about what she bought, and just like that, another crack appeared in her invisible armor. He. Was. Teasing. Her. *Wow.*

Oh god, each time all that dark-eyed intensity focused solely on her, she couldn't concentrate. *How was it that he could scramble her thoughts so completely without saying a word?*

Standing as they were, with her packages tossed on the sofa and floor, separated by just a few inches, she was enthralled by the power radiating off him. That she felt compelled to put her hands on his chest shook Lacey considerably.

He didn't skip a beat while playfully pretending to peek in her bags. "I hope there's a pair of shorts in that pile 'cause with these shoes on, your long legs would look magnificent."

How she stayed standing, she did not know.

Pulling herself together with a strong mental shake, Lacey neatly sidestepped the flirty banter with a very specific segue back to more important matters. Coughing lightly to clear the sudden thickness in her throat, she ended by tugging at her bottom lip with quick bites of her teeth.

The shoes completely forgotten, Cam had to restrain himself from reaching out his hand and smoothing her luscious lips with a stroke or two from his thumb. She was trying to look so serious but was hiding her eyes from him. Remembering his earlier instinct that he'd foolishly bullied her into compliance, he remained silent and waited.

"Cameron," she started. Hesitating and still not fully meeting his gaze, she darted her eyes in every direction as she shifted on her feet.

He held his breath for what came next because he understood she needed to own her part of this decision. The lady was no coward. *Hmph.* He grimaced. She'd probably want to lay down a few well-stated rules if he was reading her correctly.

*Okay, Ponytail,* he thought, *give me your best shot.*

Squaring her shoulders and straightening to her five-foot-eight height, she nodded in his direction. "Thank you for your incredible offer. Even though we just met, I am grateful and beholden to you for this opportunity."

Unable to stop himself, Cam blurted out, "Wait! What does beholden mean? If it has anything to do with obligation, forget it, Lacey. You won't owe me a thing. I had a rough time growing up, so I'm in a unique position to understand what you're going through." The admission of his difficult past came out of nowhere, shocking him almost as much as it clearly intrigued Lacey, if the expression on her face was any indication.

"All you need is a break; the rest is up to you. If you're like me, you'll grab the opportunity and wrestle it to the ground. Make it your bitch!" He snarled good-naturedly.

Finally, because he couldn't hold himself back any longer from touching her, he wrapped his big hands around her upper arms and rubbed slightly. "I have faith in you, Ponytail."

When he growled her nickname, Lacey flinched. She wanted to say more about sharing expenses and honorable stuff like that, but all her mind could comprehend was the way his green eyes gleamed when he said *'if you're like me'*. He was so solid and hard, focused, intense. Lacey assumed that was the military in him. Learning some of that might have come from circumstances much as her own made her stop and pause. Maybe her dark knight understood. Actually understood.

Aware of a tingling warmth spreading through her arms where his large, muscular hands rubbed, Lacey swallowed back an unwanted moan and tried to put a smile on her face. "Well, I don't know about making it my bi ... uh, you know"—she sighed—"but I promise to make the most of this unexpected opportunity."

Cam had to chuckle at her shy response. What a delight his Ponytail was. *Now if only she would touch him*, he thought. Maybe she heard his thoughts because she laid both her palms upon his chest when he used his grip on her arms to gently pull her forward.

Lowering his gaze to her mouth, he watched as her tongue snaked out to swipe moisture along her lips. *She would be his.* At some point. He wouldn't be able to stop himself. The only thing holding him back right now was that he actually liked her. That and some hidden crumb of male honor loitering in his conscience.

Liking her meant he had a hard time shutting down the other thought screaming inside his head to take her. Now. Make her his in the most primitive way possible. Mark his territory, his possession. Hell, he didn't want to scare her away, but he also wanted to taste her. Deeply.

In the end, he didn't hesitate although he should have. Common sense on hold; Cam grabbed Lacey around the waist, pulling her quickly up against his body as his mouth descended on hers for a hungry kiss that held little finesse. His libido was on fire and nothing less than a no-holds-barred oral invasion was going to satisfy his desire.

Startled by his actions, she didn't have the time to resist before his lips were feasting on hers. Lacey had never experienced anything quite like this. She had, in fact, never been kissed by a full-grown man. His tongue stroked the seam of her mouth, touching off a firestorm of awareness that had her trying to drag oxygen into her rapidly muddled mind.

When her lips parted, he took full advantage by swiping his tongue inside her mouth in a way that made her forget all about remaining independent and in control. Instinct, raw and untried, brought her inexpert tongue in contact with his as she shyly answered his incursion into the moist recesses of her mouth. Swirling her tongue around his, she was shocked when his grip became bolder, and he molded her trembling body against his powerful heat while sucking greedily on her response.

Lacey didn't know what to do; this was way outside her known world. She knew she shouldn't be encouraging this madness, but the strange force that had been between them from the moment they met kept her willingly in his bold embrace. With mind and senses on overload, she experienced a growing sensual tension that was as totally foreign and confusing to her as a trip to Mars would be. Heat deep within was spreading through her quaking form, making an explosion of throbbing awareness go off at the juncture of her thighs. She experienced a series of firsts when liquid arousal flooded her panties and a desperate need to taste Cameron shot into her awareness.

Keeping her hands on his impossibly broad chest, Lacey leaned into him and let all those feelings have their way. Operating on instinct and pure desire, she opened up to his questing tongue and voracious lips as he devoured her inexperienced response. He tasted amazing. She couldn't get enough.

Cam was on fire and sinking fast. When he lost his intention to keep her at arm's length and simply grabbed hold, the feeling was like free falling without a parachute. She tasted a thousand times better than he imagined, and the exquisite sensation of her long, lean body pressed so perfectly against his was like nothing he had ever known. And certainly nothing he was prepared to deal with. It was easier to think that what was enflaming his senses was nothing more than biology. He wanted her in the most basic of ways. He was a normal male who sensed an available female. Simple.

*Yeah, right.* Nothing was simple about this. Nothing. Pretending that what was happening was just sexual arousal and nothing else was insane, but Cam couldn't bring himself to admit to anything else. Sure, it was knocking on the door of his brain—especially now that he'd admitted to himself that he truly liked her—but he was in no way ready to accept what that meant.

Right now, all he could concentrate on was the way her trembling body moved against his when she raised on her toes to fit more intimately against him or the hushed moans of need rumbling in her chest. Both were enough to render him mindless and on sensual autopilot as he plundered her mouth with abandon. When her hands moved from his shoulders to spear unsure fingers into his hair, he lost whatever small hold on reality he'd been clinging to.

They stayed like that, wound around one another, held deep in a sensual thrall through a kiss that defined what kissing should be all about, for a long, long time. Lacey's fevered moans and shaky gasps eventually struck a chord in Cam's oxygen-starved brain. It hit him like a ton of bricks that her responses indicated she'd never been kissed like this a second before that thought expanded all on its own. He knew with absolute certainty that she'd never done any of this before. The thought sobered him up faster than an ice bath. *Shit.*

The groan he let out as he left her lips and peeled her off his body sounded harsh and loud in the silence of the small room. "Do you know what you're doing, Lacey?" he ground out a bit more harshly than intended. "Do you realize what kissing like that does to me?"

Lacey got caught completely off guard by the question. She'd been so lost in the sensation of being kissed by Cameron that the last thing she expected was for him to push her away. Embarrassment shot along her nerve endings as she cringed, knowing that her complete lack of experience with the opposite sex had been obvious to someone who clearly knew his way around seducing a female. Overcome with feelings of disappointment and self-protection, she realized how close she'd come to making a complete fool of herself.

When she didn't answer right away, Cam was gripped with frustration, which he could handle, and a sense of protectiveness for the confused female in his presence, which he couldn't. Protective wasn't something he did. On the battlefield, he looked out for his brothers, and they him, which was expected warrior behavior. However, in his personal life, he'd never felt protective toward a single human being, ever. Lorraine had seen to that. The only person he'd learned to be protective of was himself. The feelings he was forming for Ponytail were unfamiliar and uncomfortable.

Sighing, he tipped her chin up with his fingers so she had to look at him. The sheen of embarrassment and uncertainty lighting up her eyes told Cam a hell of a lot, and the pieces started falling into place. "Tell me, Lacey, are you a virgin?"

Her blue eyes, which seconds before had been smoky with arousal, turned sharp and defensive at his question. The wary shield she kept around her started to go up until she wavered under his intense perusal. Satisfied he had her full attention, he was flabbergasted when he saw a film of tears appear in her eyes.

"I don't know," she whispered lowering head before he saw any deeper than he already had into her tormented soul. Lacey didn't know why she'd answered him that way because she knew her words invited the inevitable follow-up. She never discussed this part of her life with anyone. Hell, she never discussed anything at all with anybody, but for reasons she couldn't fathom, this dark-haired man with the gruff outer shell and *don't mess with me* persona made her feel safe for the only time in her life.

Keeping her gaze lowered, Lacey waited, feeling her heart pounding with anxiety as the silence around them grew. When she finally couldn't take the suspense any longer, she slowly raised her eyes to his, quickly sucking a hiss of air into her lungs at the intense expression on his face. He looked mad, though not at her, which was a relief. She suspected his anger stemmed from having already surmised something of the dark acts that hid in her past.

Cam hadn't been prepared for the tears or for her response. He figured the question had a simple yes or no answer. Her shaken murmur of *I don't know* hadn't been on the list of possibilities he'd imagined when he asked the question. Kicking her bags out of the way and pulling her toward the sofa, he sat them down. "Explain," he grimly countered when the tense silence lingered.

Lacey wished she knew what to say. She hadn't thrown herself at him. At least, she didn't think she had. They had ended up in each other's arms when he seemed to give in to something she was just barely starting to understand.

Sitting cross-legged against the arm of the old sofa, she snatched up an ugly throw pillow and pulled it protectively against her middle. God, she hated feeling nervous and really hated the sudden jarring loss of self-confidence that she counted on to keep herself together. *Could she tell him about her past? Why in the world would she want to?* He was practically a stranger—one who could vanish from her life as quickly and easily as a puff of smoke. *Why, even though she knew that, did she feel so pulled in his direction? And why, dear god why, was she letting him so far inside her mind?*

The answer to her question was looking at her across the small distance between them. Lacey might not know who he really was or where he came from, but she did know with every fiber of her being that she could trust him, mystique and all. He had his secrets and so did she. They were strangers, yes, but somehow, they were also, quite impossibly, becoming friends.

Cam watched the play of thoughts and emotions on her face, noting each one. She was deciding whether to open herself to him. He felt like a man waiting for the judgment of a jury. His mouth ran dry, then turned to dust when she reached up and yanked the band from her ponytail, letting the brownish gold waves fall softly against her shoulders. The smattering of light freckles across the bridge of her nose taunted him with her innocence, and he wondered if it would always be that way even as she aged and matured. She had a natural beauty that left him breathless and made him forget that he didn't trust women. He suspected she could make him forget a lot of the emotional nonsense he'd been clinging to all his life but right now, he was not the person on the hot seat.

When she'd gasped at his question and answered that she didn't know, a piece of his heart squeezed in painful contraction. He'd tasted her innocence, enthralled by it, but her full reaction suggested a darker truth that made his insides churn in anger. The agonizing suspicion she'd been assaulted or abused became very real as the silence lingered. He wanted to hurt somebody in a powerfully aggressive way. Fearing that this lovely young woman had been harmed for someone else's perverse satisfaction ripped open a wound in his soul. If his suspicions were correct, he would have no problem killing the motherfucker who had harmed her.

"Just let it out. Some things aren't meant to stay hidden forever."

Lacey nodded at his choice of words, sensing he realized some portion of what she might be about to say. She wanted to be brave and fearless, and most of all, she wanted this secret to be behind her once and for all. With a deep sigh, she filled her lungs one last time, blowing away years of anger and fear as she simply dove right in and went for it.

"My mom died when I was only a baby. I don't really remember her, but I do know she loved me. For a while after she was gone, my grandmother was in my life, and I remember more of her. Dad was not around very much; he seemed to always be working so Gran did the day-to-day stuff. When I was eight, we moved to Oklahoma where Dad had gotten a job. We lived in a trailer, and all I really remember of that time was being alone and how isolated everything felt. I cried for my gran, but she was far away, and after a while, she just faded into memory."

"Right after my fourteenth birthday, Dad signed on as a pipeline foreman in Alaska. It wasn't a job that allowed him to bring his teenage daughter tagging along, so without any warning, I was dumped on an uncle's doorstep in Florida. One I'd never met or known about."

The silence lengthened as she struggled to keep a firm grip on her emotions. Lacey had hated the man on sight, and while it was apparent from the way the two brothers interacted that they weren't exactly fond of one another, that hadn't stopped her father from walking away from his only child without a backward glance, leaving her in the hands of an evil psychopath. Some things can never be forgiven. Her father's desertion was a perfect example.

"I won't bore you with the gory details except to say that this so-called uncle was a Bible-thumping jerk with a deep hatred of women. His wife had taken their son and fled to god knows where years before I arrived on the scene. He liked to use words like *Jezebel* and *harlot*. Mostly, I tried to stay off his radar, but that was hard to do when you live in a swamp. Oh, did I mention he ran gator tours for a living? Yeah, that's right," she bit out. "My darling daddy left me with a gator nut who spent his days taunting vicious reptiles for paying customers. At night, he drank and quoted the good Book. Being of the female persuasion meant I must be cleansed of my inherently wicked ways. I guess Eve really was a naughty girl because, in his mind, all women were dirty and suspect."

Cam stayed silent as she clutched the pillow a bit tighter and her words became softer, like a whisper. He was imagining all sorts of disgusting scenarios and was having trouble remaining passive while she spoke. The idea of seriously harming the gator-taunting dickhead was already forming in his mind. Justice must be served.

"By the time I was sixteen, he was locking me in my room each month when I got my cycle because I was unclean and shouldn't be around people." She snorted in derision. "I was completely cut off from other people and totally at his mercy. I had no family and no friends. We were in the middle of a disgusting swamp, and I was part of a homeschool network, so there were no teachers to see what was going on. Basically, my life was f-u-c-k-e-d."

Cam grimaced at her spelling of the inelegant word and wished he could change her life so she never had to use that expression again. It didn't take a surveillance expert to see that she avoided swearing and crude language when she spoke. He who had never given a shit about anybody suddenly and without warning wanted to be some kind of white knight, swooping in to rescue this freckle-faced beauty.

Lacey sighed again and let the worst part of the tale tumble out without embellishment and with very little show of emotion. "He started abusing me then. Not in the classic way, but in a much more vicious way that spoke to how evil and twisted he truly was. His best friend was named Jack Daniels. Good ol' Jack made his presence known almost every night. More often than not, he'd get snarling drunk and wind up in my room late in the evening. He liked to wrap his hands around my throat and whisper vile taunts while he threatened to choke the evil out of me. His favorite demand was that I touch him while he slowly cut off my air supply. If I made a move to comply, he would beat me senseless and scream about what a whore I was. Some nights, he was buck naked and would yell at me to get on my knees and pray to release him from my wanton spell. It went on like that for more than a year. Besides smacking me around and occasionally beating the snot out of me, he never touched me physically."

She threw the pillow on the floor and abruptly straightened her shoulders. He suspected the worst was yet to come, and he could not have been more right.

"One night, he forced me to drink a bottle of beer that appeared out of nowhere. He wasn't a beer guy. When I hesitated, he pushed me down on the floor and held me there as he poured the entire bottle down my throat. I choked and gagged while he screeched insanely about damnation. Afterward, he paced the room like a crazy man peeling off his clothes while he preached about women's subservience to man, and my head got fuzzier and fuzzier. The evil jerk had put something in the beer, and I was lucid enough to realize it was probably a rape drug. I went nuts and started screaming and hitting him. The last thing I remember was of him ripping my clothes as he punched me over and over until I lost consciousness." The tight shrug she ended with made him sick to his stomach. The bastard had drugged his own niece and assaulted her while she was unconscious, and all she could do was shrug.

"A couple of hours later, I came to and found him naked, covered in blood and out cold on the bedroom floor. My clothes were destroyed, and there wasn't an inch of my body that didn't hurt or have marks. Judging by how we both looked, one could presume I put up quite a fight. Something inside me snapped, and less than an hour later, I had packed what I could and gone through all his ridiculous hiding places until I'd cleaned him out of any money he had squirreled away. I was barely seventeen years old. Six weeks later, I was alone, trying to survive in a big city and pretending I was older and wiser. That was five years ago. Most of the time, I've been in youth hostels, campgrounds during the summer, or living in run-down motels while I work odd jobs and get an education any way I can. Sooner or later, I figured my luck would turn around and I'd have enough money to get an apartment someplace and a proper job so I could live like a real person."

Her bright eyes and the determination in her voice confirmed how important it was for her to make it on her own after having lost her mother, been abandoned by her father, and abused by an uncle.

"So, to answer your question, my only response can be that I don't know. Maybe he did, maybe he didn't."

She stood, wiping imaginary dirt from her butt before forcefully pushing up the arms of her shirt. With her hand held up to say stop, a grim set to her mouth and a deep frown, her body language screamed her resilience. "You're not allowed to feel sorry for me. I can't have pity or sympathy. Other people have real problems. That's who you can feel sorry for. Not me. I'm not a victim. Just because things have been tough does not mean I haven't made loads of progress." Her voice steadily rose while this emphatic declaration of independence burbled out.

"I didn't need your help to figure it out. Don't get me wrong. I am grateful for your rescue during the mugging, but if you hadn't happened along, if that situation hadn't occurred, I would have found a way to move things along to a more positive place."

"I don't doubt it for a second, Ponytail. Those freckles don't fool me. You kick ass just by being so determined."

"Thanks, I think, and I'm sorry for getting carried away before. You're good at that." His quirked eyebrow asked the question that she answered, "The kissing I mean. Um, you're quite, uh …"

"Good at it, am I?" Sighing, he reached for her, running his hands up and down her arms once again, this time to warm her up and chase away the chill of her confession. "We both got carried away and for good reason. The chemistry between us is powerful, and even without experience, you sensed it. But I'm definitely the one in the older and wiser category, and I shouldn't have crossed the line just now. Men like me don't have relationships, we get our needs met in other ways. Sweetness, you in no way come off as the type of woman who would settle for an arrangement like that. I can't start something that would only end with you getting hurt."

After that little speech, no one was more surprised than Cam when he gathered her in his arms for a tender hug. When she wrapped her arms around his waist and leaned in to him, he felt a powerful sense of inevitability. His face buried in her hair and her head against his chest, they swayed back and forth in a tightening embrace that went beyond mere friendship.

# Chapter Seven

CAM WAS HAVING a hard time concentrating on the miles rushing by due to the presence of an overly excited passenger. She was having the time of her life as they made their way cross-country from the northern part of the East Coast to the southwestern desert in Arizona. Her enthusiasm and wonder at every little thing was refreshing albeit a bit exhausting.

During the long drive yesterday, she'd been keyed up—after all, she was on an unexpected journey that could possibly change her life. He'd managed to distract her with stories about the people who made up his real-life family. This was new territory for him as he'd always been a man of very few words. To lighten the mood, he simply started talking, something he never did, and they'd basically had an eight-hour conversation after that.

Stopping for the night at an old highway motel with a restaurant and bar attached, he'd practically forced a huge steak dinner on her. That she savored the cheap cut of meat with whipped potatoes and canned green beans like it was a gourmet meal made him feel a thousand feet tall.

He'd rented two rooms and after eating and getting their signals straight for the next morning, they parted awkwardly from one another. He hadn't wanted to leave, and she didn't seem too thrilled about being left alone.

All day long, tucked in the back of his mind, was a disturbing scene they'd shared in the early morning as they met up to get back on the road. When he tapped on her door to see if she was awake, he heard the distinct sounds of her scurrying about just on the other side of the door. When she let him in seconds later, his trained eyes noted a wadded-up mound of pillows stuffed down next to the sofa and the bed that had not been slept in. He also spied her backpack off to the side of the door along with a half-drunk bottle of water. Her skittishness at his presence and the way she kept smoothing imaginary loose strands of hair from her face told a story. All signs pointed at Lacey having slept on the floor, right where his feet were now, just inside the door. Instant understanding flashed in his memory—nights spent up against a door as protection and immediate awareness against an intruder. It gutted him to see evidence of the fear she'd been going through staring him right in his face.

He wasn't stupid and was well-aware of the shift he was experiencing courtesy of his traveling companion. In just a few days, he'd developed an interest in another human being, had allowed himself to become concerned about her well-being, and most surprisingly of all, was using the friendship word quite liberally. Drae and Alex were in for a surprise when he showed up with Lacey in tow. And not just because they'd be presented with a new employee but also because they'd pick up immediately on his growing attachment to her.

Hell, he liked being around her. And not just because she smelled like a million bucks and acted like he was the most fascinating guy on the planet. He liked hearing her opinions; she had an interesting take on a variety of subjects and was well-read despite the challenges she'd struggled to overcome.

He also couldn't lie to himself or deny that he wanted her, naked and in his bed, spread open for his pleasure until he pulled her underneath him and sank into her heated depths. He conjured up a picture of those long, lean limbs of hers clutched high across his back as his hands held her incredible ass while he pounded away in a frenzied, intense fucking that would only end after he watched her come, maybe more than once, and then emptied his aching balls deep inside her. Knowing she was an innocent in the ways a man's mind worked in no way diminished the endless erotic images that flashed in his thoughts. He simply wanted her.

Recalling her unease after their first day of driving and the way she reacted to being alone, on their second night he secured two adjoining rooms in a large chain hotel boasting an indoor pool. Dropping their bags and making quite a show of opening the door that made their rooms side by side, Cam suggested they go for a swim before dinner to get some exercise. He made it sound innocent, but he was man enough to admit that what was really spurring him on was the desire to see her in a bathing suit. He wanted to find out once and for all if the luscious breasts he felt when they embraced were as perfect as he imagined. The minute the words came out of his mouth, she started clutching that damnable backpack she never let out of her sight. *Time to find out what that was all about.*

Raising an eyebrow at the worn bag, he commented, "Any chance you have a bathing suit in that bag, Lacey?"

Setting the bag on a chair, Lacey looked at Cameron in surprise. While she liked knowing that they were cautious friends, she was starting to hope for something a bit more on the intimate side. The fact was, she found him terribly exciting and sexy as hell. Two days with him in a truck cab and her nerves were in tatters.

The idea of going swimming filled her with a pleasure so keen she almost embarrassed herself. She bet he looked damn good in bathing trunks, but she was bummed she wouldn't get a chance to see for herself since a bathing suit wasn't included in her meager belongings. "No, sorry. Nothing quite as exotic as a bathing suit in here," she joked as she patted the old bag. "All my clothes are now in a travel bag, so this is just a few personal items," she muttered at the end.

"What's in the book you carry?" he asked. Cam liked that she didn't play bullshit head games. With her shining baby blues staring him down, he watched her face as she decided what to do and waited patiently while she made up her mind without a lot of drama.

Reaching swiftly into the old worn bag, she hauled out the leather book she guarded with her life. "This is my grandmother's diary," she said simply and concisely. "It's from when my mother was a young girl, and it's full of day-to-day details of their family life. I never really knew my mom, so these words feel like the only connection I have left with her."

Laying the old book on a table, she handled it carefully, as if it was a priceless manuscript, and opened it to an old photograph tucked near the back. She held the picture in her hands, staring at it with an intensity that rippled through the space between them, hitting Cam forcefully in the middle of his chest.

Speaking so quietly he could barely make out her words, she whispered, "This is me and my mom."

Gazing at the picture she held up, Cam saw the happy face of an adoring mother holding a baby wrapped in a fluffy pink blanket. Lacey had her mother's eyes. He wondered if she realized that. The loss of a mother's love at such a young age must have been horrible. He was glad she had this picture to connect her with a happier time. He had no such pictures and no happy childhood to recall. It was no wonder she guarded the bag as if her life depended on it.

He remained silent as she replaced the picture and gently closed the book before placing it into the backpack. When her hand stayed and caressed the bag, he couldn't stop himself from blurting out, "I envy you the surety of your mother's love." Lacey's bright blue eyes snapped to his in question. He had no idea what made him say that since he never spoke of the woman who had given him life.

"You didn't know your mother, Cameron?" she asked.

"Oh, no. I knew the woman. That doesn't mean she had the capacity to love anyone other than herself," he bit out with disgust.

Moving to his side, Lacey reached out and touched his arm before sliding her hand gently into his. "I'm sorry to hear that, Cameron. Even though I lost my mother, I know she loved me."

Cam stared at their joined hands and marveled at whatever had made him say that out loud about Lorraine. She'd been completely open with him about her darkest secrets, so maybe he just felt he owed her one of his. Whatever it was, now that he'd shared a little, he was anxious to move on to other things. Feelings weren't where he was the most comfortable.

Stepping away from her, he pocketed the room keys and suggested, "There's a gift shop in the front lobby. Let's go check it out and see if they have something for you to wear in the pool." *Smooth move, you asshole*, he thought. Nothing like a clumsy two-step to keep things light and uncomplicated.

"We don't have to do that. I won't have much use for a bathing suit after this. You go ahead and catch a swim if that's what you want to do. I'll hang out here and watch some TV."

"No way, Lacey. You're coming swimming with me, and FYI, you'll have *plenty* of use for a bathing suit once we get to Arizona. You do realize it's hotter than the lobby of hell there for part of the year, don't you?" he teased. "Come on. No argument. It's down to the lobby we go and no pissing and moaning from you."

Half an hour later, they were back, carrying a plastic shopping bag stuffed with sweatshirts and t-shirts from the gift shop along with a rather demure one-piece suit. He insisted on matching t-shirts with a tacky state slogan across the front that got them both laughing and then tried to tease her into a hot pink two-piece suit that was little more than patches of fabric held together by string. Trotting along with her butt hanging out of a ruffled thong was more than Lacey could handle, hence the sedate one-piece alternative.

Taking the elevator to the indoor pool, they retreated to their respective changing rooms. Cam was already in the pool, enjoying the heated water, when she hesitantly approached with a big towel wrapped around her like a shroud. He enjoyed her shyness and found it totally refreshing compared to the brazen show-offs he was used to. Most of the women of his acquaintance would have gleefully opted for the half-naked look of the hot pink thong and been more than willing to let most of their tits overflow the tiny fabric swatches. Not this one. Dolphining quickly to the side of the pool, he popped up from the water, swiping his long hair back from his face.

Holding out his hand, he said, "Come on, Lacey. I won't bite. Lose the towel and get in here with me before I come up on deck and throw you in."

His bark of surprised laughter bounced off the natatorium walls when she impishly stuck her tongue out and dropped her foot into the water to splash him. When she released the towel, though, his laughing stopped because nothing could have been sexier or more alluring than her not-so-modest one-piece suit. High-cut sides showed off her fabulously long, toned limbs while the sweetheart neckline allowed for a more than generous glimpse of the curves it covered.

Lacey should have jumped right in, but after she tossed her towel on the nearby bench and turned around, Cameron had moved into the shallow end of the pool and was standing in waist-deep water. The sight of his naked chest and impressively toned physique emptied her brain of all coherent thought. With his long, wet hair and smoky green eyes moving hungrily over her exposed skin, she shivered with awareness as she took in his usual facial stubble and the line of dark hair that covered his chest and arrowed downward into his trunks. She was glad that what lay further was under the water because she doubted her ability to look away. She remembered the way she had inspected every visible inch of his incredible body when he had lain unconscious, fevered with illness, and blushed from the soles of her feet to the roots of her hair. *Just friends, right?*

See her slight hesitation, Cam backed off a few feet to give her room to ease into the water, but his eyes never left the tempting vision she created. *Maybe insisting on a swim wasn't such a good idea.* Especially if the hard-on he was sporting was any indication of where his thoughts lay. When she dropped into the pool and gracefully sank beneath the water, the last thing he saw was her rounded bottom before it disappeared beneath the surface. That ass should be declared a health hazard. *Holy fucking shit*, was the only thought Cam could form as vibrant images of her naked body, writhing underneath him as he thrust relentlessly into her body tattooed themselves on his eyeballs. *Just friends, my ass.*

Even long after the other hotel guests had left and only the two of them remained.

Cam had the time of his life challenging her to lap sprints and engaging in some flirtatious water play. She was a very good swimmer and appeared to thoroughly enjoy splashing around in the heated pool.

*Yep*, he mused. Getting her in a pool had actually been a very good idea. Cavorting around in the water loosened them up, and by the time they were ready to get out, they'd been hanging, side by side, on a floating lane divider talking about everything and nothing for the better part of half an hour.

When Lacey paddled to the ladder of the pool, Cam followed close behind, enjoying the sight of her spectacular ass when she pulled herself dripping wet from the water. Reaching quickly for a towel, she began swiping rivulets dripping down her legs while Cam got lost in some undeniably hot and lascivious thoughts. The notion of licking the water from those long, incredible legs renewed the surge of arousal in his groin that had dogged him most of the day.

Lacey concentrated on drying off rather than on the sight of the water dripping from Cameron's hair after he pushed his long dark locks back from his face with an impatient swipe. Not following the path of those droplets as they dripped across his shoulders and down the sexy dark hair framing his chest was an excruciatingly difficult task. There simply was no two ways about it; he was absolutely drop-dead gorgeous and after their round of wild kisses two nights ago, she'd been unable to think of anything else but him. Even the excitement of the first days of their journey dimmed under the magnificence that was his body.

A couple of hours later, after a quick dinner and some quiet TV watching, she was still fighting the lure of his appeal on her frazzled, innocent nerves. As always, he had watched her more than the TV, and she didn't know quite what to make of that. He'd been just as affected by their kissing as she had, she was sure of that, but when he pulled away because he sensed her innocence, something had shifted between them. She was pretty sure he wanted her, but he also seemed hell-bent on making sure he didn't take advantage of her or the situation they found themselves in.

*Was it going to be up to her to make the first move? Oh Lord.* Lacey winced. She was in way over her head. While she desperately wanted to experience the thrill of his lips devouring hers again, she wasn't sure she was ready for whatever came after that. Her hormones might be raging out of control, but she was hardly the sexy femme fatale she imagined.

Cam watched her worry both her bottom lip and the soft throw blanket on the sofa as they sat together watching the late evening news. He was having a hell of a time ignoring the sexual tension in the air, and judging by her actions, she was too. Maybe a good night kiss would be enough to stave off the hunger building inside him.

"Time to turn in, Ponytail," he murmured, reaching for the remote control and switching off the television. "We have an early start in the morning, okay?" As the room plunged into semi-darkness, he appreciated the cat-like stretch she performed when she tossed aside the throw blanket and stood.

From where he sat, Cam enjoyed the sight of her standing at his knees, looking down at him. The breasts he'd been fantasizing about earlier bobbed slightly under the pink nightshirt she put on. Clearly, she wasn't wearing a bra, and the stretchy pants covering her legs did little to disguise her sexy shape.

Before she could answer, Cam grabbed her by the wrist and pulled her down onto his lap. Her shock at his actions gave him the perfect opportunity to press his advantage. "Any chance of a good night kiss?"

Staring expectantly at his sexy mouth, Lacey let her body relax into his. "I'd like that," she husked quietly while she waited for him to move. Leaning forward slightly, she felt her breasts press against his chest while she moved her hand to caress the side of his neck and face. "I like kissing you," was all she got out before feeling his arm move up her back and across her shoulders bringing her even closer to him.

With their lips so close they were breathing each other in, she felt his next words as much as she heard them "I like kissing you too, darlin'. Maybe too much." He groaned as he closed the scant distance between them and captured her expectant lips with his own.

Cam wasn't in the habit of taking his time and beating around the bush when his libido fired up. Used to experienced women who knew the score, every encounter with Ponytail was new, unchartered territory. The admission she had given him about her inexperience wasn't dampening any of his lustful feelings. Far from it. Knowing that every kiss, caress, and sensation he wrought from her was a first made his balls ache for her even more. He wasn't going to be able to help himself in the end, as her total seduction was all but written in stone. That his pulse kept beating out the nonstop message, *Take her. She belongs to you*, wasn't helping.

Her soft hand caressed his neck and traced his jawline, turning his blood to hot lava. Her sweet whimpers and delicate moans as he made love to her mouth had him shuddering from head to toe. When her tongue shyly began the mating dance with his, he was lost. Never had he experienced anything as achingly erotic as their tongues swirling around each other while the oxygen seeped from his brain.

Overwhelmed and consumed by Cameron's sensual assault on her mouth, Lacey never imagined that the simple act of kissing could be so raw. On top of that, being crushed in his arms as he held her fast against his hard, wide chest made her conspicuously aware of how his body molded so perfectly to her own. The low growls from the man laying siege to her senses were unbelievably sexy, and it seemed as though with each rumble her panties became more and more damp.

He was wearing a dark t-shirt that was preventing her from

satisfying the aching need to get closer to his skin. While Cameron sucked her fleshy tongue into his ravenous mouth, she awkwardly attempted to pull his shirt out of his jeans so she could finally touch him. When the shirt didn't move out of the way fast enough to satisfy her desire, she tore her mouth from his, snarling in frustration. She was impatient and half out of her mind with a desperate need to get at his skin.

It was that frantic pawing at his clothes which finally brought Cam back to his senses. He was stunned at how fast their kissing had spun out of control. He was shaking with need and ready to jump first and deal with the aftermath later. The way his cock was throbbing inside his snug jeans was robbing him of common sense.

He'd thought they'd stop at a good night kiss. Man, was he ever wrong, and as much as he wanted to bury himself in her quaking body, he had an obligation to act responsibly with the innocent in his arms. If he didn't get some control over himself, he'd be fucking her bareback in the next five minutes and to hell with the consequences. *Mental note to self: condom in pocket at all times.* Unfortunately, at this precise moment, the condoms he carried were in the bottom of his shaving bag in the other room, buried in his overnight bag. There was that and the fact that seducing Lacey wasn't exactly playing fair. She'd have emotional expectations afterward that Cam didn't know how to fulfill. *Fuck.*

Since walking away wasn't going to happen, he gave her a heady dose of very direct, dirty talk to let her know where all this moaning and sucking and gyrating was headed. She needed to know the type of man she was dealing with before this went any further.

Grabbing both her delicate wrists a nanosecond before her hands found their way under his shirt and on to bare skin, he leaned into her in such a way that there was no mistaking the depth of his arousal. With his dick throbbing in synchronized unison with his pounding heart, Cam let his body communicate with hers as his hungry mouth bit down on her neck.

"Ponytail … you taste like sin. I want to lick your skin, everywhere.

Your calves, inside your thighs. Around your belly button and under your breasts until you cry out for me to lick your sex too. Would you like that, Lacey? Do you want me to taste you? Lap up your wetness?" he groaned into her ear.

Instead of drawing back, which was what Cam expected, Lacey ran her tongue up his neck and across his jaw before asking with her lips so close to his he could inhale her words, "Do I get to taste you too, Cameron?"

*Jesus Fucking Christ, his Ponytail was full of surprises.* He was already at DEFCON 2, and if he didn't calm this interlude down, there was little chance of them making it far enough to ensure her protection. He was seconds away from pushing her down onto the cushions and ripping away her clothes so he could get inside her.

Taking a series of deep, shuddering breaths, Cam held her close but didn't release her questing hands or let her use the physical advantage that in her innocence she might not realize she had. When he felt a measure of control return, he allowed one more sweet, deep kiss before settling her back on the sofa.

"Lacey," he murmured, "you have no idea how much I want your touch, want you to taste me." His admission brought her eyes to his blazing gaze. Watching her reactions, Cam ran a finger across her plump bottom lip before pushing it into her mouth. When she eagerly sucked and swirled her tongue around his finger the same way she would around his cock, his gaze darkened even more.

Removing his trembling finger, he grabbed her chin and looked deeply into her eyes, "You're the most desirable woman I've ever met, Ponytail. You're setting my senses on fire by just sitting there." His eyes swept along the length of her voluptuous body, lingering with fierce attention on the aching, plump mounds of her breasts. When he met her wide-eyed gaze, he let the primitive male inside him rumble and growl, "Know this, fucking you once will not be enough. Once we start, I'm going to want to feast on your body till we both shatter, over and over and over. Do you understand what I'm saying?"

*Oh, she understood all right.* He wanted to command, control, and consume her. She should be wary but found herself drawn closer to his fiery heat. Crashing headfirst into her long-buried sexuality was creating havoc on her mind and senses. Lacey sensed he was trying to keep things from spinning out of control. The very notion that he was as turned on as she was made her pulse race even more.

She wasn't stupid, though, and knew she couldn't allow her raging hormones and unleashed sexual desire to rule the moment. Clearer and calmer heads needed to prevail if they were going to survive being thrown together as they were on this trip. In uncharted water, Lacey was scrambling to stay ahead of the waves crashing through her emotions.

"Are you trying to frighten me, Cameron?" she surprised herself by purring suggestively. Apparently, it was time to cross common sense off the list because even though she knew that quiet comment would throw petrol on the fire, she asked it anyway.

"You don't need to warn me off, y'know," she continued. "It's true that I may not have a lot of experience in this area, but I have enough knowledge to know that this thing," she cried as she gestured wildly between their bodies, "is strong. *Powerful*," she whispered to add dramatic emphasis. Lifting eyes to his, she asked, "It's not going to just go away, is it?"

*Was it going to simply stop the endless craving, the deep yearning to join with this woman?* At that moment, Cam couldn't imagine how. With each passing moment, he got drawn in further by ever intensifying waves of desire coursing through his veins. He was barely keeping his shit together, and she was slowly killing him with the way she responded to each new level of intimacy.

Seeing her trembling body cradled in his arms with her golden tresses all mussed up and looking sexy as hell, he knew that while she would be his, she deserved more than a frenzied sofa fuck for her first time. And she needed to hear what he was thinking.

Her tongue slowly appeared at the seam of her lips for just a second, leaving a shiny path of moisture as her cheeks flushed. Yeah, she needed more, and he intended to see she got that even if it killed him to pull back.

His eyes turned earnest as they bored into hers. "Yeah, it is strong. And no, I don't sense it going away at all. Knowing that, I think we should give this inferno some breathing room. Let us catch our breaths." Her breath hitched at his words. "Feed the fire until it can't be contained and then when the timing is right …"

Um, Lacey was pretty sure she would burst into flames from the way he was looking at her. No, wait. Not looking at, more like he was seeing *in* to her. His hot stare on her lips had all but made them sizzle. Hearing his words, she knew he was slowing things down, but when he groaned something about fueling the flames between them, she nearly shattered right there and then.

With less than a second to catch her breath, Cameron shifted gears. She was amazed to find herself upright and on her feet before she'd even realized he had plucked them both up from their entangled sprawl on the sofa. Wobbling awkwardly, she struggled to regain her equilibrium as he put on his Master of the Universe hat and took control.

Shooing her along to the bed, Lacey sat down in a daze while he nattered on about the hotel's breakfast and what time they should get started in the morning. She watched as he checked out the bathroom and flicked on the light, generally wandering around her room to make sure she had everything she needed. He made quite the point of reminding her that their room adjoined and even suggested that they leave the door open between them if it would make her feel safer.

Her senses fully returned, Lacey sat up a bit straighter on the plush mattress and grabbed her inner fearlessness as she contemplated what was before her. Cameron was suggesting she take a shower and crawl into bed while he did the same in his room next door, *but* they'd leave the door open between the rooms. The way he looked at her and the meaning interjected into his words told Lacey he was on to her habit of sleeping on the floor up against the door. He was also throwing down a challenge, and he knew it.

Where three minutes ago, she had been slowly melting down

with desire, now she was wrestling powerful inner demons. Every thrilling moment since he rushed into her world had brought Lacey one challenge after another. This, though, was a big one. She'd started sleeping against the door when she was a teenager and desperate to fend off her despised uncle. In the years since, being cautious and always aware of her safety had kept her from harm on more than one occasion.

*Could she surrender and trust him to see to their security?*

Cam knew his comment about being safe had hit the mark when her eyes blazed at the mention. He hated to leave her like this, but it really was best to just keep breathing and let the future unfold as it was meant to. Besides, she had to learn how to walk before she could run. Sleeping in the bed, not curled up in a defensive ball against the door on the floor, was a good place to start.

He waited by the door between their rooms as he tried to decipher the thousand thoughts and emotions flitting across her face. He watched as she visibly pulled herself up, nodding at the brave face she was assuming. The lady was a warrior. Her plucky resolve was appealing and, like everything else about her, turned him on. So sayeth the dick throbbing in his pants.

Counting backward in her head, Lacey took a deep breath and jumped. *Five, four, three, two, one. Go!*

"I probably will use the shower before bed. Um," she wavered slightly before charging on. "Uh, breakfast is when?" she croaked.

"Six until ten," he calmly replied.

Her tension rising, Lacey continued as if nothing important was going on. "You'll leave the door open, then?" she asked in what she prayed was a casual way.

Cameron lifted away from the doorjamb where he'd been leaning, moving till he was center frame in her view but still out of arm's reach. "The door stays open. I checked all the locks. You're bolted in tight for the night. Get some sleep and don't worry. I'm just beyond this doorway," he said, nodding his head to the space just behind him. "I'll keep us safe Lacey. Relax. I've got this." He grunted something that came out sounding rough and husky. "My manhood feels like it's being called into question."

His attempt at levity was just so damn charming that Lacey couldn't help but smile.

"Oh, your manhood isn't in question, Cameron." She sighed as the corners of her mouth quirked upward. "After all, I've felt, um … proof and can attest to you being all man."

He had to give it to her; she went balls out when she had to.

His chest grew warm around his heart when she added, "Thank you. For *everything*." The emphasis she gave the word carried a world of meaning. "And thank you for thinking of the door. I really am going to shower and then get some sleep."

Because he didn't really want to leave her, Cam tossed out one final comment, hoping it would make her eyes shine. He couldn't have hit it more right on if he'd been trying. "Your sleep shirt might be right." He chuckled while wagging his eyebrows suggestively at her.

*What did that mean?* Lacey wondered. Gazing down at her choice of sleepwear for a clue, she saw the soft pink cotton first and then what was written on the shirt. She'd barely registered any sort of print or words on it when she had spied the next-to-new sleep shirt in the thrift store's fifty-cent bin. All she cared about at the time was the condition and price of the simple garment.

It took a few seconds for her eyes to focus, but then she saw it. A trail of little hearts and flourishes up one side with the words *It started with a kiss* and a big pair of red lips. As the meaning of the words sank in, she felt heat spread across her chest and up her neck. When she realized that the big red lips were strategically placed directly over one of her pouting breasts with an engorged and extended nipple clearly visible at the center of the mouth, she didn't doubt her cheeks blazed.

*It started with a kiss, indeed!*

Catching his quiet chuckle, she shifted with arms at her waist and her legs slightly parted, she scolded him playfully with as serious a face as she could muster. "Men," she cried playfully. "Always with the one-track mind!"

When she stomped a foot and mischievously stuck her tongue out at him, it was all Cam could do to keep from jumping on her right there and then. His first priority would be to suck that wicked tongue she was wagging at him into his mouth where he would slide his own along hers. Next would be the puffy nubbins staring at him from her breasts that were begging for tongue time too.

He didn't do anything to disguise his thoughts and knew she had clearly seen what was on his mind. The glowing smile she bestowed on him was what he saw from that moment until much later when sleep finally claimed him.

# Chapter Eight

DESPITE THE INTENSE erotic dreams that visited him through-out the night, Cam woke up refreshed with an uncharac-teristic grin on his face. Okay, so maybe the grin was a tad awkward and lopsided, probably from lack of practice, but it was real and the result of the woman sprawled on the bed in the next room.

True to her word, Lacey had spent a ridiculous amount of time in the bathroom last night after he retreated from her room. She was still doing whatever women do when they bathe long after he had finished his own shower. Eventually through the open door between their rooms, he heard her rustling around in the linens of her big bed and filled with pleasure knowing she felt safe enough to take another tiny step into a different way of life.

A long time later, deep in the night, Cam crept from his bed and silently made his way to hers where he found her sprawled, hair a jumbled mess around her face, clutching a small pillow to her side. She was sleeping peacefully, her chest rising and falling with each soft breath. As he enjoyed taking in the sight of her peacefulness, his balls tightened of their own accord as he was struck by her beauty.

He thought of his king-size bed at home. Damn thing was huge, solid, and rather like himself, it was stripped down and basic. Crafted by Drae from rustic timbers he'd smoothed and finished to a deep golden glow, the four-poster bed sat along a glass wall that showcased the beauty of the southwestern desert.

It didn't take much imagination to picture a sexy, ponytailed angel lounging amidst the sumptuous, earth-tone linens he preferred. The rich hues in his bedroom would complement her dusty blond features, and try as he might to control the attraction he felt toward her, the visual of her pale beauty writhing with desire on his bed made his dick stiffen with alarming speed. In seconds, it felt like all the blood in his upper body had rushed at supersonic speed into his throbbing cock. How he managed to walk back to his room while his manhood fought to bury itself in her heat, he did not know. Nor did he know how he fell asleep not too long thereafter.

His desire for her had chased him through the night. Rapid-fire scenes of her ravishment at his hands, under his mouth, and astride his hips as he bucked wildly into her played out on a continuous loop in his dreaming mind. The final fantasy, the one that clung to his aroused body and mind once his eyes opened, was a different matter altogether. Returning to the delicious vision she had presented in her cute pink nightshirt, his thoughts settled on how mouthwatering her nipple seemed where it taunted him at the center of the red lips. It was as if the lips were suckling at her breasts. With that provocation, he claimed the turgid nipple for his own, sucking it forcefully into his mouth through the nightshirt. The perfect feel of her plump breast cupped in his big hand as he held the nipple in place for his hungry lips seared itself on his senses.

His dream self felt powerful, on the edge, and raw. Ripping away the nightshirt, her naked skin seduced him in the shadowy light of a moonlit sky. Prowling her body, he breathed in her arousing scent and let his eyes feast on her exposed flesh.

Crouching over her quivering form, he used his large hands to grasp and massage her ample breasts as her nipples stood at aching attention. Growling his approval, he lightly flicked his wet tongue against each fleshy pink nub. She arched her back, whimpering for more. The beast inside answered her cries, nipping at the tight buds and drawing them against his tongue until half a glorious breast was stuffed inside his mouth as he suckled voraciously on her bountiful curves.

Her moans and pleasured sighs echoed in the silence, enflaming his response to the woman in his dreams. She was on fire for him, so he stoked the flames even higher while his hands memorized her torso as he continued licking, suckling, and biting at her breasts and neck. Even in his dreams, he wanted to devour her.

His questing touch drew lazy circles on her stomach before grabbing her fiercely and spreading his fingers to knead the soft curves of her bottom. Time slowed when his dream lover's thighs fell open at his urging. An exquisite rush of desire greeted his questing fingers when he found the warm, soft curls that shrouded her sexy mound. Cupping her gently while his tongue and lips found their way back to her mouth, Cam swallowed her sensual gasps and moans as he pressed on.

Gently separating the fleshy lips that guarded her most intimate flesh, Cam fell through the rabbit hole when his hands discovered the wet, slick evidence of her arousal. His mind snapped when he felt the liquid desire covering his fingers. Without hesitating, he slid one long, sturdy digit into her hot, wet depths as her hips churned.

*Goddammit, she was fucking magnificent.* Undulating under his caress without abandon as little cries of excitement split the air. He stopped kissing her, and in an agony of intensifying need, he vigorously finger fucked her while she rocked against his hand. Adding a second finger, he stretched her tight passage while spreading the hot, creamy evidence of her arousal.

This dream had nothing to do with his own satisfaction and everything to do with bringing her to an explosive orgasm while he watched and savored her raw response. As his hands continued their exploration at her throbbing core, he growled next to her ear, telling her in the most basic way he could that she was magnificent. That he loved feeling her wet response as it dripped from her slit. How delicious he was sure she would taste when he first put his mouth between her legs. How he wanted to come inside her, empty his balls while buried deep as she spasmed and clutched his cock. Her moans and gasps were the only answer he needed.

She was getting close. Her hips were undulating wildly while she spread her legs ever wider, giving him complete access to her hot wetness. He watched and waited, circling his thumb against the cluster of nerve endings that throbbed at her clit. His breath husked and sounded ragged when he hooked his fingers, stroking that special spot inside her which triggered a flood of wetness, further drenching his hand. She started shaking while her inner muscles claimed his wicked fingers in a frenzy of rhythmic spasms and frantic clutches as he brought her to a screaming climax.

Her cries of completion were still ringing in his ears when his dream world finally broke and sleep receded. *What a fantastic way to start his day,* he grimaced. Nothing like a raging hard-on and an overactive imagination. The only thing to make it better would have been finding her naked in his bed so he could draw her body against his while his throbbing staff slid into her from behind.

Well, glorious as that thought was, it wasn't on the agenda this morning. Lifting from the bed, Cam did a few quick stretches and made for the bathroom where a cool shower helped calm his body and clear his mind for the day ahead.

His hope was to make it through Texas in one day with a planned stop at a military base. The Justice Agency had been invited to participate in a security round table, and he was going to attend. He was generally ambivalent about his military connections. After leaving the service, he'd pushed the memories of his years choking back the dust of the Middle East into the far reaches of his consciousness. Dragging all that baggage around only held him back. Each time he ventured onto a base or dealt with uniforms, Cam felt the military mindset closing in. It wasn't something he was looking forward to.

Dressing less casually today in deference to his business

obligations, he chose a crisp, white button-down shirt and black slacks. Later, he'd add a dark jacket and, if necessary, a tie. Having shaved thoroughly and gotten his shaggy mane of jet black hair smoothed into sensible waves, he looked to be exactly what he was, a businessman on a trip.

Thinking of the trip, he focused on the freckle-faced beauty asleep in the adjoining room. Still buttoning his shirt, he stepped through the open door and paused. Curled on her side, she had one leg crooked at the knee, arms wrapped around a huge overstuffed pillow. She looked adorable, all sleep tousled and mussed. Her nightshirt had ridden up in the night, and with one leg flung on top of the covers, Cam had a tantalizing view of her exposed buttock and thigh. She was wearing sensible white panties again, only a bit of lace softened this pair. He swallowed and sighed at the delightful picture she presented. No matter what he did, she was all he could think about.

Calling quietly to break her sleeping spell, Cam's deep voice rumbled in the silence. "Lacey, wake up, sleepyhead."

When she didn't stir, he stepped closer and gently ran his fingers across her exposed calf. "Ponytail. Rise and shine." The way his hand tingled from the simple contact guaranteed she was awake now. There was no way she hadn't felt that.

"Mmm," she moaned, floating up from sleep to wakefulness, stretching her body from head to toe. One eye opened. Then the other. She took a moment to consider where she was and then turned her head searching for him. "Cameron," was all she said. A heady satisfaction surged through his senses when he realized her first thought upon waking was of him.

"Good morning. Did you sleep well?" he asked, enjoying the moment. "We have a busy day ahead, so get your butt in gear and let's hit up the breakfast buffet before we get back on the road." She was sitting up now, rubbing the sleep from her eyes and looking like the sexiest thing alive in that silly nightshirt with her messy hair. He couldn't recall seeing a woman just as she woke up ever before.

Lacey felt different somehow. Maybe it was the long, relaxing bubble bath she took last night that made her feel so serene. Or maybe it was the luxury of the huge plush bed with the soft crisp sheets and the squishy pillows that had given her the first relaxing calm night's sleep she ever remembered having. All she knew for sure was that when she opened her eyes and saw Cameron at her bedside, she felt a rush as if an electrical charge shot through her senses. She found seeing his beautiful face the moment she opened her eyes to be the icing on her cake after an amazingly restful night's sleep. After that, everything just felt, well ... *different*.

Pulling herself up to sit cross-legged in the middle of the king-size bed, Lacey yawned a few times, pushing the wild hair from around her face and looking more closely at her beautiful sexy knight. Gone was the three-day stubble, worn t-shirt, and old jeans. Today's Cameron was clean-shaven, his hair groomed, wearing business attire and looking quite serious. In a word, he looked *yummy*. And very, very hot.

"Hey! Do I know you, sir?" she squeaked dramatically, clutching a tiny corner of the sheet to her throat. "What did you do with cowboy Cameron?" she teased. "Seriously, what's the deal? Is it formal Thursday, and I didn't know?"

He liked the way her voice sounded kind of rocky and even sexier, if that was possible, first thing in the morning. She was priceless, and he snorted at her wiseass remarks. *Cowboy Cameron?* Hey, he liked that.

Groaning in mock frustration, he gestured at his dress for the day. "Ah, yes. Well, business is on the schedule. We'll be stopping at a military base in Oklahoma for a scheduled meeting. Boring round table, lots of talking. Sorry but duty calls."

Something flashed across her face, but it was gone so quick he didn't have a chance to register what it was. But Ponytail was suddenly tense and looking a bit stern.

"Hey, hey," he murmured, stepping into her personal space. "What's with the frowny face? It's really NBD. You'll hang out in the family area because of security, but you'll be fine. There are always loads of people and liaison volunteers there. Guaranteed you'll have a better time than I will."

At the mention of Oklahoma, Lacey fell silent. Oklahoma. *Wow.* There was a place she never thought she'd ever be again. She'd lived in Oklahoma before her dad did his flit and abandoned her.

Memories flooded her mind. What she remembered of her father was muddied by age. She'd been so young when they'd lived together. He was never around, and she practically raised herself. She remembered that he smelled of cigarettes and Lava soap and had a moustache and a beer gut. He watched Mickey Mouse cartoons and made gallons of sweet iced tea that he kept in big jugs in the refrigerator. That was basically the sum total of what she could recall of her time with him.

There were snippets of being in grade school and riding in his work truck crammed full of tools and empty fast food drink cups. And shadowy memories of a time when he laughed and seemed happy, impressions from before they lost her mother. Beyond that, her mind was blank where he was concerned. She didn't blame him for not visiting—after all, Alaska wasn't exactly around the corner from south Florida—but she did feel a bitterness deep in her heart that he'd just walked away without a second's glance.

Seeing Cameron looking so hot and drop-dead sexy in the stark white shirt and dark slacks staggered her with self-doubt. She was little more than a kid, and here she was with this serious-looking businessman.

Cam was surprised when she tried suggesting that she wait for him in the truck, out of the way, while he went about his business. But he would have none of that.

"No. You're not hiding. You're with me. Don't get all worked up." A light bulb went off in his head that he thanked his lucky stars for when he told her, "Wear that pretty little sundress you picked up. Give you a chance to show off those strappy sandals I know you've been dying to wear."

The clouds in her demeanor seemed to lift and vanish after that as they busied with their morning tasks before heading down to the breakfast buffet. Cam wasn't sure what that had been all about, but he knew keeping things light and her moving forward was the easiest way to overcome whatever had appeared to dim her outlook.

By the time they got on the road about an hour later, Lacey was still quiet but not nearly as tense as she had been. Cameron tried filling in the silence with idle chitchat about current events but she didn't want to talk. Finally, he found a classic rock station on the satellite radio, and they listened to that as the scenery sped by.

The fact was, the mere mention of Oklahoma had triggered a tidal wave of emotional baggage. The only thing keeping her calmly in the seat was the solid presence of the guy sitting beside her. He made her feel safe. When he looked at her with those hypnotic green eyes, she felt bravery and courage feed into her system, drip by drip, as his gaze bored into her soul. It was unnerving and exciting at the same time.

With the breath caught in her throat and the *thump, thump, thumping* of her heart, Lacey realized her thoughts were wandering. Glancing his way, she got lost in his masculine profile, feeling small and fragile next to his large frame. From her side of the front seat, it seemed he took up much of the space in the truck's cab with his impressive height, impossibly broad shoulders, and muscled thighs. The dark shaggy hair she was used to seeing was styled away from his face, giving her a clear view of Cameron's sculpted cheekbones and perfect nose atop a pair of lips that should be declared illegal. It never failed to astonish her how readily she quickened whenever he was near.

Unable to look away, she noticed his hands where they gripped the steering wheel. Just like the rest of him, they were huge. His fingers were long and tapered, strong and sturdy, but not clumsy. Physically, he was controlled and showed an economy of movement. He wasn't all over the place, restless and edgy. That rock steadiness showed in his grasp and made her think about what it would feel like to have those big hands touch her. Explore her intimate places, learn her female secrets. The thought made heat rush up her back while a fine shudder shook her body.

Lacey knew she was developing powerful feelings for him. What started off as a wayward thought about his presence making her feel safe hadn't taken long to detour into a much more intimate territory. *Yeah, he made her feel safe. And he made her feel all flushed and sparkly inside.* She quickly bit off the gurgle of laughter that nearly burst from her throat. She added a silent snort of disbelief at her own naïveté. The sparkly feeling was commonly referred to as sexual arousal. *Lord, but she was out of her depth with him.* He was, after all, trying to play nice, and while she should be grateful for that, she didn't feel like being sensible.

A water tower in the distance caught her attention as it grew larger as they zoomed down the highway. Getting closer, Lacey spied some sort of military insignia and the name of a base on the tower and realized they must be approaching their midday destination. Shutting down brooding memories and an inconvenient attraction to her traveling companion, she pulled it together and turned her attention toward the nerve-wracking thought of going out in public with Cameron. She hoped that she didn't do or say anything to embarrass him. He appeared so mature and serious in his business attire and it sort of freaked her out.

Checking out her outfit for the hundredth time, she tried seeing herself through a stranger's eyes. With her hair in a loose ponytail, she'd added two simple white enamel clips above each ear that lent a bit of shine since she didn't have any jewelry to accessorize with. The simple summery dress had short sleeves, a scoop neckline, and a fluttery hem that stopped well north of her knees. With its breezy fabric of tiny pink flowers, the dress felt deliciously feminine. As Cameron had suggested, she added the strappy sandals, but the suggestive sway she now walked with caught Lacey off guard. In fact, she was pretty sure those swinging hips caught her dark knight by surprise too, if the way his eyes had burned off the top layer of her skin when she walked to the truck was any indication.

Hours later, Lacey was enjoying some small talk with a group of military spouses gathered for a day of recreation. She'd been left to her own devices shortly after arriving, having gone through some heavy formalities and a sobering security check. Cameron had quickly been drawn away through the security zone while she had been warmly welcomed at the base community center bustling with families and volunteers.

It hadn't taken long to overcome her initial shyness, and she found the time spent over lunch and relaxing in the outdoor courtyard with the military families heartwarming and informative. Hearing their stories helped Lacey create quite a vivid picture in her mind of what life while deployed was really like.

Tales of intense heatwaves, bugs, poor food, and a lack of simple comforts as well as the constant danger and never-ending high alert moved her beyond words. Knowing Cameron had experienced these things squeezed at her heart. He hadn't said much about the military, but she'd known from his fevered delirium that he'd been part of the special forces.

Even when he was actively seducing the breath from her body, he'd been sure to remind her that he was, as he put it, no gentleman. Even referred to himself as a complete bastard several times. Hearing what the spouses told her today, she understood that the emotional burden of war sometimes made those who'd served think they were not very nice people. Cameron clearly thought of himself as somewhat broken. She couldn't disagree more.

Escaping the heat of the late afternoon, everyone had gone back inside the center where she was standing by a vending machine chatting with two women when Cameron appeared at the end of a long hallway. He was deep in conversation, hands jammed in his pockets and walking alongside someone in an officer's uniform. The way he moved and held himself showed a strength she was starting to see through different eyes.

Keeping her eyes on him as he made his way down the length of the narrow hall, Lacey enjoyed the warmth creeping along her nerve endings. Seeing him as he was, tie loosened and the top button of the white shirt that stretched tight across his solid chest undone, he looked so gorgeous that she lost her thoughts and nearly forgot to breathe. *Damn.*

"Is that your man, honey?" the woman at her side asked. "Oh my! Girlfriend, that man is H-O-T!"

Lacey blushed and looked away, making the two women hoot in delight at her obvious embarrassment. "Don't be shy, Lacey!" the one teased. "I wouldn't mind if he put his shoes under my bed, if you know what I mean!"

She couldn't help but giggle at their easy banter, eventually making quiet, shooing gestures with her hands to halt the chatter before the advancing men entered their space.

On their approach, the older woman called out to the officer. "Colonel Davis. You know Lieutenant Turner's wife, Sarah, don't you?" she asked as the two men came to a halt.

The colonel acknowledged both women before turning to Cameron and performing the basic introductions. It didn't take long after that for the women to wander discreetly away. When the colonel turned to Lacey, Cameron quickly staked his claim with a hand at the small of her back, drawing her close to him.

"Who is this lovely young lady?" the colonel asked with a twinkle in his eye. "Don't tell me she's with your sorry butt, Justice," he added with a smile. "Ah, the injustice!"

Both men chuckled at the funny twist on his name. When Cameron answered, he did so with a half-assed salute and a smirk. "Just because you outrank me now, Frank, doesn't mean you get to flirt with my companion."

Cameron waved dismissively in the other man's direction. "Lacey, this cigar-chomping reprobate with the ugly buzz cut is Colonel Frank Davis. We had the misfortune of being deployed together a long time ago. Don't believe anything he says. As an officer, he is no gentleman and lies like a rug."

While she laughed and smiled, Cameron fixed his old friend with a searing look. "Frank, this is my friend, Lacey Morrow." Nobody missed the slight emphasis he'd placed on the word *friend*.

Reaching out politely to shake her hand, the colonel nodded his head, acknowledging Cameron's' introduction. "It's a pleasure to meet any *friend* of a Justice Brother," he said.

Lacey twitched in surprise when Cameron added hastily, "She's traveling with me to Arizona."

"Whoa, whoa, whoa! You're taking someone this pretty into the Justice compound? Cam! You old dog, you!" chortled the obviously amused officer.

Turning mischievous eyes her way, the colonel mock-whispered to her, "Watch out for that piece of work, Draegyn St. John. He's a devil with the ladies."

At the mention of Drae and his womanizing ways, Cam's stomach clenched. So did his jaw, teeth, hands, and thighs as a low growl built in his chest. "Yeah, well, Drae will be on his best behavior. Even he knows better than to fraternize with an employee. Lacey will be handling the front office for a while," he quickly added, earning a thoughtful stare from his old comrade.

Lacey watched this strange exchange and wondered what was really being said and why the man at her side had tensed to ramrod straight in a heartbeat. The conversation eventually went back to more serious matters as the three of them made their way from the rec center across the courtyard to the parking area. Cameron's hand stayed glued to the small of her back while she walked quietly at his side. She liked the sense of possessiveness conveyed by his body language.

When their business concluded, the men gave a brief salute then embraced in one of those bro-hugs that spoke louder than words. She was beginning to understand how deep the emotions ran between modern day warriors serving together on the battlefield. Theirs was a special bond that would endure a lifetime. Suddenly humbled by the man she was traveling with, she considered that while he may be damaged and been knocked around a bit, he was also worthy of her respect.

After driving hours away from the base, Cam was exhausted. His analytical mind was picking apart the information he'd learned in the security meeting while trying to squash his body's ever-growing desire for the quiet woman in the seat next to his. He was normally out of sorts anytime he had dealings with the military. Damn memories had a way of clogging his thoughts. Maybe his strong reaction to her presence was a result of that.

The moment he'd introduced her to his old buddy Frank, Cam had been overcome with feelings he didn't know how to handle. The man had been yanking his chain by suggesting Drae would have designs on Lacey. It had been nothing more than typical soldier teasing. Snarky comments were something they excelled at because sarcastic chitchat was one way they dealt with the more serious shit. But his reaction of immediate insane, red-hot, possessive jealousy had thrown him, big time.

She looked so damn pretty in her flowered dress with the sandals that made her sizzle as she walked. Releasing a heavy sigh, Cam doubled down on exercising some control before he pulled over to the side of the road and lifted her into his lap so he could get at her body.

Wanting her the way he did and not acting on that desire was making him crazy. Chalking it up to simple frustration, something physical, Cam had to admit he wasn't used to reining in his libido.

*How else could he explain his unexpected reaction?*

Really? *Really,* screamed his inner voice. *You don't know how else to explain that green-eyed reaction?* What a fucking liar. *Get some new bullshit to spew, Justice.*

Time to stop for the night. Get some food and take a hot shower. Maybe by then, his mood would shift, and he wouldn't need a virtual gun at his head to stop his hands from finding their way into Ponytail's panties. Grinding his jaw when he remembered she was off-limits, Cam reluctantly acknowledged that losing himself in the sweet heat of her surrender wasn't going to make him forget where he'd come from and everything he'd done.

Well, maybe it would for a while, but eventually, the grim reality of who he was would come back. He didn't want to use her like that.

Lacey was tired of being quiet, and she'd had enough of being cooped up in the cab of the truck while sexual tension swirled around them in the close confines. He seemed awfully dark and moody after their time on the base. For reasons she didn't self-examine, she wanted to comfort her dark knight. Wanted to get close and whisper to him how brave and wonderful she thought he was. Wanted to replace the somber scowl on his otherwise beautiful face with something less sad. Oh yeah, and she wanted all that while he was dressed, or rather undressed, and wearing only the sexy cotton briefs burned in her memory.

Sighing, she perked up quickly when the truck exited the highway. Thank goodness they were stopping. It seemed like they'd been driving forever. She needed to get her wayward thoughts under control and desperately needed to use the bathroom. Maybe after she relaxed and ate something, she'd be thinking clearer.

# Chapter Nine

HE'D CHECKED THEM in to a surprisingly comfortable hotel hours ago on a wave of tense silence that wasn't fading. Even after they'd had a bite to eat, relaxation hadn't been on the agenda. The storm of unpleasant memories kicked up by the visit to the military base had not settled one bit. Actually, Cam was feeling dark and slightly dangerous. The beast inside him was prowling quietly, straining to get off the tether that kept his baser instincts in check.

Memories, visceral and intense, were tap-dancing on his nerves. He couldn't contain the need to burn each and every one to the ground, any way he could, before they messed with his head. Those shadowy thoughts were always pushing back, reminding him of darker times when blood and war and survival ruled the day.

He didn't know how he kept up the pretense of being a card-carrying member of the human race when the primal creature inside him was snarling to be let loose. An epic, internal battle was raging. On the one hand, his better self was urging calm. Reminding him that Lacey was someone special to guard and protect. However, the other hand was pushing the boundaries in every way possible. Urging him to take her, to ease his frustration and anger at the past in the only way he knew how.

He'd arranged for adjoining rooms again but had retreated into a self-imposed isolation once they'd gotten settled. She kept looking at him with those smoky blue eyes as if she could see into his tortured soul. The way she softened each time his eyes caught hers tugged at his heart.

Growing more and more frustrated, Cam knew he was fucked, because her sweet innocence excited and rankled him at the same time. Still, he had no business dragging her gentle loveliness into the darkness of his half-life.

It had been a relief when she'd disappeared into the bathroom, and he heard the shower running. Needing time to put on his game face and get his desires in check, he kept silently chanting, *She's not for you, soldier. She's not for you.* Unfortunately, he was pretty damn sure his dick wasn't listening.

Time passed. The shower turned off. He knew this because he'd finally prowled his way into the shadows of her room, lying in wait like an animal hunting its prey. He'd reached his breaking point. He. Couldn't. Stay. Away.

When Lacey appeared wearing the button-down shirt he'd removed earlier, he lost his mind in a heartbeat. Okay, maybe it took two heartbeats. Either way, he was up and stalking her with just one thought in mind—to make her his once and for all, and to do it now.

Lacey didn't immediately realize she wasn't alone in the room until she sensed a knockout blow of raw, intense energy hit her from behind. When she whirled around, the shock she experienced wasn't from finding her dark knight in the same room but rather from the way her body reacted to the fiercely aroused look etched on his face and the way he was zeroing in on her with the precision of a heat-guided missile. She. Was. In. Trouble.

Or perhaps he was the one in trouble if the heat surging between her legs and the way her breasts plumped and nipples peaked were any indication. He wasn't wearing a shirt. *Oh right*, her brain shouted. She was wearing it and almost nothing else. His trousers were unsnapped but still zipped and had an impressive bulge she couldn't ignore.

Eyes, devoid of their green color and dark as a midnight sky, bored into hers with an intention and purpose that unleashed flames of desire inside her. As he moved through the shadows of the sparsely lit room, she saw twin shards of color infusing his cheeks, evidence of the wild desire driving him on. Jesus, she could sense his arousal. *Was she breathing?* Lacey wasn't sure.

"I surrender, Ponytail," he snarled. With a look that devoured and enflamed, he came so close she could feel the energy as it sparked between them. The small whimper escaping her throat was a direct result of the way his powerful eroticism enveloped her entire being.

"I want you. Under me, naked, legs spread wide as I sink into your body over and over and over until both of us are wrecked."

She watched, helplessly fascinated as his nostrils flared and his eyes glittered with each provocative word.

"And you want me too, Lacey. I can see it in your eyes, smell it on your skin."

He took a single step closer as her senses shifted into overdrive. It was hard to breathe. She was painfully aware of her chest heaving as she struggled to keep the oxygen moving in and out of her lungs. She thought he was beautiful, and at this second, she'd never seen anything sexier or more enthralling than Cameron Justice.

With a heavily aroused voice, Cameron growled out a single command. "Turn around and put your hands on the desk."

Lacey blinked. No more dancing around and pretending this wasn't going to happen. She wanted his hands on her. Wanted to know what it was like to be consumed by this man, to be flung into the flames of desire until he had absorbed all her fire and wrung the last drops of pleasure from her body and soul.

Slowly, with her heart thumping wildly in her chest, she turned, only dropping her eyes from his at the last second when she had to. With her back to him, leaving her essentially blind to whatever came next, she bent forward slightly, resting her trembling hands on the desk against the wall. Swallowing the thickness crowding her throat, Lacey stood there, silently aware of the way his shirt barely covered her bottom and the sound of his breathing, thick and heavy, hanging in the air.

Cam's knees almost buckled when she turned around. Enjoying the seductive view her fantastic backside afforded, even covered by the length of his shirt, was a pleasure beyond description. The outline of her ass teased him through the stark whiteness of the button-down shirt. As long as he lived, he'd never seen anything quite as mouth-wateringly sexy as her heart-shaped bottom just waiting for his touch.

Inhaling deeply, he savored the way her womanly scent mingled with the smell of coconut shampoo. Holy shit, but his mouth actually watered while his tongue seemed to grow larger and more insistent, rather like his cock, which at this moment was throbbing against the tightness of his trousers.

In a voice deepened by desire, he whispered, "I dream of you like this. Half-naked, your body calling out to me. Do you dream of me too?" His fingers lightly touched her thighs, making her legs quiver at the soft caress. "Do as I say, Lacey. Do everything I say, and if you're very, very good, I'm going to fuck you senseless just the way you pictured it in your dreams."

Cam watched as she reacted with a seductive arching of her back. Enticing her body would be easy, but seducing her mind was equally as important. Gently palming her lovely ass, he commanded that she put her legs together and not move until he said she could.

He felt intense satisfaction as he watched her legs close while her breathing got heavier. Right then and there, he wanted to tear her panties away and shove his hungry cock into her trembling body. He could smell the arousal coming from her, and it was all he could do to stay focused and not succumb to the needs of his own body.

Lacey was stunned. *He could see into her thoughts and into her fantasies and nighttime musings? Oh, no!* Secret, erotic fantasies suddenly burst to life in her brain. Cameron suckling voraciously at her breasts while his hand dipped between her thighs to test the flood of desire he'd wrung from her body. Cameron gently parting her womanly folds to flick his tongue against her throbbing nub before pulling it into his mouth as she dreamed of him doing to her nipples. Cameron pushing her thighs apart so he could thrust deep, deeper into her. Oh. My. *God.* His hands swept around her, and in seconds, the shirt drifted silently to the floor.

She was a quivering mess by the time she'd squeezed her legs together, waiting for whatever came next. Senses on overload, Lacey shook her head, feeling her long ponytail fall down her back. When Cameron's hands began tracing the skin at her knees, moving slowly up the outside her thighs, she had to grip the edge of the desk until her knuckles went white. By the time his touch arrived at the leg openings of her cotton panties, she had let out a quiet whimper that sounded completely foreign to her ears. *Was that her with the low, husky moans?* He was barely touched her, yet she was more turned on than she'd ever been before and that was saying something since their kisses had been off-the-charts hot.

Unable to stop herself, Lacey involuntarily shimmied her bottom in response to his sensual stroking, earning her a stinging swat on her butt and his growling warning to be still and move only when instructed. Her head dropped forward, and she tried to clear her mind, aware of how desperate she was becoming. She wanted more.

Lost in an erotic haze of thundering lust, Cam watched his big hands stroke her warm, soft skin. *My god.* She was sex on two legs and didn't even know it. Running just a fingertip lightly along the elastic leg openings of her panties, he almost lost it at the sight of her skin prickling under his touch. She was so sensitive, so open to what he was doing to her. He slid his hands under her panties and massaged each butt cheek bringing her head snapping up from where it had been hanging just moments before. *Hmm.* She liked what he was doing. *Good.* He liked it too.

Removing his hands from her heated skin, he moved until his aroused body was almost touching hers. He made sure not to actually touch, preferring to drown her senses with suggestions of what lay ahead. He knew she could sense him from the sounds of her erratic breathing and the way her thighs quivered as he neared.

Sliding the palms of both hands into the soft cotton laying against her hips, he very, very slowly peeled the sides of her panties down until they hung below her ass, held in place only by the fact her legs were pressed together. The sight she presented with her un-fucking-believable ass made his cock throb with need.

He placed one hand low on her abdomen so his fingers could touch the soft nest of curls between her legs. His other hand wrapped around her ponytail, yanking her head back and to the side. Affording his mouth clear access to her neck and shoulder, he leaned over her shaking body. He pulled her back to his groin, fitting his covered bulge in the seam of her butt cheeks a scant second before his hungry mouth latched onto her neck.

Lacey jerked in surprise and then completely melted down at the cascade of sensations battering her. His big hand against her tummy holding her in place while his hips ground slightly against her naked ass was sweet torture. She went up in flames when his mouth bit into her neck, sucking on her skin while he fisted his hand in her ponytail.

Long minutes passed, maybe an hour or three, as Lacey lost herself in what he was doing. He attacked her neck, leaving bite marks on her skin, before licking the same spot, drawing shudders of sensual thrall from her shaking body. He was marking her, and she liked it.

*No, she loved it.*

The oral assault on her neck and shoulder became rough and demanding. Lacey writhed and moaned her approval. When she whispered his name, he stopped, but she could feel his mouth against her sensitized skin.

"You like that. Good. *Very* good."

His hand remained fisted in her hair as he left a wet trail of kisses along her shoulder blades and part way down her back. Lacey wasn't sure how much more she could take and remain standing. When he dropped to his knees behind her, she barely registered the change in position before his teeth began nipping and biting the plump cheeks of her ass. Try as she might to stay still, she just couldn't and arched into his mouth for greater contact.

When he swatted her butt with a sharp smack, her legs shook so hard she was sure she'd be slithering to the ground any second.

"Be still or I'll stop, Lacey. You must do as I say, or I'll leave you here with your panties hanging down and your beautiful ass exposed. Is that clear?" he snarled. "I want you mindless with desire, proof of your arousal running down your legs."

Cameron reached for the closure of her bra and unsnapped the confining garment. As it fell down her arms, stopped by the placement of her hands on the desk, Lacey was mindfully aware of the wanton picture she presented with her breasts swinging free and her panties held up by her closed legs.

"Cameron," she cried. "Please." Shaking almost uncontrollably, she hung her head and begged, "Please, please touch me!" until at last she felt his hands sweep up from her belly to grab both breasts in his large hands. He didn't do much more than simply stand behind her as he molded her sensitive mounds, but it was enough for the moment.

"Mmm. Lacey. Your breasts are fantastic. Is this what you wanted? Or is there more?" he asked while caressing her aching mounds.

She felt his hardness on her naked and exposed bottom.

"More, *please*," she croaked out as he massaged her breasts, causing her nipples to peak and ache. He leaned over her and laved her ear with his tongue as his fingers sought out her dusty pink nipples, gently pinching them.

"I want to taste your nipples," he croaked. "Suck them into my mouth and swirl my tongue around each one again and again." Lacey groaned aloud and started panting in anticipation, but he slowed his stroking and laughed close to her ear.

"Ah, I see you want that too? It arouses you to think about my mouth pleasuring your gorgeous breasts. Well, you'll have to wait. And be good about it because I'm barely getting started. Before I'm done with you, I'll have tasted everywhere, not just your hard little nipples."

With that, he quickly released her aching breasts, leaving them hanging. Looping his fingers into the sides of her panties again, he began to slowly pull them down her legs. With her knees clamped together, he had to peel them off her center, making Lacey exquisitely aware of the dampness that flooded her core. His quiet murmur of pleasure at finding the cotton panties drenched from her arousal sparked a surge of piercing desire to course through her.

Lacey was amazed how he made her feel with his large, warm hands exposing her nakedness to his gaze. He was kneeling behind her, and as the panties slowly moved down her legs, she was aware of his heated breath on the skin of her backside.

Once her panties were down around her ankles, there was a long moment of silence before she heard him husk out his next demand. Wrapping a hand around one ankle, he commanded her to raise her foot while he slipped the cotton away before following suit with the other. From the corner of her eyes, she saw him toss the crumpled undies to the side in an impatient gesture that turned her on even more. He didn't say anything for a long time. She was exquisitely aware that he stayed close to her trembling body from the occasional sensation of his hot breath on her exposed skin. For someone who had never experienced any level of intimacy with a man before, Lacey was overcome by the decadence she felt knowing she was fully naked and exposed to his eyes.

"Drop the bra to the floor," he demanded, which she did in short order before returning her hands to the desk. If she didn't have something to hold, Lacey was certain she'd simply collapse in a puddle of wanton desire.

She shivered when he wrapped his hands around her ankles and tugged slightly, prompting her to open her legs. She wasn't exactly spread eagle at that point, but her legs had parted enough that she felt the dampness clinging to her thighs. He must have been aware as well because she detected a slight tremor in his grip when the scent of her arousal wafted up. It was all she could do at that point not to cry out.

Cam was almost blind with lust from the little game of seduction he'd been subjecting his Ponytail to. She was a quick learner and had done exactly as he'd asked when he slowly and deliciously peeled away her lingerie to bare her luscious body to his view. Fuck, but she was a tempting sight to his jaded eyes. Her skin was so pale and soft. Except for the freckles across her nose, the only other marks on her body were the love bites he left along her neck and a tiny, heart-shaped spot on her hip that only accentuated the shape and unbelievably sexy curve of her ass.

Peeling the panties down her incredible long legs, he'd almost lost his cool when he'd picked up on the delicious, sexy scent of her arousal. He bet she'd taste sweet and sinful. He wasn't joking when he'd told her he intended to lick and taste every inch of her body. Hell, it was all he could do not to devour her right this second.

With his big hands still wrapped around her slim ankles, he slid them slowly upward, enjoying the warmth and softness of her skin. At her calves, he stopped to knead her flesh as a vision of them gripping his waist while he ground his cock into her exploded in his mind. The thought of her delicate feet digging into his ass while he rode her made him catch his breath and moan aloud. Fucking this sweet, responsive woman would be incredible. She was made for his pleasure, and he was damn sure going to see to hers as well.

Lacey had gone from a slight tremble to shaking uncontrollably as his hands moved up her legs. She was having trouble staying upright, and even her death grip on the edge of the desk, which at the moment was her only anchor, was proving to be insufficient as her arms turned to jelly and every scintilla of strength she had evaporated under his sensual assault.

A cross between his name, a moan, a cry, and a whimper shuddered from her when she felt him press a warm, wet kiss on the back of each knee. She shook as his palms stroked the rest of the way up the back of her thighs until his fingers cupped her bottom. With his hands positioned that way, he moved his thumbs between her thighs into the soft curls that covered her womanhood. After finding the damp proof of her desire at the top of her spread thighs, she remembered what he'd growled earlier when he taunted her with his naughty words, saying he wanted proof of her arousal running down her legs. Nothing could stop the groan that rumbled from her core or the way her backside arched toward him.

Leaving his thumbs barely touching her damp curls, his strong hands gripped the cheeks of her butt as he leaned in to swipe one wet, decadent stroke of his tongue after another along the tops of her thighs.

"Cameron, my god," she moaned as her legs shook. "I can't take anymore."

Biting her ass with a sharp nip, he moved strong hands to her waist, smoothly turning her around to face him. Lacey kept her hands behind her, still gripping the edge of the desk lest she lose the ability to remain standing. The sight of Cameron crouched down on his knees at her feet, bare chested and breathing heavily, set her pulses racing even higher. His green eyes darkened with desire, gold sparks shooting at her with primal intent.

While she watched, he repeated his earlier action, slowly running his hands from ankles to thighs; only this time, his thumbs pressed against her quivering mound. Right then and there, Lacey struggled to breathe on automatic. Her mouth, already open to gulp in air, gaped and went slack when he leaned forward and pressed a delicious wet, open-mouth kiss on her abdomen right above her hairline. Her nipples peaked in agonizing response, and she feared if he didn't take them in his mouth soon, she would beg.

Cupping her sexy mound with one hand, Cam's eyes closed when an earthquake-like shudder rolled through him as he touched the wet warmth between her legs. *Jesus.* He wanted to explore her moist channel and watch while she fucked his fingers.

Locking his heavy-lidded gaze to hers, Cam ground the palm of his hand against her, feeling a surge of satisfaction crash through him when she rolled her hips against his firm touch and whimpered in that softly, husky voice of hers.

Going on instinct, he took one of her hands and thrust it between her thighs before covering it with his own. When he ground both their hands against her weeping center and she started shaking all over, the beast inside him gloried in her remarkable response.

"You're wet," he groaned. "So fucking wet. Can you feel it?" he asked as he moved her trembling fingers back and forth against her slit. "That's all you, Lacey. That's you wanting me deep inside your body, stroking in and out until you fall apart in my arms."

Lacey shook from head to toe as he continued using her hand to rub against her swollen cleft, spreading the flood of her need until she thought she'd faint from the pleasure it was giving her.

Just when she was sure she couldn't take another second of his sweet seduction without exploding, he abruptly stood. Pressing his half-naked body against hers, she was aware of how his hair-covered chest felt against her unbelievably sensitive breasts. She was desperate to feel every inch of him against her naked skin.

Wrapping his arms around her, one hand cupped her bottom pulling her into closer contact with his arousal. Reaching up to once again to pull on her ponytail, he sank his mouth into her neck. Licking and kissing his way to her ear, he whispered hot words that flooded her core.

"I'm going to lay you out before me on the bed now, with your legs spread wide so nothing is kept from my view. Then I'm going to feast on your beautiful breasts until your nipples are raw." His breath rasped against her sensitized ear, making Lacey shudder, shake, and whimper.

"If I can keep from pushing my rock-hard dick into you a while longer, I may even lick your pussy, but this first time, I intend to be buried balls deep inside you when you come. Will you cry out, Lacey, when the climax rips through your luscious body? Hmm? I want to feel you pulse around me while your muscles milk my cock dry."

Accentuating his words, he bit and licked her neck with each word he growled, "I. Am. Going. To. Fuck. You. Hard. Deep. Long. Until. You. Come. And. Come. And. Come."

At that point, her legs finally buckled beneath her. As if he'd been waiting for her to come undone, Cameron caught her as she collapsed, swinging her up into his arms as his mouth crashed down on hers. She reacted with a thunderbolt of passion, wrapping her arms around his head, squirming in his embrace, giving as good as she got in an incendiary kiss that lasted until he finally tore his mouth from hers and unceremoniously tossed her on the bed.

Disheveled and aroused, Lacey's eyes widened when he yanked the zipper of his pants down and reached inside to pull out his throbbing erection. Pushing the clothes down his legs, he stepped out of them and prowled toward where she lay. His big hand stroked his turgid flesh from base to tip where the fat, puffy head of his cock seeped with fluid and twitched in his grip.

"See what you do to me, Ponytail? I've never felt harder or more swollen with desire than I do right now."

*My God, he was enormous*, Lacey thought as her body writhed on the bed at the sight of his naked sex. She wanted to reach out and touch him, but shyness kept her frozen in place. He was magnificent. Helplessly aroused, she stared at his ferocious hard-on. Through pleasure-shrouded, downcast eyes, she watched in complete fascination as he stroked himself in an erotic display that made her whimper.

When he stepped up to the side of the bed and stood before her hungry gaze, he dropped his hand and let her enjoy the sight of his long, thick cock, which was throbbing slightly and twitching under her gaze. She couldn't tear her eyes from his body and didn't for the longest time until she heard a hoarse chuckle rumble from his throat.

"You're going to kill me with those hungry eyes of yours."

Lacey felt a hot blush start at the soles of her feet and move rapidly up her naked body until it bloomed in what she knew would be vivid color on her face. When her tongue swept from the depths of her mouth to leave a trail of moisture along her lips his amused chuckle turned to a low, almost feral growl.

Apparently, that was his breaking point because he fell on her like a starving man before a banquet.

# Chapter Ten

EVERYTHING BLURRED AS Cameron feasted on her flesh. Lacey had never known this kind of pleasure or even suspected that such desire existed. Everything about this situation was new to her, and all she could do was moan, gasp, and writhe uncontrollably on the big bed while his hands and mouth devoured her.

He was dominating her totally. Rough and greedy at times, his touch gentled when he took her sensitized breasts into his big hands. She cried out when his thumbs scraped back and forth across her tingling, beaded nipples and shook from head to toe when he began pressing open-mouth caresses along the heavy, plump bottoms of both mounds until she finally begged him to suck on her.

Cam fell into her demand to take her breasts into his mouth with insatiable abandon. With his heavy erection pressed against her squirming hips, he squeezed and massaged the fleshy orbs until her dusty pink nipples darkened with excitement. At first, he was content to flick his tongue against each beautiful nub, engrossed by the sight, feel, and sounds of Lacey moaning and writhing beneath his touch. She was fucking magnificent in her arousal. He felt waves of fiery satisfaction and sexual power raging through him.

With so many things happening all at once in his body and mind, he was scrambling to catch up. Words like succulent and voracious sounded so loud he wondered if some kind of erotic soundtrack was playing. Nothing like that had ever happened before. Her breasts were so damn delicious that he would happily take his last breath right then and not feel a second's regret.

When he pulled her engorged nipples into his wet mouth and suckled, she quivered and arched against his sex. That was pretty much it for him. While still attached to one of her magnificent breasts, hungrily pulling it deeper and deeper into his mouth, Cam shifted between her legs and roughly pushed her thighs apart. Without a second's hesitation, he reached into her dampened curls and thrust a finger into her hot, wet center as she cried out and gripped his head against her heaving breasts.

Her legs jerked and shook when his finger first entered her. The sounds of his suckling upon her breast filled the air as did her grunts and groans with each stroke of his finger. Her passage felt hot and swollen and was so fucking wet that he growled with animalistic pleasure. She gripped his shoulders and squirmed against his questing finger while she cried out his name over and over. He wanted this moment to go on forever.

Cam knew she was ready, could feel it in the way her body shook and the strength of her inner muscles when they contracted against his marauding touch. He knew she wouldn't be able to last much longer. Her response was pure and unpracticed. He didn't have to wonder if she was faking it. He knew she wanted him, and that undeniable fact filled his frozen soul with pleasure.

Letting her breast pop from his hungry mouth, Cam stilled his finger inside her, making Lacey's eyes fly open, connecting instantly with his. With his gaze locked to hers, he slowly pushed forward and then even slower, pulled back. The leisurely slide inside her wet channel made her gasp and roll her hips. When his thumb sought out and massaged the swollen bundle of nerves at her center, she arched off the bed. Keeping his finger deep inside, she groaned when he twisted it this way and that, while continuing to rub her clit. Watching her became an obsession.

When her hips started bucking wildly, Cam finger fucked her deeply for a few moments before pulling his hand from her wet heat. Waiting till she opened her eyes, he deliberately and with great emphasis brought his finger to his mouth. After licking the evidence of her creamy response away, he crushed his mouth to hers, thrusting his tongue in and out in an approximation of what was yet to come.

Wrenching her lips away from his, Lacey gasped for breath and begged. "Cameron, please. I don't know … please, please," she moaned. "I can't," she cried out as her body writhed in frustration.

Cam watched as his Ponytail started to lose control. Setting back on his haunches with his hungry cock bobbing to and fro, he lifted her ass with both hands bringing her bottom onto his thighs. "Spread your legs." He sounded ragged and desperate.

With her wet, swollen, and completely open to his gaze, Cam ran his fingers seductively along her folds with one hand and grabbed his engorged dick with the other. He was so aroused that he almost embarrassed himself with just the contact from his own hand, but he held it together long enough to roll on a condom and move into position against the entrance to her sex.

"Can I fuck you now, baby? Will you let me in so I can bury my cock inside you?" His voice sounded rough, a lot like he felt. "Are you ready, Lacey? I don't want to hurt you, but I can't hold back anymore. I need to be inside you. Now."

"Oh god, Cameron. Please, please!" she cried as her hips rolled and jerked. With the head of his dick at just the entrance to her body, he got lost in the sensation of it dipping in and out of her opening. With each slight pulse at the entrance, he heard her breathing grow heavier and more erratic. He was trying not to hurt her, but all he could think about was getting the full measure of him deep inside her as quickly as possible.

He pressed forward slowly while his huge hands pushed her knees back toward the bed to give him better access. Finding the perfect angle, he released her legs and commanded her to wrap them around his waist. Doing exactly as she was told, a keening cry of need escaped her mouth. She grasped his buttocks with desperately shaking hands, trying to force him farther inside. When he hesitated, she cried out in frustration, lunging quickly upward, grinding against him as her movements sucked him deeper and deeper and deeper into her wet depths.

"Holy fuck!" Cam cried as her swollen passage stretched to accommodate his size while her body quivered and flooded with the superheated proof of her desire. He felt the barrier of her virginity a split second before he lost control and plunged deep, filling her completely with his throbbing sex. For him, the moment when his hungry dick buried itself in her heat was nothing short of transcendent. She was tight, wet, and nothing he'd ever experienced before in any way resembled the perfection of her body accepting his.

Pulling back slightly, he eased onto his forearms to give her some space, but remained deep inside his beautiful Ponytail's incredible pulsing heat while streaks of regret and fear at having caused her any discomfort arced through him.

"Did I hurt you? Do you want to stop? Talk to me, Lacey." He was literally hanging by a thread. If she asked him to withdraw, he would, but he wasn't sure he would retain his sanity if that was how this ended. "Baby, please." His husky voice pleaded in her ear.

The shock of that powerful thrust and the momentary pain she experienced when her innocence was surrendered to Cameron caused Lacey to hiss out a small, fractured whimper. For a brief second, she almost cried, not from the pain, but from the overwhelming pleasure that intensified with each passing moment.

*Did she want him to stop? Hell, no!* After the stinging pain, all she could feel was a delicious sense of fullness and an erotic pulse of pleasure coming from the place where his groin rubbed against her core. In fact, she never wanted him to stop and hoped that there was more, much more to come.

"No, Cameron, no," she groaned. "Oh god, please don't stop."

Throwing her arms around his neck, she pressed soft kisses along his throat and chin while rubbing her sensitive breasts against the soft hair on his chest. She might not have any idea what the heck she was doing, but Lacey knew enough to realize that when she rolled her hips just so, the pleasure sparking in her core intensified. Her knees, which had gone slack the moment he pressed home, gripped his waist with intent. When she shifted her hips, it felt like his cock sank even deeper inside, bringing a low, primal groan from her throat. "Cameron. Cameron," she cried as her body began rocking insistently against his.

Cam was stunned by her response. Her soft kisses on his neck made him shudder, and when her hips began grinding against his, he brought his mouth to hers in a wet, open-mouth kiss that he hoped could go on forever. She looked amazing underneath him with swollen lips and the bite marks he'd left on her neck and breasts. With flushed cheeks and an erratic telltale pulse beating at her throat, Cam was sure she was the most beautiful woman he'd ever seen. *And he'd made her that way.* A surge of male pride made his dick swell even bigger while the fat head, buried deep, twitched and throbbed.

Coming up briefly for air, he laughed out loud and then growled like an animal in heat when her encouragement to do more, go deeper, and move faster lit up his brain. Pumping slow and deep at first, it didn't take long before he was pulling all the way out of her and slamming home over and over as her inner muscles clutched and released. They moved together in an age-old rhythm that had them groaning in the throes of intense mutual pleasure that didn't know where he ended, and she began.

Lacey was shaking, whimpering, and grinding against him on every downward stroke. She loved the way he dominated her. Spreading his thighs wider, he put his hands beneath her bottom, pulling her into him each time he stroked deep. It went on and on like that until she started to feel an agonizing tightening in her depths. She wanted more but didn't know how to make that happen.

With her inner muscles clenching his hard cock, Cameron slowed the pace, kissing her deeply as his tongue inside her mouth mirrored the actions of his sex. She was coming undone. When he stopped moving completely and held still while buried balls deep, she was aware of his wildly beating heart through the throbbing of his dick enclosed in her womanly flesh.

"Not yet, sweet Ponytail," he whispered. "I haven't had enough of your sexy body." When she moaned in protest, he soothed her by cooing, "Shh. Shh. Just breathe and relax. It will be better this way. When you come, I want to watch your beautiful eyes and hear you cry out. Promise me, Lacey, that you'll let me see your pleasure when it happens. Don't hide anything from me." His words made her shudder from head to toe.

Lacey tried to relax, but the way he swelled bigger inside her was making her arousal peak rather than back off. Her legs started moving of their own accord as if she was trying to climb his back and lodge him deeper inside her aching depths. When she looked through hooded eyes at his beautiful face, she found him gazing down at her as if she was the most beautiful and most precious thing in his world. At that moment, for the first time in her adult life, Lacey felt love for another person. He might not have realized it yet, but he'd let his guard down, and she'd found a place inside him.

Without ever taking his eyes off her, he began rotating his hips, grinding against her while buried deep. She moaned. He ground some more. She moaned and ground right back. When he began slowly thrusting again, she was overcome by the sounds coming from their joined bodies. She was so wet that moisture was running down the crack of her ass, and with each forward stroke, the sloshing sound as he slid home made them shudder.

He buried his mouth in her neck, suckling wildly, as he continued stroking sure and steady. In and out. In and out. "Hear that?" When she moaned, he said, "You're so wet. So fucking wet. *Uh… fuck!*" he groaned as his rhythm picked up. He urged her on, grunting each time her hips rose to meet his. "Yes. Oh god, more! More!" he chanted as their bodies gyrated against each other while her wet clutching heat intensified.

*It was all too much yet not enough,* Lacey thought as she climbed higher and higher on a spiraling trajectory toward an end she couldn't imagine. He kept watch on her as she whimpered and writhed under his huge, powerful body. "C'mon, baby. You can do it. Yes, that's it!" he cried when the last thread of her control unraveled. She was frantically rocking against him with each plunge, clenching her powerful inner muscles around his marauding cock.

Her eyes fluttered closed, making him growl low and fierce. "No. Don't look away. I want to see your eyes when you come. You *are* going to come for me. Just let it happen." On and on it went as he slammed into her again and again.

"Cameron, I can't!" she cried. "Oh, my god. What's happening?" she moaned. She didn't know what to do as the pleasure skyrocketed to a place beyond her comprehension. She felt his hand slide between their joined bodies and move with unerring accuracy to the tight bundle of nerves in her throbbing clitoris.

"Come on, baby," he rasped as his cock filled her completely while his fingers circled her pleasure nub. He groaned loudly when her muscles clenched and fisted around his sex. "That's right. Fuck me, baby."

Moaning as a powerful release shook her, Lacey could only cling as he continued pounding into her. The climax which had begun as a dull throb had intensified, shattering her into rapturous shards of shimmering light.

With his powerful body pounding relentlessly, he lost his way when her body went rigid, and he felt her pussy spasm in ever tightening waves. She cried out his name in a strangled moan as she went up and over in a climax that Cameron felt along every inch of his throbbing cock.

She was magnificent in her ecstasy. The sound of her husky voice crying his name was all he hoped it would be. The flood of superheated moisture drenching his cock when she came was just about the sexiest thing he'd ever felt. A hoarse, triumphant grunt split the air moments later when Cameron felt his climax explode. A lightning bolt of exquisite pleasure that shot from the balls of his feet to the top of his skull, his cock spurted and twitched inside her still churning body.

His thundering orgasm didn't halt their lusty movements. He continued grinding against her as she moaned and shuddered around his cock. He didn't want it to be over, didn't want to leave the sanctuary he'd discovered in her lovely body. Keeping her clasped against him, Cam bit at her lower lip, sucking it into his mouth until she groaned and responded with a flick of her tongue.

Rolling onto his back, he brought her astride his spread thighs with his still firm cock buried deep. She gasped at the swift change in their positions while he nodded, satisfied when he caught the spark of re-ignited arousal in her eyes. Gripping her hips, he showed her how to move on top of him. Showed her how to go after her pleasure and take what she needed. Cam marveled at her glorious breasts as they swayed and shook with each thrust. He watched through heavy-lidded eyes as she rose, and he felt his hungry cock slide from her wet depths. When she slowly sank down, he shut his eyes, growling low and deep.

Lacey was having an out-of-body experience, she was sure of it. As if the shimmering climax he'd given her wasn't enough, when he'd rolled onto his back and she'd experienced his impressive cock nudge even deeper into her wetness, she'd lost herself completely. Moving in sensual slow motion, she swallowed his sex over and over. His eyes were closed, but the strong grip of his fingers on her thrusting hips hadn't lessened at all. Something snapped inside her while she watched him lose himself in the moment. It was mesmerizing.

Not able to control herself a second longer, she slammed against him, whimpering softly at the wet, slapping sounds coming from their bodies. She was climbing fast toward a completion that was squeezing every drop of sensation from her body. Riding him with a strength and finesse that thrilled her, she grabbed at the sheets beneath them while unleashing a blistering assault on his magnificent body with her clutching inner muscles and grinding hips.

His eyes fluttered open as she flew higher and higher. For a moment, he remained motionless under her and then all hell broke loose. With a thundering grunt, he began bucking wildly as her heated response drenched them both. She moaned his name as the world tilted slightly and she fell apart on top of him. That didn't stop him at all as his thrusts intensified.

When he finally came, his hold kept her firmly against him so she felt the pulsing throbs as his cock exploded deep inside. She was undone, sobbing softly against his neck where she'd collapsed. Her body shaking, Lacey clung to him as the aftershocks from what they had done to each other slowly faded.

# Chapter Eleven

WHEN THE DREAM started, Cam lay immobile as the familiar scene unfolded in his mind. Nothing was ever different. It was always the same. Waves of fear followed by anger and then horror played out until at last he struggled awake. Only this time, just as the dream-induced terror took hold, he heard a soft, husky voice call his name.

At first, the sound of his name sounded urgent and desperate until eventually it became a sexy groan that filled up his senses and pushed the dreaded nightmare back into the dark realm of dreams. Relief followed and then awareness. There wasn't any danger. Everyone was safe. Something was different, though. He felt—peaceful. At the sound of that sexy groan calling his name, he'd known a moment of real happiness.

Shifting slightly, the warmth of a body snuggled against him infiltrated his senses. Instantly awake after that, he lay there enjoying the sensation of Lacey sleeping quietly in his arms. Gradually, he recalled in exquisite detail the heart-pounding fucking they had engaged in the previous night. He remembered trying to control her at first while he greedily devoured her innocence. She'd been incredible and surrendered willingly. It didn't take much to recall the sweet taste of her nipples on his tongue or the way her pussy had wept with arousal when he'd touched her intimately. She'd surprised him, though, when he'd shown her how to ride him for her own pleasure. The lady was the most naturally sensual creature he'd ever encountered.

Eventually, Cam's thoughts drifted to the way her voice had vanquished his nightmare. *What the hell was that all about?* Surely, he was putting too much emphasis on the importance of what had gone on between them. It was just sex, after all. Great sex. Okay, maybe it was the best sex he'd ever had, but the last thing he needed or wanted was this warm-all-over fuzzy feeling, especially when he should be feeling guilty about sacrificing her virginity on the altar of his carnal needs. The moment when he'd felt the barrier of her innocence had been incredibly intense, surreal, and to be honest, cool as shit. Knowing he'd been the first and only man to have her trembling with need as he buried his dick in her body had really affected him. He'd known going in that he shouldn't mess with her. He wasn't what she needed. Wasn't whole enough to even dream about anything more with her, or anyone, but nothing could have stopped what happened.

*Fuck. What had he done? And why had just the sound of her voice been what saved him from the agony of a nightmare that had followed him for years?* Even while he continued to lay quietly with her warm body in his arms, he knew that when the day broke, he'd have to set about putting some distance between them. Her life was just starting and his, well, his was not a place for sweet, freckle-faced ponytails. He was damaged goods with a darkness in his soul that had broken him a long time ago. Best he clean up this mess before it went any further and the soft, lovely woman in his arms got emotionally involved. No. That wouldn't do at all.

For her sake, he had to end this now even though he suspected that doing so might kill him. He'd do the right thing. Get her settled in Arizona and make sure she had the chance she deserved to get her life on track. He'd have to accept their one incredible night together was all they'd ever have. She deserved someone as special as she was. End of story.

Besides, examining his feelings was not going to end well. Men like him didn't deserve women like Lacey, and that was all there was to it.

Lacey awoke to the sound of a door slamming and instantly jolted upright in the bed. It took all of two seconds for the events of yesterday and last evening to come crashing into her mind. *Good grief.* She slept with Cameron Justice.

Actually, *sleep* wasn't exactly what they'd done. Had wild, hot, wet sex. Yes, *that was* what they'd done. Glancing down at her naked breasts, she saw tiny red marks and remembered the hungry way he'd devoured her flesh. A slight tingling between her legs and a definite soreness there made her think of his huge sex and how he'd hammered into her over and over. Remembering how later she had ridden his magnificent body until she screamed in climax caused a hot blush to shoot across her face. She'd been totally wanton in her response to him. *Yikes.*

The rumpled linens and imprint of a head on the pillow next to hers let her know they'd shared the same bed through the night. But he was nowhere to be seen right now, and the slamming door that awakened her must have been him. She might not be an old hand at morning-afters, but she knew him well enough to know he was probably having regrets.

Wrapping the sheet around her, Lacey slid from the bed and headed to the bathroom. If they were going to get into it, she wanted to be dressed. He'd been warning her off all along, and she suspected last night had happened because he'd been chasing away demons.

She let him call all the shots at first. Control seemed to be something he needed, and the truth was, she rather liked the faintly submissive way she reacted. It had been exciting to be told she would come, and when. Even now, just remembering, her core twitched in agreement.

The bright lights of the bathroom told an interesting story as she peered in the mirror. Letting the bed sheet fall away, she found a road map across her naked skin of their encounter. Tiny bite marks feathered across her breasts, collarbone, and neck while faint pink shadows here and there from where his stubble rubbed her skin told of a sexy ravishing that she wasn't about to let him run away from. *Not when she wanted to do it again.* Right now.

Life has a funny way of smacking you upside the head at the oddest times. A zillion possibilities that hadn't existed a week ago were now front and center. Her sexy and very hot dark knight had crossed some emotional Rubicon last night and given in to the erotic vibe pulsing between them. A shiver of awareness snaked up her spine. Every moment since they met had been moving them toward what happened. She was meant for him, and there was no denying it although she was certain he would try.

*Men!* Shaking her head at the bemused reflection in the mirror, she set about getting herself together for the day ahead. This was her new life. She'd been visualizing a hopeful change like this for a long time. In just a few days, she had grown up pretty quickly and even managed to get involved in a spectacular way with a very complicated man. Butterflies were doing acrobatics in her belly, but she wasn't going to be a spectator in her own life. Nope. She was going to jump in with both feet, all barrels blazing, no matter how scared she was.

"Bring it on, world!" she told her reflection.

Falling easily into an old pattern, Cam used physical activity to clear his head. The rhythmic sound of his feet thudding against the ground was like meditation. The longer and harder he ran, the more settled he felt. By the time he'd worked up an intense sweat and felt the burn in his thighs, he was much more in control than when he had escaped from the hotel like a thief in the night.

The longer he'd stayed in that bed, and in that room, with memories of the intense sexual interlude he'd shared with the warm, compliant female snuggled in his arms, the harder it was to shift gears. He knew it was arrogance on his part to believe that simply because he was the man, his decisions and actions would be for everyone's good. But that was what his oddly scattered mind was telling him this morning.

Determined not to let this thing with Ponytail get any more out of control, he flipped a switch in his brain and decided, with as much puffed up male sanctimony as he could muster, to keep her at arm's length from here on out. The voice of doubt in his head that wouldn't shut the hell up had taunted him unmercifully as he slipped from the bed and dressed. Pausing to look at her sleeping form before running off in the early dawn light, he knew it was for her own good. At that thought, the doubting voice in his head erupted in laughter.

*Shit.*

Lacey was just zipping up her overnight bag when Cameron let himself into his side of their connected rooms. She heard him toss his sunglasses on the table and yank open the mini-fridge. When he appeared in her doorway seconds later, drinking from a bottle of water, she was ready for him.

"Hey, you. Have a good run?" She surprised herself at how calm and nonchalant she sounded. Even on the worst day of her life, she'd never succumbed to being a stage-four clinger. His look of mild surprise at how matter-of-fact she appeared struck her as hilarious. *Wow.* This man was in for a surprise. She was issuing a challenge of her own by not being all a-flush with romantic fantasies.

His voice hinted at having been set back a notch or two. "Let me jump in the shower and we'll go grab breakfast before getting on the road."

"You go on ahead. I've already eaten. I'm going to run by the front desk for a newspaper. Can I get you anything from the gift shop while I'm down there?"

*Okay. Color me surprised,* Cam thought as Ponytail acted as though nothing important had happened in the bed just beyond his vision. *What the fuck was she doing,* he wondered. Expecting to find her all shy and giggly after having surrendered her innocence to him, he wasn't in any way prepared for the fully dressed and businesslike woman who presented herself.

Peeved that she wasn't moony-eyed and clingy, he was finding it hard to get in sync with this unexpected turn. Instead of letting her know that last night had been a one-off they shouldn't repeat, he was grinding his teeth with frustration that she wasn't all over him like a damn rash.

*Goddammit. Did she think she could quite literally fuck his brains out and then act like it never occurred?*

*What the hell happened to keeping his distance for the good of everyone involved?* His inner voice was falling down laughing.

When she looked at him like he had half a screw loose because he hadn't answered her yet, an actual blush spread across his face. Her manner left him feeling flat-footed and clumsy. Not at all how he envisioned this scenario playing out.

"No. I'm good. I take it you're ready to go? If we get moving soon, we should be outside Sedona later tonight." *How many times had he cleared his throat before any of that made sense? Jesus fucking Christ.* Keeping things light and uncomplicated between them wasn't going to work if he kept behaving like a smitten teenager.

Smiling, she turned toward the bed, straightening the covers. "Ready when you are, boss." Cam's jaw ground even tighter as he watched her yank the bed back into some semblance of order. Knowing what they'd done to create the jumble of sheets wasn't helping his frame of mind.

"Okay then." He slugged back the rest of the bottled water and crushed the flimsy plastic in his hand. "Yep. Okay."

"Okay," she answered sweetly.

*Really? That was it? That was all she had to say?*

He might have run to the bathroom, after that; he wasn't sure. All he knew was she hadn't reacted the way he expected, and he wasn't happy about it. Whatever resolve he'd fashioned to keep her at arm's length evaporated in the face of her response or lack thereof. *Fuck.* That damn inner voice cackled hilariously at his foolish arrogance the entire time he was in the shower.

Lacey enjoyed watching Cameron fumble and trip over her non-response to their lovemaking. *Yes. That was what she was calling it. Lovemaking.* Sure, they'd engaged in some pretty hot, steamy sex, but that didn't mean it hadn't been seething with unspoken feelings. The emotional fallout was only beginning as far as she was concerned.

She'd shocked him by not falling adoringly at his feet. Glad that she had no prior experience to go by, trusting her instincts made it easier to stay as true to her inner compass as possible. She knew without a doubt that if she'd run to him, he'd only take off in the other direction all the faster.

*Didn't take a genius to figure out that her dark, brooding knight wasn't comfortable in the world of emotions.*

He'd been prepared with a guy speech when he came back from his run. She'd seen it written all over his face. Acting like she hadn't just creamed and shuddered on top of him hours earlier was not what he expected. She would have preferred to strip him naked and do it all over again. And again. And then maybe, again. But giving in to those impulses would only freak him out, so she somehow managed to keep her tone light and her smile firm.

He said they'd be in Sedona tonight, and the thought made those butterflies appear again. A lot was coming at her, fast. She couldn't exactly ask for a time-out so she could think things through and come up with a plan. Keeping up with the changes was taking a lot out of her as the highway sped by and they neared their destination.

She'd listened quietly when he'd called and spoken to the head guy, Alex. He was using a Bluetooth device, so she'd only heard Cameron's side of the conversation, but she knew he'd let Alex know he wasn't alone. Silence and the way his jaw clenched after that announcement led her mind on a rambling journey of possibilities as to how his friend and business associate had reacted. Watching him in the shadows of the evening light, her stomach performed a series of impressive cartwheels when a storm of doubt and uncertainty blew through her thoughts.

She wanted these people to like her, even if just a little, and to give her a chance. If there was one thing she was terrifically adept at, it was adjusting quickly to whatever situation she found herself in. Cameron had told her about Betty, the woman who ran the office for the Justice Agency. She'd been the only person in that position, having started in its earliest days. A family matter had called her away, leaving them in a bit of a bind. Three weeks had turned into six weeks, and things got out of control at the office. Since Betty wouldn't be able to return to Arizona for some time, they were forced to find a replacement to fix the mess.

Even without knowing how things ran, Lacey was sure she was up to the task. Looked forward to it, in fact. However, Cameron was another matter altogether. Figuring him out was likely going to be a hundred times more difficult than running an office. Proving herself in both instances was a challenge she would willingly take on.

He'd had precious little to say during the final leg of their drive as the desert southwest dominated the vistas rushing by her window. Biting her lip for the thousandth time, she had to stop from dithering on about the beautiful scenery. Fascinated by the endless colors found throughout the landscape, she'd been dying to share her excitement with him.

Instead, she had played his game, staying calm and quiet as the hours ticked by. She might not know what he was thinking exactly, but she could hear his mind working overtime. She didn't care what had come before; she was only interested in what the here and now was offering. Unfortunately, he was caught up in old beliefs about himself that prevented him from imagining a future.

When they passed Sedona, she knew this would be the last hour they would spend together before the world intruded. *Should she say something about last night?* If she wanted to, this would be her best opportunity. *Or should she remain quiet and wait for his next move?*

Squirming restlessly in her seat, Lacey made quite the show of removing the band from her hair and allowing her ponytail to collapse around her shoulders. Not knowing what to do next, she scratched her nose and cleared her throat, hoping for divine inspiration. When it came, she nearly choked with laughter. Keeping him half a bubble off-plumb was essential if she was going to get inside that complicated head of his.

Cam's thoughts were wandering all over the place. Thank god they were almost home. Without saying a word, she'd been invading his senses with her scent, soft sighs, and small gestures. He wanted to hear her voice so badly that his stomach was in knots with yearning. He'd never known a woman to be so fucking quiet. It was driving him nuts.

She'd caught him off guard this morning, and he'd struggled all day to understand his uncharacteristic reaction. Instead of being the one to put on the brakes, it seemed like she was in the driver's seat. With every passing mile, the silence from her side of the truck cab grated more heavily on his nerves. As a grown man who had plenty of experience with the opposite sex, he was wholly unaccustomed to dealing with a woman who didn't spend every waking minute trying to grab and keep his attention. His silent Ponytail was unnerving the shit out of him with her cool poise and lack of communication.

So much for wanting to keep things chill between them. If she kept this up much longer, he was certain he'd be begging for her attention.

*My, my how the mighty have fallen,* sneered his inner voice. Right now, he'd like to grab his conscience and kick its ass.

"Do you ever smile?"

Glancing her way quickly to make sure she actually spoke and it wasn't his desperate imagination, he mumbled an inelegant, "What?"

"Do you. *Ever.* Smile?" He could feel her blue eyes studying him in the darkness. "C'mon, Cowboy. You know what I mean. Smile, as in laugh. When the corners of your mouth turn up so you don't always look like something bad is about to happen."

He contemplated what she said for a moment and then shrugged. "I guess if I have to stop and think about it, the obvious answer would be no. Not really."

"You're kidding me, right?" Her tone and the snort that accented her words spoke of disbelief. "Cameron, everyone smiles sometime. Even you."

"Maybe there's not a lot to smile about." *Lame answer, dude.*

"Betcha I can get a smile *and* a laugh out of you," she taunted.

"Mmhmm. Many have tried. All have failed."

She laughed outright at that and then fell silent again. *Shit.* He didn't want silence. He wanted to hear more of her sexy voice. Searching like a bumbling idiot for something to say, he didn't expect what she did next.

"Why did the one-handed man cross the road?"

"What?" He seemed to be saying that a lot.

"Why did the one-handed man cross the road?" Her delivery suggested she thought he was dumb as dirt.

"I don't know why."

"Well, to get to the second-hand shop, of course!" she responded playfully.

*Oh, my fucking god.* She was trying to get a rise out of him with a joke. Could she be any more adorable? Was that half a smile working its way onto his face? Why had he thought they needed to keep their distance? Damned if he knew.

"Knock, knock!"

Okay. So she wasn't going to give up. Thank god. "Who's there?"

"Cows go."

*Hmm.* He didn't know this one. "Cows go who?"

"No, cows go moo!" The giggle in her voice wrapped around his heart in the darkened truck. "Wow. Still no smile? What's a girl gotta do to wipe that somber look off your face? Oh, I know," she trilled excitedly, turning her body toward his as he drove them on into the night.

With a charmingly dramatic throat clearing, she cooed the next joke in that sexy, husky voice that turned him inside out. "What do you see when the stewardess bends over?"

He thought about it for a second and then gave in when nothing obvious sprang to life in his mind. "Uh, you got me there. I have *no* idea. What do you see?"

"You, silly!" She chuckled. "Why, the co ... *ooomph*," came her reply when she suddenly clamped her hand over her mouth.

"The what?" he asked.

"Oh, uh, never mind. I forgot the punch line."

"Like hell, Ponytail! You can't leave me hanging like that. C'mon! Tickle my funny bone and tell me the rest."

He watched her shake her head from the corner of his eye. "I can't!" She laughed.

"Why not?" This was getting good. She started it, and he intended to make sure she finished it. Whatever *it* was.

Slapping her hands on her thighs, she turned back to him giggling in what sounded like embarrassment.

"Let me guess," he said. "There's a naughty word involved, right?" He'd noticed her reluctance to swear and found the trait charming. The expression, *swearing like a Marine*, was true for him in so many ways.

When she laughed some more, he lightened at the sound. He really, really liked this woman. "Please."

"Nuh-uh," came her reply.

"Pretty please! With a cherry on top?" *Good Lord. Where the hell did that come from? Was he actually engaging in some foolish banter?*

She sighed theatrically and threw up her hands in surrender. "Oh, okay. For a cherry on top, I suppose I have to."

Yep. A smile was threatening to break out across his face. "So, tell me, Ponytail. What do you see when the stewardess bends over?"

Cupping her hand to her mouth as if she was telling a secret, he heard her blurt out, "The cockpit. You see the cockpit!"

No amount of self-control could help the enormous bark of laughter that rumbled from his chest at her reply. For the first time in forever, Cam threw back his head and laughed like fucking hell. The cockpit! *Holy shit.* Priceless.

She giggled right along with him as they spent the next half hour exchanging horrible jokes and one-liners. He smiled. She beamed. They both laughed.

*Now what was he supposed to do?* With very little effort, she'd pierced the dark veil of brooding that he'd been wrapped in for far too long.

# Chapter Twelve

I T WAS LATE when they finally arrived. Lacey hadn't a clue what to expect, and in no way was she prepared for the reality of where Cameron lived and worked. Far from the nearest town, they turned down a darkened road and drove for a bit before coming upon an ancient-looking arched gate complete with a state-of-the art keypad and an obvious security camera. Punching in a series of numbers, alerting whoever was on the other end of their arrival, they drove on.

In the looming darkness, Lacey made out tall trees, bushy shrubs, and cacti lining their drive. She detected the faint smell of sage and experienced a sensation much like coming home. The feeling rattled her. *Big time.*

Continuing around an outcropping of rocks in a hilly landscape, she saw the first glimmer of lights indicating the presence of buildings. Her small gasp of surprise when they drew closer to the main house hung suspended in the air when she caught her first view of the old Spanish villa that served as the home base for the Justice Agency.

Words could never adequately describe that initial sight of the rambling, multi-storied hacienda with its massive cobbled courtyard nestled among cypress, piñon, and juniper trees. It was huge, sprawling, and even in the darkness, absolutely beautiful. She was surprised when they continued to drive a short distance away from the courtyard to a series of spread out buildings.

This wasn't at all what she expected. *Had she imagined a sterile office building or a warehouse full of high-tech security toys?* She couldn't remember now that she was presented with reality. Under the twinkling lights of the big house, the heavy Spanish influence of the architecture and the undeniably romantic setting awed her.

*Wow.*

Before too long, they stopped beside a charming, single-story casita with a red tile roof and a large front window. Spanish-style lantern lamps glowed in welcome next to an arched front door under a sturdy pergola. If this was Cameron's home, the unexpected simple beauty of it enchanted her.

"Welcome home, Ponytail. This is Casita de Corazon which, if you know any Spanish, means Home of the Heart. It's a guesthouse that Alex keeps for his sisters and mother when they come to visit. He's invited you to stay here while you're working for the agency."

*He was kidding, right?* Lacey couldn't quite wrap her mind around what he was saying. *This quaint little house was where she'd be staying?* No. This couldn't be for her. She'd been so grateful for the chance to start fresh that she'd have willingly set up a tent in Cameron's backyard. Learning she was moving into the small guesthouse was so much more than anything she ever dreamed of.

Cameron was out of the truck and yanking open her door before she recovered her composure. Turning eyes filled with questions to her traveling companion, she could only blink in speechless silence at the hand he held out to help her from the truck.

"Cameron, n-no," she stuttered. "This is too much. Isn't there a room someplace or maybe …" She didn't get out another word as he reached into the truck and lifted her out.

"No, Ponytail. There is no maybe. You'll stay here, and that's all there is to it. My home is a little farther along the main road. Alex lives in the main house, and Drae, if he's even here, has a place another quarter mile behind mine. I know it's hard to see in the darkness, but there are a dozen or so buildings in the main compound and another bunch spread out around the property. Tomorrow, I'll introduce you to everyone. Several people live here full time, and a world-class security system connects all the buildings. You'll be well-protected here, Lacey."

He must have sensed her reticence and confusion because he just kept shuffling her along the path from the truck to the door of the casita before she could resist. Just like at the front gate, he punched in a security code on the entry keypad and pushed open the heavy wooden door. Just like that, Lacey's world tilted on its axis again.

Small but unique, the inside of the modest casita had Moorish arches, tiled floors, and low wood beams across the ceiling. A stone fireplace took up one side of the quaint living room, and through another beautiful archway, she spied a modern, tiled kitchen. The overall effect of the tiny home was undeniably welcoming and warm.

Leaving her to look around, Cameron returned to the truck to grab her meager belongings. When he reappeared and walked through to the bedroom at the rear of the house, she followed in his footsteps. Tossing her bags on the high, queen-size bed, he looked around and motioned with his head toward the en suite.

"Bedroom, check. Bathroom, check. Kitchen, check. Everything is right here. It's small but cozy and just a short walk from the office."

"I don't know what to say. It's really too much." Lacey was struggling for composure. She wanted so badly to walk into his arms and let his embrace soothe her frazzled nerves. She didn't, though, because even overwhelmed as she was, she hadn't missed that Cameron seemed equally so. For some reason, he was avoiding looking directly at her and had started nervously prowling the room, making sure all the lights worked properly. Flicking on the ceiling fan, he made quite the project of setting it on low.

"Th-thank you. It's perfect." Running her hands across a magnificent wooden armoire she tried to quell the upwelling of emotions clogging her throat. "I don't know what to say, Cameron. You might have to pinch me so I know all of this is real."

Just like that, he wasn't avoiding her eyes any longer. In two long strides, he reached out, pulling her into his arms. "I can think of better things to let you know this is real than a pinch," and with those few words, his sexy mouth swooped down on hers. Unlike the fevered kisses they'd shared previously, this one was tender, almost reverent.

He used his tongue to trace her full bottom lip before sucking on the flesh in a way that elicited a quiet moan from her. When her tongue shyly swiped across his, it was Cameron's turn to moan. About the last thing she expected after the day's tortured silence and the way he'd pulled away following their wild night together was for him to kiss her like she meant something to him. *Maybe his guard was coming down.* She wished it would. There was something so special about the way they were with each other.

Unfortunately, the kiss ended before her thoughts went much further. "If you need me, dial nineteen on the phone system, and you'll be connected to my private line. I can be here in minutes if … well … if you need me."

*God, he was something else.* He wanted to stay, but she was certain he wouldn't. He wasn't ready yet and she knew he needed time to work out some of his issues on his own. She had to let him run this time, but she was damn sure going to make certain he ran with a solid case of wood in his jeans. Reaching up, she ran her fingers along the side of his beautiful, brooding face and across the sexy lips she wanted to devour. His eyes flared at her touch.

"Last night was … well, it was amazing. I'll let you leave this time. But if *you* need *me*, I'll be here." The emphasis she placed on those two words was meant to give him something to think about as he walked away.

He nodded just once at her words and then quietly left the room. She walked silently behind him to the front door where he turned around and fixed her with a searing look that left her breathless. One glance down the front of his jeans, and her mind shouted, *mission accomplished!*

"I'll come by in the morning and take you up to the big house."

As the door clicked shut and she heard his truck starting up, Lacey turned back to the interior of the charming house and crossed her fingers.

Letting himself in to the enormous Spanish villa that dominated the property, Cam headed quietly to the back of the main floor where he knew Alex would be holed up. While other guys fashioned man-caves, Alexander Valleja-Marquez, Don of all he surveyed, went the high-tech route with something a bit more cybergeeky.

The property that housed the Justice Agency assets was the hereditary home of the Valleja-Marquez family. The glorious hacienda-style villa at the heart of it all was a masterpiece of Spanish architecture. Alex had inherited the house and nearly six hundred acres of land years ago. He, of course, lived in the main house while Cam and Drae built separate homes set apart from the central compound.

At the entrance to Alex's tech cave, Cam leaned indolently against the doorjamb and studied the scene before him. As usual, the dark room hummed and throbbed with blinking lights and flashing screens. Classic rock turned low on the sound system hung in the air while at the center of it all sat the man himself.

Major Alex Marquez hunched over a piece of machinery that appeared to be emitting a hologram. *Typical.* Dude always ran light-years ahead from where most of the cybergeeks were stuck. Seeing him dressed in a ridiculous pink golf shirt and an ugly pair of patterned pants, Cam smirked, knowing he'd come here straight from the golf course. When Alex had something on his mind, he was like a dog with a bone. Distract him and he'd snarl. Fuck with him in any way when he was on to something and get your head neatly ripped off, shredded to bits, and then handed back to you on a silver tray.

Cam also knew that even though he hadn't announced his

presence in any way, the Major was well-aware he was standing in the darkness. The guy had unreal spider senses, something he and Drae taunted him about unmercifully. That those senses helped propel their exclusive services to a realm where money was no longer an issue was a fact Cam never overlooked. The man was nothing short of a genius.

"Are you going to lurk there all night?" Turning toward Cam with unerring accuracy, Alex raised one eyebrow in a look that said, *Gotcha!*

Levering away from the door, Cam strode into the room toward his friend for a hearty hug and a bit of backslapping. He'd noticed that Alex was favoring his bad leg, a sign of strain and discomfort. Going to him so he didn't have to get up was an old habit, one that developed during Major's long rehab and the years that followed. They rarely spoke of his injury anymore. Didn't have to. All their lives had changed that awful day. The day that still haunted his dreams.

Alex had been lucky to survive, and although he was one of the three left with visible scars, they'd all been pretty thoroughly fucked up in one way or another. Coming together as the Justice Brothers, a nod to their past, had started the real healing. This compound, tucked away in the Sonoran Desert, had morphed over time into a small town that Alex oversaw with all the tight corners and command his rank as Major demanded. He was also something of a father figure, in addition to being a brother, if only in name.

"Hi, Alex. You look like bloody hell, by the way."

Rubbing his sturdy hands through his mess of a haircut, Alex sneered at Cam although the twinkle in his eyes was genuine. "Blow me."

Slapping Alex on the back one more time, Cam moved aside and swung his hand out at the mess where they stood. "Jesus. What the hell happened in here? Looks like a hurricane blew through, dude."

"Yeah, it did. Nice try ignoring the elephant in the room. I'm damn glad you're home, and that you made it one piece. Okay. That was the polite shit. Now tell me what is *really* going on. You brought someone back with you. A woman? Explain."

*Damn.* Cam didn't want to get into this conversation. Not right now, anyway. *How could he explain something that he didn't understand himself?* Wandering around a workbench strewn with god-only-knows-what, while trying to act all cool and matter-of-fact was a lame stall. When he'd informed Alex during their phone call that he wasn't alone, his announcement was initially met with deafening silence. Shocking Alex was something hard to do, so it was just best to just plow ahead. Make like it's no big deal. Yeah, that's what he'd do.

"Uh, so ... let me see. Yeah. Her name is Lacey."

*Goddammit.* He sounded like a bad kid reporting to Dad. Picking up some random device as he gathered his wits, he turned it over in his hand like it was actually of interest. *Get your shit together, man.*

"She, uh, she ... well, the fact is I sorta rescued her."

*Oh, fuck, had he actually said that?*

"Wait a minute! You *rescued* someone?"

The incredulity in his friend's voice shamed Cam. *When did acting like a decent person seem like such a stretch for him?*

"Watch it, man. I might be a prick, but that doesn't mean I'd stand by and let someone get hurt right in front of me."

The eyebrow rose again. "Uh-huh. Go on. I'm listening."

Resting against the workbench, Cam's arms folded against his chest. In a gesture similar to the one he'd seen Alex make just minutes ago, one hand crept up while fingers speared through his long hair before grabbing the nape of his neck. Alex seemed content to wait him out. He'd even lowered onto the massive desk chair that made him look like James T. Kirk in the captain's seat. Nothing like saying something without actually saying anything.

He almost blurted out the part about how he'd been watching her before pulling the words back. *No.* Right now, some things were best left unsaid. Stick to the facts. Just the facts. Alex wasn't stupid. He'd know there was more.

"Bunch of teenage thugs tried to snatch her bag. She fought back. Probably made it worse. Must have been the last thing those shitheads expected. I came upon what was happening as it spiraled out of control."

"Okay. Understood. Continue."

*Jesus.* This was starting to feel like a debriefing. "Anyway. Getting mugged was kinda the last straw. She was going through a tough time, you see."

The arched eyebrow on Alex's face shot into his hairline.

Unfolding his arms, Cam stood with his hands on hips. "I knew Betty bailing on us for the foreseeable future was creating chaos, so I offered her a hand, that's all. She can get the office under control and settle here. Win, win." Shrugging like all of it was absolutely no big deal, he hoped that would be enough to satisfy curious minds.

Alex being Alex, though, cut right through his bullshit. "How old is this *woman*?" The unspoken question in his delivery reverberated off the walls.

The word *twenty-two* got stuck in his throat and went no further.

When Cam didn't answer, Alex snorted. "For fuck's sake, Cam. This isn't like you. Lacey is her name?" Cam nodded, then looked away.

"What does this Lacey mean to you, bro? There's like a shit ton of detail you're not sharing, and last time I checked, getting to the bottom of things is what we all do for a living, so how about you tell me what's really going on."

Cam couldn't answer. The problem was, he didn't know what she meant to him. It was all coming at him too fast. He heard the surprise and concern in Alex's voice, but all he could think about was how he wanted to go back to the casita and take Ponytail to bed. He'd pretty much thought of nothing else since he'd crawled from her embrace this morning.

Being back at the compound only reminded him that he was not what would be considered 'relationship material.' His life was vaguely dangerous at times, he kept to himself as much as he could, and he had enough darkness in his past to qualify for disaster relief. None of that sounded like a guy who should be messing with a twenty-something all-American beauty with her whole life ahead of her.

Even so, he couldn't stop his thoughts from picking up the thread of their intense sexual encounter. She'd been so willing, so receptive. He knew if he marched into her room right now, he could have her panties in his pocket in moments. Could have her under him while he pounded into the wet, tight warmth of her body.

*How did he get to be such a mess?*

Alex watched his friend intently. No one knew the man known as Cameron Justice like he and Draegyn did. They'd been through hell and back, the three of them. There were no secrets between them.

They were complicated men. *Who the hell wasn't these days?*

Drae had trust issues and he—well, Alex—was their conscience. Every dark and deadly event from their shared time on the battlefield was his to atone for, being the leader of the group, and not just because he'd outranked them in the end. There was a reason the Justice Squad had been successful. He'd been a master tactician. Focused on their mission. Ruthless. Responsible for countless lives—some of which were lost on his watch.

He knew that the conflicted man before him wore the burden of some of those deeds like a hair shirt of penance. Cam's castaway up-bringing gave him a sense of not quite being good enough. Add that to some real-world blood, guts, and gore, and it was easy to see the recipe for dysfunction it all was. Cam truly believed he was an island unto himself where no emotion meant no regret.

Alex said nothing. He simply waited. When Cam was ready to talk, he'd be there to listen. It was curious, though. Him bringing any-one, let alone a woman, into the compound. He couldn't wait to get a look at the mysterious Lacey. *What would she be like,* he wondered. *What sort of female had it taken to stop Cam dead in his tracks?*

"Is Drae here?" Cam eventually muttered in a tone that piqued

Alex's curiosity.

"Why?"

"No reason. Just wanted to set him straight about a few things."

"Well, isn't that fucking great?" Alex grunted. "First, Betty runs off, then Mister Roboto joins the dark side, and now sibling rivalry. It's awesome being me!" Cam's look of surprise at the mention of Alex's right-hand assistant, Liang, was a reminder of the mess the business was in.

"Liang's playing with the big boys now? Shit Alex. Is that why the place is such a mess? How long's he been gone?"

"Don't try to switch subjects. Yes, Liang is off to more lucrative pastures. A black ops team offered him the sun, moon, and stars. End of story. Now let's get back to the grumbling about Drae. C'mon, bro. What's going on in that head of yours?"

Cam pulled himself upright until all six-foot-four inches of his bulk seemed to be straining at the seams. This was getting interesting.

"Look, there's nothing going on. Yeah, I brought a woman back with me, but she's just a ... *friend*. Drae needs to keep his dick in his pants where she's concerned. That's all. You know how he is."

Alex considered everything Cam just said along with his body language. Yeah, right—there's nothing going on. Unless he was totally blind, something pretty damn big was happening right in front of his eyes.

Nodding, Alex could only grimace at the mention of Draegyn's track record with the fairer sex. The man had personally bedded nearly every available female on the planet.

"Understood, man. Understood. He's off doing the security for a concert tour. Y'know, that little putz with the saggy pants and screaming teenage fans? There's a break coming up before the European leg starts. He'll turn up soon, I suspect."

"All right, man. Thanks for the heads up."

"Cam, I'm here if you need to talk."

His friend's hesitant nod was all the conversation he was going to get. Sometimes, Mr. Tall, Dark, and Brooding was a pain in the ass. This was one of those times. A series of beeps and clicks from an array of computers happened at the perfect moment, giving Alex the opportunity to switch gears.

Turning to see what was up, he murmured over his shoulder, "Bring Lacey 'round in the morning. At least Carmen and Ria are still on the job. I'll tell them we have a guest in the casita and to set an extra place at the table."

Cam shuffled to the door and then stopped, earning the return of Alex's complete attention. He couldn't wait to see what the man said next.

"Uh, Alex?"

"Yeah?"

"Do I smile?"

Alex's slack-jawed, blinking response made Cam scowl.

"That's what I thought," was all he said before turning to make his way from the room.

# Chapter Thirteen

S OMETHING ABOUT THE desert at sunrise, when a million colors and hues lit up the harsh but beautiful landscape, made Lacey feel, well ... happy. Peaceful. She'd pulled on a pair of jeans and a thin t-shirt before stepping onto the brick patio under the kitchen widows to survey her temporary home. The casita was perfect in every way. Small, homey, and comfortable, just as Cameron had said.

Luckily, she'd found a tin of organic tea in the cupboard that was quickly turned into a hot, steaming beverage. She loved tea at sunrise. Never having learned to appreciate the black sludge some people drank first thing in the morning, she preferred the soft, subtle flavors of a good tea blend. She always had a stash of Dollar Store brand teas in her old backpack.

This morning, she filled her mug with a red, tinged fusion of black tea and rooibos that had mercifully not needed a splash of cream or a spoonful of sweetener. There really wasn't anything in the cupboard except some spices and a few other nonperishable staples. She'd have to stock some supplies, a simple task that filled her with excitement. The idea of making a shopping list made her giddy and lighthearted.

She wondered what Cameron was doing. Half-expecting him to

turn up at some point last night, she had finally given up waiting and gone to bed. No one was more surprised than she was when, hours later, she awoke to find the sunrise creeping onto the horizon. *When was the last time she'd crashed so completely that she slept through the night?*

*Oh yeah*, she remembered. That would be the night before last when she'd passed out cold in Cameron's comforting embrace.

Stretching, Lacey reached overhead with both hands and let left-over nighttime kinks work out. Bending slowly forward and relaxing her spine, she let her chest fall toward her legs. With both hands planted firmly on the ground, she felt the stretch of her thigh muscles two seconds before she noticed a tiny green lizard darting between the scraggly shrubs that lined the patio. She certainly wasn't on the East Coast anymore.

Remembering that Cameron had said he'd come by and get her in the morning, she wondered when he'd make his presence known. He was an early riser, so she had better get her butt in gear if she wanted to be ready to step into this strange, unexpected opportunity that had come her way.

Hating to leave the beauty of the morning's unveiling, she drank in the spectacular scenery for a few more seconds before turning to go back inside. A shower was definitely in order. There was nothing like greeting a new day with clean hair and fresh clothes.

*Okay, maybe what she really meant was she wanted to greet Cameron fresh from the shower.* Damn the hair and clothes.

Hot water pounded his back where he stood, hand braced against the muted colors of the travertine tile in his shower, head bowed, while long minutes ticked by. From that vantage point, with his eyes cast downward, Cam could only grimace at the sight of an erection that simply didn't want to cut him a break. The shower had begun in freezing fashion but even that hadn't helped. Eventually giving up, he'd turned the temperature steamy while his dick mocked him by jutting out straight from his body under the pouring water.

He'd dreamed about her all through the night. Hot, insistent dreams that cranked his awareness level to high and stiffened his manhood. *Fucking, eh.* Any hope that a new day would bring the return of reason to his mind was shot all to hell. *Reason? What was that?* All he knew was his cock was throbbing like a son of a bitch.

Sighing, his free hand reluctantly lowered until he had his rock-hard dick in a firm grip. The last thing he wanted to do right then was jerk-off but taking himself in hand was clearly going to be the only way to dispense the raging case of wood he'd awoken to. Talk about a Louisville slugger.

In the end, he'd been so turned on that it hadn't taken but a few quick tugs to have him shaking like a leaf. Visions of his Ponytail with her gorgeous legs wrapped around his waist while her feet dug into his ass as she bucked and shook under him was all it took to send him straight into an orgasm that seemed so out of place in the solitary shower. His shoulders heaving, Cam squeezed his staff low around the base and then quickly stroked it with a tight fist. When the explosion came, his growls of completion echoed in the tile enclosure.

*Fuck. Fuck. Fuck.* Orgasm accomplished and he still felt like hell. Coming by himself and by his own hand was a far cry from his true desire. He couldn't ever remember feeling like this. Handling the crude demands of his sex, when what he really wanted was to lose all awareness inside a soft body, was not improving his mood. He wondered if she would take him into her mouth, and just like that, his cock woke up yet again. Slamming his palm against the tile wall, he let loose a series of vulgar oaths that pretty well summed up how fucked he was.

*Screw the shower.* Apparently, he was doomed to have a perpetual hard-on that wasn't going to back off. The way he felt, he could stand there the whole damn day, stroking himself, and it wasn't going to bring any real relief. He needed to see Ponytail. Wanted to hear her voice.

Toweling off with a brutal intensity, Cam tried to bring his emotions into check. His conversation last evening with Alex had been a disaster, as had the struggle to leave her be. He couldn't even count the number of times he'd considered going to her. Time to get his head on straight before he lost control. As if jerking off in the shower like a horny teenager wasn't a damn good sign of how little control he actually had.

Sighing, Cam went about his morning business. He had some damage control to do with Alex and a new life to introduce to Lacey. It was going to be an interesting day.

She felt her breath quicken and heart race as the low growl of a truck signaled its approach.

*He was here!*

Checking her reflection in the mirror and nodding at the plain scoop-neck tee and newer jeans she'd picked to wear, Lacey liked what she saw. Confidence restored, she drew a deep breath to steady her nerves and pulled open the arched door just as her dark knight strode up the cobbled walkway, clutching a large box.

Trying for lighthearted, she chimed, "Hola, Cameron! It's a beautiful morning, isn't it?" as she held open the door for his arrival. She seriously hoped some of the self-assured poise she was hoping to project was hitting its mark. Eyeing the carton in his arms, she quirked an eyebrow at him, laughing. "What's in the box? I hope it's nothing slimy. So far I've made friends with a lizard and something I think was a jack rabbit, but I'm definitely not ready for anything that slithers just yet."

After getting him to laugh at her silly jokes during the long ride in his truck, she hoped that his smile might make a brief appearance at her jovial attitude. Judging by the hooded gaze he kept to himself, she was, as they say, shit out of luck. There was no way she would give up that easily, though. It was going to take a whole lot more than his brooding nonsense to deter her.

He was achingly gorgeous, sexy, and very, very yummy to look at first thing in the morning. True to his habit of dressing mostly in black, today he wore what at one time passed for a concert t-shirt and faded dark jeans. A pair of broken-in cowboy boots completed his attire. Taking a cue from the t-shirt he wore, she kept up a nonstop stream of verbal drivel, hoping to get some sort of a reaction from him.

"You don't strike me as a Foo Fighters kind of a guy. I figured you were more the Keith Urban type," she joshed good-naturedly. "I must say, Cameron, that your t-shirt has seen better days. Looks like it is going to end up in a bucket full of truck-cleaning suds any minute."

*Holy cow.* Was that the faint glimmer of laughter shimmering in his eyes? If she wasn't mistaken, he was clinging pretty hard to that somber thing he had going on while fighting to keep a smile from cracking his usual reserve. *Good. She was making headway.*

The truth was, she'd thought of nothing but him since letting him take her to bed. He might be running, but she was in close pursuit. Mr. Cameron Justice was mistaken if he thought for one minute she wasn't going to do everything in her power to knock some sense into his thick skull. He couldn't scare her away with a few dark looks and some ridiculous narrative about being broken and without real emotion. Even if he wasn't quite there yet, she knew better.

"Do you always start rattling off the minute your eyes open, woman?"

*Nice try, cowboy*, she thought. *Game on!* "No, of course not! Must be your sparkling wit and clever repartee that sets me off. You need to learn to be quiet more, Cameron. Sheesh! Give it a rest, why don't you?"

Sashaying ahead of him into the kitchen, she left Cam staring at her crazy, sexy ass in the snug jeans while she continued to needle him with her sassy mouth. No wonder he couldn't get his rampaging dick under control. All she had to do was smile like that and tease him with her sexy voice and he was struggling to catch up.

Following close on her heels, he picked up on the subtle scent of her shampoo and marveled at how something so simple could strike such a blow to his senses. Dropping the carton of provisions brought from his own kitchen, he reached into the box and pulled out a huge travel mug that he thrust at her. "Tea. Hot and sweet. The way you like it."

Her gasp of delight, when she whirled around to accept the mug, cracked a tiny hole in his reserve. "Okay. I'm letting you off the hook because of this," she said while waving the steaming container at him. "Thank you."

He expected the thanks. The swift, soft kiss she placed on his cheek took him by surprise. It was all he could do not to turn and capture her lips in a searing kiss that would tell her all the things he couldn't.

"Seriously. What's in the box?"

*The box. Oh, yeah, right. The box.* He pulled out a bunch of ripe bananas, a loaf of store-bought bread, and some packets of sugar and dropped them on the counter. A couple of cans of soup followed as did a container of eggs, a carton of milk, and boxes of cereal. He pretty much grabbed whatever he had in his kitchen until the box had been crammed full of all sorts of stuff she'd need.

Lacey watched him while taking small sips of the tea he'd brewed specifically for her. It had come as a surprise that he even had tea bags, but once he found them, he quickly set about making the hot drink. Noticing the small scrap of paper on the counter with a modest shopping list, he told her, "There's a lot of ground for us to cover this morning, but we can head into town later to do a grocery run."

"It was hard to see much in the darkness last night, but I gather this place is enormous. How many people work and live here?" she asked.

Opening the refrigerator, he stowed away the eggs and milk, and he paused at her question to consider his answer. Leaning his hips against the counter, he did a quick mental count. "Besides Draegyn, Alex, and myself, several others live here on the compound. Carmen 's quarters are in the Villa, but Alex's cook, Ria, lives behind the barn with her husband, Ben, the property manager. He looks after things. One of his projects is a sustainable garden, a greenhouse, and a bunch of other things that get put to good use when there are clients or consultants staying." He shared her surprise because the incredible amount of vegetables and fruits Ben harvested throughout the year was staggering. The man had a serious green thumb.

"There are others, mostly seasonal people, like the guy who trains our security dogs. You'll meet Gus, too. He's in charge of everything from the horses to the ATVs to the motorbikes. That's who to see if you need a vehicle of any sort. We have clients and security personnel who get training and brush up on their skills throughout the year. Those folks are in a residence a ways from the main house."

"Wow. I had no idea. Did Betty have an office, then?"

"Yep. The office is here in the main part of the compound. I'm afraid it's something of a mess at the moment. You have your work cut out for you, Ponytail."

"I won't let you down, Cameron," she whispered. For a brief second, he saw something that looked like anxiety flash in her eyes.

*Why did he have this need to reassure her?* He probably should be examining his motives and responses, but that sort of straight thinking seemed to be in short supply of late. Instead, he reached out and tucked a wayward strand of blond hair that escaped her ponytail behind her ear. Touching her had been a mistake because he couldn't stop from tracing the shell of her ear with his fingertips. The shiver that shook her at his touch almost brought him to his damn knees. He cleared his throat and stepped away, desperately trying to rein in the desire to lift her up onto the nearby wooden table and step between her thighs, so he could do a whole lot more than caress an earlobe.

"Uh ... so. You ready to meet the lord and master of this crazy place? Alex will be waiting for us. He's, um ... well, he's curious to meet you."

"I bet." She snorted in amusement. "I'm thinking you don't bring many girls to the old homestead, huh? Well, don't worry. I'll be on my best behavior." She laughed while elbowing him playfully in the ribs. "Oh, and I promise not to tell anyone that you really do know how to smile. That'll be our little secret, hmm?"

He tried not to, but it couldn't be helped. It took a few seconds, being as out of practice as he was, but eventually a half-smile twitched on his lips. "What have I gotten myself into?" He groaned in mock dismay. "C'mon, Ponytail"—he chuckled while smacking her firmly on the ass—"let's get moving before I teach that sassy mouth of yours a better way to drive me crazy."

Her smoky laugh rang in his ears as they left the casita and climbed into his truck for the three-minute drive to the main house. He seriously hoped Alex was ready for the surprise he was about to get. There was no way his ripe imagination had conjured up a picture of Lacey that would even come close to reality.

It took all of Lacey's strength to keep things light and easy with the man at her side. She hadn't missed the telltale bulge in his jeans and had done everything in her power to keep from staring at his groin like a hungry predator. *Did he know how desirable he was?* Probably not. Men seemed to think that desire was a one-way street inhabited only by them. He'd no doubt be shocked by how naughty her thoughts were where he was concerned. At one point, she even put her hand on the kitchen table to test how strong it was while her imagination went crazy with erotic fantasies of lying back on said table, naked and begging for his possession.

*Good grief.* Two days ago, she'd been a complete innocent, but after a couple of hot kisses and one night of total surrender, she was practically overcome with arousal whenever he appeared. Pressing her thighs together in the tight jeans, she tried to quell the slow burn starting between her legs. *Mental note to self: get more undies.* She was sure to destroy the few pairs she had with the way his dark good looks made her panties damp with each encounter. Even an innocent conversation turned her into a wet mess.

She was relieved that he didn't seem as driven to push her away this morning. If anything, a pulse of protectiveness coursed that he wasn't trying all that hard to hide. Maybe the walls around his heart were breaking down. She could only hope that was the case. They were good together, in more ways than one. She'd even gotten an unexpected grin by teasing him about the smile thing.

In the daylight, the magnificence of the Spanish influence on the rambling villa was nothing short of breathtaking. Pulling into a large, courtyard driveway, Cameron pulled the truck to a slow stop near a stone walkway that led to the home's massive front door. The subtle scent of desert sage and the flowering yucca trees filled the air. From her seat in the front of the truck, Lacey tried to take it all in. Nothing about the place had been what she expected at all.

Sensing his eyes upon her, she turned toward his gaze, smiling softly. "It's so beautiful, Cameron. Thank you again and again for bringing me here."

He didn't say anything; he just sat still and watched her. When he exited the truck and came around to her side to help her jump down, she put her hands upon his shoulders when he offered his assistance. As her feet hit the pavement, she moved her hands from those impossibly broad shoulders to the back of his neck and leaned in for a swift kiss.

When she stepped back to look him straight in the eye and said "Showtime!" he looked shocked. And pleased.

*Showtime, indeed.*

# Chapter Fourteen

T HEY'D BARELY STEPPED through the wide, heavy front door when he heard a shouted greeting in lightly accented English. "Welcome home, Meeester Cameron!"

"Hola, Carmen," he replied, his voice heavy with tenderness. "¿Cómo estás?"

Alex's trusted housekeeper glided down a set of massive wooden stairs from a long, second-floor balcony that looked down into the huge foyer. Carmen Delgado was one of those ageless women who could have been anyone's favorite grandmother. With dark hair mixed with gray and a wide mouth set with a hearty smile, she ruled Alex's roost with great aplomb.

"You've been missed, you scoundrel!" She laughed as Cam drew her into a warm bear hug.

"Ah, scoundrel, huh? Your English has gotten too good, señora! Next, you'll be telling me how good looking I am," he teased.

"Big chance!" She snorted while beaming her obvious fondness at him.

"Uh, it's fat chance, and one can hope."

"Oh. Did you hear about Liang? Meeester Alex, he was …

*peeessed?* Is that right?"

"Pissed covers it quite nicely, I think, and yes, I heard. The bat cave looks like someone was more than pissed, if you ask me."

Carmen laughed. "Bat cave! Good one, amigo! I must use that word with Javi. My grandson, he loves the superheroes, that boy."

For a moment, Cam recalled another young boy who was into all things Batman. A shadow gathered in his mind that he just barely managed to dismiss, but the reminder was there nonetheless. *Great.* Without warning, he felt a trickle of sweat roll down his back.

"Hola, Miss Lacey. *Meeester* Alex told me you are staying in Casita de Corazon. My name is Carmen. Whatever you need to make your stay comfortable, please don't hesitate to ask."

Cam watched the two women greet each other. Carmen, of course, was welcoming and direct while Lacey offered a shy greeting that made the older woman grab her in a firm hug.

"Welcome, welcome! It's good to have another woman around this old house now that Betty has been away. These men"—she gestured with her head in a conspiratorial fashion—"they need us to keep them in line!"

When Ponytail laughed, he knew a bond of friendship had been formed between the two.

"All right, all right. Enough of that! The only person needing to be kept in line is you, old woman. Why, you're lucky we don't hire some fancy New York butler instead of putting up with your antics." Without realizing at first what he was doing, Cam finished the teasing with a simple smile.

Carmen looked back and forth between he and Lacey, and a devilish grin spread across her face. Apparently, she also noted the unusual appearance of a smile on his face. *What the hell was happening to him?* The sparkle in Lacey's eyes told him she approved. He rather liked that blue sparkle. It lit up her face in the most charming way. Maybe he could try smiling some more if that was the reaction he could expect.

"Off with you two, now. *Meeester* Grumpy is prowling out in the back. Good luck. He's already made Benito's life a living hell this morning over something silly. Whatever you do, don't ask about that ridiculous fishpond they're planning. Apparently, fish don't like living in a desert. Nice meeting you, Lacey. We'll see each other again at lunch." She nodded in their direction and strode away.

"Fish pond?"

"Yeah. Don't ask. Sometimes, Alex gets these ideas. It's hard to explain. Takes his mind off … other things." He didn't elaborate that the other things generally referred to the flare-ups of pain and mobility problems brought on by his old injuries.

Taking Lacey by the hand, another new experience he rather enjoyed, Cam pulled her along in search of Alex. They found him, prowling, just as Carmen had suggested. Cam saw the slight limp and tried not to let concern show on his face. Alex would have none of that and wouldn't appreciate any mention of his physical infirmities.

He was on the rear patio, pacing back and forth beneath one of the two wide cabanas that flanked the enormous pool. As always, his big black Labrador Zeus was by his feet. He felt Lacey's brief hesitation as she took in what he knew looked like a luxury resort. The pool area had been completely renovated several years ago to Alex's precise specifications. Water therapy had been key to his rehabilitation, and he continued to swim regularly as a way to keep the discomfort in check.

"G'morning, Alex," Cam barked as he dragged Lacey into the lion's den.

Alex's head snapped up at their approach, and even behind the dark sunglasses he was wearing, Cam knew his friend was sizing up the woman at his side. Instead of dropping her hand, he held firm, sending a clear signal he hoped Alex heard. Squeezing her fingers for encouragement, he pulled her in front of him for an introduction.

"Lacey, allow me to introduce Alexander Valleja-Marquez. Don't let the scowl scare you off. He just does that for effect." Spearing Alex with a *fuck you* glare, he finished. "Alex." The warning in his voice was unmistakable. "This is Lacey Morrow. Be nice, bro. She's not used to figuring out which hat you're wearing." He provided an explanation when Lacey glance at him turned to confusion.

"Some days, he's the Major. Other days, the Don of a Spanish Villa. Most days, he's just an asshole with a shitty attitude."

When Lacey pressed her lips together to bite back a smile, he felt some of the tension ease from her body. He had to hand it to her, she recovered quickly, and knowing she was undergoing an intense inspection, she offered up a fabulous smile while stepping forward, out of Cam's protective reach, to extend her hand in greeting to Alex.

"Good morning, Major. You have a beautiful home. Thank you for allowing me to stay in your guest house."

Short, sweet, and to the point. Smart girl.

Alex pushed the sunglasses up his head as he reached for her hand. Cam watched their exchange in gritty silence. If Alex so much as stepped a toe out of line, he was ready to let him have it.

"Ah. Lacey. What a pleasure to meet you! Welcome to the Villa. We could use a bit more female influence around here. I hope a bunch of crotchety old bachelors don't ruin your stay."

When Alex folded her delicate hand in his big one and held on, Cam almost jumped on him to separate them. Just like his reaction to Frank, a searing jolt of white-hot jealousy made his jaw clench. The smirk on Alex's face let him know his reaction hadn't gone unnoticed.

"Please, sit under the awning before the sun devours your pale skin."

Cam's jaw, as well as his hands and gut, clenched at his friend's words. Devour, my ass. *What game was Alex playing?* He knew the suggestive power of the phrase he chose. Motherfucker was trying to get a rise out of him.

Before he could regain control of the situation, Alex stepped in and smoothly guided Lacey to a comfortable swinging chaise placed at the rear of the cabana. Dude was in for a serious ass kicking if he kept this up.

"Cam tells me you've signed on to clean up the mess we've made in the office now that Betty has taken a leave. Brave of you, I must say.

Especially if all you've had to go on before now was the character and behavior of the dark one over there."

Hearing him referred to as the dark one made Cam's hackles rise. Lacey's snort of amusement didn't help. *Mothergoddamnfucker.* He was definitely going to kill Alex when he got the chance. He thought Drae would be a fly in the ointment, not stuffy old Alex.

"Thanks for the warning. May I call you Alex?" she asked.

He nodded before pointing at the puckered skin on her arm. "What happened here?" he inquired.

Lacey glanced down at her arm and just stared for a moment as if the healing wound was something she'd never noticed before.

"Oh, that." She shrugged. "Had a bit of a run-in with … well, with a couple of America's troubled youth. They were what you would call earnest."

Smiling shyly at Cam, she pulled her arm away from Alex's inquisitive gaze. "Cameron saved the day. Didn't he tell you? Showed up in the nick of time and then did a fine job of stitching my little boo-boo."

Alex fixed him with a look that could strip the paint off an old car. *Shit.* He was definitely going to have some explaining to do when the time came.

"Well, my dear, I, for one, am glad he intervened. Someone as sweet as you shouldn't be subjected to such harsh treatment. It's good to hear that my partners have the good sense to jump in when necessary although it may have been more appropriate for Cam to have been the one who ended up sliced and diced."

Apparently, his choice of words struck her as funny, and she giggled. "Seriously? Those two morons didn't stand a chance. The way he laid out the biggest guy with one punch was pretty impressive." Her look of beaming approval struck him between the eyes, and once again, Alex didn't miss a thing.

"Hmm. I see. Well, you'll have to tell me more later. I'd love to hear all about our hero and his rescue of such a fair maiden. For now, though, you'll have to excuse me. I have a video call that requires preparation. I'm sorry to cut this short, but you're in capable hands with Cam."

It was the Valleja-Marquez Don in all his noble glory that reached out and snatched Lacey's hand for a chivalrous kiss on her knuckles. Cam stood by with a heavy glower directed entirely at Alex.

What. A. *Dick.*

The belligerent sneer from his old friend let him know that they'd be having a serious talk. Soon.

When Alex walked away, Cam threw himself down on the chaise next to Ponytail. She searched his face with a question in her lovely eyes.

"Did I say something wrong? Why are you looking at me like that?"

Laying his head back against the cushions, he pushed on the pavement to get the chaise slightly swinging. Turning to look at her, he sighed. "You handled him beautifully."

"Well, then why are you scowling at me? Did I miss something?" She jumped up and stood with her hands on her hips as she practically shouted at him. "What was all that about? Is he always so …" She searched for a word with a grimace of confusion shadowing her face. "I don't know. So, um … gallant?"

*Gallant? Was she fucking kidding?* Yeah, he was going to kill Alex. Easing forward with his forearms resting on his thighs, Cam looked up at her where she stood fretting before him.

"It's cool, really. Don't let his nonsense bother you. He just does all that suave European bullshit to get under my skin. No red-blooded guy would get caught going around kissing hands."

"Oh, is that so?" The haughty look she froze him with and the way her eyes blazed told Cam he'd just experienced his first ever foot-in-mouth moment with a woman.

"Okay, wait. That came out wrong." *Was it possible to breathe back words that were already out there?* Before he could get another word out, the tables turned on him so completely and with such ease that Cam was left speechless.

"Whatever. Don't you have an office to show me? Let's get this tour back in gear. I'd like to get started right away, if that's okay with you."

Her unspoken *you are a dick* hung out there in the silence between them. *How the fuck had he so completely lost control of the situation? Goddammit.* This was Alex's fault. He was going to strangle the asshole.

His talent of knowing when to give in had served him well over the years, and this was one of those times. Determined to demonstrate that he too could behave like a gentleman, Cam motioned with his hand for her to precede him as he guided her through a series of courtyards and walkways that led to the converted barn housing the state-of-the-art office where Lacey would be working.

*Why the hell was it that even when she was clearly annoyed with him, all he could think of was getting his hands in her pants?*

He found her lovely and sexy as hell with her baby blues and freckles. When she got all fired up, like she was right now, he could barely contain himself. Sexy didn't come close to covering how he saw her right then. Screw keeping her at arm's length. He wanted to absorb the sparks shooting from her eyes. Wanted to tame some of that fire. Hell, he wanted to jump on her and make her come over and over before finding his own satisfaction. Now *that's* what he called gallant.

*Head in the game, Cam,* he chanted silently when they arrived at the wing of offices and conference rooms that made up the business center. She'd gone ahead up a short flight of stairs, giving him a tantalizing view of her sweet backside as she stomped along. *How the hell was he supposed to stay focused when the woman had such a fantastic ass?*

Betty's inner sanctum was a large room with huge windows along one wall that looked out onto a magnificent desert vista. File cabinets and large pieces of wood furniture made up a seating area while a massive executive desk dominated the center of the room. Computers and an assortment of electronics were clustered everywhere. Lacey went immediately to the desk, hissing quietly when she found stacks of mail and papers covering the wide space.

Still acting the gentleman, Cam quickly ran her through some basics about the setup. He showed her how to access the agency email and even set her up with an email address of her own. He demonstrated how to operate the special window treatments that managed the relentless sun. Still silent, she took everything in, asking direct questions when necessary and nodding in understanding as he laid things out.

When finally there wasn't any more reason to stay and he'd run out of excuses to keep talking, Cam looked around, surveyed the damage done through Betty's absence, and silently headed for the door. *She was, after all, ignoring him completely, so what was the point?*

He liked this feisty side of Ponytail. Liked the way her stubborn fire issued a challenge that the primitive beast inside him was champing at the bit to accept. Maybe that was the reason he remained determined not let things get crazy between them. She was innocent, and he didn't imagine for one second that she was aware of the signals she was sending or the way she was turning him inside out. His primitive side almost got off the leash the other night, making him cringe when he remembered the raw, demanding way he'd taken her. His conscience scolded that he should have at least tried to be gentle, but fuck it if her responsive sweetness hadn't set him on fire. All the more reason to back off. Every indication was that he couldn't control his urges around her no matter how hard he tried.

Looking at his watch, Cam spoke up one more time before hightailing it the hell out of there. "Ria puts out a small lunch around noon. I'll come get you, or you can try to find your way back to the big house. Whatever works for you." Thank god, he'd managed to sound businesslike and casual.

His statement required a response from little miss icy freeze, and he wasn't disappointed when she lifted her frigid baby blues and met his gaze.

*Oooh, arctic blast.* Score one for the lady.

"I'd like to try to find the way on my own, thanks."

*Hmph.* Dismissed just like that. Taking the hint, he nodded, and with his tail firmly between his legs, he slid out the door. He needed a workout after their encounter with Alex and the way she'd shut him down following his insensitive gaffe. He'd probably be picking his teeth up off the floor if he'd finished what he had been saying about Alex's so-called gallant behavior. About to call him a fucking pussy for the unctuous hand kissing, he'd cut himself short when the sparks began coming off her.

Dammit. *Enough.* Changing direction, Cam headed to the gym complex and what he hoped would be some welcome relief from the turmoil Lacey's presence in his life had wrought.

*Women!*

Glad to see the back of him when he finally turned and left her alone, Lacey wanted him gone before she said or did anything stupid. She didn't really know why Cameron's sarcastic remark about his friend peeved her so much. Maybe it was because his attitude was another layer in that *emotions are bullshit* nonsense he excelled at.

*What was the big deal anyway about Alex kissing her hand?*

She'd found it charming and almost giggled like a starry-eyed teenager.

*Was the dark knight a tad jealous of other men?*

She'd picked up on something similar when they'd been talking with Major Frank.. Here she was, all but panting after the man like a bitch in heat, and all he reacted to was other guys being socially polite to her.

*What was she doing wrong?*

The Major was cute and all, in that Ryan Reynolds meets Lumberjack Larry way. He was good looking, solidly built and had a messy haircut along with a half-assed beard covering his face. Alex struck Lacey as one of those burly, sexy types that would make an uptight judge giddy, but that sort of appeal wasn't her cup of tea at all. The man couldn't hold a candle to Cameron's smoldering hotness.

No, apparently, she went for silent and brooding with a dash of *it's just sex*, and a double dose of *I'm unlovable*.

*Sheesh.* Nothing like making it difficult.

Well, Mr. Cameron Justice was a matter she'd just have to deal with later. Right now, she had to dive in to the mess on Betty's desk and try to figure out how bad things were.

An hour later, she discovered that from the moment their office manager left, the Justice Agency hadn't paid a bill, created an invoice, answered an inquiry, or opened an email in all that time. In other words, it was chaos. At least she'd found a starting place, and with that thought in mind, Lacey threw herself into the immediate tasks that needed urgent attention.

Right before lunch, as if on cue, Alex wandered into the weight room where Cam was relentlessly punishing his body with a grueling workout. Covered in sweat, every muscle pumped up and a dark scowl plastered on his face, he stood in front of a mirrored wall swinging heavy hand weights as he watched his friend's approach.

He knew Alex would turn up eventually. It had been clear that Lacey wasn't at all what he'd expected. She was younger, fresher, and a hundred times more girl-next-door than anyone Cam had ever been with before. Her explanation of his rescue and how she'd gotten hurt had painted a vivid picture for Alex to consider. Apparently, the contemplation was complete, and now, he'd come expecting answers.

Cam dropped the weights with a heavy thud and stripped off his lifting gloves while watching in the mirror as Alex came to stand behind him. His expression was impossible to read, making a frisson of unease wind through Cam's nervous system. More than just friends and business partners, Alex and Draegyn were Cam's family in every way that it mattered. Even though they were all close in age, Alex's position as the eldest of the trio sometimes came off as a parental figure, and it looked to him like Dad was about to issue a lecture.

*Sigh.*

They all knew each other too well to bother with niceties or beating around the bush. Alex's posture—one leg cocked slightly, hand shoved in a pocket, and the other running back and forth through his perpetually mussed hair—let Cam know he wasn't entirely comfortable with wherever his thoughts had led. No surprise there because he wasn't entirely at ease with what was going on either.

Turning to face the other man, Cam sank down on a weight bench, forearms on his legs with his hands hanging limp between his spread thighs. The workout had kicked his ass, and he still wasn't settled. This wasn't a great time to have a heart-to-heart, but it didn't seem like he was being given a choice in the matter. Reacting to the inevitable, he raised what he knew were troubled eyes and waited.

Both hands shoved in his pockets, Alex grumbled, "Jesus Christ, Cameron. Please tell me you know what you're doing. That girl is … well, dammit if she isn't just that, a girl! Do you wanna do a rewind on that story about her being just a friend? I'm not blind, dude. You're practically eye fucking her every time you look in her direction."

Cam winced at Alex's indelicate words. He might be trying to pretend it was just fucking, but he didn't want anyone else thinking in those terms about his Ponytail. A new beast roared to life inside him. One he'd never encountered before. This one was a snarling menace hell-bent on protecting what was his.

"Watch your mouth, Alex." His reaction surprised them both.

"Ah. So that's how it is, hmm? You've fallen for her."

"What? No!" The denial tasted bitter as it burst from his mouth.

"Nobody has fallen, bro. I just don't want anyone thinking that kind of stuff about Ponytail. She's not like that."

Alex's wide-eyed shock hit him square in the face. "Holy god, Cam! *Ponytail*? What the fuck?"

Realizing the mistake he'd just made, Cam twined his fingers together at the base of his skull as his head hung low. A deep sigh rumbled from his chest when he straightened and looked at Alex.

"I know. I know," he muttered. Nervous energy propelled him from the bench as he moved to stow away the weights. Turning toward his friend, he shrugged one shoulder, closing his eyes as he shook his head in confusion.

"I don't know what happened, man. One minute, she was an intriguing distraction to be watched from afar, just for the hell of it. The next minute, I was punching the lights out of some kid and playing the fucking hero for all it was worth." Chuckling at the absurdity of hearing all that out loud, he fixed his friend and brother with a serious look. "Haven't had a sensible thought since then."

Alex quietly considered what he'd said as a heavy silence fell between them. Discussing women and feelings wasn't where they did their best work. This was virgin territory in every way. Cam was glad his other brother wasn't there to complicate his thoughts even more. Drae's ice-blue eyes matched his cold-blooded approach to the opposite sex. Women were for pleasure only. Nothing more.

After a long pause, Alex spoke. "Just be careful, Cam. You're not ... well, what I mean is, you don't have the best mindset when it comes to the ladies."

"That's just it, man. I know that leaving her alone would be what's best. For her, anyway. I don't do hearts and flowers and wouldn't know where to start even if I wanted to. Believe me. I'm trying to do the right thing."

Alex sighed. Cam felt a weight sink to the pit of his stomach. *What a fucking mess.*

"Maybe you should consider going to Seattle next week instead of sending one of the juniors. It's a straightforward setup, nothing very involved. All you'd have to do is a systems check and a final run-through and then turn it over to the client. Would give Lacey some time to settle in and you a chance to step back. Gain some perspective."

"I don't know, Alex."

"It's cool, man. I'll personally keep an eye on things. Make sure she's okay. Think it over and get back to me."

"Thanks. Will give it serious thought, I promise."

# Chapter Fifteen

D AYS LATER, LACEY was tapping away at a computer in the office while nonstop thoughts of Cameron invaded her mind. She'd seen very little of him since their frosty last words and figured he was avoiding her. *Just as well*, she supposed. While she ached to be near him and wanted nothing less than his complete attention, she knew he was giving her time to adjust to her new surroundings.

She'd been crazy busy and had loved every second of the past days. Managing to get things in some semblance of order, she familiarized herself with the running of the agency every chance she got. She wandered around the stables, kennel, and motor pool; she introduced herself to Ben and the veterans he employed to help manage the impressive organic garden, met a dozen people, and had been thrilled by how affable and helpful everyone was. She felt accepted.

It had been Alex who surprised her the most, though. Every day, he made it a point to show up in the business center, usually with Zeus trotting at his heels, to check on how she was doing. He was unfailingly polite and friendly, and she suspected he was keeping tabs on her, maybe even reporting on her progress to the dark knight himself.

Luckily, she really did like Alex, so it was easy to be around him. He was an unusual man, stoic in his demeanor, and quite brilliantly fascinating when the subject was anything related to technology. He'd patiently explained, in excruciating detail, how a hologram functioned—something he'd been working on perfecting. She hadn't understood but every fifth word of what he was saying and struggled to keep up with the man's obvious genius.

Each evening, the Valleja-Marquez Don himself came to the casita to fetch her for dinner at the main house. Cam was present sometimes, silently brooding as usual. More people from the inner circle gathered at night around the rough-hewn table in the massive dining room. There she'd met Ria, Ben's wife and the ultimate drill sergeant when it came to feeding the giant household. Gustavo, or Gus as he asked to be called, came over from the stable most evenings. He managed the stuff that moved. Horses, trucks, ATVs, Hummers, electric golf carts—you name it, and he had it. She'd met Brody Jensen, the dog guru with the magic talent, who trained their highly sought-after guard dogs but who kept mostly to himself when not in the kennel.

Everyone had made her feel welcome and been incredibly helpful. Everyone except the one person she wanted attention from. *Damn that man.* His cool, detached, civility was getting to be like fingernails on a chalkboard. When he was around, his eyes followed her, but he kept a polite distance, deferring interest in her well-being to Alex.

Tonight, he was distracted and edgy. When Ben announced that Drae had surfaced and would be returning to the compound in a couple of days, she saw Cameron's gaze snap to Alex's. Some sort of unspoken communication passed between them. Every time Draegyn's name was mentioned, he went on high alert.

*What in the world was that all about?*

Ria was saying something sweet and supportive of the outfit Lacey was wearing. Ben had driven her into town right after her arrival, and besides stocking her little pantry with necessities, she had splurged in a local department store with this particular impulse purchase. The denim pencil skirt and soft jersey top were the perfect accompaniment to her favorite strappy sandals. The ensemble was new, not something hastily grabbed in a second-hand store, and fit her perfectly. She liked the way it made her feel. Feminine but modest, she knew she carried off the look pretty damn well.

The way Cameron's eyes burned when she sashayed with her sexy sandals into the large open dining room had been supremely satisfying. Now that the stress of the first days in an office going down for the third time had passed, she was back to thinking about the problem of *them*. Lacey wasn't even going to try to pretend the warmth flooding her core and the way she nearly devoured his presence wasn't happening. No, she wanted to be with him, and while running seemed to be his only move at the moment, Lacey realized that she'd have to put on her big girl panties and grab the proverbial bull by the horns if she wanted to get a reaction out of him. The man was very, very good at appearing detached. Of course, the substantial bulge he was attempting to hide told her otherwise.

Halfway through their meal, she overhead Alex casually ask Cameron when he was leaving. Leaving? *No, no, no,* her mind cried! *What did that mean?* Panic slowly fed its way into her nervous system.

Overcome with anxiety, Lacey tried to concentrate, but all she could think about was Cameron going away from her. She fidgeted and worried the end of her cloth napkin into a twisted mess. *How could she find out what was going on?* They had barely spoken to each other in days. It took a tremendous effort not to burst into the conversation and demand answers.

Finishing her meal in silence, Lacey retreated inward as old concerns and fear of abandonment crowded her mind. *Wow.* It hadn't taken much to stick a fork in her newfound confidence. He was ignoring her, and it was all she could do to keep tears from welling in her eyes. *Damn.*

Catching Alex's observant gaze upon her, she coughed in embarrassment and sat up straighter. If she wasn't mistaken, he was going back and forth, watching her reaction and then considering his friend. Intrigued, she glanced Cameron's way and saw his jaw clenched tight and his mouth set in a firm, tense line. Didn't seem as though her dark knight was a happy camper at the moment.

After dinner, people drifted away while Carmen and Lacey stuck around to help Ria clear the table and straighten things up. When she went to say her good-byes for the evening, Alex surprised her by suggesting that Cameron walk her back to the casita since he was busy.

The dark knight turned unreadable eyes her way, and with an abundance of politeness that brought a flashing smirk to Alex's otherwise bland expression, asked, "Are you set to go?"

They walked behind the big house along a landscaped path that led to the guest quarters. The twisting path was softly illuminated with solar lights. Lacey was acutely conscious of the sound their slow steps made on the crunchy gravel. With hands jammed in the pockets of his jeans, Cameron stayed close but silent. When she nearly stumbled in her high sandals, he reached for her hand and threaded it through his arm for support.

*How gallant,* she thought, a split second before a sly smile twisted her lips.

So that was how they were going to play this. *Okay then. He wanted to be all smooth and controlled?* She didn't think so. Not if she had any say in the matter. Knowing that her attitude about Alex had no doubt sparked this gentlemanly behavior gave Lacey pause. *Well,* she thought, *let's see how far he was willing to take it.*

Hugging his arm to the side of her breast, she sighed theatrically and gazed at the moonlit sky. "It's so beautiful here at night, don't you think?"

*Yeah,* he thought. It *was* beautiful. Being with Ponytail under a carpet of stars that stretched across the heavens was wonderful. In fact, in the perfect world that was his mind, he wanted to take her out into the desert and make love to her while thousands of twinkling stars stood watch over them. Something was wickedly sensual about the notion of being naked with her out in nature. He bet she'd be magnificent nude, with only the light from a half moon illuminating her sexy body.

"Do you like the desert?" he asked while glancing up just at the moment a meteor raced across the ink black sky.

"Did you see that, Lacey? A meteor," he cried as his arm squeezed her hand. "Quick, Ponytail, make a wish," he murmured while acknowledging a silent yearning of his own.

Her quick gasp of delight told him she had seen the sparkling trail as it arced across the sky. It seemed special to witness her sweet reaction while he let the warmth that her closeness brought him spread through his body.

"I love the desert," she eventually answered. "It's so calm even though I know it can be dangerous." *A little like you, dark knight,* she added silently.

Ice broken, silence forgotten for now, they walked on.

"Are you going somewhere? I heard Alex say something about you leaving," she boldly blurted out when she couldn't keep the question in any longer.

"Uh, yeah. I am. Business in Seattle," was all he said.

"When do you leave?"

"Tomorrow."

Her stomach sank. *Tomorrow.*

Cam felt her fingers tighten slightly on his arm and wondered about her reaction. *Why hadn't they spoken in days?* He couldn't remember. All he cared about was this moment and how he wanted to talk to her, be with her, and absorb the lightness that her presence brought to his somber world. He'd agreed to Alex's suggestion that he step back from Lacey and get his shit together, but in truth, he was reluctant to leave her even if they weren't exactly talking.

Knowing that Drae would be returning soon only ramped up his reluctance to be apart from her. The last thing he needed was the James Bond of their trio trying out his man-whore ways on the woman clutched at his side.

*My god. When had he become such a cynical bastard?*

Arriving at the casita, his intent was to escort her politely to the door, see her safely inside, and then bolt. When she turned toward him at the last second and whispered, "I'll miss you while you're gone," he forgot that intention and swiftly replaced it with another.

He didn't give her any warning, simply pulled her flush against the length of him and crushed her mouth under his. She barely flinched when he set about devouring her sweet, succulent lips, and responded with a moaning enthusiasm that set him on fire.

They stood at her door, clinging to each other in the darkness, engaging in a kiss that quickly got out of control. He grunted with deep satisfaction when her mouth opened to his questing tongue, allowing him to delve deep. She answered by sliding her tongue around his while her hands clutched the front of his shirt.

She was so unbelievably delicious. He'd never tasted anything quite like this Ponytail with the cute freckles and sexy backside. Drowning in her response, Cam dueled greedily with her naughty tongue while the fire inside him shot flames out of his pores.

He eased off before shit got crazy, vowing to go slow and be the gentle lover she deserved that first time. He was also well-aware that his thoughts had turned from screwing her brains out to indulging in a sensual mating that was more lovemaking than fucking. *She'd done that to him.* Made him think outside his narrow emotional box.

It took but a quick second to bundle her in his arms and push through the door into the privacy of her little home. While he would have been satisfied under normal circumstances to drop her to the floor where they stood and bury his hungry cock in her seething wetness, Cam was much more interested in savoring the slower plan he had in mind.

Swinging her up into his arms, he never left her mouth, continuing to nibble at her sweet lips and stroke his tongue against hers, letting her know what he wanted to do with her.

Making it to the bedroom proved a challenge when the soft female in his arms turned hungry tigress, spearing fingers into his hair and rubbing her breasts against his chest. Every one of her movements caused her insanely sexy ass to wiggle and squirm in his arms, making Cam painfully aware of the hard-on pressing against his zipper in a most uncomfortable way.

When they arrived beside the bed, he let her body slide from his grip until her feet were once again on the floor. When he came up for air after tearing his mouth away from hers, she responded by all but ripping off his shirt as she clawed her way to his skin.

He wasn't the only one on fire.

Catching her hands in his, he laid them just above his thumping heart. His chest was heaving as though he'd just run a marathon. She stared straight ahead, at her hands and the skin she'd exposed while he watched her lips pulse in the aftermath of their sultry kissing.

Calmer now, with his mind firmly set on Ponytail's total seduction, Cam released her hands and finished unbuttoning his shirt. Taking his time, he undid the buttons at the cuffs, then slid the shirt from his shoulders, letting it drift to the floor. Her breathing was heavier now, unsteady.

She lifted blue eyes to his green ones, and he saw for himself the arousal that was shaking her from head to toe. He also saw her appreciation for his body. The lady liked what she saw. All those shit-kicking workouts had enhanced his already toned physique into something harder, more defined. Masculine. For the first time in his life, Cam felt something that resembled pride about his looks.

He noted that her eyes had turned smoky blue while a soft pink blush set her skin aglow. When her delicate hands began stroking his chest, he urged her on with a rumble of pleasure. *Holy god.* The way she touched him melted his brain. He heard little gasps of pleasure when her hands swept lower, mapping his abs in slow, exquisite detail. By the time her fingers had finished rubbing through the hair that led into his pants, he was shaking too.

*This was how he wanted things to go.* Slow, unhurried. He wanted … no, *wanted* didn't do his desire justice. He *needed* to know every inch of her body and was pleased that she wanted the same of him. Letting her touch to her heart's content was hardly a chore. He hoped that before too long she'd be willing to use her lips and tongue the way she was using her hands. The thought of her sexy mouth on his skin made his breath hitch.

As if she'd read his thoughts, Lacey leaned into him and let her tongue swipe tentatively along his collarbone.

*More.* He wanted more.

Rolling his head back to give her better access, Cam groaned into the darkness when she took the encouragement he offered and went to town on his neck with her teeth, tongue, and lips. She was greedy, sucking on his skin while he spread his fingers across the back of her head to hold her close. When she rose on her tiptoes and swirled her tongue in his ear, he had to plant his feet more firmly or he would have stumbled from the pleasure. She nipped at his earlobe and then sucked it into her mouth while her hands searched for and found his nipples. What she did there sent his heart rate into overdrive.

"One of us has too many clothes on," he growled low and soft next to her ear.

Her hands dropped to his belt as she licked his neck in a long, slow swipe, then whispered, "That would be you, I think."

*Oh, fuck.* He needed to stop her, but dammit, what she was doing felt so good.

He let her go on for a bit while he worked his big hands under her top and lifted it. She seemed shocked when he pulled it over her head and tossed it aside, as though she'd been so wrapped up in him that she hadn't realized he was undressing her. He took advantage of her hesitation by reaching around her waist to pull down the zipper of her skirt and push it over her hips until it hit the floor. In a few smooth moves, he had managed to get her half-naked. Stripping her bare was the plan, but not quite yet.

Gazing at the soft blond beauty visible in the moonlight, Cam found her seductive appeal mesmerizing. Seeing her pale loveliness next to his shadowed body turned him on to no end. They complemented each other perfectly. He was big and hard, dark haired and powerful. She was smaller, rounded, soft, and pale with a compliant streak hidden within her courage and a strength that pleased him immensely.

She didn't need sexy, barely there lingerie to be desirable. Her plain bra with molded cups that hid her bountiful breasts from his view was easily as alluring as anything he'd ever seen a model wear. There was something about the way her tits plumped up and pressed against her bra the more aroused she got that made the vision she presented absolutely perfect.

The hi-cut white cotton bikini panties she wore were nothing short of mind-blowing. Fuck the G-string. Her incredibly long, lean legs and sexy hips made those simple panties look good. *Damn good.* He drank in everything about her and let the excitement she sparked inside him ignite a raging bonfire of desire.

Watching her tremble under his intense perusal, he reached out and ran a finger lightly down the center of her chest, over her bra, and down her stomach, stopping only when he reached the elastic band of her panties. Christ, she was so responsive. Her skin prickled from his gentle touch while her breathing quickened.

"You are so damn beautiful, Ponytail. I don't deserve you one bit, but that's not going to stop me from having all of you."

She smiled into his eyes and said, "Didn't you say one of us has too many clothes on?"

It was his turn to smile. *Smartass.*

Should he have her undress him, or should he slowly strip and fuel the flames he felt growing all around them?

When she took the initiative and reached for his belt, he decided on the latter. Served her right. He'd make her wait and watch until he let her touch … eventually.

Pushing her back against the edge of the bed, he pressed her hands to the mattress. "These stay here," he growled while quickly squeezing her fingers.

"Hmm. I like this," he said when he took in the sight of her clasping the bed behind her, the position pushing her chest up practically in his face.

The half-smirk on her face almost got him to laugh.

"Tsk, tsk, Ponytail. So impatient. Is this what you want?" he asked, stepping back to give her a good view.

Sure that he had her undivided attention, Cam looked down his front, drawing her eyes to his body, before running his hand down his chest, fingers leading the way. When he got to his belt buckle, he popped it open with a quick snap, loosening the edges so both ends dropped down, framing the tent his hard cock was creating in the front of his pants.

*Fuck!*

Even he was impressed by how awesome a move that was. The visual made his dick look huge.

*Hey, he'd take it any way he could get it.*

When she bit down on her lip and then swiped her tongue along the bottom of her mouth, he assumed it was her way of agreeing.

Lacey certainly didn't disappoint when she pursed her lips, looking pointedly at his straining bulge.

"I like those slacks, by the way. They're a good, uh, fit," she purred.

Yeah, that got a shit-eating grin on his face faster than any joke could. *God, she was awesome.* He loved that she gave as good as she got, and that he never knew what to expect.

Deciding to give her something to look at, he turned and walked a few steps away, grabbing the post at the foot of the bed with one hand for steadiness as he bent forward slightly to toe off his boots and peel away his socks, one at a time. Hopefully, she liked the way his pants fit his ass too. When he swung back to catch the expression on her face, the downright lascivious way she was devouring him with her eyes captivated Cam. He'd reward her for that natural, unguarded look later.

The way her breasts quivered in their white covering and heaved with each breath she took was almost hypnotic. Her hands twisted in the bedclothes but stayed where they were. Those legs of hers, though, were a different matter. One second, she seemed to be pressing her thighs together, and the next, she was shifting restlessly back and forth from one foot to the other.

She growled at him. "You have till the count of three to drop the pants, or I'll come over there and do it myself."

He threw back his head and laughed at her command.

"Ah, you laugh now, but we'll see who's laughing when I get to three."

In two long strides, he was on top of her, so close he could feel her breath on his skin. He traced a finger over the rounded top of one breast and grinned down into her face. "Go on then. Start ..."

Smiling sweetly like the she-devil she was, Lacey turned her face up to his, hesitated for emphasis, and then bit her bottom lip for good measure. "One ..." she said while her eyes blazed with naughty pleasure.

Before her mouth had closed on the word, Cam had deftly reached behind her back and unhooked her bra. She gasped in surprise as he pushed it down her arms and quickly discarded the garment while pressing her hands back in place.

Raising an eyebrow at her, he leaned in and let his tongue caress the seam of her lips. "Were you saying something?"

"Uh ..."

He reached for her breasts with the beaded dusty pink nipples, caressing the magnificent plump orbs with obvious delight. Squeezing gently, he lifted one of her mouthwatering tits in offering to his own mouth that was lowering with slow motion guided precision.

"Yes?" he murmured against her flesh. "Go on."

"T-two," she moaned as his lips closed around the nipple that stood in stark relief before his eyes.

*Mmm.* She tasted heavenly. Sucking tenderly, he felt the nipple grow firmer as her arousal increased. Letting the tiny, sensitive nub pop from his mouth, his tongue flicked relentlessly for a few moments before leaving a wet kiss on the beautiful tip of her breast. He was already cupping the opposite breast in readiness for the same attention, which he bestowed in good measure.

"So do you jump on me at the next count, or is three just a warning shot?"

She was quaking all over by this time. Not waiting for her answer,

he stepped back again and put his hands on his zipper. Her eyes zeroed in on the movement like a heat-seeking missile.

Being super careful not to injure his aching dick with any careless
moves, Cam pulled down the zipper, trying not to wince at the touch
of his fingers as they moved over the large bulge. With his eyes glued
to Ponytail's heaving breasts, he slowly pushed the fabric over his hips
and down his legs.

Once he'd kicked away the pants and stood before her in a pair of
gray cotton boxer briefs that molded to his body, leaving very little to
the imagination, she started and then stopped from reaching for him.
It was thrilling to watch as she struggled with her needy response to
his strip tease. Keeping her hands on the bed was costing her big time.

Stepping close enough to crowd her body, Cam shifted until his
bulging cock pressed against the juncture of her thighs. He caged her
in by putting his hands on the bed next to hers, Her slight whimper
sent a shockwave of intense arousal ricocheting through his body.

He didn't get the chance to play out his next planned move because
without warning she raised her arms to clutch him tightly around his
neck and shoulders. She levered back a bit and then climbed his body
with her strong legs until they wrapped firmly around his hips. The
heat between her legs seared his stomach where she ground against
him.

"I win. You dropped your pants by the count of three. Now, kiss
me and we'll call it even."

The way she was staring at his mouth made him think all kinds
of erotic things.

With his hands holding each butt check in a firm grip, he walked
them to the side of the solid wood armoire where he slammed her
back against it and lowered his mouth to her needy lips. She went
wild, gripping his shoulders and hips with such strength that he
groaned in sensory overload.

The whole time he was ravaging her mouth, she was wiggling in
his arms. The sensation of her bountiful breasts rubbing against the
hair and skin on his torso got his heart racing. If she got any better

at this, she'd probably give him a damn heart attack. Time for her reward.

Taking her back to the bed, Cam physically pulled her from his body and tossed her down on the mattress like a ragdoll. She lay there momentarily stunned, which gave him a few moments to enjoy her dishevelment and the tantalizing way her swollen breasts bobbled and swayed when she landed.

She looked … well, she looked ripe. Ready for what he wanted to do next. He caught the subtle scent of her arousal and instinctively reached for his cock, squeezing his hard-on through his briefs while she watched his actions and panted with excitement.

The nighttime shadows in the darkened room did nothing to diminish the sight of her blue eyes, staring at him with undisguised hunger. He doubted she had any idea what was coming next. That first time, he had been too out of control for anything that resembled finesse and had succumbed to the pounding desire to be inside her as quickly as possible.

This time, he intended to pleasure her first with everything at his disposal. Hands, lips, teeth, mouth. His dick would have to wait its turn.

He leaned over, pressing a wet, open-mouth kiss on her bare abdomen as he inhaled her delicious scent. He was suddenly ravenously hungry. Licking her was the only way to satisfy the desire surging through him.

Hooking his fingers into the side of her panties, he yanked while telling her to lift her hips. Whisking off the last of her clothing exposed her to his voracious gaze at last. The dusty blond curls between her legs were a perfect match for the rest of her pale coloring. He'd never seen anything quite so achingly beautiful as his Ponytail, naked and fiercely aroused, spread out in front of him.

"Open your legs for me, Lacey. Let me see all of you."

Her legs parted as she dug her heels into the mattress and wantonly rolled her hips.

Placing his hands on her ass, he lifted her slightly, bringing her closer to the edge of the bed as he sank to his knees. *Jesus.* He hoped the sight of her wet, open slit didn't render him blind. He'd never seen anything so luscious or smelled anything so sweet and sultry.

He used both hands to gently spread her lips open as she gasped in surprise. Being the first and only man to see her like this was a heady experience. What he did to her now, she would remember forever. *Shit.* He hoped he was man enough for the task. She deserved every pleasure he could wring from her body and more.

Making her wait would only increase the arousal and anticipation she felt, so Cam took his time parting her flesh and running his fingers through her soft curls. When her legs fell open wider, he gloried in her response and drank in the quiet moan that split the air. A creamy wetness gathered at the entrance to her passage that he ached to touch. With slightly trembling hands, he used a single finger to trace her opening with the gentlest of strokes. Her legs twitched, and he watched in utter fascination as her pussy clenched in response.

The soft moan from a few seconds ago turned into a rumbling groan of need that she punctuated with an involuntary shudder. She was incredible. So hot. So deliciously wet and ready for his tongue. Cam's dick twitched and throbbed in anticipation.

Nestled beneath the wet curls at her center was a nubbin covered in shiny wetness that was more tantalizing than any gourmet treat he could imagine. Pursing his lips he zeroed in on the tiny bundle of nerves, dropping a hot kiss on her swollen clit before laving his tongue across the same spot.

She writhed in response, fisting the bed linens and crying out his name. That seemed to go pretty well so he did it a few more times until she was pleading with him to stop because she couldn't take it anymore.

*Foolish girl.* He wasn't stopping; in fact, he was only just getting started.

Running his tongue back and forth along her open slit, he forgot his pledge to go easy when her response infiltrated his sense and set a fire of need crawling along his nerves. She had a sweet tangy taste that poured over his senses like hot lava. He couldn't get enough.

Lapping at her delicious wetness, Cam used his lips to draw her engorged nub into his mouth where he sucked and nibbled on it as he had her nipples. He knew if he kept that up for much longer, she would come in his mouth, and while the thought had a definite appeal, he wasn't ready to send her up and over just yet.

He liked squatting between her open legs. It gave him the most mouthwatering view. Not wanting to waste a moment of such a glorious opportunity, he kept one hand busy spreading her open while he slowly inserted his long middle finger deep inside with the other. Just like before, he watched in wonder when her inner muscles clenched tight. The sight of her sweet pussy closing around his invading digit was tattooed forever on his brain.

Slowly pumping his finger in and out became a growing torture for them both. She was shaking and rolling her hips, and he felt a bead of sweat roll down his neck, as he struggled to maintain control. Flicking his tongue against her clit, he plunged his finger in over and over with deep strokes that increased her excitement, and triggered a flood of creamy wetness.

He knew she'd reached her breaking point when she cried out and bucked wildly against his marauding finger. Quickly adding a second long, sturdy digit, Cam continued stroking in and out with increasing vigor, placing his mouth once again over her swollen nub and suckling it with a pulsing rhythm meant to trigger an orgasm.

Her climax, when it hit, was like nothing he'd ever seen or experienced before. Arching off the bed, her back bowed while powerful shudders ripped through her. A heated flood of moisture gushed from her body as her pussy clenched and spasmed over and over and over in wave after wave of intense pleasure that moved him more than words could say.

To his amazement, she was crying softly. The aftershocks continued to pulse through her even as he removed his fingers from her hot core. Laving one last kiss on her beautiful pussy, Cam kissed and nibbled his way up her shaking body until he reached her mouth. He didn't hesitate to swirl his tongue against hers, sharing the taste of her sweet response still on his lips.

Glad he had the foresight to place a condom on the nightstand when he shucked off his pants, he wriggled out of his briefs in a frenzied rush and sat back on his haunches with his cock sticking straight up. Ripping open the foil packet with his teeth, he rolled the condom down his patient dick while the woman spread open before him watched with half-closed eyes. He let his throbbing staff bob and twitch under her heated gaze for several moments while his hand remained clutched at the base making the fat head plump even more.

To his everlasting surprise, Lacey widened her open thighs even more in clear invitation. He wasn't going to wait for another. Moving between her legs, he levered his hips to allow the sensitized tip of his cock to stroke her wetness, covering the length of his hardness with creamy delight. Cam's body was coursing with exquisite arousal as he placed his hands under her knees so he could push her legs up and open even farther.

She was breathing heavily as she helped him hold her legs open. It turned him on even more, if that was possible, to see her all but begging for his dick. He knew what she wanted so he gave it to her a little bit at a time.

At first, he only let the bulbous head of his sex slide inside her. Each time he pulled back, her pussy made a quiet slurping noise. He knew when he told her how, she would quickly get the hang of letting her tight pussy grab on and suck him deep in with the strength of her inner muscles alone.

For now, though, he was in the driver's seat, so he kept teasing her with just a portion of what he had to offer. It didn't take long for her to lose control as she desperately tried to draw him deeper into her body. When she cried out, "Please, Cameron. Please," he swiftly surged home with a mighty thrust and a satisfied grunt that echoed in the darkness.

*Dear God.* The feeling of her incredibly tight, wet pussy stretching around his pulsating cock was enough to satisfy his hungry sex, but only for a moment. Planted deep and firm inside her, Cam rotated his hips, shuddering at the sound of her wet response as he let the beast off its leash for the finale.

Releasing her legs, he fell on her with randy abandon, licking and sucking her nipples as his powerful thighs unleashed a thunderous pounding. She responded with strong upward thrusts each time he pressed home, causing him to pump harder, deeper, and longer. The incredible rhythm they found seemed natural and about as erotic as anything he'd ever imagined. With each stroke, he pulled almost all the way out of her luscious body. The mind-blowing strength of her tight pussy wouldn't release him, and the sensation of her sex clenching the fat head of his dick on every retreat became heaven and hell at the same time.

When he hammered forward, each plunge sent him deep enough to tap against her womb. The feeling was extraordinary, and he never wanted to stop. That wasn't going to be possible, though, because his body had been patient and cooperative long enough. He felt the fire growing in his balls each time they slapped against her dripping center. Picking up the tempo, Cam issued a serious volley of powerful thrusts that caused her to cry out in sweet agony.

The moment her pussy exploded he felt a shockwave of molten heat shoot along his spine. She ground against him as her body milked his cock in a series of earth-shattering convulsions that vapor locked his brain. Grunting like a wild animal, Cam experienced long moments of indescribable pleasure when his dick, that had been locked and loaded long enough, fired off inside her. Churning wildly, he pumped into her over and over while his balls emptied and her pussy clutched him through it all.

When it was over and they could both breathe again, Cam dealt with the condom and then pulled her close, fitting his exhausted body against hers as they drifted off. His last thought before sleep claimed him was that they hadn't talked, not really. Except for some sexy teasing, not much had been said between them. Communicating with their bodies seemed to be what they did best.

*So much for backing off and getting some perspective.*

# *Chapter Sixteen*

FOUR DAYS HAD gone by. Four long, busy days and not one word from Cameron. Lacey felt like kicking a dog. If she had one, that was. Well, she wouldn't actually kick the animal just because the guy in her life was behaving like one.

After their unforgettable night together, she hadn't been totally surprised to wake up alone in her rumpled bed. *Okay, maybe a little surprised.* After all, the way he had behaved, driving her wild with wanting before staking his claim inside her body, had been nothing short of mind-blowing. Expecting a bit of tenderness the next morning shouldn't be such a big deal, but with Cameron, it most certainly was.

*Poor man,* she mused. She wondered if he realized she'd been poking and taunting him, attempting to crack the polished veneer he'd been trying so hard to maintain. His testy version of Alex's noble gallantry didn't suit the dark knight, making her glad when he'd tossed in the towel. A delicious tremor rushed up her neck remembering how his polite, respectful distance vanished the second he put his lips on hers.

Heaving a huge sigh that broke the silence of the office where she toiled each day, Lacey leaned back in the big plush desk chair and contemplated the ceiling. Anything to divert her thoughts from the man with the sexy mouth and the brooding good looks.

Filling the hours that made up her day, working brought a rhythm she looked forward to. Once the original crisis had been dispatched, she'd taken over the business side of the agency with ease, earning kudos from everyone, especially Alex. He had been charming, solicitous, and made every effort to include Lacey in the inner workings at the Villa. If only she could stop pining for a man who seemed to have no problem walking away. He was very good at it, in fact. The walking away.

Another dramatic, heavy sigh ripped through the air.

Twirling around in the big chair like a bored two-year-old, she thought about the paycheck Alex gave her that she hadn't been expecting. She'd been mortified and said so. The amount had startled her. Apparently, the agency compensated their employees quite well. Even though the payroll was farmed out to a professional service, she knew that Betty was being taken care of during her absence. She liked the message such loyalty and caring suggested.

Leaving the merry-go-round of a chair, Lacey stood and wandered to the wide windows that looked out onto a desert scene that was so perfect, it almost resembled a painting.

The conversation she'd had with Alex about the payroll had been highly illuminating. When she'd tried to reject the paycheck on the grounds that letting her stay in the casita had been payment enough, what she learned next had hit her like a ton of rocks.

"You're staying in the guest house because that's where Cam wanted you. It wasn't my decision, or any of my business for that matter," he had said.

Normally pretty quick on the uptake, she'd been confused and asked for an explanation. What had he meant exactly by *that's where Cam wanted her*?

"C'mon, Lacey, think about it. There's a dormitory for visitors and clients who stay over, and a bunch of studio apartments throughout the property. He could easily have put you in any of those spaces, yet he chose to plant you between the main house and his. We save the Casita de Corazon for family. It's for our exclusive use, Cam, Drae, and myself. Clearly, he wanted you close by."

Jolted by the implication of what she'd learned, Lacey was hit with an avalanche of conflicting emotions. Disbelief came first. Followed by embarrassment. Eventually, though, a whiplash of female satisfaction had her sitting up and taking notice. By setting her up in the guesthouse, Cameron made a silent statement whether he wanted to admit it.

She'd been moved when Alex put a hand on her shoulder and squeezed before telling her not to give up yet. She could only take the comment one way—Cameron's closest friend was giving his approval of their involvement and encouraging her to stick it out.

*If only he knew how complicated the whole thing truly was.*

It was clear that neither she nor Cameron had the slightest clue how to go about having a relationship. To make it more complicated, he believed his less-than-stellar upbringing and sometimes gritty life experiences made him unworthy of love or caring.

*Why couldn't he could see himself the way she did?*

The conversation with Alex became even more revealing when, deciding to go for broke, she delicately asked about his injury. Most of the time, he did a bang-up job of hiding the slight limp in his gait. When he was stressed or tired, though, the hesitation in his walk became almost painful to watch. Other times, he rubbed his hand back and forth against his thigh in an absentminded gesture that told of the discomfort plaguing him.

Lacey hadn't been sure if he would answer. Maybe the story was too personal, and perhaps, she'd just stepped way over the line. When he boosted his backside up onto the desk and fixed her with a wry smile, she breathed a sigh of relief.

"In the end, it was one bad day out of a thousand bad days. You get used to it, you know," he murmured with a chuckle that didn't sound joyous in any way. "The heat, the dust, the smell. After a while, you barely notice. Being alert, watching out for everyone, staying alive … it was a twenty-four seven proposition."

He stared into space as the rewind played out. "Had the misfortune of getting promoted. Damn military. Liked to reward foolishness they thought was bravery. Anyway, getting pulled out of our team to play officer was the last thing I wanted. That's where the Justice name comes from. Me, Cam, Drae, and a bunch of others were called by that name since that was what we did. Meted out justice to the bad guys."

Lacey made note of that tidbit of information. *Hmm.* Another puzzle piece. Justice Squad? Team Justice? It wasn't her first inkling that Cameron might not be who he said he was. She'd been introduced to Alex by his formal surname, Valleja-Marquez. And she knew that Draegyn's last name was St. John. Only Cameron seemed to have no identity prior to the one he'd created for the agency.

A chill tingled along her spine. *Interesting.*

"That day started off like any other. Visiting politicians and some dog and pony show bullshit had just wrapped up. I was out of sorts and distracted. Being in an office isn't my thing," he said with a twisted grin while taking in where they sat, "in case you haven't noticed." She smiled at that. Alex was a lot of things, but organized and businesslike weren't on the list.

Rubbing his thigh absently, the story rushed out as if he didn't want to say the words.

"I don't remember much except that all hell broke loose, and then there was a tremendous explosion in the HQ. Half my staff either died or was injured. Everything was blown to smithereens. It was a complete shit show. The guys tell me when they arrived on the scene, I was buried under a pile of debris. The bottom half of me looked like a pile of raw meat with my leg taking the worst of it."

She shuddered at the picture he was painting, but he didn't notice. Lost in the memory, Alex had turned to stone right before her eyes.

"Gotta hand it to the medics, though. They did a bang-up job of keeping all my body parts attached. Spent a couple of months in Germany, touch and go most of the time. Then a year of rehab back in the states. The leg was saved, but it looks like a fucking patchwork quilt and aches like a bitch at times."

Looking out at the desert scene, he sat quietly for a few moments. Lacey could feel the anguish radiating off him in waves.

"Damn lucky the family homestead isn't farther north. The cold lays me out."

He looked at her with eyes that had seen way too much. "Draegyn and Cam were there that day. They helped pull me out of the rubble. In case you haven't put this together yet, we're all pretty fucked up in one way or another after what happened. It's way more complicated than the story tells."

Lacey listened, emotion clogging her throat with each word. He was being matter-of-fact, but she heard the torment in his voice and saw a slight hesitation just before that last statement. Something unsaid was swirling in the air. He slid from the desk, shaking out his leg as he did so, and ambled to the windows. She waited him out.

"Turns out the explosion was the work of a suicide bomber. Someone we all knew. A woman. Her name was Badirya … she worked as a translator for the coalition forces."

Lacey sucked in a surprised breath. Someone they all knew. And it was a woman. She was gaining insight into the complicated mindset that led Cameron to be so detached from his emotions, particularly where women were concerned.

Alex reacted to her surprise with a dark scowl. "It gets worse, unfortunately. She had a young son, maybe nine or ten. Everyone liked the boy. He was too young to understand the war, but he liked hanging around with the guys. His father had been killed years earlier. She took him with her when she blew everything up. It was deliberate, too. We lost a lot of good people that day. And for what? None of it makes sense. Didn't then. Doesn't now." His hand was absently scrubbing back and forth through his hair.

Lacey went and stood next to Alex, laying her hand gently on his arm. "I think you're unbelievably brave."

"No!" he vehemently replied. "I hate that word. No one was brave! We were just men, trying to stay alive. Hoping to make it home in one piece."

"I know that, Alex, but you *are* brave. All of you! Past couple of years haven't been a cake walk for me. Hearing what you've said reminds me of that people were fighting and dying in my name all that time and I barely paid attention. I don't care how desperate someone's existence gets. We should always be aware of and support the men and women who go into harm's way for us."

He gave her a lopsided smile. "You have a good heart. I hope telling you my story helps you see Cam in a different light. He's a good man, Lacey. It's just that his situation is ..." He struggled to find a word. "Complicated. Yeah, that's it. Complicated."

"I don't understand any of this, but believe me, I'm trying. And, um ... things between Cameron and I may not be what you think."

"Well, before you waste any time trying to convince yourself, or me, that it's not *what I may think*, I know that his truck stayed in the driveway at the main house after he walked you home. And it was still there the next morning when he came to get it for the trip to the airport."

"Oh."

"Yes. *Oh*."

Lacey turned beet red at the thought that Alex knew what they'd been doing in the little guesthouse.

"As I said, don't give up. I know he's probably being a dick, but in all the years I've known him, you are the first girl he's ever let get close. Fuck, the first *person*! That has to count for something."

She hung her head and nodded. Of course, it counted, but if the man never got past that point, all of this would be moot. He was either angry and brooding or cool and detached. There was no middle ground, and she was completely inexperienced in dealing with men.

"Look, why don't you plan to come over to the barn tonight? Got talked into a karaoke get-together. Everyone will be there, plus a few townies you should meet. Will take your mind off ... work."

"Thanks, Alex. Sounds like fun. What time?"

And with that, the rhythm of her evenings fell into place too. It was work, work, work all day and then hanging out with the Justice crew after supper. Some evenings, they went to town and bowled, and sometimes, it was cards. But mostly, it was simple camaraderie at its pleasurable best. On day eight, though, everything changed.

She, Carmen, and Ria were up to their eyeballs in baking supplies, churning out several dozen cookies for an upcoming church bake sale, when Zeus began barking up a storm. Lacey startled at the sound because the big Lab was not a noisemaker. She'd made friends with the dog almost immediately and was delighted to learn that Zeus was a 'she.' The women joked that the men couldn't handle being guarded by a female, so they gave the poor girl a guy's name.

Whatever, or whomever, had gotten the dog so riled up was causing quite the commotion. Curious, three sets of eyes turned to look into the rear courtyard at the exact moment shouts of *hola* and *welcome home* filled the air.

Lacey's heart picked up a few beats, hoping this meant Cameron had returned, but the sleek Lamborghini sports car that was slowing to a halt most certainly was not his style.

"Who's that?" she asked her companions.

Ria laughed at her surprise and said, "Oh, that's right! You haven't met Draegyn yet, have you? Well, get ready for a treat. Things are sure to get lively now that he's back."

The next thing she knew, the back door flew open and in strode what could only be described as one impressive doppelgänger for 007 himself. Not as tall or wide as Cameron, nor as outdoorsy or messy as Alex, this final piece to the Justice puzzle was tall and lean, with ramrod straight posture and a laconic swagger that probably made the ladies swoon. *And dammit if he wasn't actually dressed in a tuxedo!* The bow tie was hanging undone and the suit looked like he'd been wearing it for days, but it was an honest to goodness tuxedo.

*Was that her mouth hanging open?*

"Carmen! You're a sight for sore eyes!" he cried, obviously delighted. "Can I beg you to whip me up a turkey sandwich, mamacita? I'm starving."

"M*eee*ster Draegyn! You've been missed!" the woman said with a smile curling on her lips. "The tuxedo, it's overkill, yes?" she added, laughing at his appearance.

Draegyn waved his hands at the wrinkled attire and grinned. "Oh, come on! No good?"

When Carmen mocked him with an indulgent sigh, he leaned in and gave her a theatrical kiss on the cheek, ending it with an exaggerated, "Mwah!" She swatted him on the arm for good measure and giggled like a schoolgirl.

Turning his attention to the other woman beaming at him, he wagged his eyebrows while looking her over and making a 'twirl around' gesture with his finger that had the woman pirouetting gracefully in what was obviously a private joke.

"Ria. You look fetching as ever," he teased with an amusing leer. "Where's that husband of yours? Can I get a hug before he turns up with that awful scowl?"

Lacey watched fascinated while Ria and Draegyn hugged and teased each other with clear affection.

When he turned his attention to her, she felt like she'd been pulled into his force field.

Draegyn St. John was blond and had the iciest blue eyes she'd ever seen. His hair was short and immaculately cut, quite the departure from his brothers. A mouth that looked almost cruel sat on a face that suggested a broken nose at some point with a small, barely visible jagged scar on his right temple. Despite all the joking, his look was serious. Slightly dangerous. Mysterious. Oh yeah, and he actually tugged at the cuffs of his immaculate white shirt while he checked her out from head to toe.

"Who might this lovely lady be?" he quizzed her two companions. Stepping close, close enough to catch the scent of his spicy aftershave, Lacey was left almost speechless by his approach.

*Good Lord.* This guy was something else!

Trying to overcome a sudden bout of shyness, she stepped up and offered him her hand. "Hi. I'm Lacey. I'm …"

When he enclosed her small hand in his and held on, Lacey almost died laughing. It didn't take a psychic to understand why Cameron had been so worked up about Drae coming home. The man was as a complete ladies' man in manner, style, and attitude. Her heart lit up with happiness when she realized Cameron *had* been jealous. *Awesome.*

"She was about to say that she's taking Betty's place for a while," came a booming voice. Lacey hadn't seen Alex enter the kitchen, but he was right there and looking like a rather stern parent. *Uh-oh.*

Still clasping her hand, Draegyn's eyes twinkled as he laughed. "Well, this is one replacement I heartily approve of!"

She couldn't believe he was actually flirting with her. *If only he knew.*

"Drae!" Alex's voice threatened. When he had his attention the big man quite succinctly stated, "She's staying in the casita."

"Ah, is that so?" Drae still smiled at her.

"As Cam's guest."

The look the two brothers exchanged was heavy with meaning, and just like that, her hand was dropped and the flirting halted. Taking a respectful step backward, Drae's entire demeanor changed in a nanosecond.

"Where is Cam?" he asked. "I got a message from him a few days ago. Is he still in Seattle?"

"Yes. Yes, he is," Alex offered. "But I spoke with him earlier, and hopefully, he'll be finished in a day or so. He's anxious to get back." The steady-eyed look he shot Lacey was filled with meaning.

"Well then, that's great. We'll all be here together for a while. I've got a fantastic little toy I picked up in London that I can't wait to show you. Fashioned after one of MI5's listening devices. You'll love taking it apart, Alex!"

Slapping the man on his back, Drae seemed to forget all about the three women as he bent his head to Alex's and the two went deep in conversation.

The gloominess in Lacey's outlook vanished upon hearing that Cameron would be returning soon. She watched Alex and Draegyn wander into the drive and head toward the luxury sports car. Now that she had all the pieces of the Justice puzzle, she marveled at how different the three were. Alex had so clearly let Drae know she was involved with Cameron, causing him to instantly change his behavior toward her. He'd gone from unabashed flirt to respectful and courteous in seconds.

And so it was, three days later, that the missing Justice Brother made his way back to the compound. By then, Lacey and Drae had formed a friendship that equaled the one she had with Alex. There was never a moment when she wasn't aware that the two men were keeping an eye out for her during Cameron's absence. She almost felt like part of the family. Everything was good, work was going great, and all the people who made up the agency treated her with kindness. Life had certainly changed. *Now if only the dark knight would let her in.*

# Chapter Seventeen

THE ARIZONA HEAT hit him like a speeding train the second he stepped outside the airport terminal and made his way to the long-term parking lot where his truck would be waiting. After the cold and rainy weather in Seattle, he was glad to be home.

It had taken forever to get clear of the airport after having to wait an eternity in baggage claim, giving Cam good reason to be edgier than usual. The project he'd just wrapped up had gone well, and though he'd been working with a bunch of smart people who knew what they were doing, he'd still been unusually short-tempered and touchy.

Tossing his gear into the back of the truck cab with more force than necessary brought him up short. Getting a grip was priority number one now that he was home. There was no use in trying to compartmentalize what was causing his tension. He'd thought of nothing else but Lacey since the second he'd left her bed and ran away. *Some war hero*, he snorted into the silence. Surviving the battlefield didn't hold a candle to keeping his damn shit together in the face of some freckles and a sexy backside.

*Why did he keep running? Why was it so hard to turn off his emotions where she was concerned?* It had never been a problem before. Maintaining his distance, complete with radio silence, had seemed like the way to proceed a week ago. Today, though, he was regretting both those decisions. On a rare surge of conscience, Cam deeply regretted not having tried to call her at least once during his absence. He was behaving like a pig. Each time they were alone for more than a minute, he was all over her like a fucking rash. Sleeping with the lady and then walking away without so much as a word or a nod had been bad manners. Trying to pretend he was a gentleman had backfired spectacularly.

Well, time to face the music. He supposed he'd have some groveling to do. In fact, he expected that. *Isn't that what usually happened in these matters?* He'd realized halfway through the week away that he wasn't going to be able to keep on kidding himself where Ponytail was concerned.

He wanted her. Plain and simple. Well, in truth, the wanting wasn't exactly plain or very simple. Overriding years of keeping away from all emotional entanglements, he was cautiously admitting that wasn't going to work where she was concerned. The urgent need to be with her was killing him.

Thinking about the small box in his suit jacket with the delicate pearl earrings he'd bought for Lacey got his heart pounding. He'd never, *ever* bought a gift for a woman. This time was different. During some downtime, he had scoured jeweler's row in downtown Seattle looking for whatever struck his fancy. He wanted to give her something she would wear next to her skin and make her think of him.

*Fuck, if he wasn't going all soft over a girl.*

Checking the time as his big truck pulled onto the highway, Cam relaxed into the drive and focused on how he would handle seeing Lacey again. He'd be at the Villa soon. Hopefully, by then, he'd have it all figured out.

It was the midafternoon when he pulled off the main highway and started the long, slow drive into the compound. He liked this part of the trip the best, when he knew that home was just around the bend. For an orphaned kid, having that sense of arriving and a place of permanence never lost its importance.

This time, Cam experienced another rush. A surge of emotion at the prospect of seeing Lacey again. More than simple pleasure, the feelings of happiness she lit up inside him were changing the way he viewed his life. He was taking a huge leap of faith in hoping that the emotionally broken life he'd been living could be saved, having found his salvation in a pair of blue eyes.

Whatever warm, fuzzy feelings he'd been entertaining quickly shut down the moment the truck pulled into the drive at the main house. Drae's shiny red sports car stood out like a sore thumb. A thumb that was suddenly poking Cam right in the eye. Adrenaline shot through his system with the velocity of a bullet.

*Fuck.*

Parking his truck with a decided jerk by standing on the brakes, Cam was out of the cab and stomping toward the door when the raucous sound of voices and yelling caught his attention. Following the noise, he rounded the cookhouse and headed toward the commotion that appeared to be coming from the stables.

What he came upon was a familiar scene. About twenty or thirty people gathered around the outdoor horse arena, cheering on a riding competition. Dogs were barking. People were laughing. *Great.* He'd walked into an agency barbecue.

The training and workshops they were known for were serious business. The attendees had rigorous sessions, both mentally and physically. It was an agency custom to end each session in a way that gave everyone a chance to blow off steam and get ready to go back to the real world. The riding event was part of a full day of fun that was probably headed to the pool before too long and a gathering that would go on well into the evening with great food and easy times.

Not too far from where he stood, several people, men and

women, hung out by the arena fence. Some were standing on the bottom rail while others were milling about flashing high-fives and cheering loudly. Feeling out of place in his white button-down shirt and tailored slacks, Cam started to turn toward the main house when something caught his eye.

Perched on top of a fence rail was a backside he'd know anywhere. *Lacey?*

Cam shook his head as if that would help clear his vision. Sporting a cowboy hat and dressed in a snug pair of jeans with a light colored western shirt tucked neatly at her waist, she was hollering and cheering along with everyone else. As he watched dumbfounded, she hopped down from the rail, high-fiving the people around her, looking like somebody having the fucking time of her life.

*Well, isn't this just dandy?* Here he figured she'd be slumming about, boo-hooing over his absence, a scenario that he had to admit suited his aims where she was concerned.

Not able to take his hungry eyes off her, Cam memorized every motion and felt his gut churn when the sound of her husky laughter hit his ears. She looked adorable in her western wear—from the cute straw hat to the very sexy boots. When she took the hat off and smacked it against her butt, he almost fell over. In place of the ponytail, she was sporting a pair of cowgirl pigtails that made her look incredibly young. Suddenly, he felt like a dirty old man, lusting after someone much, *much* too young for him.

Her group began walking toward the stable, and for a second, all he could do was admire the delicious sway of her hips in the form-fitting jeans. What he wanted to do to her ass at that moment wasn't for the faint of heart.

Stepping from his vantage point against a stone wall, Cam decided to go after her when suddenly she turned and saw him. For a brief second, she looked shocked. Then, if he wasn't mistaken, a flash of happiness appeared on her face a second before it evaporated. He thought she would walk to him, but instead, she hesitated, half-smiled, waved a greeting, and then turned back to her group and continued to walk away.

Uh, no way was that a good sign. *What the fuck just happened?* She'd been happy to see him, he was sure of it. *But if that were the case, why had she twinkled some fingers at him and then just turned around?*

"Oh, fuck me! Is that the great and powerful green-eyed wizard of odd I see lurking in the shadows?"

Before he could answer, Drae had grabbed him in a bear hug that quickly turned into a brotherly slapping match.

"Still driving that pretentious pussy magnet for a car?" Cam taunted as they danced around each other, taking the occasional half-hearted punch.

They kept it up for a few minutes, hurling insults and calling each other out for an array of manly shortcomings. It was good to see Draegyn. His irrational jealousy forgotten for the moment, Cam enjoyed the light teasing. This was what coming home meant. Being with his family, such as it was.

Drae slapped him on the back as they both made for the driveway. "Seriously, Cam. It's good to see you. I've been gone for so long that this place started to seem like a dream. Seeing your sorry ass here makes it all real again!"

Cam tried out one of his newfound half-smiles on his old friend, earning him a quizzically arched brow and another backslapping.

"So is that the way it is?" Drae's full throated laugh as he threw his head back and let loose surprised him. "Well dude, I'm glad somebody can smile. Alex is practically chewing iron nails, so I hope Seattle went well. The man is like a caged animal all of a sudden. Do you know what he's going to do about finding an assistant? I'm not stupid enough to ask. Crazy bastard almost ripped my face off last night for daring to suggest he needed help."

Cam eyed him with amusement. "Don't look any worse for wear, Drae," he drawled. "Since when do you shrink from a bit of tension?"

"Are you fucking kidding me?" He laughed heartily. "Spend three months in Europe babysitting a teenage heart throb with an empty head, and even you will avoid more stress! I must say, though, that your Lacey certainly lightens things up around here. Alex treats her like royalty, and she's everyone else's new best friend! What's up with that, Cam?"

He'd frozen when Drae mentioned Lacey. "How long have you been here, Drae?" he asked as smoothly as his thumping heart would allow.

Trying not to wince when he heard the edge in his voice, Cam stood silently under his friend's intense perusal. It was like being in the glare of an interrogation lamp. Draegyn was the cold, analytical one of their group. A black belt with impressive skill, he had an icy ruthlessness about him that helped earn him the James Bond comparison. At Cam's indelicate reaction to Lacey's appearance in the conversation, his antennae must have gone up.

Drae's eyes narrowed, and his mouth thinned to a tense line. Cam might be bigger than him in stature, but this guy's mad skills in hand-to-hand meant he'd get his ass kicked if he challenged him physically. *What the hell was he thinking?* He didn't want to challenge anybody. This was his brother. One of the few people he trusted and knew he could count on.

Stepping back to ease the hovering confrontation before it got out of hand, Cam shook his head vigorously. "Sorry, man. That was uncool." He winced as if he'd been sucking on a lemon and turned away.

"C'mon, brother. Let's go find Alex and crack open a bottle of scotch. It's been too long since we got shit-faced for no reason."

Crisis averted, Cam nodded. "Uh, about Lacey ..." Unfortunately, nothing else came out after that.

Draegyn fixed him with a steady gaze, saying, "I've got your back." He didn't need to say anything else. Cam's insane jealousy was misplaced, and that was all there was to it.

Alex had nixed the booze fest by reminding them that they had business to deal with in the form of a huge barbecue around the pool in an hour followed by an evening bonfire before their guests ended their stay. At the mention of the festivities, party master, Drae made his excuses and headed out to make sure all the arrangements were in place.

When he took his leave, their eyes met for a moment before they both nodded, and then he was gone. He spent the next half hour talking about business and the project he'd just completed. Alex, as usual, was full of detailed questions about how the equipment functioned.

Eventually, the topic turned to more personal matters as Cam knew it would.

"You should have called her."

*Ouch.* Talk about short and sweet.

Keeping his face composed and showing little emotion, Cam pussied out at the last moment and went with a slight shrug. The truth was, Alex was right, and he didn't know what to say.

"Let me save you from wasting my time by beating around the bush. The night before you left … when I asked you to walk Lacey to the casita. Your truck stayed in the driveway up here until the next morning."

Cam swallowed while his conscience laughed its little ass off. He was busted, and the look on Alex's face told him he was none too pleased.

"Not exactly keeping your distance, hmm? I thought you knew what you were doing, brother, so I have to ask again … what the fuck, Cam?"

The silence that followed was deafening. *How could he admit to his friend that he'd lost control and taken her?* Alex wasn't a fool. Her innocence was a given. Even though he'd thought of nothing but her the entire time he'd been away and had even gone so far as to bring back a gift, he still wasn't comfortable with or entirely sure what the hell he was doing.

*Was he in love with her?* He didn't know. *Was he just scratching a sensual itch? God.* He hoped he wasn't that big of an asshole. To use someone so young and dependent on him for sex. The thought didn't sit well with him.

"Y'know, Cam, sometimes your brooding silence pisses me the fuck off. Talk to me, man. Tell me what's going on. I like this girl." The look of white-hot fury that shot off Cam didn't miss its mark.

"As I was saying before the dagger eyes, I like this girl. She's got a good head on her shoulders. If you mess with her, there's going to be a whole crowd of folks standing in line to kick your ass. That's my way of letting you know that she has friends here. Everyone likes her, so watch yourself."

Cam knew he was being a dick. First, jealousy about Drae, and now, wanting to punch Alex's lights out. Goddammit, the girl had him twisted inside out.

Alex watched his friend, marveling at the heavy emotional burden Cam's broad shoulders carried. He needed someone by his side who cared about him. It was clear to even a blind man that Lacey was that person. Seeing him struggle with the enormity of his personal baggage, Alex felt some responsibility for at least a portion of what was tying his friend in knots.

The three of them escaped the battlefield but not the brutal aftermath. He didn't need to ask to know that Cam and Drae still carried harsh memories and vivid nightmares from their wartime activities. As always, Alex assumed a heavy share of the responsibility for them as their commanding officer. He had been the one who gave them their marching orders.

Finally, Cam spoke up. "I seem to be apologizing a lot. First Draegyn and now you." Jamming his hands deep into pockets that barely held his big paws, he hung his head and slowly shook it back and forth. "She's too young and too ... well, you know. Someone like me is no good for the likes of her. I knew that, but it didn't stop what happened. Fuck. Didn't even slow it down." The look he gave his friend was the most honest he'd ever shown.

Alex solemnly nodded. "If it helps any, she put on a good show, but believe me, the lady was seriously bumming without you here.

If you ask me it's a fucking pity that someone so lovely fell for your tortured soul bullshit! Time to fish or cut bait, Cam. Make a damn decision. Either stake your claim or cut her loose."

When Cam finally looked at Alex full on, he added, "And that's an order."

"Fuck you."

"No, dude! Fuck *you*. Now go grab some swim trunks and get your sorry butt out to the pool. Time to party!"

The poolside gathering felt like water torture to Cam. Too many people were around to do more than nod at Lacey, so he did the next best thing. Staked a claim on one of the padded loungers, slid his dark sunglasses across his eyes, and watched her every move.

Dammit if she wasn't wearing the one-piece suit he'd gotten her during their trip. Thinking it modest before, he considered it practically indecent today with so many sets of eyes checking out her alluring figure. She had an ass that made men and women alike turn and take a second look.

The insistent hard-on triggered by watching her required careful towel placement to avoid knowing looks. It didn't help that she seemed to be deliberately ignoring him. Nor did it help that she fit in so well with the others and was all but the life of the damn party.

Drae lived up to his reputation and zeroed in on a fierce-looking woman who Cam was fairly sure his friend would be banging before the night was out. The lady looked like she could take care of herself and was clearly enjoying Drae's secret agent charm. He was relieved that the man didn't approach Lacey because keeping a lid on his jealousy was proving a bit difficult.

The barbecue wasn't any easier on Cam. He'd caught her peeking at him throughout the day. Quick, covert glances that were making his nerves stand on end. He decided to wait until the bonfire and then make his move. They needed to talk.

Unfortunately, once dinner was over and nightfall had thrown them into darkness, the alcohol started flowing around the same time that the bonfire lit up the nighttime sky. Cam pretended to nurse a beer, but none of it ever passed his lips. Not if he intended to keep his shit together.

He noticed she had what looked like a mixed drink with a colorful umbrella poking out of it. On closer inspection, he noted the pale pink color of the umbrella and realized she was drinking a non-alcoholic beverage. Good. He didn't want to deal with an inebriated Ponytail.

Years of surveillance work meant Cam could patiently wait her out. He was prepared to bide his time all night if he had to.

# Chapter Eighteen

L ACEY WAS BESIDE herself. When Cameron appeared at the rodeo earlier, she'd nearly whooped with delight and flung herself into his arms. It had taken a supreme effort on her part to act unmoved by his return. She'd been pleased with herself for managing a halfhearted wave of hello before she left him standing slack-jawed in the Arizona dust.

*Serves him right*, she thought. *Did he really imagine he could come into her bed, melt her bones with mind-blowing sex, and then vanish without a word?* Nope. That wasn't going to be how this played out. If he didn't want her, *all* of her, he would have to say so. The silent act was not going to cut it.

Now that he was back, they were sharking around each other in this ridiculous dance that wasn't fooling anyone. She was careful not to let the cocktails being passed around find their way to her hands. Tossing back a few drinks might make her brave but they would also impair her judgment and that wasn't a good idea. No. The longer he kept his distance, the more she must be on high alert.

Eventually, Alex produced a guitar, and the mood started shifting. One of the things she'd discovered about this particular Justice

Brother is his amazing talent and hard-core grasp of every song made popular in the past twenty years. The guy could sing.

He was playing a classic Eagles song while the others sang along when she noticed Cameron slip away into the shadows.

*Good Lord! Was he kidding?* She was surprised when her quarry made a hasty retreat in the direction of his home. *Was he really just going to walk away? Again?* Lacey's heart sank. She had truly believed they had at least a chance. Watching him turn his back on her, and everyone for that matter, killed her. He said he was broken. Maybe he was right.

Hesitating didn't seem like a good option, so she got up and quietly followed him. Maybe she was being a fool, she didn't know, but the time had come to stop all this idiocy. She wanted him, and she was absolutely sure he wanted her. Getting him to admit it was more than casual sex was the real problem. The distinct possibility he wasn't going to let her in was still there.

Squashing the soul-crushing fear, she crept into the shadows with fingers crossed. Oh yeah, and her panties were damp. Not much about that situation had changed during the time he'd been away. She still wanted him with all her being.

Slowing her steps, she searched for what to do next. There wasn't any reason to confront him. The back of him said more than any words could. She couldn't smile and be the happy friend, either. That would just kill her too, only slower.

*What the hell was she supposed to do?*

The sound of his door shutting with a firm push brought her senses snapping back to the present. She looked around, realizing she'd followed him as far as his driveway. This was the first time she'd come so far down the lane past her little house.

Not having given much thought to what Cameron's home would be like, she gasped at the gorgeous wood cabin nestled among a stand of trees that gave it privacy from the lane.

The two-story structure had broad wooden steps leading from the driveway to a wide stone porch under a heavy wooded pergola.

At night, the lights from the house illuminated the welcoming porch littered with comfortable looking wood furniture and terra cotta pots brimming with desert succulents. It looked so homey. *Was it weird that she was so surprised?* Nothing about Cameron's demeanor would lead anyone to envision his home being so warm and inviting. The man was full of endless surprises.

Cam made it to the cabin in quick time once he realized he'd left something vitally important to his plans at home. When he'd changed into casual clothes earlier, he'd left the small jewelry box with the delicate pearl earrings he'd bought for Lacey on his nightstand. Slipping away once the music started, he figured that it would take but a few minutes to run home and get back before anyone missed him.

Not that the 'anyone' he had in mind was paying much attention to his whereabouts anyway.

Regardless, he was determined to draw her aside someplace quiet where they could talk. They had to find a way to handle what was happening between them. Or rather, *he* had to find a way. She seemed to be handling herself fine. He was the mess.

Grabbing the box, he paused and opened it. Tiny pearl drop earrings were set in the plush padding. The low lights of his bedroom gave the delicate pearls a warm glow. He hoped giving her jewelry wasn't a step too far. The moment he saw the pretty earrings, he wanted her to have them. *They were like her. Charming. Light.* He sighed.

Lowering the lights as he made his way through the house, Cam stopped dead in his tracks when he flung open the front door and spied a startled freckled face staring at him from the driveway. She had a deer caught in the headlights look that matched how he was feeling inside. Remembering the box in his hand, he slid it into his pants pocket while his eyes drank in the sight of her.

She'd worn a very short summery dress to the barbecue that

molded perfectly to every one of her curves. The sexy cowgirl boots were a nice touch. He was bummed that the pigtails were nowhere to be seen, but the sight of her blond tresses falling about her shoulders was recompense enough. She was beautiful.

So far, they'd flirted like crazy, kissed like the possessed, fucked liked animals, and indulged every sense in a coupling that stormed his soul. Seeing her hovering and uncertain at his front door tore at his senses.

His feet propelled him right at her even though his mind urged a more thoughtful approach. She'd shown how fearless she was by coming after him, so Cam let instinct be his guide. Nothing short of a cataclysm was going to keep him away from her.

Not now.

The sound of his feet thumping down the wooden stairs echoed in the silence. With just a few wide strides, he reached her, and without missing a beat, he swung her into his arms and headed back toward the house. The only sound she made was a short gasp when her feet left the ground. After that, all he heard was her shallow, rapid breathing.

Inside the house, he secured the door and then walked her to the massive stone fireplace that dominated the living space. Placing her carefully on her unsteady feet, he switched on the gas to bring the flames to life and then retreated several steps to look at her.

She took in in the high ceilings while Cam watched her with satisfaction. He'd helped design his home, and Draegyn had put his impressive woodworking talents to use in every inch of the interior. It was massive and masculine, and he loved every inch of it.

When she eventually returned her eyes to his, he let the energy arcing between them go wild while he held her gaze.

"Take off your dress."

*Jesus, had he just told her to strip?* He had. He'd also surprised the shit out of her, judging by the way she straightened up.

"Wh-what? Don't you want to kiss me first?" She looked confused. "Not even a hello, Cameron?"

"No. I said, take off your dress."

*Mmmhmm. So that's how it's going to be*, Lacey thought.

She was starting to know this side of him quite well. It was his default setting. Control. Iron control. By calling the shots, he got to pretend no emotions were involved. Well, that crap was coming to an end right now.

Praying she wasn't about to make a fool of herself, Lacey let her gut lead the way. It was clear that every time she and Cameron were alone, they lost their clothes with alarming speed. Not that she minded. Not at all. But this time had to be different if they were going to make real steps forward.

Sucking in a deep breath to boost her resolve, she gathered her hair, lifting the tresses away from her neck as she walked toward him. Turning around, she murmured, "Unzip me, please?"

Nothing happened for a series of heartbeats. He could, she knew, simply take her with little effort if that was what he wanted. By allowing her to have a say, they'd be entering new territory, and if she had her way, that territory would include more than sex.

Relief and indescribable pleasure surged through her when his fingers moved to the clasp at her neck and then to the zip of the dress he'd demanded she remove. Even though he was putting on a good show of being controlling and demanding, the slight trembling she detected in his touch was more endearing than any words could have been. She had to give him credit. He certainly could give as good as he got.

It was her turn to tremble after the zipper finally descended, as slowly as humanly possible, and she felt him run his fingers along her spine. The soft caress was enough to send sparks of want and need shooting through her.

*Keep breathing*, she thought. Just keep breathing.

Taking a few small steps forward but keeping her back to him, Lacey pushed the dress from her shoulders and let it fall to her waist. Though she might be fighting a deficit of confidence, she had enough experience to know he wasn't missing a single action. Feeling a small burst of female satisfaction at that thought, she went for gold with a deliberate wiggle while she bent forward slightly, easing the garment down her hips and stepping out of it. Tossing the dress aside, she ran her fingers along each thigh to adjust the scrap of stretch lace boy undies she'd worn.

*Take that, Mr. Control*, she thought.

Glad for the warmth coming from the fireplace, she turned around and immediately searched his face for clues to what he was thinking. The half-lidded gaze that had quite obviously been checking out her backside sparked and smoldered, calming the butterflies dancing in her belly.

Standing before him in her lingerie and a pair of cowboy boots, she struck what she hoped was an attractive pose with a hand on one hip while the other fluffed her hair. She almost said *come and get me* but bit back the words at the last minute because she wanted more than that.

Noting his big hands clenched at his sides, Lacey figured he was having a hard time staying put. She didn't doubt for a second that if she crooked her finger at him, he'd have her naked and spread out under him in a flash. But that wasn't the way this was going to play out. Not by a long shot. Mr. Cameron Justice was about to learn he couldn't always control the situation any more than he could ignore the feelings swirling in the cool desert night around them. She wasn't going to let him.

"Is this what you wanted?"

Although a question, the words sounded like a challenge to her ears. When she saw his chest rise and fall from the answering breath he'd sucked in, Lacey thought, *Game on!*

Cam couldn't believe it when she'd answered his demand to strip by calmly asking him to pull down the zipper and then stepping out of her dress. The sight of her mouthwatering ass in the lace underwear nearly blinded him. Hell, her body was so goddamn perfect that it looked photoshopped. Add the unexpected boots to the feminine lingerie, and the lady steamed up the room by doing nothing more than standing there.

His rational side knew his behavior was caveman at best, in a situation that he'd already determined required some motherfucking finesse. When he was away from her, his conscience worked overtime, telling him to play it cool, be detached, and let her be. As soon as he saw her, though, all that flew out the window in record time.

She looked different somehow. His training meant he picked up on even the smallest clues in the overall picture. After forcing his mind from the haze of lust fogging his thoughts, a thousand tiny details rushed at him.

First, everything she had on was new to her wardrobe. Gone were the baggy second-hand pants and nondescript hoodies. The style she chose now complemented her glorious figure. His Ponytail had good taste.

Second, she'd gotten some sort of makeover. Nothing drastic, more like a haircut that gave her beautiful blond mane a very sexy swoosh. Each time her head moved, the hair swung and shifted on her shoulders.

She was also wearing nail color, making him wonder if she'd had her toes painted as well. While he liked the kick-ass boots, he suddenly had an aching desire to see her bare feet.

While those easily discerned subtleties were important, there was something else. Something way more nuanced. Being at the Villa had been good for her. In just a few short weeks, she'd blossomed into an even more beautiful and self-assured woman than the one he'd first met. Her courage turned him on. She'd faced danger and survived challenges that would make most people crumple.

And then there was the provocative come hither look she was sending his way, which hinted at a confidence that made his balls ache. When she fluffed her hair and pouted so prettily at him, he was a goner.

"Is this what you wanted?" she purred. And just like that, he was hard as a rock and out of his fucking mind with need.

Lacey didn't wait for his answer. Being on a one-woman mission to open up the incredibly hot, sexy man standing just out of her reach was important, yes. But standing there half-naked while he devoured her with his eyes had sparked a throbbing in her core that got more insistent with each passing second. She needed to put her hands on him, wanted to taste him, and planned on getting him out of his clothes so she could do just that.

Hearing the *tap, tap* of her boots on the hardwood floor, she went at him head-on in a hip-swaying saunter that snagged his gaze. "My turn," was all she said while her hands landed on the buttons of his shirt. He was breathing heavily now but continued to stand rigid and straight as she slowly slid each button through its hole, one by one, until she'd arrived at the waist of his pants. Yanking the shirttails free, she finished with the buttons, opening the shirt so she could gaze upon his magnificent chest.

*My God*, she thought. It wasn't right that he was so beautiful. And he smelled so good, too. Lacey couldn't help herself from leaning in close to breathe in his enticing scent. *He was all man, that's for sure.*

"You're playing with fire, woman."

*Oooooh, she liked it when he growled.*

"I know." She sighed as her nose crinkled with glee.

His eyes narrowed at her playful taunt. Putting both hands on his rock-solid abs, she stroked his skin, whispering close to his ear, "Let's feed the flames a bit, shall we?"

That was all it took for him to reach for her, but she'd been waiting for him to relax some of his formidable restraint and easily side-stepped his touch. Sliding quickly behind him, she peeled the shirt down his arms, exposing his massive shoulders and the bicep tattoo that never failed to catch her attention. Tossing the shirt aside, she placed her lips gently on one shoulder as her hand palmed his butt. The other hand snaked around the front and crawled across his torso in a possessive embrace. *Touching him was like an aphrodisiac.* The more she caressed his skin, the deeper she fell into the sensual thrall that was sweeping her away.

With her lips still on his shoulder and hand on his chest, she felt as well as heard the lusty grunt that broke from his throat.

*How could he continue to pretend this was nothing but sex?* They had barely started, yet he was already trembling. So was she, just thinking about what she wanted to do to him. Poor man. He had no idea what was coming his way.

"Mmm. You smell good. Feel good, too," she added with another hearty caress of his ass. Pressing against him so he could feel her breasts on his back, Lacey reached around to his front, running her hands very slowly down his chest, pausing to rub his hardened nipples, and then zeroing in on the fastenings of his pants. His hands covered hers for a nanosecond, as if he might stop her, but she nipped his shoulder and shrugged off his attempt.

It didn't take but a moment to deal with the snap and reach for his zipper. Despite the trembling in her limbs, Lacey kept going before she lost her nerve. She'd been naked with him before but never because she took the initiative. Until now, she'd been happy to let him be the aggressor. After all, he did so quite well.

*Ah, what the hell*, she thought. Even though this was new territory for her, she wanted him in the worst way. Pressing herself against his back, she relished the feel of being so close to him while carefully tugging on the zipper. Instinct and desire took over when she felt the firm bulge of his erection with her fingers. Quickly swallowing the moan about to escape her mouth, she instead bit his shoulder as her hands finished their task.

Lacey slid her hands into the waistband on each hip to help ease them down his legs as she followed them to the floor, crouching behind him to help as he toed off his shoes and raised each foot until the pants joined his shirt on the floor. From her crouch, she had a dizzying view of his muscled thighs and tight butt.

*Oh yes,* she thought with lascivious delight, when she discovered he was wearing the cotton boxer briefs she found so damn sexy. Standing, Lacey made sure to drift her fingers softly over his fabulous backside, causing him to clench the muscles in his butt. She couldn't help but smile. The guy was positively drool-worthy from the rear. Impossibly broad shoulders, narrow waist, lean hips, muscular legs, and an ass that deserved its own billboard in Times Square.

She let him stand there for a moment as she admired the enticing, masculine view. Quickly unsnapping her bra, Lacey shimmied out of it and draped it over his shoulder. His surprise was apparent when he reached up and gathered the silk and lace in his hands before throwing it aside. As her lingerie landed on a nearby chair, she pressed back against him, shuddering slightly when her hard, aching nipples touched his skin.

For a while, her mind went blank and all she could concentrate on was how his body felt against her. He was hard in all the right places. *Mmm.* Both of them were breathing heavier while her hands wandered, eventually ending up splayed across his chest. Everything about him set her senses on fire.

Pressing eager kisses across his shoulders blades, she moved her hands in a tantalizingly slow descent, mapping every inch of his magnificent torso. When she reached the bulge of his erection, Lacey never paused, using both hands to mold his hardness in the confinement of his briefs. Cameron's shudders emboldened her actions, making her cup and fondle his swelling cock until his head fell back and a tortured moan rumbled from deep inside him.

*She definitely had his attention now.*

His passionate response made her want to spend an eternity exploring his heated flesh with her questing fingers. There was something uniquely erotic about touching him so intimately through what was left of his clothing. The way his briefs molded his enflamed manhood made her mouth go dry. It was almost as gloriously enticing as seeing him naked.

He surprised her by reaching back, grabbing her ass in both hands, and dragging her forward until her mound slammed against the curve of his rock-hard ass.

*Whoa!* Lacey couldn't stop the corresponding response that ripped through her as she gripped his erection and ground herself against him. As her body flooded with desire and urged her to chase the orgasm building in her aching core she struggled to get hold of herself, before all control was lost.

She was enjoying this too much to draw away from him just yet, so she stayed behind him, grinding against his backside while her greedy fingers continued to stroke him through his clothes. He groaned and shook when she placed a very wet, open-mouth kiss between his shoulder blades.

*Time for round two*, she thought, kicking off her boots.

She slid slowly around his body, leaving a trail of wet kisses along his shoulders and then finally across his chest. Standing in front of him, she moved her hands on his bared skin and look deeply into his smoldering gaze.

The only thing she could do was go for broke. She had to lay it all on the line if she wanted this giant of a man. Since he obviously couldn't, she must be the one to share what she was feeling. Hopefully, hearing how she felt might reach inside his walled-off emotions and find a way to release his heart.

"I missed you while you were gone, Cameron. Did you know? Could you feel me thinking about you?"

Sparkles of emotion lit up his green eyes. He *had* been thinking about her, she was sure of it. Now if only he would say so.

*C'mon, big guy,* she chanted silently. *Be brave. Take a chance. You can trust me. I'll be here to catch you when you fall.*

He looked at her so pensively that she worried he would reject what she was offering. Biting her lip to stop it trembling, she silently prayed she was doing the right thing. It would kill her if he walked away again.

"You are a*lways* in my thoughts, Ponytail," he murmured in a deep, throaty growl as he pushed a strand of her hair out of the way. His gentle touch tracing the shell of her ear got her senses cranking on all cylinders.

"I was a prick for not calling you. Believe me, I know that." His lips quirked in a wry, half-smile that melted her wildly thumping heart.

*Aww*, she thought. He was being so brave and sweet. She knew just the right way to reward him for his honesty.

"Well, I'll have to think about forgiving you," she replied with an arched eyebrow and a look she hoped suggested how peeved she'd been by his silence. "For now, though, I think you need a reminder for the next time you think being all tough and brooding is the way to go with me."

Her last words she'd accented with a firm stroke against his huge bulge and a naughty squeeze for good measure.

# Chapter Nineteen

DROPPING DOWN IN front of him and tugging at the waistband of his briefs, she knew he'd been shocked when he reflexively tried to stop what she was about to do.

As if! Absolutely nothing was going to get in the way of what she wanted, which was his twitching hardness, gripped by her hands. Against her tongue. In her mouth. The desire to explore him with all her senses had been haunting her dreams. This was her chance to let those desires run free.

Pushing the cotton down his massive thighs ,the sight of his rigid cock springing from its confinement made her giddy with need.

*Did he know how magnificent he was?*

A brief surge of jealousy for every woman who had ever seen him like this invaded her brain. Doubts, born from inexperience, battered her composure. She'd pictured him before with supermodels and beautiful women by the dozens. After all, he was too damn hot and gorgeous to be living like a monk. Surely, women lined have up for a chance to experience his smoldering sexual prowess.

*Well, be that as it may.*

He was a grown man in his thirties and hardly inexperienced.

Only what was happening right here and now mattered, not the ghosts of his sexual past.

It was up to her to take what she wanted. Waiting for him to lose his reluctance and let honest feelings anywhere near his broken heart wasn't going to get them anywhere. Men, apparently, did not excel in the realm of emotions. He'd more than proven that with the foot dragging and running away.

She liked what she saw once the briefs were stripped away. He looked like one of those statues depicting male perfection. The heavy-lidded expression on his face and the way his nostrils flared with each of her caresses gave Lacey the boost of confidence she needed to continue her innocent exploration of his flesh.

From her position on her knees, she sat back and drank him in without embarrassment. Frankly, she was content to simply stare at how beautiful he was forever. Seeing him in all his naked glory made a flood of desire drench her already damp panties. His cock was huge. She studied the size and shape of it and marveled that something so big had been inside her. Feeling her sex clench at the memory of the way he'd pounded into her brought a small smile to her lips.

Reaching out with tentative fingers, Lacey explored his hardness, gasping slightly when it throbbed at her touch. She'd never considered the male penis all that much before now. Sure, she knew basic anatomy, but *this* was something else entirely. Knowing his sex had swelled with desire for her was a heady realization. He was hard because of her. The thought made her shiver with satisfaction.

Both hands were on him now, running gentle caresses along his impressive length. Not sure what to do, she looked up into his face as she cradled his balls in one hand and gripped his staff with the other.

"Show me," was all she said.

He knew what she was asking because he moved her hands away and proceeded to give her a bird's-eye view of him stroking from root to tip while he cupped his balls. She watched in fascination, her breath hitching every now and then, while he showed her how to handle him.

What a glorious instrument the male cock was with skin much softer than she imagined, stretched taut by desire. She really couldn't help the involuntary way she licked her lips while she sat there transfixed by what was before her eyes. As if the turgid length of him wasn't enough to scorch her panties off, the plump, bulbous head held a definite fascination for her. Remembering how it felt to have that fat knob push her lips wide as it sought entrance to her body made her moan out loud.

His knowing gaze told her he remembered what it felt like too. When a glob of clear fluid leaked from the tip, Lacey gathered it with her finger and brought it to her mouth. He tasted, well ... he tasted yummy. After inserting the finger into her mouth, she was rewarded with a look so hot and scorching, from where he loomed high above her, that she winced from his intensity.

Now it was her turn to be the one stroking. She wanted to turn him on, yes, but she wanted to answer her own desires as well. It was a tiny bit shocking to realize how much she wanted to lick him with her tongue and take him into her mouth. Considering the size of him, she wondered just how much she'd be able to take. It was time to find out.

Rising onto her knees, she reached out and swept his hands aside, so she could replace his touch with her own. He was so tall that being on her knees brought his cock and balls within easy reach of her mouth. Holding him with both hands, she aimed him at her lips while dipping down swiftly to leave a wet, sucking kiss on the fleshy tip that emerged from her grasp.

Cameron groaned like a man in agony while readjusting the stance of his trembling legs. Drawing away from his tense, sexually charged body, Lacey employed one of the oldest coquettish ploys known to women the world over when she gazed up at him through lowered eyes, head slightly tilted. The primal man inside would recognize her actions as flirtatious and submissive. It was seduction with modesty.

Using her hands to mimic the strokes he'd shown her, it was easy to fall into a heart-pounding trance as she watched his flesh slide through her fingers. He was harder and wider than she imagined, and the skin she touched felt hot and flushed. When his hand reached out to cover hers, she gasped as he showed her just how tight she could grip him.

*Gentle not required!*

Before long, she had explored him enough with eyes and hands. Feeding the pulsing in her core, she let loose the hungry need to take him into her mouth. This was what she'd been fantasizing about.

*Was she supposed to feel this needy for his taste?* She didn't know.

Lifting his cock with her hand to expose the underside, Lacey flattened her tongue against the throbbing vein she found and licked her way along his length. When she arrived at the head, she swirled her tongue around the ridged flesh and once again, kissed him gently right on the tip. His dick quivered, and she smiled.

Cupping the twin spheres below, she angled his hard-on to make it easier for her to slide her open mouth down his shaft in slow, sucking waves that found her taking more of him than she first thought possible. She liked the way he felt sliding along her tongue. Even liked the slight gag that let her know he was deep in her throat.

It was thrilling when she felt his hands slide into her hair and grip the back of her head. In the darkened room lit by glowing flames in the big fireplace, their shadows blended as one each time her mouth sank on his staff. She was moaning, saliva spilling from her mouth as she tongued his swollen flesh and sucked him with greedy delight. She loved his big hands holding her tight as his hips tensed and bucked from what she was making him feel.

*It wasn't enough.* He was holding back—she could feel it—and god, but she wanted him wild and out of control. The same way he had made her feel each time they'd been together. Suspecting he was only indulging her needs rather than addressing his own, she doubled down with a ferocious onslaught of sucking and licking intended to bring him to his knees.

He growled at her, low and serious. The sound made her ache with need but he didn't want to come in her mouth, and she had no intention of letting him play the gentleman. No, she wanted to know what it felt like when he lost his reserve and let her have all of him. Every inch. Every drop. Every spasm.

Plunging her head up and down, she took him deeper and deeper into her mouth until she was desperate to taste that last part of him. He gave up trying to pull her away from his straining cock. The way it throbbed and twitched against her tongue made Lacey whimper as he fucked her mouth while he swelled even larger. Grabbing his ass, she submitted to the pressure of his hands and the thrusting of his hips.

An explosion of raw heat detonated in her pussy at the same time his hips bucked involuntarily. Cameron threw his head back, letting go a throaty growl while his cock jerked uncontrollably against her tongue and he came in rapid spurts of heated liquid. It was like nothing she could have ever imagined. The heat, his helpless response, her wildly sucking mouth. It was all so hot. She worked on his glorious cock until she'd squeezed the last drop from him. He tasted wild and musky, and she loved it.

When it was over, she let his softening sex slide from her mouth and sat back to study her handiwork. The sight of her saliva mixed with his come glistening on his flesh hit her like a sledgehammer. His hand was still tangled in her hair when she leaned forward one last time and sweetly kissed his beautiful, beautiful cock.

She wasn't sure what she looked like but assumed her hair was a mess. Her mouth seemed a bit swollen too. A shy smile that she wore like a badge of honor spread on her face when she thought about what had just occurred.

He lifted her up, guiding her with the hand still clutched against her head. She rose and found herself crushed against his much larger frame when he grabbed a handful of her ass and hauled her tight against him. He looked at her for a long moment then crashed his mouth down on hers. *Yes!* her heart cried as he devoured the response that leaped from her soul.

Flinging her arms around his neck, she lifted her body against his, rubbing her aching breasts against the soft hair on his solid chest.

His kiss was rough and insistent. She went wherever he led, gave when he demanded more, and opened to him as completely as she could.

Somewhere in the midst of that incendiary kiss, she lost herself so completely that it hadn't registered when he'd swept her into his arms and moved them into his bedroom. It wasn't until she heard the door slam and felt herself flying through the air that she came to her senses. She was sprawled rather ungracefully on a huge wood bed large enough for an entire family. He yanked the bedspread from under her ass, tossing it to the floor.

Trying to right herself into some sort of position that didn't resemble a quivering mess, she was stopped by his grasp on her hips. Pulling her forward to the edge of the bed, he tugged her panties off and spread her thighs before she had time to process what he was doing. The position completely exposed her to his gaze. All she could do was slump back onto the cushioned mattress and tremble while his eyes devoured her the same way she had gazed at him.

Lacey knew he could see how excited she was from sucking him off. She was wet and aching for his possession. He mimicked the way she had tasted his fluid, when he ran a single finger up and down her slit, unfurling her pussy lips and coating his finger with her excitement. When he licked the creamy fluid from his finger, she undulated and moaned. He didn't miss the message in her rolling hips because he suddenly thrust his middle finger deep into her and wiggled it around.

"Oh, Cameron," she cried over and over.

Hearing his heavy breathing mixed with her quiet moans took her to the edge and fast.

He removed his finger from her wet heat but kept his hands between her legs, holding her open.

"I love how fucking wet you are."

Her sex clenched at his words.

"Mmm, that's right, Ponytail. Squeeze that beautiful pussy for me. I want to see you explode with cream. For me, babe. Only for me."

He licked her then. First along her gaping hole and then at the cluster of nerves that made up her distended clit. She dug her heels into the mattress and bucked against his tongue. He laughed and said, "My lady likes that, hmm?" while he flicked his clever tongue against those nerves over and over until her insides were clenching frantically.

"You're playing with fire, y'know," she murmured just as he had done earlier.

Sinking his teeth into her inner thigh, he sent shockwaves up and down her spine. "I know," he answered. "Paybacks are a bitch, aren't they?"

Then it was *her* hand tangled in his hair, holding his head the way he had done to her. This time, it was her hips bucking wildly as his tongue and lips worked her sensitive nub. When he pushed his finger back into her dripping wetness and sucked her clit into his mouth, she went up and over so fast she could only cry out in helpless abandon as a pulsing climax ripped her apart.

Instead of calming once the tension from her aching body eased, Lacey took advantage of the release to gather herself together and push forward. He still wasn't ready to open up completely, so she had more work to do. Before her orgasm had subsided, she pulled him onto the bed, scooted back to give him room, and then pushed him onto his back. Straddling his hips, she put her hands on his and made a halfhearted attempt to hold him down. His laughter at the attempt to subdue him brought a huge smile spreading across her face.

"Don't think I can hold you down?" she taunted.

Leaning forward, she let her breasts swing slightly across his chest. The harsh breath he sucked in wiped the laugh from his face as her pebbled nipples connected with his skin.

Suddenly, he sat up, gathering her snugly against his groin with his hands on her ass. "Witch," he replied a scant second before his mouth latched onto her neck.

Sensing her control was fading, she whimpered quietly in his ear, "Don't leave like that again. I won't be ignored, Cameron."

He looked at her, nodded and asked, "Have you forgiven me yet, Ponytail?"

"No," she answered bitingly. "What are you going to do to make it up to me?"

In their present position as she straddled his hips and sat high in his lap, her breasts danced near his face in a clear invitation he didn't hesitate to take advantage of. Cupping both breasts, he scorched her skin with his hot breath as he kneaded her aching flesh. Finally, when she couldn't take anymore, he guided a tightly beaded nipple into his mouth and sucked hard.

Lacey really, *really* liked the visual of his dark head feasting on her flesh. She found watching him suckle her breasts profoundly sensual. The way his mouth opened wide to take in as much as he could brought a moan of pleasure from deep inside. When he released her nipple and her breast popped from his mouth with a heavy jiggle, something snapped inside her. Taking the other fleshy mound in his hand, he applied the same torturous suckling until she was writhing in his lap, both hands clutching his head as he brought her swiftly to the edge.

Only the sensation of his chest, heaving deep with each breath, stopped her from falling apart. Proof that he was as equally as undone as she was reminded Lacey that breaking down his barriers and getting them to a place where he could admit to feeling something for her was key.

Reaching between their bodies, she quickly enfolded his reawakened cock in her hand and brought it to the opening of her body. It took but a second after that to forcefully impale herself on his surging staff, causing Cameron's head to roll back in surprise. She seriously doubted he was prepared for her to be the aggressor, taking from him what she needed.

With his hands clutching her hips, he grunted once or twice as he physically moved her around on his rapidly swelling dick. She let him have his way for a bit, enjoying every minute of his possession. He showed her how to bring her knees up tight to his side, with her feet on the bed as he pumped up into her. It felt incredible. She rocked against him, whimpering and gasping. He was so damn big. With her arms locked around his neck, his hands were free to explore every inch of naked skin on her body.

Eventually, their motion slowed and became less frenzied. Lacey could feel his heart banging against his chest where she pressed up against him. Each thundering beat throbbed in his cock as well. Connecting with him on such a basic level was exquisitely erotic and deeply satisfying.

When he softly groaned she hoped that meant he felt it too. This was where she belonged. Somehow, this was home. Cameron buried deep in her body, the two of them plastered against one another, lover's moans and the delicious sound of her wet pussy devouring him. It was so perfect. *She felt complete.*

The scorching realization that she loved the man quivering in her embrace filled her heart and caused a tidal wave of intense heat and creamy desire to flood her core. His hands grabbed her ass and held her firmly while his pulsing cock danced inside her.

His nipped where he nuzzled her neck and groaned her name. Happiness welled up in her heart. Pushing upright and rearranging her legs so she could ride him home, Lacey silently prayed he was finally close to flying without a parachute.

He kept his eyes locked on hers, and his hands on her voluptuous breasts as she began moving on him. In this position, she had all the control, so she took them on a guided tour of every stroke and angle imaginable. Occasionally, she would stop moving and lean down to kiss him with an awful lot of tongue and a good deal of saliva flowing between them. Everything really was better when wet.

He tried to force her to pick up speed by bucking his hips, but she refused to relinquish control. No, she preferred a slow, languid rhythm intended to drive him wild. She knew it was working when he began thrashing beneath her.

"Is this what you wanted, darlin'?" she drawled next to his ear, wanting to remind him that while he might have started this, she intended to finish it.

His response was something between a menacing growl and a

helpless moan. She lowered slowly onto his cock, taking him balls deep, and then stopped. His gaze smoldered while his cheekbones flushed, and his neck tensed. When she ground her pussy against his groin with a slow rolling of her hips, his eyes closed and a frustrated hiss tore from his throat.

She leaned in, nipped at his ear, and then licked the same spot. He groaned out loud.

"Tell me. I need to know," she growled while letting loose with a flurry of hard slapping thrusts that had them both grunting and shaking with raw need.

With her pussy tightening, she could feel the orgasm building from a place so deep inside that it almost hurt. He was pressing against more than her cervix. This complicated man, her dark knight, was invading her heart and soul.

Slowing once more, she asked again, punctuating her words with deep, rolling stabs of her hips. "Tell me, is this what you wanted?"

When she tightened her inner muscles for emphasis, his control snapped. Surging up into her, he cried out a strangled, "Yes! Yes! Oh, my god, Lacey. Yes!"

Hearing her name burst from his lips in the throes of their passion made her seriously lose her shit.

He didn't stop there. As she continued rolling and grinding her hips while her pussy clenched and contracted around him, he went wild underneath her, bucking and groaning, calling her name over and over.

Hearing him shout her name pushed her body to maximum sensory overload, splintering into a million shards shot with a pleasure so exquisite she cried out as her hips rode his. He came undone as her climax overtook them.

*Was that her screaming?*

Suddenly, he wrapped her in his arms and pulled her down for a blazing kiss that stopped at nothing. With his tongue mimicking each upward thrust of his cock, she felt him go rigid and swell even larger. When he exploded deep inside her, she whimpered into his neck, chanting his name.

What happened next was completely unexpected. As his balls emptied into her wet depths and he cried out her name over and over, just as his orgasm began to subside he murmured low and deep, "I need you, baby. Need you," tightening his arms until she was crushed to his still shaking body.

*Wow*, she thought. *Mission accomplished.*

# Chapter Twenty

SLOWLY COMING AWAKE, Cam absorbed a shit ton of sensory input before his eyes even opened. A feeling of peaceful calm, like none he'd known before, enveloped his body and mind. Remembering how his Ponytail had taken them on a sensual journey that had ended with him shouting her name as he exploded inside her made his morning hard-on spike higher and harder with each passing second. Her delicious scent hung in the air and clung to his skin. It was going to be a very good morning.

Turning on his side, Cam prepared to reach for her when his opening eyes caught sight of the empty space next to him. Sitting up in a hurry, he found the imprint of her head on the empty pillow but absolutely nothing else lingered in his room to suggest she'd even been there. The panties he'd torn off her weren't anywhere to be seen.

*What the fuck? Where the hell was she?*

Flinging aside the sheet tangled around his hips, he left the comfort and warmth of his bed, prowling naked into the main part of the house in search of his sexy lover. It didn't take but a few seconds to understand she wasn't there.

*Shit.* Finding her gone was the last thing he expected.

Standing there naked, sporting a quickly diminishing erection, Cam scrubbed both hands back and forth through his hair and across the stubble covering his face. Grabbing at his chest like a man in the midst of a heart attack, he was overwhelmed with a crushing sense of loss. As if her absence foretold an impending doom.

*Had he done something stupid? Fuck.* He couldn't remember anything except a handful of memories swirling with so much passion and emotion that he could barely take it all in. His intention to sit down with her and talk about what was going on between them had been completely circumvented when his dick got hard at the sight of her in those damn cowboy boots and not much else.

Finding his pants laying on the floor where they'd landed after she'd pushed them down his legs, Cam quickly stepped into them commando style in his increasing hurry to find out where she'd gone and why. Yanking up the zipper, he snapped the waistband closed a second before the slight bulge in his pocket registered.

*What the …?* Pushing his hand into the pocket, he withdrew the small black jewelry box containing the delicate pearl earrings he had wanted to give her as a peace offering.

*Oh, Jesus,* he thought. *Had he really been that stupid?*

Instead of explaining his ignorant behavior while he'd been gone and softening her up with some modest bling, he'd once again reverted to type and simply demanded she get naked. So he could fuck her. The sour taste in his mouth let him know what an asshole he'd been. ·

*What the hell was wrong with him?*

One minute, he wanted to keep her at a distance, and the next, he was going at her like his dick was a divining rod in search of her sweet pussy. Fuck. Fuck. *Fuck!* That wasn't what he intended. Or was it?

Hurrying to find the rest of his clothes, he quickly pulled on an old t-shirt plus a pair of ratty house shoes and headed for the door. He didn't care that he looked like hell. He didn't care that anyone seeing him would know how his night had ended. All he cared about was finding Lacey and fixing whatever he'd done.

Slamming out of the house, he decided against firing up his

truck, opting to stomp like a madman along the dirt lane that would take him to the casita. And if she wasn't there, he would move on to the big house.

With each pounding thud of his feet on the packed dirt, Cam remembered more about the previous night. He was ashamed of his earlier thought that what they did was just fucking. The sharpening memories of her seduction, not just of his body but also his heart, invaded his mind. She'd asked for more, and as a shiver of awareness shot along his spine, he remembered giving it to her. Remembered crying her name a thousand times, remembered telling her of his need. For her.

At the casita, he tapped on the front door even though there were no signs she was home. Shit. That meant she was in the office or at the big house. Neither of those options appealed to him since they each involved the possibility of other people being present.

*Ah, what the fuck.* Screw all this sneaking around crap. She deserved better from him. Time to buck the hell up and act like a man. He only hoped he hadn't blown it with her completely.

Finding Drae and Alex in deep conversation as he entered the Villa's large kitchen, Cam searched for evidence of Lacey's presence but found none. He didn't especially want to talk to anyone but her right now, but since both men saw him, he couldn't exactly turn his back and walk away.

"Yo, dude!" Drae chuckled. "You look like shit. Too much partying last night? Couldn't help but notice that you and Blondie went missing at the same time."

The man's smirk did nothing to lighten Cam's mood. "Shut up, Drae."

Holy crap, he sounded like a wounded animal even to his own ears. The knowing look Alex fixed on him didn't help.

Drae held his hands up in mock surrender. "My bad, my bad. Sorry. Who you sleep with is none of my business."

Cam caught the flash of a conspiratorial look between his two brothers but didn't slow down long enough to consider what it meant.

"I mean it. Shut the fuck up! You don't know what you're talking about."

"Well, I know enough to see more is going on than just the naked rhumba with someone who, I might add, is technically your employee."

Barely acknowledging Cam's stern look, Drae laughed and continued, "Oh, like I'm gonna shrink from one of your dark scowls! Get real. Look bro, all I'm trying to say is I really hope you know what you're doing. That girl is out of your fucking league, man."

Alex nodded in agreement.

"Everyone here thinks she's the tits *and* the balls. Even that grumpy bastard over there," Drae added with the jerk of his head in Alex's direction. "And by the way, if you don't get an assistant soon," he said, still looking at Alex while swinging his finger back and forth between himself and Cam, "we're gonna fucking mutiny. Capisce?"

Cam reluctantly admired the way Drae had diplomatically placed himself as antagonist and co-conspirator with each of them. Smart move. Meant he could say whatever the fuck he wanted and he'd have to stand there and take it.

"Back to *Ponytail*," Drae challenged with dripping emphasis on the endearment Cam had let slip earlier. "She's got quite a posse of friends and admirers. The lady's smart and quick as shit. Word around the barn is that not only did she get the office back in shape, but she's also added a few touches of her own to our management style. I believe you'll be getting a MEMO about Throwback Thursday. Apparently, we're all gonna bond over crappy eighties music and grungy nineties fashion!"

Alex and Drae laughed in unison, shaking their heads in wonder at the idea. Cam wasn't surprised that she'd fit in so easily or that she'd taken on her new life with determination. *Why had he been trying so hard to act like her appearance in his life had been no big deal?*

Drae moved a few feet from his shoulder and crossed his arms over his chest. "What I'm trying to say is, if you're just messing with her, you might want to think that through. She's not like your usual emotionless fembots. She deserves better, man." He shrugged. "If you think you have some obligation to look after her, that's cool. But believe me, she won't be by herself for very long. There isn't anyone here, ladies included, who doesn't have some form of a crush on her."

Drae and Alex both laughed in unison again, and Cam felt the white-hot flare of insane jealousy rise again in his mind.

The feeling scared the shit out of him, making him feel hot and cold at the same time. He didn't like it, not one bit. Jealousy set the beast inside him on an angry prowl the minute it shot through his mind. Feeling out of control and not knowing how to contain the flood of feelings and emotions sweeping him away, Cam reverted to form while he tried to get a grip.

"You looking for a new conquest, Drae? Need a fuck buddy? Well," he growled, "won't be the first time you had my sloppy seconds."

The startled gasp that split the air behind him brought three pairs of eyes in search of the source. The last thing Cam expected was to swing around and find Lacey hovering in the doorway, a bunch of papers in her hand and a look of absolute horror on her face. She'd clearly heard what he'd said.

He reflexively moved toward her, gesturing as if in supplication. "Lacey, I can ..."

*Crack!* Her hand hauled back and smacked him so hard he staggered for a moment. From somewhere behind him, Cam heard Drae mutter, "Whoa!"

He silently wished a hole would open in the floor and swallow him whole before this awful moment got any messier.

"Fuck you, Cameron!" a white-faced Lacey screamed at him. "Who the fuck do you think you are?"

She had never uttered a single swear word in his presence until now. All three men gasped at her foul language.

"I can explain," he gritted out, hating that Alex and Drae were witnessing what was essentially going to be his downfall.

"No!" she spat out as she slapped the stack of papers she'd been holding on the marble counter. Turning on him with both hands on her hips and a look of complete disgust on her face, she looked him up and down with derision dripping from her every pore.

"There is no explaining *sloppy seconds*. Ever! You're a fucking pig. And I hate you!"

Her words hit him square in the face even harder than the slap. He'd been right all along, that she was too good for him. Too real. Too honest. Look what he'd done to her. The self-loathing that lashed at his soul was too much for him to bear.

*She hated him.*

Escape seemed like the only option in the face of what had just detonated between them. He made for the door, looking back one last time to see her shove trembling knuckles against her mouth as her body shook with the emotion she was choking back. Seeing her like that cracked open a hole in his heart.

Now, he really *was* broken.

Lacey stood there frozen but not numb. No, the pain from what she'd overheard was tearing her apart inside. She'd been such a fool to hope they were moving to a better place in their relationship after last night. They hadn't shared anything but body fluids. *Sloppy seconds? How could he say that?* She felt sick.

She heard Alex, dear grumpy, disorganized Alex, issue a single terse command. All he needed to say was "Draegyn" in that tone he used that said it wasn't a good idea not to obey.

When Drae moved to go after Cameron, she snapped.

"Oh, sure! Run after him, the poor thing. Y'know, gentlemen, all that tortured soul bullshit is just that—BULLSHIT!"

She almost laughed at the shocked expressions on both their faces, but that didn't stop her from speaking her mind.

"Shit happens. In everyone's life. News flash! You three aren't the only ones who've had bad stuff happen. The thing is, though, in Cameron's case at least, he's still pissing and moaning about stuff that happened … what? Like decades ago? When is it enough? Seriously! Why does he get to cling to past hurts and traumas but everyone else is expected to move past those things? Run after him if you have to. Clearly, you'd know better than sloppy old me."

*Had she imagined it, or did they both just cringe at her choice of words?*

Exasperated, she glanced around the big, modern kitchen where this strange turn of events had gone down. She liked it here, but this was Cameron's home. He belonged here, not her. That Alex and Drae's first instinct was to chase after him said a lot.

She was startled, and it showed when Alex moved silently to her side and put his arm around her.

"Honey, everything's gonna be all right." He tightened his hold on her and jostled her in a friendly way. "C'mon, Lacey. Trust me, okay? Let me and Draegyn calm things down. We were taunting him when you walked up. He didn't mean what he said. Really. He has a habit of running away from the obvious. We all do."

The look he and Drae exchanged was fraught with meaning she didn't understand.

"You don't have to tell me he's a runner, Alex. He's been running from what's been happening between us from the moment we met. I think the message here is loud and clear. This is what he does. I'm no different or more special than anything or anyone else he's ever turned his back on."

"Ah, but you are. That's the whole point, and if you hadn't appeared when you had, I'm pretty sure he would have admitted just that … eventually. Please trust us, Lacey. Don't do anything rash, okay?"

She nodded hesitantly but didn't look at either man.

Alex left her side and told Draegyn, "You know what to do."

He started to go after Cameron but stopped to squeeze her shoulder. His look asked her not to rush to judgment, and she nodded again.

"I'm going back to work," she announced twenty seconds after Draegyn left the room. "Those papers"—she pointed at the stack she'd thrown on the counter—"all need your signature." Clearing her throat, she shifted into business mode. "If you need me, you know where I'll be."

After leaving the house, Cam made a beeline to the vehicle garage, jumped on an ATV, and headed to his house. From there, he grabbed a bottle of whisky, his sunglasses, and a side arm for good measure.

About two hours later, Drae found him. By then he'd gotten as far as an old cabin, miles from the main area of the compound, where he'd pulled over and plopped down on an ancient, rickety chair by the cabin's door. A good portion of the whisky bottle now stood empty, and a fence post some distance away was riddled with bullets from the inebriated target practice he'd been doing.

His old friend didn't say anything, just climbed out of the truck and sat down next to him. A minute went by and then Drae's hand shot out to take away the gun. Not that Cam minded. He hated guns. After the military, he'd had enough of that sort of thing. He wasn't sure why he'd grabbed it in the first place.

Once the pistol was safely put aside, Drae handed him an ice-cold bottle of water. "Take it, dude. Either that or I'll pour it down your throat myself."

The heat from the midday sun was frying his alcohol-fueled brain, so he grabbed the bottle, tore off the cap, and drank the entire thing to the head.

"Thanks."

Silence descended. Drae was waiting him out. Probably a smart move considering how crazy he'd been acting. In the end, he could only think of one thing to say.

"Is she all right?"

Drae leaned forward with his forearms on his thighs and didn't say anything at first. Cam got nervous because his friend was rarely so cautious or tentative.

*Fuck. Was Lacey all right or not?*

He hung his head, catching it with one hand, and covering his eyes. The whisky and the heat had given him a thumping good headache that one bottle of water wasn't going to cure. The fact that his conscience had been screaming at him from the moment he left the Villa probably hadn't helped.

Turning to the side with his head still supported by his hand he groaned at his friend, "Please."

Draegyn straightened in the chair he'd claimed, throwing Cam a serious expression before finally responding. Unfortunately, it wasn't the answer he wanted to hear.

"She said something after you left that I keep thinking about. Basically," he snorted, "she accused the three of us of being whiney pussies when it comes to the past."

The smirk on his face told Cam her comment had hit its mark.

"I think she may be right." Grabbing another bottle of water from the rucksack he'd carried, Drae tossed it to Cam, and then retrieved one for himself.

They sat there, downing the water, each lost in their own thoughts about the meaning of her words.

"Look at us, man. Successful in every sense of the word, with solid reputations, and more money than we need. But at the end of the day, I'm a fucked-up trust-fund baby, Alex is shouldering the aftermath of an entire war, and then there's you, my old friend. You've been carrying a tremendous chip on your shoulder because of shit your mom did decades ago. Lacey reminded us in no uncertain terms that all of that is in the past. Dragging it along like luggage through our lives means we each need a personal valet just to handle our bullshit. She wasn't wrong."

Drae stood and gathered his stuff, making moves to leave him alone. He still hadn't told him whether she was all right or not. Cam started to ask again but got cut off.

"Are you in love with this woman? You do know it's all right if you are. Fuck, dude. If you can fall in love, maybe there's hope for the whole world, y'know?"

Cam's chest heaved as he answered. "She means everything to me, Drae. I don't even know how or when that happened, but it's the truth. Believe me, I know she deserves better than someone who's irretrievably broken, but that's the way it is."

Draegyn nodded at his assessment but added, "You might be a little banged up, but you're not any more broken than I am. Or Alex, for that matter. We're survivors, Cam. That's what counts, not how we got to this point. And the hard truth of the matter is that the lady in question doesn't think you're a lost cause. How often in life do you think something like that's gonna happen? You'd be a fool to let her go without a fight. It's something that would haunt you forever, and then you really would be a broken man."

He flipped his sunglasses on and turned to walk away.

"To answer your question," he said while striding to his truck, "she's confused. Mad as hell, yeah, but what she walked in on really hurt her. To be honest, I think she'll probably bolt. If that's what you want, then by all means, stay here. If it's not, I suggest you get your shit together and go try a bit of groveling."

With that, Drae climbed into the truck, started it up, and drove away with a cloud of desert dust coming from under his wheels.

It was a while before Cam finally made ready to leave the ramshackle cabin for the ride home. He'd had a lot to think about, and he needed time to let some of the whisky-haze fade away. He wasn't surprised by what she'd said about the past being the past. She was proving the truth of that statement by just being who she was.

*Why did he presume that his painful childhood had more importance than the years of neglect and abuse she'd suffered?*

Lacey had survived a mountain of challenges and managed to stand tall. He, on the other hand, wore his challenges like a hair shirt. Never letting any of it go, living his life as though a difficult beginning was the only thing that defined him.

*Goddammit.* He'd been such a complete ass.

# Chapter Twenty-One

LACEY HADN'T FELT much like having dinner, so she settled on her back patio with a cup of yogurt and a spoon. Anything more substantial would probably make her gag anyway. How she'd held herself together and stayed busy in the office all afternoon was a mystery and a miracle. After the dreadful scene with Cameron speaking about her in such a degrading way, she'd gone numb with shock and heartbreak.

Right before the office closed for the day, she'd spied Draegyn slipping into Alex's bat cave, but no sign of the man he'd been sent to bring back.

*Just as well*, she figured. *What was the use of trying to fix this mess?*

Even though Alex had asked her to trust him, she'd spent a good portion of the afternoon contemplating what she should do now. She certainly couldn't stay here, no matter how much she wanted to.

By the end of the workday, she'd decided to finish up whatever loose ends she could and then clear out over the weekend. She still had most of her nest egg plus the generous salary the agency had provided for the work she'd done, so finding other accommodations wasn't going to be a problem. Registering with a temp service seemed like her best bet for employment, so she'd researched a couple of local agencies on the internet.

It all sounded so simple and easy compared to the heavy, crippling, Humpty Dumpty feeling around her heart. She didn't think anything could make her feel whole ever again. Losing Cameron felt like a piece of her soul had been ripped, painfully so, from her body.

The emotional lump in her throat erased any hope of choking down the rest of the yogurt.

When two fat tears welled in her eyes and ran down her cheeks, Lacey was taken by surprise. She didn't cry anymore. Life had been too serious to be distracted by boo-hoo thoughts. Feeling the hot tears streak across her face shook her up.

*Was she feeling sorry for herself, or was she weeping for the man who, by giving up on himself, had broken her heart?*

Drawing her knees up to her chest in a protective posture, she huddled in the big wood patio chair and tried not to fall apart. Staring blindly at the stone patio beneath her, she hadn't noticed another set of boots making their way across the terrace to where she sat.

"Hi."

*Good Lord!* He startled the crap out of her with his silent approach, making her jolt with surprise and almost causing her to tumble from her seat. He looked like she felt. Reflex made her want to make room for him next to her and reach out to comfort him as best she could.

*Screw that,* she thought. He could stand there until hell froze over.

"Go away," she hissed. There was no way she could take anymore. Just being around him was smashing even more of her heart to pieces.

"No. I'm not going anywhere, Ponytail. We need to talk," he said while jamming his hands into the pockets of his jeans.

When she didn't make any room for him to sit, he sighed heavily and then scooped her up into his arms, striding quickly inside the casita where he dropped her gently onto the sofa.

"We don't have anything to say," she snapped at him while arranging her body in a posture that said *Stay away!*

Letting her have the space she needed, he pulled a side chair close and lowered himself into it.

"Okay, fair enough. Maybe you don't have anything to say right now, but I hope you'll listen to what I need to tell you. Maybe after that, you'll change your mind."

Lacey tried her hardest not to look at him, but his quiet, earnest tone intrigued her until at last she lifted her shrouded eyes to his.

"I am more sorry than you can imagine for what I said earlier. It's not an excuse, but Alex and Drae were yanking my chain and I overreacted."

She blinked at him a few times as her belligerent frown turned to confusion. *What did that mean, he overreacted?* Calling her easy was a bit more than an overreaction.

"It seems I have an insane case of jealousy where you're concerned."

She punctuated her look of disbelief with a half-sneer. A jealous, possessive guy wouldn't keep walking away, as he had, over and over.

"Last night … well, last night was like nothing I've ever felt before. When I woke up this morning, I hoped we could, maybe, talk. But finding you gone meant I wasn't thinking clearly."

"Well, now you know how it feels!" she bit out. "How many times have I awakened to find you vanished into thin air?"

*Well, I told him!*

"Again, fair enough."

She gave him a hostile look and drawled, "For the record, I have a job here and a clock to punch. You were sleeping soundly, and I didn't want to disturb you. That's why I wasn't there, Cameron. I'm not your beck and call girl, and I didn't need your permission to get up and head off to work!"

So far, his so-called explanation was an epic fail. He better do a lot better if he expected her to soften. Just like that, her emotions snapped.

"You know what? I just can't take any more of this. You've made your feelings known. Can't you allow me the dignity of walking away without a post-mortem? It's the least you could do."

He reached out and snagged one of her hands in his. "This will be easier if you shut that pretty mouth of yours and let me finish."

When she started to answer, he put two fingers to her lips to silence her.

"Shh, Ponytail. Let's do this my way for now."

She almost bit him when he silenced her with his hand. It would serve him right if she drew first blood. Still, he was being awfully solemn as he tried to explain himself. That in and of itself couldn't have been easy for a man like Cameron. She doubted if he'd ever had to defend anything he'd ever done.

*Arrogant prick.* She amended that thought pretty quickly to hot and sexy arrogant prick.

He hadn't let go of her hand and turned it over on his thigh, palm facing up, while his thumb drew lazy circles on her sensitive skin. *Ooooh,* damn but he was good.

"As I was saying … I wasn't in my right mind when I ran into Drae and Alex. All I could think of was finding you. Hell Lacey, I'm not sure now what I would have said when I did. Something was driving me. It was … well, it was need. I needed you."

His admission froze her to the spot. He'd told her he needed her last night too.

*Damn,* she thought. *Double damn! How could she have been so stupid?* Those words meant a lot and him saying them to her, even in the aftermath of a blinding climax, had been important.

Wait, no—not important. They were life-changing words., When she crept quietly from his bed and toddled off to work. Lacey knew she hadn't considered his reaction to revealing his emotions. She hadn't even left a note.

"They started giving me shit right away. About you. I know now that they were just trying to get me to be honest about what was going on, but at the moment, all I heard was every other word, and the next thing I knew, Drae was pointing out that you were out of my league and would be better off with anyone else. He may as well have dropped a grenade in my lap. The idea of you with another man pushed me over the edge with jealousy and rage. What you walked in on was me being a king-size dick because I couldn't deal with the feelings running around inside my head."

She let out a deep sigh. "I've never understood why you think that. This opinion you have of yourself as some evil, damaged monster just doesn't fit with the man I know you to be. There were two of us in that bed last night. It wasn't just you. Do you really think I would be with someone I didn't respect or think was an honorable person?"

"I hear what you're saying, honey, but there are things in my past, things I've done, that weigh heavily on me. The kind of stuff that makes you feel unworthy and spoiled. Like second-hand goods held together with duct tape. Forget the drug addicted mother and the endless group care homes in my childhood. Something about a warzone that doesn't play by conventional rules can fuck up a guy's head. Every day, I live with regret and nightmares that never let up. You're so young and beautiful. It felt wrong dragging you into my personal hell."

"I won't try for even half a second to imagine that I understand what you experienced," she whispered.

His demons were parading in his head, evidenced by his tensely clenched jaw. *What could she do to ensure he was concentrating on their conversation—important as it was—and not his inner turmoil?*

Levering up from her spot on the sofa, she sat on his lap, and *BOOM,* had his undivided attention.

Shocked into silence at her unexpected action, Cam was totally distracted by her sitting on his groin. He knew what she was doing, and for some odd reason, as she was talking, he suddenly laughed.

"You're talking with your butt."

"What?"

"I know what you're doing, Ponytail. Plopping down on my lap was meant to keep me focused on what you are trying to say. Planting your sweet little derrière on my, uh … zipper, well, of course that's going to get my attention. Therefore, you are communicating with your butt. Period."

He paused as his words sank in and grinned at her stupefied expression.

She wanted to strangle him. Here she thought they were having a moment only to learn that his thoughts were entirely on her ass. The man was exasperation in dark jeans.

*Well,* she figured, *two could play at that.*

Tossing a bit of faux righteous indignation at him along with a randy squirm of her bottom, she deliberately and provocatively shifted to look directly at him and paused.

*Bingo!* The tense line around his mouth let her know how effective her ploy was. *Now* she had his attention.

"Cameron. Whatever dark impressions you brought back from the battlefield are things from the past, yes?"

At his slight nod and near grimace, she knew he understood what was coming next.

"Weren't you the one telling me that the past shapes who we are today, and that it doesn't have to bring us down or define who we are in the present?"

This time he squirmed as her words blew past the barriers he'd erected in his mind.

The *"Yes,"* he mumbled in reply to her question came out in a half-hiss as her rounded bottom into direct contact with his groin.

"So … the man you are today, is he for real? I mean, is he a real person? When you do things like rescue a person in distress or when you bend over backward for your friends, does all that come from inside you? Or are you just playing a game with everyone? Which is it, Cameron? Are you caring and concerned about the people you've let into your life or not? You don't get to have it both ways."

She hadn't raised her voice a notch even though the passion in her words came through with damning precision as she aimed and hit her mark over and over.

Going for broke, she moved her hands to frame his face and looked deeply into his eyes so he could see not just her feelings but also her determination. She wasn't going to let this go.

"You're not a bad person. You're a man who has faced extraordinary challenges and somehow managed to survive. It's the *somehow* that bothers you, and I totally get that. For your friends, though, the people who care about you, they're only mindful of the survival part, not the somehow part."

"Are you one of those people, Lacey?" he asked quietly as he sat perfectly still. "Even after everything you've been through and the way I've treated you, is it possible that you *care*?"

*Wow,* Lacey thought. This was supposed to be about him, yet he had turned the tables on her so deftly and with such exactness that she was taken slightly aback.

*Did she care?* Of course, she cared. She was human, after all. However, that wasn't what he was referring to, and she knew that.

He'd behaved like a shit this morning and nearly destroyed her heart in the process, but she could see how a lack of communication combined with the strength of their confusing feelings had set the stage for the mess they were in.

She'd been trying to help him see that whatever experiences he'd faced in the past had made him the man he is today. He was showing her the same. Everything she'd experienced made her strong and independent. Someone who could face anything, as she'd proven she could.

He was asking her to be brave and answer a question honestly, in a way that might liberate them both. The future was quite literally in her hands and completely under her control in the looming silence as each of them waited for her answer.

*Big, deep breath.* "I care, Cameron. Truly, I do."

She glanced away as her hands dropped from his face. A surge of determination bubbling up from her soul helped her continue.

"I've been falling in love since the moment you swooped in like some dark angel to save me from certain doom."

Her openness made him feel incredible. Cam couldn't help but feel humbled by her bravery and moved by her trust. She deserved the same from him.

"I'm not playing a game with you, Lacey. The man you see today *is* the real person, and what I feel for you very much comes from the inside."

It took one mighty effort not to punctuate that sentiment with the thrust of his hips against her bottom, but he held fast because he damn well knew that this was a huge moment for them. A moment that stood alone, outside the potent sexual pull they each felt toward the other and deserving of its singular importance.

Feeling her heart fill to almost bursting for the first time in her known life, Lacey was overcome by the emotions drenching her soul. He was telling her he had feelings for her, and truth be known, no words had ever sounded more wildly thrilling or quietly satisfying as those did.

Laying her head on his shoulder as her hand moved to a place above his heart, she sighed out, "Oh, Cameron."

Instinct told him to offer it all, so he grimly countered with a somewhat terse, "Um, Lacey? My name is Jason. Jason Cameron."

Her head snapped up with his admission and pinned him to the spot with those flashing blues. Without missing a beat, she simply asked, "Is that what you want me to call you? Jas ..."

"No!" he bit out, cutting her off from saying that name.

He didn't hate his name, nothing quite as glamorous as that. He remembered too clearly the way his mother slurred it, though, along with the sound of her distaste for his existence in every syllable. It was an association he didn't need in his adult life.

"I'm Cameron and have been for way longer than I was Jason. Just wanted you to know, that's all."

A silent shrug followed, moving his torso in a way that reminded Lacey of the very warm and aroused male's lap in which she sat. The trust in her that he was admitting matched the trust in him that she had confessed.

She searched his face and bit back a laugh when she found his expression, while full of sincerity, plastered on a face taut with sexual desire.

Sighing melodramatically, Lacey leaned in to snuggle his neck a moment before placing a wickedly lascivious kiss next to his ear that ended with a wet tongue stroke and a whispered, "You're really too old for me, though."

This brought the immediate reaction she hoped it would.

"I beg your pardon?" he snarled as he flattened her onto the nearby sofa so fast she hardly had time to react.

By the time she did, he was already firmly between her thighs pinning her beneath his hard, male body. "Wanna try telling me that from this position?"

The way her hips welcomed his presence with a naughty roll spoke for itself, and besides, she'd been teasing. Him getting all caveman-like was exactly the reaction she wanted.

"I suppose you can try to prove me wrong."

*Jesus, was that her cooing?*

"I don't want to get stuck with some old guy."

Not said with a coo. Something more like a taunt or better yet, a challenge. True to his nature, Cameron took up the dare without hesitation.

"This old man has satisfied your desires, surely?" he purred a second before his lips found that spot on her neck that wiped her brain of coherent thought.

When she bit back a whimper, he went with a fully engaged ravishing of just three-square inches of her skin.

*How did he do that?* she wondered.

He wasn't touching her anywhere else, and except, of course, for his body stretched out atop hers, he wasn't using his hands at all. All he was doing was licking and kissing a small segment of her exposed neck. Being reduced to a puddle in mere seconds had her thinking she had to try this teasing thing more often.

Cam feasted on her skin for long moments, enjoying the way he reduced her to a quaking heap without much effort. Her heated response made him feel alive. While it wouldn't take much to get them both naked and groaning as he buried himself inside her, it was way more fun at the moment to just hold her close and thank his lucky stars that they had weathered the storm that nearly destroyed what they had.

Nipping her ear, he growled low and deep. "You're right. I'm too old for such a young innocent."

When he went to rise from the cushion of her voluptuous body, she tightened her arms around his shoulders and held him firmly where he was.

"Not so fast, mister!" she cried. "Aren't you supposed to be proving me wrong?"

Their teasing had been fun. Enjoyable even. Especially after they had revealed their true feelings and taken a leap of faith. Cam felt there was one more thing to be said which didn't want to be denied or held on the sidelines for a better time.

"I'm falling in love with you, Lacey. Have done so since the moment I first laid eyes on you. I think you're amazing and probably the bravest person I've ever met."

Considering where and how he'd spent most of his adult life, Lacey fixed him with a 'yeah, sure' look.

"I'm serious. Look, when people get sent to war or find themselves in the middle of a threatening situation that they've trained for, they know what to expect. It's not a surprise. You were no more than a toddler when your world started falling apart. You weren't a trained warrior, yet you've done a double-digit tour of duty, all alone with no help or backup, and managed to survive. And not just survived but also turned out to be an amazing woman in the end. I think that makes you pretty brave."

Her shy smile wound around his heart.

"I can't even be bummed out by those experiences anymore. Not if, in the end, they led me to you."

Now that he knew how to smile again, it was easy to let a big grin spread across his face at her words.

*My god. What had he done in his life to deserve such perfection?* He had no idea, but he knew without a shadow of a doubt that he was blessed beyond measure to have found such a treasure.

"I have something for you, Ponytail. Here, sit up," he said as he tugged her upright onto his lap and reached into his pocket.

Pulling out the small box, he pushed it into her hands, saying, "I brought you a souvenir from Seattle."

Her look of stunned disbelief made the moment even more special. He waited while she gently cracked open the little box with trembling hands. Happiness, pure and undisguised, leaped in his heart when he heard her gasp of delight. Tear-filled eyes blinked up at him. He felt a million feet tall.

Taking the box from her hands, he removed one of the pieces and deftly placed it on her ear. Quickly doing the same with the other, he admired the way the tiny pearls accented her delicate features.

She reached up and touched the earrings, asking, "You got these for me in Seattle?"

Cam nodded and confessed his truth, "I may have tried running, babe, but nothing could keep you out of my thoughts. At first, I figured I'd hunt down some cheesy northwest souvenir, but that thought was quickly dismissed and was replaced by an obsession to search for something special. Just like you. I may not have been ready to say the words, but the feelings were already there. I had the box with me last night, and if we hadn't ended up in bed so fast, I would have given them to you then."

He wasn't exactly prepared when she flung herself into his arms and started dropping kisses all over his face and neck. "Thank you, thank you, thank you," she whispered.

It would have been so easy to just let that moment unfold, but they needed to discuss one more subject.

"Uh, sweetheart," he murmured as she licked his neck with reckless abandon and kissed him everywhere her beautiful, sexy mouth could reach.

"Mmmhmm."

"Unless I'm mistaken, we didn't use a condom last night, did we?"

Her head shot up so fast he almost dropped her off his lap from the reaction.

"Oh my god!" she cried out in alarm. "I wasn't thinking. I'm so sorry. This is all my fault!"

He had to bite the inside of his mouth to stop from laughing. Fuck, she was adorable, taking all the blame as if he'd been an unwilling participant. He could have stopped her seduction anytime he wanted, or that was what he told himself anyway.

"Hey, hey, hey," he muttered as he ran his hands up and down her arms. "There's no fault here. I just wanted you to know that it didn't escape my attention."

She looked a bit frantic even as he tried to reassure her. "It was my responsibility last night, Cameron. I should have been …"

"What? Prepared? C'mon, sweetheart. It's not like anything we did was planned. Besides, whatever happens, happens. We'll deal with it together, all right?"

Something made him lay his hand on her tummy as his mind filled with visions of her swollen with his child. He couldn't imagine anything more precious than a baby that they'd made together. She'd be a fantastic mother, and while he had some serious doubts about his abilities as a father, he knew with her by his side, he'd be willing to take the chance.

"C'mon," he said, lifting her from his lap.

"Where are we going?"

"I'm taking you home. We'll pack up your stuff tomorrow. You're moving in with me. I don't want to wake up another morning without you in my bed."

"Is that a request or a command?" she asked as she jammed a hand on her hip and tried to look stern.

"It's both!" He laughed as he hefted her over his shoulder and smacked her backside. "This is me, dragging you off to my caveman retreat."

Her laughter was still ringing in his ears minutes later after he'd gotten her safely to the ATV.

"Your chariot awaits, m'lady."

She laughed all the way down the lane as he wore a shit-eating grin spread so wide he thought it'd split his face.

The End … for now

*Want more of Cameron and Lacey's story?*
*Find out what happens next for the two lovers in FIXING JUSTICE*


THE JUSTICE BROTHERS
*Three extraordinary men and the women who love them...*

BROKEN JUSTICE

FIXING JUSTICE

REDEEMING JUSTICE

*One Justice Brother down, two to go!*
FIXING JUSTICE
The second book in the JUSTICE BROTHERS series
*Draegyn and Victoria' story...*
*Sometimes the last thing you need is exactly what you get...*

He's the sexy 007 type complete with tuxedo and an icy blue stare.

She's a tomboy waif who's more nerd than goddess.

When Tori Bennett ends up at the Justice Brothers compound in the Arizona desert, she's running away from an epic scandal with her in the starring role as a whistleblower. Sometimes having a moral compass means you're the one who gets shredded. She'd had enough of powerful, arrogant men, and just wanted to fly off the radar for a while and get her confidence back.

Draegyn St. John was all that and then some...and he knew it. As if being raised in society and having more money than sense along with the blonde good looks of a Nordic god wasn't enough, he was also a battle-hardened vet with a serious attitude. Women fell at his feet. It wasn't even a challenge.

Until Victoria Bennett rocks his high and mighty world in a very big way. Sparks fly each time they meet.

When an agency crisis throws them together for an out-of-town trip, their business relationship becomes personal in a hurry.

For Drae, it's an itch he needs to scratch and for Tori, it's a flat-out case of lust.

No harm, no foul, right?

What happened in Vegas, didn't stay in Vegas! Find out what happens when her smart mouth and refusal to take anybody's crap meets his powerful arrogance.

Everyone is in for one shock after another!

W HAT A FUCKING mess. Standing in the aftermath of a celebration that had been more than memorable, Draegyn St. John surveyed the carnage left behind. Everywhere he looked was evidence of the Valentine's Day nuptials that had taken place littered throughout the massive Spanish-styled courtyard at Villa Valleja-Marquez.

Taking a hearty slug from the champagne glass clutched in his hand, Drae contemplated the past few days while shaking his head in amazement. After jumping on a plane in Washington, D.C., he'd returned to Arizona and landed in the midst of an off the hook celebration.

The compound where he lived, along with his two business partners and one-time military brothers, technically belonged to the oldest and most senior of their group, Alexander Valleja-Marquez. They called it the Villa, a sprawling complex spread out among hundreds of acres of breathtaking Arizona scenery, dominated by an enormous Spanish influenced hacienda.

The glorious southwestern weather he loved was a welcome respite from the bitter cold and the never-ending snowfall he'd dealt with in D.C. Not one to usually gripe about anything remotely connected to being out-of-doors, he'd come to despise the winter weather back east. Having to clear off his car every morning, from either a coating of ice or inches of snow, had seriously pissed him off.

After leaving the nation's frigid capitol, he'd found himself immediately immersed in a thousand last-minute details for a wedding that had surprised them all. He still couldn't fathom how the dark and brooding mass of contradictions that was Cameron Justice had ended up married.

*Married*! Jesus H. Christ. Just the word brought shudders of distaste racing through his mind.

*Ugh, no thanks.*

Marriage and its false promise of commitment were a social

convention that he'd vowed never to allow in his life. His parents had taught him the hard way what a charade all that was when he'd been shocked out of his perfect family bubble as a hormonal fourteen-year-old.

Having fallen hook, line and sinker for the faultless picture of social, marital, and domestic bliss that defined the St. John family, he'd been duly horrified after happening upon his, *Do as you're told!* father, diddling the giggly twit who worked for the family as a quasi kid minder for him and his younger sister.

Dear old Dad had been dismissive of Drae's shock and cruelly arrogant when explaining his actions to his only son. Learning that his parent's marriage had been an arranged affair between two old-school, upper-class families had destroyed the image of who he'd thought they were. It had all been a lie.

His mother hadn't made it any better. Not only did she not care about her husband's wandering penis, she sarcastically informed him that '*this was how things were done*' in their world.

A cold, intolerant bitch on the best of days, Draegyn had tried more ways than his teenage brain could count to be the son she wanted, only to never feel any warmth or genuine approval from the woman. Now he knew why.

She'd married for social status and prestige and did what was expected of her in the deal, popping out the perfect set of perfect children for their perfect family.

Even now, all these years later, the thought made him sick. She made it sound like she'd consented to be bred in order to live an affluent lifestyle. *Who fucking did that?* He'd never trusted any woman's motives from that moment on.

Wandering to a bench swing beneath strands of tiny white lights strung around the decorated courtyard, Drae flung his half-inebriated ass onto the seat and forced his thoughts back to the present. All around him was evidence of the romantic, country chic wedding that had joined Cam to the blond-haired lovely who had changed everything with her quiet smile. He liked his new sister-in-law very much.

She was unique and absolutely perfect for his old friend and one of the few females Drae hadn't immediately mistrusted.

Lacey Morrow had been a surprise when she'd turned up last autumn in Cam's company. That the two ended up together hadn't shocked anyone, except perhaps Cam himself. Drae couldn't help the half grin each time he thought about the unusual parade of events that had brought his old friend to his knees where Lacey was concerned.

Miraculously surviving the minefield of bullshit surrounding their relationship, once they became an official couple, his friend had become an A-1 besotted, romantic fool. Drae supposed it was probably just an overreaction to the years of emotional isolation that defined Cam's life.

Once the floodgates of hearts and flowers had been breached, though, the man had gone ape-shit with one over-the-top romantic gesture after another, culminating in the red and white wedding he'd insisted take place on the one day every year when true love was supposed to be celebrated.

*Ha*! True love. *What the fuck was that, anyway?*

Despite his pessimism, he was happy for Cam. Truly. Knowing that one of them hadn't been doomed to an eternity of solitude made the burdens each carried lighter. It sure as shit wasn't easy dealing with what they'd done and witnessed during their time together in the puke-fest that was Afghanistan.

Swinging absently, Drae tilted his head back and watched a million twinkling stars shining overhead. Stretching his arms wide on the back of the swing, he sat there in his perfectly tailored Tom Ford tuxedo and let his champagne-fueled mind wander.

He'd gotten into special operations as an extra special *fuck you* to his parents. He could still remember the way his cold-hearted mother, with her tight-assed need to control him and his little sister, had gone ballistic at his announcement. She'd been apoplectic learning that he'd already enlisted by the time they found out what he'd done. Hidden in the dark memories that haunted him, he remembered the woman freaking out on her husband.

"Fix this!" she had screamed. "Arthur, you fix this right away. He's *your* son, after all. Do something about his attitude before he ruins everything I've sacrificed for."

*Ah. Yes.* He'd been Arthur St. John's son. Not hers. She'd made that abundantly clear. Understanding that he and his sister held no emotional importance in her world-view beyond the parts they were expected to play had been the final straw.

Of course, her *fix him* attitude had landed on his psyche and stuck like fucking fly paper.

His parents tried to fix him to no avail. The military tried to fix his bad attitude too and while he'd certainly adjusted somewhat, he always managed to ride the outer edge of insubordination.

He didn't need fixing, thank you very much. He was just fine as he was, calling the shots, and answering to no one but himself.

So what if he was also a card-carrying, male chauvinist pig with a scornful arrogance about the travesty of marriage. Staying well clear of powerful women, because they all but ate their young and generally came with a shit ton of issues, hadn't been all that difficult. He wasn't the sort they'd be interested in anyway. That left the rest of the female population in the sex toy category. Except for the innocent, of course—they were out of bounds. He wanted no responsibility, *ever*, and virgins came with a truckload.

Allowing that Cam was an exception to the rule, Drae wished his old friend nothing but happiness. Lacey was one in a million and if the emotional wedding they'd just pulled off was any indication, they'd be wallowing in contentment for all time.

He'd been honored to serve as Best Man *and* Maid of Honor while Alex had done his Big Daddy duty by walking the beautiful bride down the flower-strewn aisle. Standing as a second to the bride and groom had touched Drae's heart although he wasn't going to admit that anytime soon. His job was to perform his role as the sarcastic, conceited brother to perfection and make sure to keep the ribald comments flowing.

He'd gotten a good laugh at the devious way Lacey's mind had worked when she chose an outrageously elegant mermaid style gown that framed her ass because as she'd put it, 'Cameron was a dog for her backside.'

Drae fell over laughing at her admission and the two had giggled like conspiratorial girlfriends plotting his lovesick friend's downfall.

Serves Cam right, he chuckled, because guys enjoyed nothing more than laughing at their buddies when a woman turned the tables.

Well, the deed was done, and the Justice Brothers had expanded to include a wife. Wonders never ceased. Now that the happy couple had flown off via the agency's private jet to an extended honeymoon in Hawaii, some semblance of order and calm would return to the Villa.

He hoped.

During the month he'd been gone before the wedding, Alex had finally found an assistant to keep him organized, busy, and out of everyone else's hair.

*Thank fucking god too.* Drae had been ready to strangle the man, even from a distance, because Alex without a rudder was like a never-ending shit storm of angst. He'd gone for months without someone to trot along after him, cleaning up the crap he always seemed to leave in his wake. Luckily, Betty had finally returned too, so the office continued to run once Lacey relinquished her temp duties to focus on the wedding.

After deciding to stay put in Arizona while the newlyweds were gone, he'd been making secret plans to create an addition to the happy couple's cabin as a wedding present. Taking advantage of Cam's passion for black and white movies and old-time Hollywood gave Drae the idea to create a small home theater that he knew the couple would enjoy. Starting the very next morning, once his hangover eased, work would begin straight-away as the clock was officially ticking.

Enjoying the post-reception solitude and what was left of his Cristal buzz, Drae was startled when movement along the periphery of his vision had him shifting to high alert. He wasn't alone anymore although who or what was prowling in the shadows was a mystery since everyone else had long since staggered away to sleep off the over-partied aftermath of the day's events.

Tori had been quickly scurrying along the outskirts of the courtyard where a family wedding had taken place, on her way from seeing off the caterers to her tiny, functional studio apartment above an old barn that served as meeting space and offices for the Justice Agency.

She was exhausted after a long day of holding down the fort so the entire kit and caboodle of interesting people who made up the Justice family of partners, workers, and friends could join in the wedding festivities.

Having only been at the Villa for little more than a month, she'd been happy to pitch in wherever she could while also managing to stay invisible. She liked these folks, especially Alex, who she'd been hired to assist. With her personal life in shambles, she'd jumped at the job opportunity hidden away in the middle of a desert. Preferring to stay clear of social situations, she'd insisted on taking over on the day of the event so everyone else could enjoy it. Ever since the scandal that rocked her word had exploded in the press, she'd been working overtime to stay off the radar.

She hated being the center of attention, for any reason. There was a reason her dad had lovingly referred to her as his little mouse. Lighting up around his only child, the two had shared a special father - daughter bond. Being something of a tomboy with a serious streak a mile-wide, the times they spent holed up at the library or exploring museums had helped her forget that she was a simple girl. No great beauty like her glamorous mother, as a child Tori had been every inch the quiet, bookish mouse her childhood nickname implied.

When her dear father had passed away, she'd been too young to understand at the time what having cancer meant. After the shock of his death receded, her day-to-day reality became even more introverted. With a mop of bushy brown hair that never, *ever* did what she wanted it to and a slight frame with little in the way of feminine curves to grab a guy's interest, Tori was content to disappear behind ugly eyeglasses a shade too big for her face and basically hide from the world. That didn't however make her a pushover by any means. Schoolyard bullies had been the scourges of her childhood and she'd learned early to stand up for herself. With a fierce determination to level the playing field by leaving her peers in the academic dust, she'd mastered the art of the scathing verbal put down and never looked back.

Possessing an astute mind and a brilliant reputation for anything having to do with numbers meant she'd been labeled a financial genius while still in grad school and ended up at a world-class investment firm based out of London. Europe had been an eye-opening experience for the plain twenty-four-year-old that included hobnobbing with royalty, travel, and an inside view of sophistication and power fueled by the sort of wealth that boggles the mind. That new life had offered exciting challenges and the opportunity to shed some of her natural reserve.

When Tori and her remarkable skills had fallen under the attention of a senior partner who also happened to be an Earl, it seemed like angels had touched her as a new and fascinating world opened up. Before too long, she was working side by side with the Earl, Wallace Evingham, and enjoying one bold success after another.

At his insistence she'd undergone a complete makeover at an exclusive Hyde Park spa and revamped her wardrobe. In the end she got what she deserved for being so naïve, she mused. Wallace had been using her financial skills while distracting her with a rather public interest that led many, including herself, to believe he was grooming her to be his future Countess.

God, she'd been such a twit.

It all blew apart in rather spectacular fashion. Just when speculation had peaked that an engagement was days away, she'd stumbled upon evidence that Wallace was up to no good. He'd been raking in tons of cash in schemes that, while not necessarily illegal, were certainly unethical. And she'd been unwittingly helping him by being so trusting and free with her business acumen.

Oh yeah, and he had a string of mistresses to boot. Asshole.

She hadn't hesitated to alert the authorities to what was going on. The blowback had been dreadful and a major scandal ensued. Wallace was detained and their relationship paraded through the nightmarish British tabloids with headlines like 'Billionaire Earl Tricks American Plain Jane'.

A particularly vile tabloid reporter had referred to her as a spinster as if being twenty-six and unmarried qualified one for such a loathed status. One minute she'd been the darling of the financial sector and the next a laughingstock.

To make matters worse, it came out that the mistresses knew about each other and were all too happy to join together to cry foul at her betrayal of poor Wallace. The whole thing was embarrassing, sordid, and ugly. She'd been the injured party yet, as the American outsider, she was shunned and ridiculed by everyone. Within weeks, the firm had paid her off handsomely to simply go the hell away. That was three months ago.

And now, here she was tucked away in the Arizona desert with a bunch of former military men. Her mother had some kind of connection to the Justice Agency and through that association had asked for a favor.

Discovering that Alexander Marquez was in need of an assistant experienced with technology, it seemed a perfect fit. Tori needed to fly off the radar for a while and losing herself in the desert with some nerdy computer geek seemed like the perfect solution.

When her new boss turned out to be more of a handful than the dweeb she'd imagined, Tori had welcomed the intense, thrown in the deep end quality of work she was confronted with. Alex was a brilliant man but something of a mess when it came to practicalities. She spent just as much time trailing behind him and the loveable dog that followed him everywhere, keeping things organized and running smoothly as she did working with the mind-boggling array of technology and cutting-edge electronics that the agency had.

Right now, though, she was exhausted and feeling cranky. Knowing that Alex had been fully invested in making sure the intimate wedding event was something unique and special, she had been tap-dancing on the head of a pin all day, running from one challenge to the next. She was beyond tired but satisfied with how everything had turned out. Thank god she knew a bit of Spanish. Came in handy when she had to put out a particularly vexing fire between the obnoxious and uppity caterer and the troop of ladies from town that'd come out to work the reception.

There was an intense camaraderie among the people at the Villa that she privately envied. The radiant bride and handsome groom had smiled and kissed to the satisfaction of one and all before going on their merry way to a honeymoon that was so perfect it sounded like a movie producer had planned it. Their guests had been partying hard most of the evening. The place was a mess now that the festivities had wrapped up. Tomorrow would be soon enough to set about putting everything back in order.

She was stomping along, unconcerned that she looked like holy hell in a pair of sensible flat shoes and a nondescript skirt outfit, when she came up short spying what must be the most beautiful man she had ever laid eyes on.

Holy shitballz, the guy looked like a movie star!

About forty feet away and sitting on a swinging bench, he was staring at the sky. An empty champagne flute was on the seat next to him. She actually put her hand on her chest in both surprise and instantaneous attraction as she took in the whole of him with hungry eyes that missed nothing.

Wearing the same style black tuxedo that Alex and the groom had worn, the collar button was open with the formal bow tie hanging around his neck. Bright silver cuff links, sparkling at her under the twinkling lights, adorned the sleeves of his impossibly white shirt.

From where she stood it was easy to see the exposed skin on his neck as his head lolled on the bench's high back. The chin angled up at the stars suggested a take no prisoners attitude making Tori shiver at the enticing visuals flooding her mind with that thought. Even without seeing his face, she knew he'd be gorgeous. And dangerous. Everything about him screamed of something wild and exciting.

She must have made a sound because quite suddenly his head lifted and searched the shadows. Not having more than a second or two to school her expression into passivity, she found herself trapped in the laser-like beam of his stare when ice-cold blue eyes zeroed in on her.

*Uh-oh.*

"I WONDER IF IT makes a difference," Lacey muttered out loud. She studied each of the spice jars giving her a hard time. One had a label that said poultry seasoning and the other said Thanksgiving spice.

Uncapping both, she gave a quick sniff to be sure one wasn't masquerading as pumpkin spices.

"Boo. The same."

She tapped a manicured nail on her pursed lips and thought back through every session of Thanksgiving prep Ria and Carmen gave her.

Was she overthinking it? Definitely! Anyone in her position would. Not only was she making her and Cameron's first Thanksgiving, but this occasion also marked her debut as a hostess, and she just had to get it right.

Leaning against the kitchen island, she ended up bent over with her tummy on the marble as she shuffled through her recipe printouts.

"And what do we have here?" asked a deep, manly voice oozing sex appeal.

A warm hand ran up her left leg and caressed her bare bottom. She was naked except for a pair of naughty heels and a frilly bib-style apron.

Turning slowly, she'd thoroughly bitten her lip by the time she faced him.

As it did so often, her heart did a little happy dance when she saw him. Cameron Justice was the most handsome man on this or any other planet. His dark hair with its casual long style gave the man a swashbuckling look that fired up her fantasies. Soulful eyes that saw straight into her heart stared back at her.

She sighed. He was just so doggone beautiful.

And then his lips quivered. Cameron flashing a smile was a guaranteed panty melter.

"Thought I'd help stuff the bird." He sniggered.

"Innuendo intentional?" she inquired.

"You know it!"

"We already made love, remember?" She put on a complete performance of eye rolls, lip wetting, crossed arms, and stoic sighs.

"This is true. The journal entry for today will begin like so … Our First Thanksgiving. Something to be grateful for; we woke up and made love."

He pressed her back against the island. She loved how perfectly their bodies fit. Because she was cooking, her hair was up, so he had no trouble undoing the tie on the apron's bib.

"We're keeping a journal?" She asked the question in a breathy murmur due in large part to his beautiful hands helping themselves to her boobs.

"We are now." He laughed. "And since we want our first major holiday together to be memorable, we should think about what we're doing."

She arched a brow and smirked.

He continued in an amused drawl. "Gather content. You know. Performance material."

"Mmmhmm. Content. Got it."

His head was at her breasts doing wicked things. Cameron knew just how to touch her and what enflamed her senses. Lacey experienced a dizzying rush when he pulled the entire end of one boob into his wildly sucking mouth. Her knees wobbled slightly. The sound she heard was her own moan.

He did more things to both breasts until she was a quivering mess. Then and only then did he wrap his big hand around her neck and kiss her. His busy tongue and wicked hands drove her crazy.

When she was on fire and fighting for oxygen, he chuckled triumphantly and set her on the empty island. She lay back on her recipes, and he wasted no time spreading open her thighs.

"Journal entry number two. Time to kiss the cook. On her pussy lips."

It was all kinds of decadent and terribly exciting to be naked save for hooker heels and an apron around her waist that was easily shoved out of the way so her demanding lover could devour her. She was a wet mess. He held her legs open, gorging with animalistic passion.

It was so beautiful and perfect that she shot quickly into the stratosphere where an orgasm waited for her.

She heard slurping noises and his grunts every time her excitement grew. In no time at all, she fell apart and grasped his head. Bucking, she ground onto his marauding tongue until a silent scream and a freakishly powerful climax tore her apart.

When she came back to earth, he helped her sit up and slide from the island counter. The apron's bib hung her down her front, and she wasn't exactly steady on her feet.

Cameron was grinning like a proud idiot as he washed his hands and face at the sink. "My favorite protein supplement."

She pursed her lips and pretended outrage. "All well and good for you, but how am I supposed to cook a darn turkey now that you've distracted me?"

"Easy," he told her. "Just think about riding my dick with me in that chair you like so much."

She snorted. Was he serious?

"And how exactly is that supposed to be helpful?"

He turned her around, pulled up the bib and tied the ends around her neck. Then he helped himself to a handful of her ass as he leaned close and growled, "Because you can't have my dick until after our feast."

*Well, Cheese Whiz on a cracker.* He had a good argument.

Whipping around, she kissed him quickly and then pushed on his chest to get him moving.

"Then you'd better scram, buster. I have turkey day feast to make, and you are in the way."

She watched her gorgeous man head into the great room and turn the TV on. "Hey, look! Replay of the Macy's Parade."

He plopped onto the sofa with the remote in his hand and turned his attention to the colorful parade on the big screen.

Looking about her at the supplies she laid out, Lacey smiled to herself. She could do this. Grabbing the instructions labeled with thick black letters reading Step One, she started.

"One fabulous, romantic Thanksgiving feast, coming up."

# About the Author

*Suzanne Halliday* writes what she knows and what she loves—sexy contemporary romance featuring strong men and spirited women. Her love of creating short stories for friends and family developed into a passion for writing romantic fiction with a sensual edge. She finds the world of digital, self-publishing to be the perfect platform for sharing her stories and also for what she enjoys most of all—reading. When she's not on a deadline you'll find her loading up on books to devour.

No longer wandering because the desert southwest finally claimed her, these days instead of digging out from a snowstorm you can still find Suzanne with 80's hair band music playing in the background, kids running in and out, laptop on with way too many screens open, something awesome in the oven, and a mug of hot tea clutched in one hand.

Suzanne is the proud mom of *USA Today* Bestselling Author, Ella Fox.

The mother-daughter writing duo shares laughs and plots bunnies over Starbucks.

Social Media

Website: authorsuzannehalliday.com

Facebook: www.facebook.com/SuzanneHallidayAuthor

Twitter: twitter.com/SuzanneHalliday

Instagram@suzannehalliday

Book+Main Bites

# Other Books by Suzanne Halliday

*JUSTICE BROTHERS SERIES*
Broken Justice
Fixing Justice
Redeeming Justice
Original Justice (novella)

*FAMILY JUSTICE SERIES*
Always
Desert Angel
Sanctuary
Unchained
Unforgettable
Everlasting
Unstoppable
Dear Bella (novella)
Honeymoon Angel (novella)

*WILDE WOMEN SERIES*
Wilde Forever
Wilde Heart
Wilde Magic

*JUSTICE ~ WILDE CROSSOVER*
Bishop's Pawn
Checkmate (novella)

*AFFAIR SERIES*
The Gideon Affair
The Wedding Affair

*STAND ALONE TITLES*
Cupid in Heels

Made in the USA
Lexington, KY
16 June 2019